THE TEXAS
MOONSHINERS

THE TEXAS MOONSHINERS

WILLIAM W. JOHNSTONE
and J. A. Johnstone

PINNACLE BOOKS
Kensington Publishing Corp.
www.kensingtonbooks.com

PINNACLE BOOKS are published by

Kensington Publishing Corp.
119 West 40th Street
New York, NY 10018

PUBLISHER'S NOTE
Following the death of William W. Johnstone, the Johnstone family is
working with a carefully selected writer to organize and complete Mr.
Johnstone's outlines and many unfinished manuscripts to create additional
novels in all of his series like The Last Gunfighter, Mountain Man, and
Eagles, among others. This novel was inspired by Mr. Johnstone's superb
storytelling.

All Kensington titles, imprints, and distributed lines are available at special
quantity discounts for bulk purchases for sales promotions, premiums,
fund-raising, educational, or institutional use. Special book excerpts or
customized printings can also be created to fit specific needs. For details,
write or phone the office of the Kensington sales manager: Kensington
Publishing Corp., 119 West 40th Street, New York, NY 10018, attn: Sales
Department; phone 1-800-221-2647.

PINNACLE BOOKS, the Pinnacle logo, and the WWJ steer head logo are
Reg. U.S. Pat. & TM Off.

ISBN-13: 978-0-7860-4410-8
ISBN-10: 0-7860-4410-1

First printing: November 2019

10 9 8 7 6 5 4 3 2 1

Printed in the United States of America

CHAPTER 1

"Hey, mister! I'm talkin' to you. Are you deaf . . . or just dumb?"

The joke—if anybody wanted to dignify it by calling it that—brought raucous laughter from the man's companions. They sat at a table on the other side of the tavern's main room, where they had been passing around a jug until one of them decided to come over to the bar and harass the tall, dark-haired stranger.

Pike Shannon didn't look around. He stood there with his right hand hanging at his side, not far from the butt of his holstered Colt. His weathered, hard-planed face made him look somewhat older than he really was. In his left hand he held a tin cup half filled with colorless liquid. He raised the cup slowly and took a sip.

The 'shine wasn't particularly good, but at least it had a little bite to it. Enough to warm his gullet going down. Pike nodded to himself.

That's not the way his would-be tormenter took it. The man called to his companions, "Lookee there, boys! He nodded, so he ain't deaf. Just dumb!"

The other three men cackled again. "You are a caution, Billy Ray," one of them said. "I'll be a ring-tailed coon if you ain't!"

Pike took another sip of the corn liquor. It was still raw, but it went down a little smoother the second time.

The man standing a couple of feet down the bar from him looked and sounded more serious now as he said, "I'm gettin' tired of you ignorin' me, mister. Around here, when I talk, folks pay attention."

"I imagine most folks notice when a jackass starts braying."

For a couple of seconds, the man didn't respond. Pike glanced at the bartender, a fat man with a little mustache, a few strands of black hair plastered across a bald dome, and a red nose that indicated he probably consumed more of his own product than he should have. The drink-juggler's watery eyes were wide with alarm.

"Why, you son of a—Did you just say what I think you said?"

Pike took a third sip of the 'shine. Still without looking at the man, he said, "Called you a jackass, if that's what you're thinking."

Billy Ray's friends whooped. One of them asked, "Are you gonna let him get away with that?"

"Not hardly!"

A heavy hand fell on Pike's right shoulder. Finally, he turned to face the loudmouth, and as he did he flicked the rest of the liquor in the cup into Billy Ray's eyes. He dropped the cup and followed the 'shine with a perfectly thrown left that crashed into Billy Ray's jaw. Billy Ray was a big man, tall and rangy, but

Pike was almost as big and hit like a mule. The punch twisted Billy Ray's head on his neck and made him stumble backward.

Pike would have just as soon avoided this, but his mouth had gotten the better of him and he was in it now. He took a step and hooked a right into Billy Ray's belly. Billy Ray grunted and leaned forward, but he didn't double over, so the left uppercut Pike had hoped to throw wouldn't do any good. Instead Pike hit him in the face again with the left, aiming for the nose this time. Cartilage popped when the fist landed. Billy Ray's head jerked back so far it almost looked like his neck was a hinge.

Pike heard chair legs scraping on rough floor puncheons as the other three men jumped up. The odds were about to be against him, and Pike knew he couldn't look for any help in here. The bartender was the only other person in the tavern, and he was already backing away, clearly determined to stay out of this fracas.

Blood streamed from Billy Ray's nose as he reeled against the bar. With three other men to deal with, Pike wanted to put him out of the fight. He lifted the toe of his boot into Billy Ray's groin, not hard enough to do any permanent damage but with sufficient force to make sure the fella wasn't thinking about anything else for a while.

It wasn't a gentlemanly thing to do, of course—but Pike Shannon had never claimed to be a gentleman.

As Billy Ray howled in pain and collapsed, Pike shifted quickly away from the bar. He didn't want to get pinned up against it. With some room to move, he kicked a chair and sent it sliding into the path of one of the charging men, who cursed, stumbled over it, and went down, one of the chair legs busting off underneath him.

Pike scooped that broken chair leg off the floor and ducked a roundhouse punch at the same time. As he straightened, he slapped the makeshift club against the side of the man's head and knocked him sprawling.

That left only one of the trio still on his feet, but he was too close and moving too fast for Pike to avoid. Pike twisted his body so the punch struck him on the left shoulder instead of the face. This hombre was big and strong enough that Pike's left arm went numb for a second. He couldn't stop himself from taking a step back.

His attacker took that as an invitation to bore on in. Pike kept turning, used his right hand to grab the front of the man's shirt, and heaved him forward, using the man's own momentum against him. Pike stuck a foot out and tripped him, and the suddenly out-of-control gent flew forward and landed belly down on a table that collapsed under him.

The one who had tripped on the chair was back up. He tackled Pike from behind. Pike's hat flew off as he fell. A thick layer of sawdust was spread on the floor to soak up spilled booze and blood and anything else that might happen to leak, and some of the gritty stuff got in Pike's eyes as he and the man who had tackled him slid forward a few feet. He blinked rapidly to clear his vision as he tried to struggle free.

Maybe what he should have done, he thought bitterly, was just shoot the four of them when the trouble started. That would have been a lot simpler.

He rammed his elbow into the stomach of the man he was grappling with. That bought Pike enough room to writhe around and get a hand on the man's throat. With his lips pulled back from his teeth in an angry grimace, Pike bunched the muscles in his arm, shoulder, and back and drove the man's head against the floor. Skull met puncheon with an ugly thud. The man went limp.

A boot toe smashed into Pike's ribs in a vicious kick that rolled him over. The man he had clouted with the broken chair leg had recovered enough to come after him. The man charged in, foot upraised to stomp. Pike caught hold of it as it came down and twisted as hard as he could. The man had to go with it or suffer a broken ankle. He yelled as he fell to the floor.

Pike scrambled onto his knees, clubbed both hands together, and brought them down in the man's solar plexus. Eyes and mouth opened wide as the pile-driver blow forced all the air out of his lungs. Pike made it to his feet and kicked the man in the head, knocking him cold.

That left just the man who had fallen on the table and busted it to pieces. He was trying to get up, but he seemed stunned and disoriented. He must have hit his head when he went down, Pike thought.

One good wallop deserved another. The tabletop had split in two when it broke. Pike lifted one of the irregular halves and smashed it down on top of the man. The fella didn't move after that.

Pike straightened, hooked a toe under the piece of table, and flipped it aside to make sure he hadn't killed the man. He was relieved when he saw the man's chest rising and falling. All four of his opponents were alive, three of them unconscious, the other curled around his private parts, whimpering. Pike was glad none of them were dead. Killings could get complicated.

He slapped sawdust off his butternut shirt and denim trousers, then picked up his hat and swatted it against his leg to get the sawdust off it. He put the hat on and stepped over to the bar, where he dug out another coin and dropped it on the hardwood.

"Didn't get to finish that first cup," he told the bartender. "I'll take another one." The man stood there staring at him without moving. Pike grinned and added, "Hell of a homecoming."

The light got brighter in the tavern as the door opened and let some of the afternoon sun spill in. A man cursed, and something about the voice was familiar enough to make Pike turn around. With his eyes adjusted to the tavern's gloom, the light from outside was too bright and he couldn't make out anything about the newcomer except the man's burly shape. He raised a hand to shield his eyes as he heard the man's startled exclamation, "Pike Shannon?"

Followed immediately by the unmistakable sound of gun hammers being cocked. The man stepped farther into the room, and now Pike could see the dark, ominous maws of a shotgun being pointed at him.

"I never thought I'd see you again," the man said.

Pike had heard enough. He knew the voice now. He said, "Put that Greener down, Ramsey, and I'll fight you, too." He grinned again. "I can't think of anything I'd rather do."

A foot scraped on the floor behind him. Caught between dangers, Pike twisted his head and caught a glimpse of a blood-smeared, pain-racked face as the man he had kicked in the groin lunged at him. The man had gathered enough hate-fueled strength to make it to his feet. He swung a bung starter with strips of leather wrapped around its long handle that he must have gotten from the bartender.

Pike couldn't get out of the way in time. The bludgeon smashed against his head and sent him spinning into black oblivion.

CHAPTER 2

Pike hadn't expected to come across a tavern. In the last few settlements he had ridden through, he had noticed that there didn't seem to be any saloons, and finally he stopped to ask an old-timer sitting on a wagon if people around these parts didn't drink anymore.

The man, who had a leather patch over one eye and wore a farmer's overalls and floppy straw hat, had leaned over and spat in the dust of the street.

"Reckon they would drink," he answered, "if they hadn't gone and changed the law. Texas has got what they call 'local option' now. Those stuffed shirts down in Austin passed it a few years ago, back in '76. Seems that if enough folks in the county want it, they can hold an election and decide whether or not it'll be legal to sell liquor. If they vote not to, the county goes dry. That's what they call it. Dry. Might as well say thirsty, since that's what it amounts to."

Pike stared at the old-timer. "And people actually vote for such a thing?"

"Yeah. Ain't nobody quite as zealous as somebody who don't want to do somethin' and thinks you shouldn't ought to do it, either." The old man spat again. "Plus I reckon a good number of the folks who might've voted against it was too hungover to make it to the polls."

"Is it just this county or . . . ?"

The old-timer was already shaking his head. "This 'un, and the ones to north, south, east, and west. Son, you got to ride north clear to Fort Worth now to get a drink, believe it or not!"

Judging by the glum expressions on most of the people he saw, Pike believed it.

The farmer took out a pouch of chewing tobacco and started digging a finger in it. "How come you don't know about this? It was in all the papers."

"I haven't been in Texas for a while," Pike answered. He didn't go into detail about where he had been, and the old-timer didn't ask him. "I'm headed home, though."

"Where's that?"

"My family has a place in the hills northwest of Warbonnet, on the Brazos. They grow cotton and raise horses."

"Good country for that. What's the name?"

"Shannon," Pike replied.

The old man had cocked his head to the side and narrowed his single eye. "You wouldn't be . . . Pike Shannon, now, would you?" Before Pike had had the time to answer, the old-timer raised a hand and said, "No, ne' mind. I don't reckon I want to know."

Pike had ridden on, mulling over what he had learned. He had a hard time wrapping his mind around the fact that there were no saloons in this part of Texas. It was more difficult to believe that people would voluntarily accept such a thing, even strive for it.

Then he had come across the squat, stone-and-frame building at the side of the trail with four horses tied at the hitch rail in front. Pike had seen plenty of saloons, taverns, inns, road ranches, whatever you wanted to call them, and he knew one when he laid eyes on it. But maybe that's what this place had started out as and the owner had had to give up the liquor business once the local option election passed.

In that case, what was he selling that had attracted four customers?

Pike had given in to curiosity, tied his dun at the rail, and gone inside to find out.

As soon as he stepped into the shadowy den, he had known the answer. This was a tavern, all right. He smelled the sharp tang of moonshine right away, along with the yeastier odor of beer. Those two things were all that a tavern really needed to sell. Anybody who wanted anything fancier would never set foot in a place like this to start with.

The floor was made of rough puncheons fitted together well enough that the inevitable gaps between them were small. The tables and chairs and benches were crude but serviceable. The bar consisted of wide planks laid across the tops of barrels and nailed in place. The hills along the Brazos River were heavily wooded, so there was no shortage of lumber around here. There were only a few windows, and they were so small and dirty they didn't let in much light, but enough for Pike to see the four men sitting at one of the tables, having a good time, from the sound of their laughter and ribald talk as they passed around a jug.

They were rough-looking hombres, but he didn't recognize any of them, didn't have any business with them. He had walked over to the bar, ignoring the way their voices trailed off. He felt their eyes on him. Did they recognize *him*? It was possible. His picture had turned up here and there, in places that he'd just as soon not think about.

He had nodded to the bartender and said, "'Shine." The man got a tin cup from a shelf, uncorked a jug, poured the clear liquid until the cup was half-full.

Pike hadn't yet sampled it when one of the men stood up, strolled toward him, and said, "Mister, I don't recollect ever seein' you around these parts before. We got a, what do you call it, tradition around here. Newcomer buys a round for the house. Ain't that right, boys?"

His friends had hooted in agreement.

Pike ignored him, smelled the 'shine, looked at it as best he could in the bad light. All that was left was to taste it . . .

That was when the man had gotten obnoxious enough that Pike was no longer able to pay no attention to him.

And as it always did, one thing had led to another, and that old Shannon fighting spirit had welled up inside Pike, and for a few minutes it had been a good ruckus.

Then Doak Ramsey had stepped into the tavern, pointed a shotgun at him, and the whole world had fallen on Pike's head.

* * *

Awareness seeped back. The pain in his head, throbbing in time to his pulse, was the first thing he was aware of. When he tried to open his eyes, it was like somebody hammered railroad spikes right through them into his brain. He didn't attempt that again for a few minutes, and when he finally did, he made sure his eyes were only narrow slits.

Gradually he got used to the light. He could tell he was lying on his back on some sort of hard surface, looking up at an ugly, water-stained ceiling. Wherever he was, the roof must leak.

The hard surface underneath him was a hard, bare mattress, he decided. That told him a lot. He was in jail. Not the first time, either. Had the bartender in that tavern sworn out a complaint against him for fighting and helping to destroy some of the furniture? That seemed hard to believe, considering that the place was operating in defiance of the law. But anything was possible, Pike supposed.

He tried to sit up so he could take a better look at his surroundings, but that made things worse. The whole world spun crazily around him, as if the earth had lurched suddenly in the wrong direction. Pike sagged back, closed his eyes again, and did his best not to move until the drumming agony inside his head had settled down again.

"Hey," a high-pitched voice called, sounding close by but somehow hollow and distant at the same time. "Hey, I think this fella's awake back here."

Bootheels thudded on the floor. A man said, "You sure about that, Fiddler? He's not movin'."

"He did just a minute ago. Looked like he tried to sit up but couldn't make it. He's awake, I tell you." Pike heard something that sounded like a man licking his lips. "You gonna let me out now, Deputy Hanratty? You promised you'd let me out if the fella woke up and I told you about it."

"I gotta be sure he's really awake first." Hanratty chuckled. "Why don't you reach through the bars there and give him a good shake?"

"Ohhh," Fiddler moaned. "I don't want to."

"Go on, he can't hurt you. It ain't like he's a rattle-snake curled up in his den, just waitin' to sink his fangs in you."

Through the pain in his head, Pike thought there was something familiar about Hanratty's voice, but he couldn't come up with what it was, or summon up the energy to care.

"Ohhhh . . ." That was Fiddler again, somewhere close by Pike's side. Pike figured the man was locked up in the cell next to his. A moment later, he felt a tentative touch on his shoulder. Fiddler shook him gently. Pike couldn't hold back a groan.

"See? I told you he was awake. You can let me out now."

"Naw, I don't believe it yet. Here's what I want you to do. You pick up that slops bucket that's in there with you, Fiddler, and toss what's in it through the bars at him. That'll wake him up, for sure." Hanratty paused, then went on in a hard, mean voice, "Go on, do it. Or else I'm comin' in there and you ain't gonna like it if I do."

"I'm awake, blast it." Pike forced the words out and pried his eyes open the rest of the way. He saw now that the bunk on which he lay was next to the bars between his cell and Fiddler's. He reached up, grasped one of the iron bars, and clung to it for support as he struggled to sit up. His head whirled again, but he made it, and after a moment, the spinning actually got a little better.

Fiddler was a little man, mostly bald, with a fringe of gray hair around his ears and the back of his head. Weak eyes peered through thick spectacles. He shifted his weight nervously from foot to foot and looked about as harmless as a man could look, which made Pike wonder what he was doing in jail.

The deputy lounged in front of the cell, thumbs hooked in his belt, an arrogant sneer on his rawboned face, which sported several prominent bruises, including one large purple one in the middle of his forehead. Pike recognized him as the man he had slammed the broken table down on, back there in the illegal tavern.

"You're . . . a deputy?" Pike grated.

"That's right. Now who's the jackass?"

"And . . . the others?"

"The forces of law and order in Warbonnet County," Hanratty said, taking obvious pleasure in it. A heavy footstep sounded from the hallway leading into the cell block. Hanratty went on, "And speakin' of the forces of law and order . . ."

The bulky figure that entered the cell block was familiar to Pike, too. Now he could see the man's face, which looked like it had been hacked out of a block of granite. He said, "Ramsey . . ."

"That's right, your old friend Doak Ramsey." The man tapped a blunt fingertip against the badge pinned to his shirt. "But you can call me *Sheriff* Ramsey."

CHAPTER 3

That made Pike's head spin almost as bad as sitting up had. The idea of Doak Ramsey being sheriff made even less sense than folks voting to do away with drinking liquor.

Ramsey was in his midthirties, a few years older than Pike, the same age as Pike's older brother Tyree. At least, the same age as Tyree would have been now, if he hadn't gone and gotten himself killed a year earlier by a mule that kicked him in the head.

The letter telling Pike about that tragedy had caught up with him in Montana, where he had hired out his gun to some ruthless cattle baron who was having trouble with some other ruthless cattle baron. Pike had thought then that maybe he ought to head home and see his family, but fate had intervened, as it had a way of doing, and he had found himself in Utah, Nevada, and California, working on various gun jobs, before he finally started back to Texas.

He might not have gotten around to it even then if he hadn't received another letter from his sister, this one telling him that their father was dead.

Pike shoved those bitter feelings away and glared through the iron bars at Doak Ramsey. He said, "How in blazes did somebody like you wind up being sheriff?"

"Somebody like me," Ramsey repeated as he sauntered farther into the cell block. He didn't have the shotgun now, but the butt of a revolver stuck up at a jaunty angle from the holster on his hip. He wasn't wearing a hat, revealing the thinning brown hair on his head. "You Shannons always did think you were better than us, didn't you? Whatever gave a bunch of shanty Irish the idea that they could put on airs, I'll never understand."

Pike swung his legs off the bunk. He knew it would make him dizzy to stand up, but he wanted to be on his feet while talking to Ramsey. He held on to one of the bars between his cell and Fiddler's for support and pushed himself upright.

It wasn't quite as bad as he expected. His mother had always said he had a hard head. Sometimes it came in handy.

"We never put on airs," he said, "and we never thought we were better than everybody else. Just the Ramseys."

The arrogant grin on Doak Ramsey's face disappeared. He looked like he wanted to come in that cell and give Pike a beating. Well, let him try. Pike knew it might be the death of him, but he'd get in some licks first.

Then Ramsey got control of himself. He took a deep breath and said, "You can run your mouth all you want, Pike. You'll still be on that side of the bars, and I'll still be on this side."

Pike's mind still struggled with the idea of one of the biggest hell-raisers in this part of the state winding up as the sheriff of Warbonnet County, but he was a practical man who had learned to deal with things as they were, whether they made sense or not. He said, "Why am I locked up?"

"I reckon you know that as well as I do. You assaulted four officers of the law. Deputy Hanratty here is the only one who's not going to be laid up for a few days. It'll take longer than that for poor Billy Ray Briggs to recover."

"Yeah," Hanratty put in. "The doves at Miss Maudie's place are gonna miss him, too."

"They weren't wearing badges then," Pike said. "I didn't know they were deputies. I was just defending myself from four bullies."

Hanratty snorted. "Defending yourself, my hind foot. You threw the first punch, Shannon, after you threw moonshine in Billy Ray's face. As loco as you were actin', you could've killed all four of us."

Pike smiled at Ramsey and said, "Doesn't speak too well of your deputies, does it, that one man could thrash four of them that way?"

Hanratty took a step toward the cell door. Ramsey made a lazy motion to hold him back.

"You're charged with assault, disturbing the peace, and destruction of property," Ramsey said. "Now that you're awake, you'll go before the judge directly, and he'll decide your fine."

"Don't you mean he'll decide if I'm guilty?"

Ramsey just grunted, as if *that* was a foregone conclusion. Pike had a suspicion that it was.

"For now, you just keep on cooling your heels in there. I've sent some wires around to see if you're wanted on other charges, now that I've got you locked up."

"Not in Texas," Pike said, shaking his head.

"We'll see." Ramsey jerked his head at Hanratty. "Come on. Let's let Shannon stew in his own juices for a while."

In the next cell, Fiddler cleared his throat and said, "Uh, Deputy Hanratty, you promised you'd let me out if I told you when Mr. Shannon woke up . . ."

An ugly grin stretched across Hanratty's face again. "I don't recall sayin' that. You just hush up and don't cause no trouble, rummy. You'll get out when your time's up, not before."

Fiddler lowered his eyes and sank onto his bunk. He looked like a whipped dog.

The cell block door slammed closed behind the two lawmen.

Pike took hold of the bars with both hands now and stood there trying to breathe deep and steadily. His mouth was as dry as cotton, but there was nothing in the cell to drink.

After a couple of minutes, Fiddler said, "I'm sorry, Mr. Shannon. I shouldn't have called Deputy Hanratty. It's just that . . . well, he promised to let me out early, and I figured . . . I figured the sooner I got out . . ."

"The sooner you could get a drink," Pike finished

for him when Fiddler's voice trailed off. "So you could wind up right back in here."

"Well . . . everybody's got to be somewhere, I reckon."

Pike couldn't help but laugh. It made his head hurt, but he did it anyway.

"That's true. You spend a lot of time here, Mr. Fiddler?"

"Considerable," the older man admitted with a shrug. "You don't have to call me mister. Fiddler isn't my name. People call me that because I used to make my living playing the fiddle. I was right good at it before . . ."

"Before you started drinking too much."

"We just met, but you seem to know me pretty well, Mr. Shannon."

"Call me Pike." Feeling considerably steadier now, he let go of the bars and sat down on the bunk.

Fiddler put his hands on his knees, looked over at him, and said, "So you're one of Elijah Shannon's boys, are you?"

"Yeah. Did you know my pa?" Pike didn't remember the man, but that didn't mean anything. It had been a dozen years since he had "borrowed" one of the family's horses and ridden away at the age of sixteen. Lots of people had moved in and out of Warbonnet County since then.

"Oh yes, I knew Lije. I'm acquainted with the whole family. I know your mother, Mary; your sister, Vanessa; your brother Torrance." Fiddler paused. "I knew your brother Tyree, too, may he rest in peace along with your father. Terrible to have two such losses only a year apart."

"Yeah," Pike said. He leaned forward and clasped his hands together between his knees. "Especially when one of them may not have been an accident."

Fiddler swallowed hard and shook his head. "I wouldn't know anything about that."

"Nessa wrote me a letter." Pike's voice was flinty now. "Said Pa's body was found at the bottom of Warbonnet Gorge with a broken neck. They found his mule on the trail at the top, where it runs along the rimrock. Nessa said the judge ruled the death an accident, claiming Pa must have been thrown when he was riding along there and went over the edge."

"That was the ruling, all right. A tragic accident."

"Just like Tyree getting kicked in the head by a mule. Funny how there's always a mule around when a member of my family dies."

Fiddler held up a slightly shaking finger and said, "Now, that really *was* an accident. Tyree's unfortunate death, I mean. There were several witnesses, your own father and sister among them."

"I don't doubt it," Pike said. "Just strange, that's all."

He sat back and leaned his head against the stone wall behind him. When he'd heard that Tyree was gone, he hadn't quite known what to feel. Tyree was his brother, so there was some family loyalty, and in some ways Pike had admired Tyree because the eldest son of Elijah and Mary Shannon always excelled at whatever he put his hand to, whether it was breaking horses, fighting, sparking the prettiest girls in the county—or beating his younger brother black-and-blue.

To tell the truth, Tyree was a big part of the reason Pike had turned his back on the family. Tyree had run roughshod over him as far back as Pike could remember, knocking him around in order to toughen him up, as Tyree put it. When he was younger, there hadn't been much Pike could do about it, although he tried from time to time to put up a fight.

But by the time he'd turned sixteen, he had enough size on him that he could make a decent showing in a tussle, and he had enough rage bubbling around inside him that he knew if it ever busted loose, he might just kill Tyree. His own brother. He couldn't live with even the possibility of that—so he'd lit a shuck and never looked back.

The silence in the cells dragged out until Fiddler finally said, "Why *have* you come home, Pike? After all this time? I, uh, I know your father believed they'd never see you again."

"Probably because they didn't know whether I was alive or dead."

"Oh, they knew you were alive. They'd heard about—"

Fiddler stopped short and looked down at the floor again. Pike laughed.

"They'd heard about how I'd picked up a reputation as a fast gun and gotten in trouble with the law. I reckon I was nowhere near as notorious as Jesse James or famous as Wild Bill Hickok, but the stories got around, didn't they?"

"They did," Fiddler admitted.

"And some of them might have even had a smidgen of truth to them," Pike said. "But I didn't answer your question, did I? You asked why I came back."

Fiddler held up both hands, palms out. "It's not any of my business—"

"My sister's letter said the family needed help," Pike said simply. "Said they were having a hard time making it. Not even a sorry son of a gun like me could turn his back on that."

"Oh, I never thought you were—"

Fiddler stopped short again as the cell block door opened and Hanratty stepped in with a ring of keys in his hand. "The judge is here and wants to get this over with," he said. "Come on, Shannon."

CHAPTER 4

Pike thought briefly about jumping Hanratty, taking his gun, and shooting his way out of the jail. That idea vanished when three men wearing deputy badges and holding guns followed Hanratty into the cell block. One man had a shotgun, the other two gripped revolvers. They spread out to cover Pike from different angles through the bars as Hanratty approached the door.

Smirking as if he knew what Pike had been thinking, Hanratty thrust a key into the lock with his left hand and twisted. He pulled the door open and stepped back. His right hand fell to the butt of the Colt on his hip.

"Come on out," he invited. "But don't try anything. The sheriff might be a tad upset if we was to fill you full of lead, since he has his own plans for you, but he'd get over it. Doak's a reasonable man."

Pike had never known Doak Ramsey to be reasonable about anything. Or any of the Ramseys, for that matter. They and the Shannons had never gotten along, the rivalry going all the way back to the Ozarks before both families moved to Texas and wound up as neighbors again. When Pike was a boy, Doak's father, Wilfred, had claimed some bottomland next to the Shannon ranch, but he hadn't been able to make a go of it and had lost it for taxes. Somehow in Wilfred's mind that had gotten twisted around so that he blamed Elijah Shannon for what happened.

Ever since, that heightened friction between the families had existed. That it had never boiled over into a blood feud was mostly just a matter of luck. As it was, Tyree and Doak had gotten into it more than once when they were growing up, slugging it out until neither of them could stand. Brawls between other family members had taken place as well. There were a lot of Ramseys, and other assorted relatives, in the county, while the Shannons were basically on their own.

Pike hesitated while those memories went through his head, long enough that Hanratty drew his gun and gestured curtly with the barrel. "Come on, blast it," the deputy ordered. "I'm gettin' impatient, and I reckon the judge probably is, too."

Pike walked out of the cell. Hanratty backed away, keeping him covered. The other deputies fell in behind him. Pike followed Hanratty through the cell block door. As he left, he glanced over his shoulder at Fiddler and called to the little drunk, "Good luck."

"You'll need it more, most assuredly," Fiddler said.

Pike figured he was right about that.

On the other side of the cell block door was a short corridor that led to a flight of stairs. That reminded Pike the jail was in the basement of the Warbonnet County courthouse. He'd never been locked up here, probably because he'd left home before he was old enough to get into any serious trouble, but he recalled coming there once with his father to see Tyree, who'd been arrested for disturbing the peace because of a fight. With a Ramsey, of course.

At the top of the stairs was an office with several desks and a door on one side of the room with the word SHERIFF painted on it in gilt letters. The deputies marched Pike through that room and into another hallway. They turned right, went through a set of double doors into a courtroom.

Doak Ramsey was there, standing and talking with another man at a table in the front of the room, before the judge's bench. Pike didn't know the other man, who was tall and skinny, with slicked-down hair, a little mustache, and a small, pointed beard. His swallowtail coat and genteel-but-shabby air told Pike he was probably a lawyer. The county attorney, more than likely.

Ramsey and the other man were the only ones there. No judge, no spectators. But when Pike and the deputies came in, Ramsey turned and looked at them for a second, then went to a door at the side of the room and knocked on it. He went back to the table where the lawyer-looking fellow waited. Hanratty pointed to another table and told Pike, "You stand there."

The door opened and a heavyset man in a black robe came out. He had graying red hair and a beefy red face that reminded Pike of a bulldog. He seemed vaguely familiar, but Pike couldn't place him.

"All rise," Ramsey called, unnecessarily because everybody in the room was already on their feet. The judge went up a step to the bench, sat down behind it, and rapped a gavel.

"Court's in session," he growled. "Be seated."

Hanratty put a hand on Pike's shoulder and pushed him down into a chair behind the table. Ramsey sat down at the other table, but the other man stayed on his feet.

"Go ahead, Mr. Galbraith," the judge told him.

"Thank you, Your Honor. Warbonnet County would like to enter into the record the following charges against Mr. Pike Shannon: four counts of bodily assault, two counts of destruction of private property, one count of disturbing the peace, and one count of consuming an illegal drink, that is to say, moonshine whiskey. These charges stem from a violent incident that occurred earlier today in the general store and trading post owned by Mr. Edgar Bennett."

The judge cleared his throat. "Do you have witnesses who can testify about this incident, Mr. Galbraith?"

"I do, Your Honor: the four men who were assaulted by the defendant, all of whom are deputies serving under Sheriff Ramsey." The lawyer paused. "Well, three out of the four are prepared to testify, I should say. Deputy Briggs is still indisposed from injuries he suffered in the altercation."

Couldn't walk because he was still hurting too bad from getting kicked in the crotch, Pike thought as a faint smile touched his lips.

Not so faint that the judge didn't notice it. He scowled at Pike and said, "How do you plead to these charges, Mr. Shannon?"

Hanratty poked him in the back with the gun barrel. "Stand up when you're talkin' to Judge Conway."

Conway . . . He knew the name, Pike thought as he rose to his feet. Not Phineas Conway, surely. He was a shirttail cousin or something to the Ramseys, and when Pike had left a dozen years earlier, he'd been a mostly unemployed handyman. It just wasn't possible that Phin Conway had risen to be a judge in that amount of time . . . was it?

But Pike saw familiar lines in the man's face, though much softened by time and dissipation. That was Phin sitting up there, all right.

And with that realization came the knowledge that any forlorn hope Pike had had of fair treatment in this court was gone.

"I plead guilty to having a drink of 'shine, *Your Honor*." Pike couldn't keep the mocking tone out of his voice, even though he knew he should have. "To the rest of it, I plead not guilty."

"Do you have any witnesses to support that plea?"

Pike shook his head. "Just my word."

Conway looked back at the county attorney. "And you have three witnesses, you said?"

"Four, actually, Your Honor," Galbraith replied, "since Mr. Bennett is also prepared to testify as to what occurred in his place of business."

Of course he was, thought Pike. Bennett was running a tavern, pure and simple, despite Galbraith calling it a general store and trading post. Pike hadn't seen any trade goods in there. With the laws the way they evidently were in these parts now, the only way Bennett could get away with doing that was by being tied in with Ramsey. He was probably paying off part of his profits to the sheriff.

Judge Conway toyed with his gavel as he said, "So

what we have here is a case of one man's word against the word of three deputies and a reputable local businessman. I see no need to hear testimony, since there's no question that it will support the prosecution's case beyond a shadow of a doubt. In the interests of saving time, trouble, and expense for the court, I'm going to go ahead and find the defendant—"

"Your Honor," Pike said, "doesn't a man get to say anything in his own defense? That's sort of what having a day in court is all about, isn't it?"

"Why, you—" Hanratty moved in quickly behind him, the Colt upraised in his fist, ready to chop down with the gun on Pike's head.

"Deputy!" Conway's voice was sharp. "Sheriff, tell your man to desist immediately."

Ramsey glared, as if he'd been reprimanded and resented it, but he said, "Back off, Hanratty."

Conway leaned forward in his chair and looked intently at Pike. "You are correct about the nature of these proceedings, Mr. Shannon," he said. "What would you like to say?"

"Just that I didn't know they were deputies, Your Honor. They weren't wearing badges and they didn't say anything about being lawmen. And while I may have thrown the first punch, I say it was self-defense, because they were about to gang up on me and I knew it." Pike shrugged. "When you're outnumbered, sometimes the only chance you have is to hit first."

Conway nodded slowly and said, "Your theories of martial combat notwithstanding, Mr. Shannon, you have just convicted yourself with your own words by admitting that you did indeed start the fight." He banged the gavel down. "I find the defendant guilty as charged and sentence him to either pay a five-hundred-dollar fine or spend one year in the county jail."

Five hundred bucks. Might as well be five thousand, Pike thought. He didn't have that much, and Doak Ramsey was bound to know that because he would have gone through all of Pike's belongings by now. It wouldn't have taken that long. He didn't have much in his saddlebags. Even if he sold his horse and gun, he couldn't raise five hundred dollars.

Which meant he would have to spend a year locked up in that cell block down in the basement. A year of being at the mercy of Doak Ramsey and his brutal deputies. When Billy Ray Briggs recovered, he would be especially glad to find that Pike was a prisoner.

Phin Conway had just given him a death sentence, Pike realized, because he would never leave the jail alive.

"Which will it be, Mr. Shannon?" the judge continued. "Do you have the wherewithal to pay your fine, or shall I remand you to the custody of Sheriff Ramsey so you can begin serving your sentence?"

Pike glanced around. He was still being covered by the four deputies, and Ramsey was packing iron, too. He had no hope of busting out of here. He took a deep breath and began, "I don't have—"

A loud, angry voice came from the back of the courtroom. "Wait just a cotton-pickin' minute!"

CHAPTER 5

Everyone turned to see who had just pushed through the double doors. A burly, barrel-chested old man in overalls strode forward in the aisle between the rows of spectator seats. A white beard came down to his chest, and a floppy-brimmed felt hat sat on a thatch of white hair.

"Grandpappy!" Pike said.

"This is none of your business, Dougal Shannon," Doak Ramsey said. He had gotten to his feet. He moved to keep the newcomer from entering the railed-off area where the defense and prosecution tables were.

"You got my grandson on trial here, don't you?" the old man demanded as he waved a knobby-knuckled hand toward Pike.

"He's no longer on trial, sir," Judge Conway said. "He's been convicted and duly sentenced to a year in the county jail."

"Convicted?" Pike's grandfather snorted. "Railroaded is more like it, I'd say."

"Mr. Shannon, any more comments like that and I'll hold you in contempt of court!"

"And you'd be right, because I durned sure—"

"Grandpappy," Pike broke in, "you're not helping things."

Dougal Shannon looked a little older than he had when Pike left home, but not a dozen years' worth. Pike knew that if anybody asked the old man the reason for that, Dougal would say that a stiff drink of corn liquor every day kept him young. It was hard to argue with that theory since Dougal seemed as vital as ever.

He looked at Pike now and asked, "Where's your lawyer? Ain't you got one?"

"Nope."

Dougal glared at the judge and said, "Then this ain't a proper trial! A man's entitled to have a lawyer when he's hauled into court."

"The defendant raised no objection when the trial began," Galbraith said as he hooked his thumbs in his vest pockets. "Therefore it can be stipulated that he waived his right to legal counsel."

"I concur," Judge Conway said from the bench. "These proceedings have been concluded and cannot be reopened now. Of course, the defendant has the right to engage counsel and file an appeal if he wishes to do so, but in the meantime he must begin serving his sentence."

Which was a death warrant. Doak Ramsey would see to it that he died down there in the basement, Pike knew—"accidentally," of course—before any appeal could go through.

"Wait a minute," Dougal said. "Exactly what is his sentence?"

"I told you. Since he's unable to pay the five-hundred-dollar fine I levied against him, he must serve one year in the county jail—"

Dougal stomped forward, reaching into the pocket of his overalls. Instantly, Conway flinched and looked like he was about to dive for cover underneath the bench. Ramsey drew his gun, and Hanratty and the other deputies swung their weapons toward the old man.

Instead of a gun, Dougal pulled out a roll of greenbacks, tied with a string around them. He slapped it down on the bench in front of Conway.

"Five hundred dollars, you say? Well, there's your durned five hundred dollars! Now let my grandson go."

Nobody in the courtroom was more amazed than Pike, although they were all staring at his grandfather. Pike had no idea where Dougal had gotten that kind of money, but right now, he was just grateful that he might not die after all.

At the same time, five hundred dollars was a fortune, and he didn't like seeing the old man sacrifice that much just to save his prodigal grandson, who hadn't contributed a thing to the family except worry for more than a decade.

"It's too late," Ramsey protested. "Shannon already said he didn't have the money, so he's got to go to jail!"

"I never said that," Pike spoke up. "I didn't get to finish. I was about to say that I don't have any objection to paying the fine."

Judge Conway frowned and pooched his lips in and out, obviously thinking about this unexpected turn of events. Ramsey said, "He can't do that, can he, Your Honor? I mean, it's the old man paying the fine, not Pike."

"Legally, it doesn't matter where the money comes from, as long as the fine is paid," Conway replied with obvious reluctance. He looked at Galbraith and added, "Do you concur, Counselor?"

Through gritted teeth, Galbraith said, "The law forces me to agree, Your Honor, although I very much doubt the veracity of the defendant when it comes to what he was *about* to say."

"You can't prove different," Pike said.

"That's enough," Conway snapped. "I won't have this sort of squabbling in my courtroom." He scooped up the roll of greenbacks. "I accept this payment as full settlement of the fine owed by the defendant."

"Your Honor, you can't," Ramsey said.

"I have no choice, Sheriff." Conway rapped the gavel on the bench again. "Mr. Shannon, you are free to go."

Pike turned to smile at Hanratty and the other deputies. "You fellas heard the judge. Put those guns up and get out of my way."

"We don't take orders from you, you no-account—" Hanratty began.

"And I'll be wanting my gun, my horse, and all of my gear, too."

Hanratty looked at his boss. Ramsey angrily flapped a hand. He glared at Conway and Galbraith, and Pike had a feeling the sheriff wasn't too happy with those two "officers of the court." He wondered idly what Ramsey would do about it.

Hanratty said to one of the other deputies, "Eagleton, take him back to the office and give him his gun and the rest of his gear. I don't reckon I trust myself to be around him anymore."

Eagleton, a slender, sandy-haired man in his twenties, nodded and jerked his head toward the doors.

"Go on, Shannon. And if you want to try anything else, you go right ahead. It'd be my pleasure to arrest you all over again."

Pike grinned and said, "You don't have to worry about that, Deputy. I'm going to be walking the straight and narrow from now on."

"Never mind about that," his grandfather said. "Let's just get your things and get out of here."

That was probably pretty good advice. The sooner Pike put some distance between himself and Doak Ramsey, the better.

When they reached the sheriff's office, Eagleton took Pike's gun belt, holstered Colt, hat, and saddlebags out of a cabinet and placed them on one of the desks. "Your horse is at the stable the county does business with, in the next block," he said. "Your gun's unloaded. Don't put bullets back in it until you're out of the courthouse."

Pike nodded. He buckled on the gun belt, then opened the saddlebags to look through them. Everything seemed to be there. He wouldn't have been surprised if the deputies had helped themselves to anything they wanted.

The little leather pouch he was especially looking for clinked when he bounced it in the palm of his hand. Just because he hadn't had five hundred dollars didn't mean he was flat broke. He had a couple of double eagles and some smaller coins in here.

"How much was Fiddler's fine?" he asked.

Eagleton looked surprised by the question. "Fiddler? That little drunk? He's supposed to stay locked up until tomorrow."

"The judge didn't give him a choice between a fine or jail time?"

"Well, yeah, I guess he's supposed to do that, but Fiddler doesn't have ten dollars. If he ever got his hands on that much money, he'd drink it up in an afternoon."

Dougal frowned and said, "Boy, what are you doin'?"

Pike opened the drawstring on the pouch and took out a ten-dollar gold piece. He put it on the desk and said, "I'm paying Fiddler's fine, Deputy. Go turn him loose."

"I can't take the responsibility for that," Eagleton said. "You'll have to talk to the judge."

"You sure about that?" Pike added another eagle to the first one.

Eagleton swallowed. Pike would have expected anybody Doak Ramsey hired as a deputy to be at least a little crooked. It looked like he had guessed right.

Eagleton's hand moved, and the two gold pieces disappeared. "I'm gonna get in trouble for this," he muttered.

"Tell him to come to the stable."

Eagleton nodded. Dougal put his hand on Pike's arm and said, "Let's get out of here."

Pike was more than ready to do so.

He and Dougal walked out the courthouse's front door and down the two steps to the flagstone walk that crossed a narrow lawn to the street. As they did so, Dougal asked, "Why'd you want to help that little rummy? He ever do anything for you?"

"He talked to me," Pike said. "Didn't seem like a bad sort. And I got the feeling that fella Hanratty enjoys tormenting him. I don't like to see things like that happening to anybody."

"Well, I can't argue with that," Dougal admitted. They had reached the street, where the old man paused and went on, "Let me look at you, boy." He gazed at Pike from head to toe. "You haven't changed a bit, except you ain't a scrawny kid anymore. Still got that same go-to-blazes look in your eyes, though."

Suddenly, Dougal threw his arms around Pike, pulled him into a rough embrace, and pounded him on the back. Somewhat uncomfortably, Pike returned the hug and the backslapping.

"Blast it, boy," Dougal said in a hoarse voice, "I was mighty afraid I'd never see you again before the time come for me to cross over the Jordan. No matter what brought you home or what happens from here on out, I'm plumb grateful just for the chance to lay eyes on you again."

"I'm glad to be home, too, Grandpappy." They started walking toward the livery stable in the next block. Pike added, "And on the way, you can tell me how in blazes a good-for-nothing skunk like Doak Ramsey wound up being the sheriff of Warbonnet County!"

CHAPTER 6

Dougal stopped at a hitch rail to untie the two mules coupled to the wagon he had brought into town. He led the team as he walked along the street with Pike.

"Isn't that the same wagon we used to have?" Pike asked.

"Yep. Still works just fine, so your pa and I didn't see no need to replace it."

"It's good to know that some things haven't changed." Pike looked around. "Warbonnet's grown some."

"Yeah, the town's doin' well for itself."

"Seems odd not to see any saloons open for business, though."

Dougal sighed. "Yeah, 'twas a lot of folks movin' in from elsewhere who wanted that, more than the ones who'd been here for a while. But change ain't necessarily all bad."

That seemed like an odd thing for Dougal to say, but Pike didn't press him on it. They came to the stable, where a middle-aged hostler said he'd get Pike's horse.

"Your saddle and rifle are in the tack room," the man added.

"Do I owe you anything?" Pike asked.

The hostler chuckled and shook his head. "No, I didn't have the horse and the gear more than a few hours. Sheriff Ramsey told me I'd probably wind up getting to sell the horse to settle the bill. That's why I'm a little surprised to see you show up this way, mister."

Pike nodded and said, "Yeah, I imagine Ramsey and the rest of that bunch were surprised I made it out of the courthouse alive, too."

He didn't say anything else. He knew that Ramsey couldn't have become sheriff without having some support in the town, and this stable did business with the county, after all. It made sense to think that while the liveryman might not be a friend to Ramsey, he wouldn't throw in with the sheriff's enemies, either.

Pike was tightening the cinches on his saddle when Fiddler came into the livery barn, his feet shuffling in the dirt.

"So Eagleton went ahead and let you out," Pike said as he lowered the stirrups into place.

"Yes, sir, he sure did. Said you paid my fine, so I was being released early." Frowning, Fiddler cocked his head a little to the side. "Not that I don't appreciate it, Pike, but why would you do that?"

Pike grinned and said, "Because I knew it would annoy Hanratty, and Ramsey probably wouldn't like it, either."

"You're right about that. Deputy Eagleton told me you said to meet you down here, but I would have done that anyway to thank you. So . . . thank you, Pike, and maybe I'll see you around . . ."

Fiddler was turning away as he spoke. Pike put a hand on his arm and said, "Hold on. You have a place here in town?"

"I . . . uh . . . the widow Jefferies has a chicken coop behind her boardinghouse, and she lets me sleep there some of the time, when I help out around the place . . ."

"Anything there that means anything to you?"

"Not . . . not really." Fiddler shuffled his feet a little more and seemed to be on the verge of saying something else. Pike waited, and after a few seconds the little man blurted out, "My fiddle."

"All right, we'll stop by there and get it. Climb up on the wagon there, next to my grandpappy. You're coming with us."

"Wait a minute, Pike," Dougal said.

"Oh, I couldn't take advantage of your kindness like that," Fiddler said.

"You're not taking advantage of anything," Pike said. He looked at his grandfather. "And I don't recall the Shannon family ever turning their backs on somebody who was down on his luck."

"Bein' down on your luck is one thing," Dougal said with a frown. "Crawlin' into a bottle's another." He paused, then shrugged. "But I reckon it ain't my place to be passin' judgment on anybody, especially for that." He rolled his eyes but gestured to the little man. "Come on, Fiddler."

"If you're sure . . ."

"Don't fool around and make me change my mind," Pike said.

"No, sir!" Fiddler scrambled up on the wagon seat. Dougal slapped the reins against the mules' backs, hauled on the lines, and turned the vehicle while Pike swung up into the saddle. They went up Main Street for another block, then turned onto a cross street that Pike recalled became a wide, well-traveled trail leading northwest when it reached the edge of town.

Before they got that far, Fiddler pointed to a two-story frame building and said, "That's the boardinghouse. The chicken coop's right around back. Won't take me but a minute to fetch my fiddle."

"You wouldn't happen to have a bottle stashed in there, too, would you?" Pike asked.

"Well . . ." Fiddler licked his lips. "If I do, it wouldn't have more than a swallow left in it."

"We won't wait any longer than that minute you mentioned."

"You won't have to." Fiddler jumped down from the wagon and hurried around toward the rear of the property.

"He ain't drunk right now, because he's been locked up for a couple of days," Dougal said, "but don't expect that to last. You may be makin' a mistake here, Pike."

"Maybe so, but I believe in giving a man a chance."

"More of one than Tyree ever gave you, huh?"

Pike squinted at his grandfather. "You knew he was making things so rough on me?"

"Shoot, we all did. Figured it was up to you to learn how to handle it." The old man's tone was wistful as he said, "Your pa and I had a little bet goin' on how old you'd get to be before you turned on Tyree and gave him what he had comin'. But you borrowed that horse and left before you ever did."

"You mean stole a horse."

"You were family," Dougal said. "Your pa and me never considered it more than borrowin'."

Pike grunted. "Generous of you."

Pike's dun was well trained. As they waited for Fiddler, he looped the reins around the saddle horn and thumbed cartridges into his Colt's cylinder. When he was finished, he pouched the iron, feeling better now that he had a loaded gun on his hip again.

Fiddler, carrying his fiddle and bow in his left hand, trotted back to the wagon. He put the fiddle and bow in the back and pulled himself onto the seat next to Dougal again.

"I'm ready," he said. He seemed steadier now. His eyes were clearer. Pike would have bet there had been more than a single swallow in the bottle cached in the chicken coop. But Fiddler hadn't dallied too long and the hair of the dog had settled his nerves, so Pike didn't care.

After they had followed the trail about half a mile, Pike hipped around in the saddle to look behind them and make sure no one was following them from Warbonnet. No one appeared to be, and he had a pretty good eye for such things. He wouldn't have lived as long as he had without it.

"All right," he said to his grandfather, "tell me what's going on around here."

"Where do you want me to start?"

"With Pa getting killed, I reckon."

Dougal looked straight ahead and said, "It goes

back farther than that. If you want the whole story, you got to start with Tyree."

"What about him? From what I've heard, his death really was an accident."

"Oh, it was, it was, no doubt about that. That mule kicked him, right enough. Sent him flying a good ten feet, and he was dead by the time he landed. Head stove in like somebody'd taken a two-by-four to it and walloped him half a dozen times in the same place."

Pike grimaced. Fiddler said, "I heard about that happening. I sure was sorry, Mr. Shannon."

"Why?" Dougal asked roughly. "We didn't mean nothin' to you."

"I'm sorry when any man gets cut down before his time. It seems so tragic, especially compared to a man like me, who doesn't really contribute much to the world anymore, or have anything to live for—"

"If you're gonna sit there feelin' sorry for yourself, just climb in the back of the wagon. I don't want to hear it."

"Sorry." Fiddler looked down at his feet. "I won't say anything else."

"Anyway," Dougal went on heavily, "even before that, the family was havin' trouble gettin' by. Cotton prices ain't been any too high to start with, and we had a couple bad years in a row. Did a little better with the horses, but not enough to make up for it. And we lost some, too, to thieves."

"Rustlers?"

"That's right. Some folks like to talk about how the West is gettin' tamed down, but that ain't true everywhere. Not by a long shot." The mules had slowed.

Dougal flapped the reins again to get them moving faster. "So Tyree got to thinkin' maybe it was time to start up the *real* family business again."

"Making moonshine," Pike said.

"Yup. Just like your pappy done when he was a young man in the mountains back in Arkansas, and I done before him, and my pappy before that. Of course, we never had really stopped completely, just kept our runs small enough we didn't produce more'n enough for just the family. But Tyree said we ought to build more and bigger stills and start sellin' it again, since that durned local option had passed and all the saloons was shut down. Your pappy was dead set agin that."

"Why? Seems like there would have been some good money to be made."

"And trouble with the law to be gotten into, as well! You know good and well, Pike, that one reason us Shannons come to Texas in the first place, besides pure cussed fiddle-footedness, is because things had got a mite hot for us, legal-wise, in Arkansas. Lije didn't want that. He wanted to be able to raise his family in peace. So he held his ground—you know how stubborn he could be—and Tyree got madder and madder."

"And then Tyree got killed," Pike said.

Dougal nodded. "And then Tyree got killed, and I swear, the heart just went right outa your pappy, Pike. He regretted all the hard feelin's and wished he'd gone along with what Tyree wanted, so they wouldn't have been at odds that last year. With all that eatin' at him, he knew he couldn't bring Tyree back, but he thought maybe he could honor his son's memory by honorin' Tyree's wishes."

"So the Shannons got back into the moonshine business," Pike guessed.

Dougal nodded and said, "Yup. The Shannons got back into the moonshine business."

CHAPTER 7

They rode along in silence for a few moments while Pike mulled over what his grandfather had told him. Finally he said, "Shannon 'shine was always popular back in Arkansas, from what I've heard you and Pa say about those days. I expect it was around here, too, once word got around."

"You're durned tootin' it was. Things started lookin' up for a while. Folks came not only from Warbonnet County but rode in from the counties hereabouts, too, just to buy some jugs. We had four stills runnin' all the time to keep up with the demand, especially after some of the fellas who ran taverns and saloons before the local option put 'em outa business started back up and bought the stuff by the wagonload."

Dougal fell silent again and ran the fingers of one hand through his long white beard while holding the reins with the other hand. Pike waited for the old man to go on, and when Dougal didn't, he said, "What happened then, Grandpappy?"

"Well . . . the problem was, the Shannons weren't the only family to go into the moonshinin' business."

"So did the Ramseys," Pike guessed.

"Yup. You recollect hearin' stories when you was a youngster about how the Shannons and the Ramseys did some feudin', back up yonder in the Ozarks where we all come from?"

"I remember the stories," Pike said. "All that trouble was over moonshining?"

"Most of it. There was more—some insultin' words bandied about, some of those Ramsey boys cornerin' a Shannon gal and treatin' her disrespectful-like—but mostly it was because of the moonshinin'. Nobody ever got kilt, as far as I know, but more than one fella on both sides got shot. Then, back in the '40s, when I was just a young man and your pappy was only a boy, my pappy decided to move the whole clan to Texas. So that's what we done, and we all thought we'd seen the last of the Ramseys."

"Shame it didn't work out that way."

"It sure is. Things went pretty well down here startin' out. We had to fight off Comanch' war parties from time to time—that's how come so many things around here got called Warbonnet, from the town to the county to the peak to the gorge—and then the War of Northern Aggression come along and caused a lot of hard feelin's on both sides . . . but mostly we just raised cotton and hosses and built a good life." Dougal turned his head and spat to the side. "But then Wilfred Ramsey showed up and a bunch of his kin straggled in behind him, and . . . Shoot, boy, we're up to the part of the story you ought to remember."

Pike nodded and said, "I do. I remember . . . but I don't know what happened after I left. Every so often a letter from Ma or Nessa would find me, but that's all the news I ever got. And they tried to make everything sound all right, never talked about problems."

"Even with the Ramseys causin' trouble now and then, things still weren't too bad," Dougal went on. "But then Wilfred passed away and Doak took over the leadership of the family, and Doak was a different story. He'd always been a troublemaker, but he's smart, too."

"Doak Ramsey? Smart?" Pike had a hard time believing that. "Just plain mean is more like it."

"Don't you underestimate him, boy," Dougal said sharply. "He's smart, all right, and ambitious, to boot, not shiftless like his pappy, and that there is a bad combination, especially when you throw in that meanness you mentioned. He got the idea that the best way to latch on to more power for his bunch was to go into politics. He didn't do it himself at first. He got a Ramsey to run for county commissioner, his cousin Thad, and durned if the varmint didn't get hisself elected. Some folks thought there was somethin' a mite crooked about the election, but nobody could ever prove it. And anybody who tried too hard to find proof, or even talked too much about it, wound up gettin' a nighttime visit from fellas who give him a good beatin'. Funny how nobody could ever say just who it was who done that beatin'."

"Yeah," Pike said. "Funny."

"Anyway, with one Ramsey in county gov'ment, it was easier to get another one in there, and another 'un after that. Come to the point where Ramseys was pullin' most of the strings around here. By that time, Doak had gone to work as a deputy, and when the sheriff decided to retire—"

"Or was persuaded to retire, I'm thinking," Pike said.

Dougal shrugged again and said, "Either way, the upshot was that Doak ran for sheriff and won, of course. This wasn't long before that blasted local option business come up. They had to hold a special election for it, and it passed, and ol' Doak—"

"He was in the perfect position, being sheriff, to go into the moonshine business himself," Pike finished. "He wasn't ever going to arrest himself or some of his family, now, was he?"

"That's the gospel truth, all right. Since the whole thing started, he's been determined that the Ramseys are gonna be the only ones sellin' 'shine in this whole part of the state. Them and us ain't the only ones who set up stills. Andy Burnett had one goin' for a while. The Dawson brothers, Cloyd and Hebner. You might remember all of them. Plus some folks who moved in after you left, like Will Fisher and Sam Crow. They all tried their hands at it, and one by one, bad things happened to 'em. Andy's still got busted up. He'd fix it, and then it'd get busted up again. Cloyd and Hebner got burned out, and the shed where they had stored some jugs from their last run blowed up. Hurt Hebner pretty bad. Sam Crow's got a daughter, and somebody grabbed her and told Sam what'd happen to her if he didn't get rid of his still. He didn't have any choice but to go along with 'em."

Anger grew inside Pike as he listened to his grandfather talk. When Dougal paused, he said, "And the Ramseys, headed up by Doak, have been behind all this trouble."

"Knowin' somethin' to be true, and provin' it to the law, are two different kettles o' fish." Dougal made a clucking sound at the mules. "Anyway, the law in these parts *is* the Ramseys."

They grew quiet again. Pike looked around at the countryside through which they were passing. The trail followed a broad valley bordered to the southwest and northeast by rolling, wooded hills. About a mile to the right was a thick line of trees and brush that marked the course of the Brazos River. Along this stretch, lush grass covered most of the bottomland between the trail and the river, broken in places by cultivated fields. Here and there rose rugged limestone outcroppings. It was pretty country. Not as spectacularly beautiful as some of the places Pike had seen in his wanderings, but a good place to live and work and raise a family, if that's what a man was of a mind to do.

"Is anybody else still making 'shine around here besides the Shannons and the Ramseys?" he asked.

"Not that I know of. Doak went after all the smaller operators first."

"So it's down to them and us."

"Yup."

Pike's voice was harder than those limestone ledges as he asked, "Did Doak Ramsey kill my pa?"

Dougal sighed and said, "I honestly don't know, boy. Could've been Doak or some of his bunch, I reckon. Lije was a good rider, not likely to get throwed. And I don't know what he was doin' over by Warbonnet Gorge that day, neither. He was headed for town, I thought."

"The Ramseys could've caught him, forced him to ride to the gorge, and then thrown him in."

The huge, brush-choked slash in the earth called Warbonnet Gorge had sheer walls and was close to a hundred feet deep. Anyone thrown into it would stand almost no chance of surviving. Elijah Shannon certainly hadn't.

"They could have," Dougal agreed with his grandson's suggestion. "But if you're thinkin' you ought to go ridin' up to the Ramsey homeplace with guns blazin', that wouldn't do a blamed thing except get you killed and add to your ma's misery."

Pike shook his head and said, "I'm not going to do that. I've learned a few things about not throwing your life away when the odds are against you."

"I'm glad to hear it."

"But that doesn't mean I'm going to back down. From the sound of it, Ramsey wants a war. He might've just found somebody who's willing to give him one."

Dougal turned his head to look at Pike and said, "I don't know whether I'm happy to hear that, son . . . or plumb scared."

Pike didn't have an answer for that. He rode on and after a minute brought up something that puzzled him.

"Grandpappy . . . how in the world did you manage to show up in that courtroom at just the right time, with just the right amount of money, to get me out of that trouble?"

Dougal didn't answer right away. Instead he looked over at Fiddler, who had been listening to the discussion quietly, as he'd promised. The little man said, "If you're worried about me, Mr. Shannon, you needn't be. I'm no friend to the Ramseys, I promise you. The sheriff's men have arrested me every chance they get, and the treatment they've given me in jail has been . . . unpleasant, to say the least."

"You'd best be tellin' me the truth," Dougal warned. "I won't take kindly to it if I find out you went runnin' off to Doak Ramsey and told him anything we been sayin'."

"That will *never* happen. You have my word on that, sir."

Dougal grunted. He looked back at Pike and said, "There's a fella who's part of the Ramsey bunch—not a member of the family, but he works for them—who's sort of friendly toward our side, when he thinks it'll benefit him. When you got brung in from Bennett's place, after they'd knocked you out, this fella got word to me. He overheard Doak talkin' to that crooked tub o' lard Phin Conway and knew how the trial was gonna turn out. So he told me to bring the five hundred bucks with me."

"This hombre got a name?" Pike asked.

"Sure, but you don't need to know it. Safer all around that way, I reckon."

Pike wasn't so sure about that, but he wasn't going to argue with his grandfather.

"Five hundred dollars is a lot of money," he said instead.

"Yeah. Most of what we had saved up."

"Are you sure I'm worth it?"

"I reckon we'll find out," Dougal said.

They rode on, past fields where cotton was growing and pastures where horses grazed. This was Shannon land now, Pike knew. Up ahead, the trail curved toward the river and led past a clump of towering cottonwood trees at the top of a long, gentle slope overlooking the Brazos. Pike caught a glimpse of the sprawling, two-story frame house in the midst of those trees and felt his pulse quicken.

He was home.

CHAPTER 8

When old Garvan Shannon, Pike's great-grandfather, moved the family from Arkansas to Texas, the first shelter he had built was a small log cabin that everyone crowded into while he and his sons and sons-in-law hewed lumber from the trees and put up a proper frame house.

That house had been added onto half a dozen times over the past decades, which had given it a rather haphazard look with the additions sprouting off every which way from the original structure. The last thing to be built was a covered, railed porch that ran across what was now the front of the house.

To Pike's eyes right now, the house looked wonderful, since it was the place where he had grown up. He didn't have the fondest recollections of childhood, due mostly to Tyree's bullying and the benign neglect of his father and grandfather, but it was human nature for memory to paint those days in a more favorable light. After all, he'd been young. Anything was possible. *Everything* was possible.

It had taken time for Pike to learn that wasn't exactly true, although it was still a worthwhile goal.

So as he reined up in front of the house now, a lot of reminiscences warred inside him, some good, some bad, but all quite vivid. On top of those feelings was the relief he experienced at actually *being* here, alive and relatively well, because for a good while today, it had looked as if he would never make it but would languish and die in that basement jail instead.

The family must have watching through the windows as they waited inside. The front door banged open, and Pike's sister, Vanessa, rushed onto the porch. She was moving so fast that her long red hair flew out behind her head. She was down the steps and throwing her arms around him by the time he swung down from the saddle and turned toward the house.

Nessa had been a scrawny, flame-haired ten-year-old tomboy in overalls when Pike left home. Now she was a full-grown, lush-bodied woman wearing a green dress, and she hugged Pike so hard he had to take a step back. He managed to get his hands on her shoulders and grinned down at her as he said, "Whoa there, girl! You're going to bowl me over if you're not careful."

"Oh, Pike," she said, "we were all afraid we were never going to see you again!"

"I worried about that myself," he told her. "But I'm home now."

"Home to stay?" a new voice asked from the porch. He looked in that direction and saw the small woman standing there with a severe look on her face. Mary Shannon had been a lovely woman in her youth and still retained quite a bit of that beauty. Her thick brown hair, pulled back into a bun, was only lightly touched with gray.

"Home for now," Pike answered her, "and glad of it."

"Well, I suppose we'll have to settle for that," Mary said.

"Ma," Nessa said, "can't you just be glad that Pike's here and all right?"

The thin line of Mary's mouth curved into a slight smile. "I *am* glad," she said. "Come up here and let me look at you, son."

Pike climbed onto the porch. His mother put her hands on his arms and looked him up and down. "You've grown so much," she murmured.

"I was gone a long time."

"I know." Her bottom lip trembled, and for a second Pike was afraid she was going to start crying. He didn't know if he could stand that. But then her expression firmed and she said, "Welcome home, son. I just wish . . . I wish it were under better circumstances."

"So do I, Ma. So do I." Pike looked past his mother at the stocky man with curly brown hair who stood in the open doorway with his hands stuck in his pockets and a scowl on his face. "Torrance?"

"Just wanted to see what the commotion was about. Now I know. What I figured." A bitter edge came into Torrance Shannon's voice. "The prodigal son returns. Somebody go find a fatted calf."

"Torrance, there's no need to talk like that," Mary said to her oldest surviving son.

Torrance was between Tyree and Pike in age. Despite the burly adult he had grown into, as a child he'd been sick quite often, and so he had developed a taste for books. There was nothing wrong with that—Pike enjoyed reading, too, and usually had a novel or two in his saddlebags—but Torrance had turned inward to the point that he didn't seem to want anything to do with other people.

Pike had wondered sometimes why Tyree hadn't picked on Torrance the same way he had done with him. The only answer he'd ever been able to come up with was that Tyree realized he wouldn't get a satisfying enough reaction from Torrance. Torrance just didn't care.

He turned away now and disappeared back into the house, shadows closing around him. Mary sighed but let him go. "I'm afraid your brother hasn't changed a lot in the time you've been gone," she said to Pike.

"I'm not sure either of us have," he said.

Nessa had come up onto the porch beside Pike and her mother. She said quietly, "Pike, who's that?" She inclined her head toward the wagon, where Dougal and Fiddler had climbed down from the seat and now stood next to the team of mules. "I think I've seen him around Warbonnet, but I'm not sure."

"He's a friend," Pike said. "He was locked up in jail with me, and when Grandpappy got me out, I decided to bring him along, too."

"If he's a friend of yours, he's welcome here," Mary said. "Does he need a place to stay? We have some extra rooms. Nothing fancy, you understand . . ."

Pike thought about the chicken coop where Fiddler had been sleeping and said, "I reckon it'll seem fancy to him." He turned and motioned the little man up onto the porch. "Ma, Nessa, this is Fiddler. My mother, Mary, and my sister, Vanessa, Fiddler."

"If I had a hat, I would doff it, ma'am and miss," Fiddler said with a little bow. "Mrs. Shannon, we've never been formally introduced, but I, ah, did a bit of business with your husband from time to time, when I had the wherewithal to do so. Unfortunately, I usually had to make do with an inferior but less expensive substitute."

"You've got to pay for quality," Dougal said as he came up the steps.

"Yes, sir, and I always did whenever it was in my power to do so."

Mary said, "You're not here as a customer, Mr. . . . Fiddler, was it?"

"Just Fiddler. No mister."

"All right. You're here as a friend of the family, Fiddler, and as such, you're welcome to stay as long as you like. The Shannons don't turn away our friends."

"I'm humbled and honored by the invitation, Mrs. Shannon."

"You may regret it after he's been here awhile," Dougal said. "He likes to talk."

"He can talk to Torrance," Nessa suggested. "Half the time most of us don't know what he's saying, anyway." She linked arms with Pike. "And you're going to tell us where you've been and what you've been doing for the past twelve years."

"Vanessa," Mary said, "your brother just got home. Don't pester him."

Pike figured his mother didn't want him talking about what he'd been doing since he left home. And she would be right to feel that way, he thought. Most of the stories he could tell were pretty ugly.

"Maybe we'll get around to that some other day," he said to Nessa. "Right now it's getting on toward suppertime, and I've sure missed Ma's cooking!"

CHAPTER 9

The stew was as filling and delicious as Pike remembered it, the thick broth loaded with chunks of beef, potatoes, carrots, and onions. He mopped up the last of the savory juices with a fluffy biscuit, one of several he ate, and washed everything down with a couple of cups of strong, hot coffee. He still had some aches and pains from everything that had happened today, and weariness lurked in his bones, but for the most part he felt human again.

Fiddler seemed to appreciate the meal even more. A lot of drunks Pike had known over the years didn't have much of an appetite for anything except booze, and as a result they started to waste away over time. Not Fiddler. He tucked into the vittles with gusto and eagerly accepted seconds when Mary offered them.

"I must admit, Mr. Fiddler, such enthusiasm for the food I've prepared is gratifying," she told him.

"I've been in jail for nearly a week, ma'am," he said bluntly. "Any home-cooked meal would seem a veritable feast right now, whether it was actually good or not. In this case, the food really is wonderful. I feel as if I've been transported to heaven, Mrs. Shannon, heaven, I say."

Nessa laughed and said, "You'd better save a little room for a bowl of peach cobbler, Mr. Fiddler, if you want to experience something really heavenly."

"More food?" he said, widening his eyes in mock dismay. "Oh, I don't know if I could possibly . . . well, I suppose I might find a *bit* more room . . ."

Nessa brought out the cobbler, along with a small pitcher of heavy cream for topping. By the time Pike was finished eating, he felt like shoving his chair back, loosening his trousers, and groaning, although he didn't do any of those things except move his chair. Fiddler moaned softly, a sound of pure satisfaction.

With the meal done, Pike said, "I reckon we ought to talk over what needs to be done about Doak Ramsey and his bunch."

Torrance had been sullen all the way through supper, saying hardly anything and keeping his eyes on his plate most of the time. Now he said, "It's our problem to deal with, not yours."

"It's the whole Shannon family that Ramsey's trying to ruin, isn't it? And the last time I checked, I was still a Shannon."

Torrance's brawny shoulders rose and fell. "In name only, I'd say."

Anger at his older brother flared inside Pike. It had been an enjoyable meal, but now Torrance seemed determined to ruin any good feelings that might have lingered.

Mary said sharply, "Pike is a member of this family and always will be. If he has any ideas about what should be done, I think you and Dougal should listen to them, Torrance." She scraped her chair back. "Why don't all of you menfolk go out on the porch and talk? Vanessa, help me clear away and clean up in the kitchen."

Nessa looked like she didn't care for being excluded from the discussion, as well as being less than enthusiastic about the cleanup chores. But she didn't argue.

Pike, Dougal, Torrance, and Fiddler stepped out onto the covered porch as Mary had suggested. Dougal took an old briar pipe and a pouch of tobacco from a pocket in his overalls. Torrance reached inside his vest to his shirt pocket to pull out a cigar. He saw Fiddler eyeing it and asked, "Would you like one?"

"I would dearly love one, Mr. Shannon," the little man replied.

Torrance took out a second cigar and handed it to Fiddler. He scratched a match to life on the sole of his shoe and lit both cheroots. Dougal had finished packing tobacco into his pipe and also lit a match to hold to the bowl as he puffed on it.

Pike moved to the side and perched a hip on the porch railing. He watched his grandfather, brother, and newfound friend getting their smokes going and tried not to shake his head. Full night had fallen while they were eating, and the shadows were thick out there. Anybody could be hiding in them, drawing a bead on the three men as they obligingly lit themselves up as targets. Pike's right hand never moved far from the gun on his hip, and his eyes never stopped moving.

It was a very pleasant evening, warm with just a hint of coolness in the breeze. Pike couldn't enjoy it as much as he might have otherwise, though, because of what he had found when he got back here to his old stomping grounds.

"What do you plan to do about Ramsey, Grandpappy?" he asked bluntly.

"What *can* we do?" Dougal replied, his tone equally straightforward. "Countin' cousins, second cousins, in-laws, and the like, we got a dozen or so able-bodied men of fightin' age scattered through the county. Doak can raise three, maybe four times that many kinfolks and friends. Plus he's the law and has that power behind him. There are plenty of folks in Warbonnet County who ain't fond of the Ramseys, but they ain't gonna stand up against Doak as long as he's got that badge pinned to his shirt."

"So we can't go straight ahead at him," Pike said. "That doesn't mean there's nothing we can do."

Torrance puffed on his cigar. The coal at the end glowed a brighter orange, lighting up his face for a second. As the light faded, he blew out a cloud of smoke and said, "We don't have the money to hire a bunch of cold-blooded killers of your ilk, Pike. So if you were thinking maybe you and some of your friends could profit off our unfortunate circumstances, I'm afraid you're going to be disappointed."

Pike straightened from his casual stance and said, "Blast it, Torrance, I've only been home a couple of hours and you're already trying to pick a fight."

"I'm not trying to pick a fight, and you know it. I'm not a fighter. Never have been."

Yeah, because you're too gutless for that, Pike thought. He reined in the words before they escaped from his mouth.

He turned back to Dougal and went on, "You mentioned some of the other fellas in the county who tried making 'shine after that local option business went through. Andy Burnett and the Dawson brothers and some others. If the Shannons can't stand up to Ramsey, what chance did they ever have?"

"None at all," Dougal said.

"But what if they threw in with us? They're bound to have friends and family who would follow their lead. We might be able to come up with a dozen or more men who would help us fight back against Doak and his bunch."

Dougal frowned, puffed on his pipe, and ran the fingers of one hand through his long, white beard. Finally he said, "Are you talkin' about havin' a meetin' of some sort with those fellas?"

"It seems like a place to start. If we could persuade some of them to join us, it would cut down the odds against us."

"Yeah, it might be just two to one instead of three or four to one," Dougal said. "Those still ain't good odds, son. You might not get killed quite as quick . . . but you still wind up dead."

Fiddler said, "I'm not sure I have any right to join this discussion . . ."

"No, go ahead," Pike told him. "I've got a hunch you have a few grudges of your own against Doak Ramsey."

"And against those so-called deputies of his." Fiddler shivered a little. "Especially Chuck Hanratty. That man is just . . . *vile* is the only word I can think of to describe him." Fiddler cleared his throat and went on, "What I was going to say is that I'm acquainted with those men you were talking about, Andy and Cloyd and Hebner and the others, and they're good men, no doubt about that, but they're not . . . well, professional fighting men of the type that you appear to be, Pike. They're never going to be a match for the Ramseys in a gun battle."

Fiddler had bought white lightning from all those other moonshiners at one time or another, Pike supposed. And even though Pike didn't know any of them personally, he was sure Fiddler was right about their abilities. A man could have all the courage in the world and still lack the necessary skills to stay alive in battle.

Despite that, a man could work only with what was available to him. The alternative was to give up. He supposed the whole Shannon family could pull up stakes and leave Warbonnet County. Head somewhere else and try to start over. Abandon this spread on the Brazos River and allow Doak Ramsey to finish the job of taking over not just the moonshine business in these parts, but the whole county. All the Shannons had to do was swallow their pride and slink away with their tails between their legs.

Just the thought of doing that made a ball of sickness form in Pike's belly. Only once in his life had he ever given up and run away, and that was when he had left home a dozen years earlier.

Now that he was back, he was never going to do that again.

"Like I said, we can't fight him head-on. But there are other things we can do, especially if we can round up some help. Grandpappy, can you get word to those other men, and any others you think might be willing to throw in with us, and ask them to come here tomorrow evening?"

"I reckon I can do that," Dougal replied. "If you're sure you want to get yourself mixed up in our troubles."

"If I'm sure?" Pike repeated. "Why wouldn't I be?"

Torrance said, "You ran out on the family once before, remember?"

Pike took a step toward his older brother, his hands balling into fists as he did so. Torrance was a couple of inches shorter but probably forty pounds heavier than he was. An old familiar rage bubbled up inside Pike, and he wanted to swing at Torrance, plant a fist right in the middle of that beefy face.

But being hotheaded had gotten him into trouble more than once in his life, Pike reminded himself. And even if he walloped his brother, Torrance wouldn't fight back. Even if his face was covered with blood and his eyes were blackened, Torrance would just give him one of those smug, superior smiles . . .

Pike took a deep breath and turned to Fiddler. "What about you?" he asked, surprising himself with how calm and under control his voice sounded. "Do you want to be part of this?"

"I'll probably regret it, because at the moment I'm sober and I *never* make good decisions when I'm sober . . . but yes, Pike, I believe I would. You've treated me today as if I wasn't something you'd scrape off the sole of your boot. That's more than enough reason for me to declare that I'll do anything within my power to assist you and your family."

"You coulda just said yes, you know," Dougal told him.

"All right, it's decided, then," Pike said. "We'll get those other fellas here tomorrow night and see what we can come up with. And if nothing else, before this is all over with, Doak Ramsey will know he's been in a fight."

CHAPTER 10

In the past twelve years, Pike had slept in vermin-infested jail cells, on the cold, rocky ground, and in the fanciest hotel rooms in Denver and San Francisco. He had never slept any better, though, than he did that night in the bed in his old room. The mattress was new since he'd left home, and the curtains over the single window were different, but not much else had changed, not even the hooked rug on the floor next to the bed.

He wondered if his mother had kept everything mostly the same on purpose, in the hope that someday he would return.

Feeling more rested and refreshed than he would have thought possible, he got up early the next morning and followed the smells of coffee and bacon and fresh biscuits to the kitchen. He found his mother, sister, and grandfather there, but not Torrance. Pike didn't ask about his older brother, not really caring if it was Torrance's habit to sleep late.

"I'd like to help out around here," he said as he sat down to a plate of food and a steaming cup of coffee.

"If I remember right, there are always plenty of chores to be done."

"Of course," Mary said. "Torrance has already ridden out to check on the horse herd, but the pigs need to be slopped."

Pike winced, which brought a laugh from Dougal. "That'll teach you to volunteer, boy," he said.

"Torrance is already up and gone?" Pike asked.

Nessa said, "You shouldn't sound so surprised, Pike. He's a hard worker."

"We wouldn't have made it without him," Mary added.

Grudgingly, Dougal said, "They're right. He don't shy away from hard work. Hasn't ever since he grew up and got to where he wasn't sick all the time."

Pike drank some coffee and said, "Well, I'm glad to hear that, I suppose. The two of us rub each other the wrong way, though, and I don't expect that to change."

"It won't if you don't let it," his mother said. Nessa nodded.

They were just trying to keep peace in the family, like all womenfolks did, Pike told himself. He wouldn't go out of his way looking for trouble with Torrance, but there was never going to be any real brotherly love between them, either.

"Maybe what we ought to do today is just ride around and let you take a look at the spread again, Pike," Dougal suggested. "Never hurts to get the lay of the land."

Pike nodded. "That's a good idea."

He glanced around as a footstep sounded behind

him. Fiddler, looking a little bleary-eyed, came into the kitchen. Even though the little man had gone several days without drinking—without drinking *much*, anyway—the need was still there inside him. He had probably woken up craving the jolt of whiskey.

"Good morning, everyone," Fiddler said.

From the stove, where she was cooking more bacon, Mary gestured toward an empty chair at the table and said, "Sit yourself down, Mr. Fiddler. I'll have breakfast ready for you in a few minutes. Nessa, pour Mr. Fiddler some coffee."

"Coffee sounds good, but I . . . I'm not sure about eating—"

"Nonsense. A hearty breakfast is just the thing you need, Mr. Fiddler."

"You don't have to call me . . . Oh, I'm fighting a losing battle here, aren't I?"

"Indeed you are, sir."

Fiddler sat down and summoned up a weak smile as Nessa filled the cup in front of him with hot coffee. "Thank you, my dear," he told her.

Pike swallowed a mouthful of flapjacks, molasses, and bacon and said, "We were talking about taking a ride around the ranch, Fiddler. Want to come along?"

"You mean on a horse?"

Dougal boomed, "Fresh air'll do you good! Put hair on your chest."

"I, ah, suppose I could give it a try. I haven't done much riding in recent years . . ." Fiddler swallowed hard as Mary put a plate of food in front of him. He looked at Dougal and said, "I don't suppose we could sweeten this coffee a bit . . . ?"

The white-bearded old-timer chuckled. "There's a

jug in the cabinet, if that's what you're askin'. Never any shortage of white lightnin' around here. But you'll be better off in the long run if you do without it for a spell, I'm thinkin'."

Fiddler shuddered. "I suppose I can make an attempt." He picked up his cup of coffee. It rattled a little against the saucer as he lifted it. Using both hands, he guided the cup to his mouth and sipped. The coffee steadied him a little. He began to eat, hesitantly at first, then with greater enthusiasm.

"I must say, Mrs. Shannon, these flapjacks are delicious. And the bacon is perfect. A meal like this goes a long way toward restoring a man's strength and well-being."

"Well, you just eat hearty, sir," Mary said. "There's nothing like hard work and good food to make a man healthy again."

Fiddler smiled, although he didn't appear entirely convinced. Pike leaned over to him and said, "Speaking of hard work, I hear that the pigs need to be slopped."

Fiddler smiled, but it was a weak one. "I shall endeavor to earn my keep," he said.

Nessa laughed and said, "You got out of that one pretty neatly, Pike."

After breakfast, Pike surprised himself by helping Fiddler throw several buckets of slop to the pigs rooting around in a muddy pen a good distance from the house so the smell wouldn't carry as easily. Fiddler commented, "I knew your family raised horses, but I didn't know they raised pigs, too."

"Where do you think that bacon came from?

They've got some cattle for milk and beef, too, and chickens for eggs."

"I must confess, I've never given much thought to such things. I suppose I believed food just appeared by magic."

"No such thing as magic," Pike said. "Just hard work."

"Yes, I'm beginning to realize that," Fiddler said as he dumped a bucket of slop over the fence into the pigpen.

When they walked into the barn later, they found Nessa saddling a horse. She wore trousers now, as well as a man's shirt with the sleeves rolled up over her forearms. An old brown hat with the strap tight under her chin was on her head. Her long red hair was tied into a ponytail.

"You look like you think you're coming with us," Pike said.

"I am," Nessa said. "Grandpappy's rheumatism started acting up after breakfast, so he asked me to show you around."

"I grew up on this ranch, remember? I think I can find my way around without any help."

"Some things have changed," Nessa said with a shrug. "Anyway, Grandpappy said I could go, so I'm going."

Pike narrowed his eyes at her. "As I recall, arguing with you was always a losing proposition, even when you were a little girl."

"It still is," Nessa said, smiling.

"Have you got a rifle, at least?"

She picked up a lever-action carbine that leaned against the wall and slid it into a sheath fastened to the saddle. "Yeah, and I'm a darned good shot with it, too, if I do say so myself."

Pike just grunted, not surprised by her response, and said, "Come on, Fiddler, let's find you a horse."

They settled on a brown mare for Fiddler. Nessa swore the horse was gentle to ride, and Pike didn't think his sister would play a trick on a visitor, especially one as easygoing and friendly as Fiddler. With an apprehensive look on his face, Fiddler swung up into the saddle. The mare just stood there calmly. Fiddler appeared to relax a little, but not completely.

Pike rode his dun, Nessa a feisty paint that matched her personality. The three of them headed away from the house and barn. Nessa led the way toward the Brazos.

"I suppose there's still a river trail?" Pike asked.

"Of course. The main road doesn't follow it because of all the twists and turns, but the old trail's still there."

As they rode, Pike's mind drifted back to summer days he had spent swimming in the river, swinging out on vines from overhanging trees and dropping into the stream with splashes that threw glistening drops of water high in the air. Mostly his childhood and adolescence had been devoted to hard work, since there was always cotton to pick and other chores to do, but those moments of leisure and play had come along, as well. He recalled one particular sun-dappled afternoon in a meadow beside the Brazos, when he and one of the local girls named . . .

Pike frowned as the recollection slammed up against a rock wall. He remembered distinctly what he and the girl had done on that long-ago afternoon, but what in blazes was her *name*? Pike racked his brain trying to recall it but failed. Wasn't that a heck of a thing? he asked himself. Seemed like he ought to be able to remember something like that.

But he probably didn't need to be musing on such while riding along with Nessa and Fiddler. Instead he looked at the river, flowing slowly but steadily toward the Gulf of Mexico between flower-dotted meadows and hills covered with post oaks and cottonwoods, mesquites and bramble bushes. Being back here made him feel more of a sense of homecoming than he really had expected.

They came to an even smaller trail leading away from the river. Nessa turned her paint into it. The trees and brush crowded in close on both sides, which made Pike frown a little. There would be plenty of hiding places in that thick growth.

"You know where you're going?" he called to his sister.

Nessa reined in and looked back over her shoulder at him and Fiddler. "Of course I do," she said. "We're still on Shannon range, and I know every foot of it."

Pike didn't doubt that. He motioned for Fiddler to follow Nessa and said, "I'll bring up the rear." He didn't want anybody sneaking up on them from behind. Such caution was a habit with him, and one he couldn't afford to break.

The trail was wide enough for only one person on horseback. It twisted and turned through the trees for what seemed like a mile, but Pike knew that, actually, they had come only a couple of hundred yards from the river. He wondered where in blazes Nessa was taking them, but then a smell drifted to him and he knew. It was a peculiar odor, the sharp tang of woodsmoke mixed with something else, something earthier, almost rank. It had been years since Pike had experienced this particular smell, but he realized now that he had never forgotten it.

"That's corn mash," he called to Nessa. "You're taking us to a still!"

CHAPTER 11

Nessa grinned back over her shoulder at him and Fiddler. "Grandpappy thought you might like to know where they are these days," she said as she reined in. "The one that Pa had before you left has been moved several times, and we've added more. We had to in the past year to keep up with the demand."

"Nobody ever made better white lightning than Lije Shannon," Fiddler said.

Nessa's smile went away, to be replaced by a wistful expression. "That's right," she said.

"Oh dear," Fiddler said. "That was unthinking of me. I mean, Lije has only been gone for a month or so—"

"No, it's all right, Mr. Fiddler," Nessa told him. "Sure, it hurts that he's not here anymore, but Pa would have been the first one to tell you, life has to go on. Otherwise, all the hard work a man's done, all that he's accomplished, well, it just goes for nothing if his family can't carry on without him, doesn't it?"

Fiddler nodded slowly and said, "That's a wise way of looking at things."

"Don't think we're not mourning him. At night

sometimes, I hear Ma crying in her room, and I know she's got this raw, aching hole ripped inside her. But when she comes out, she's got a smile on her face and she's ready for the day's work. The rest of us try to be the same way."

Pike leaned forward in the saddle and thought about his own reaction when he read in Nessa's letter that their father was dead. To be honest, he'd been angry more than anything else. Any grief he'd felt had been because an hombre was *supposed* to feel sad when his pa died. Too many years, too many miles had passed since he'd left home for him to feel the sort of gut-wrenching sorrow Nessa was talking about.

But the anger was still there, maybe stronger than ever now that he suspected Doak Ramsey might have had something to do with his father's death.

Nessa put a brave face on again and motioned with her head for Pike and Fiddler to follow her. "Come on," she told them. "It's not far now."

They resumed their ride through the woods. A few minutes later the trail entered a straight stretch that ran for about fifty yards to the base of a slope. The tree limbs overhanging the trail formed a tunnel cloaked by shade. Nessa paused and whistled like a bird. Pike knew that was a signal. As they rode forward again, he looked over the woods on both sides of the trail and spotted a stray beam of sunlight reflecting off something to their right. A rifle barrel, more than likely. A guard was posted out there, but Nessa's whistle had let him know that it was safe to let the riders pass.

They reached the slope and climbed about twenty yards to a hilltop. Some of the brush had been cut down and hauled away to form a clearing under the tall post oaks. The mash smell was strong in the air now.

A small, three-sided shed stood to Pike's right, the fourth side open to the elements although a large piece of canvas was attached to the sloping roof so it could be pulled down to form a wall of sorts. The shed had a couple of cots and a potbellied stove in it, as well as a round table made from a barrel and a wagon wheel and a couple of rickety-looking chairs.

The still dominated the clearing, though, with its large, round boiler, the pipe connecting the boiler to the thumper made from a barrel, and then the keg containing the worm, as the unseen coil of pipe was called. The worm was the final stage of the process, and from the tap attached to the keg would flow the pure corn liquor, the white lightning, the moonshine that people came from miles around to buy once it had been strained into jugs.

No fire burned in the stone furnace underneath the boiler. The mash was in there ripening, getting ready for a run, Pike knew. He could tell that from the smell—although he was a little surprised that he actually remembered such a detail after all these years.

Along with Nessa and Fiddler, he reined in as two young men came out of the shed to greet them. They had been sitting at the makeshift table playing cards. A jug was on the ground next to one of the chairs. Pike wondered if the boys had been passing it back and forth, even though it was pretty early in the day to be guzzling 'shine. One thing about being around the stuff all the time, though—a fella didn't exactly develop a tolerance for it, but swigging a little white lightning came to be almost as natural as breathing, something you could do any time of the day or night.

"Howdy, Nessa!" one of the youngsters called. They were little more than boys, Pike saw now, fifteen or sixteen years old. Both redheaded and freckle-faced, one a few inches shorter and built stockier than the other. Pike could tell they were brothers. Possibly even twins, though not identical.

They both held weapons, the shorter one an old Henry rifle, the taller boy a shotgun. They were dressed in overalls and homespun shirts.

The shorter one had spoken first. Now the taller one said, "Gee, it sure is good to see you again!" then immediately gulped and looked embarrassed. It was hard to tell with so many freckles on his face, but Pike thought a pink flush was stealing across the boy's features.

"And you as well, Charley," she told him with a smile that made him blush even more. The youngster had a crush on her, that was obvious.

The shorter boy nodded toward Pike and Fiddler and asked, "Who are these fellas?"

"Charley, Davey, this is my brother Pike and his friend Mr. Fiddler."

The boys ignored Fiddler and stared openmouthed at Pike. Davey, the shorter brother, said, "Pike Shannon, the famous gunfighter and outlaw?"

Pike smiled and said, "Most folks would say infamous or notorious. But yeah, I'm the Pike Shannon you're thinking of. Now that I'm back in these parts, though, I'd rather just be known as one of the Shannon boys."

"But you gunned down that fast-draw *bandido* Hector Ortiz out in El Paso!" Charley exclaimed.

"And killed a bunch of men in one of them range wars up in Montana," his brother added. "We read about it in the *Police Gazette*!"

Pike grunted. "Just did what was necessary at the time, or it seemed so, anyway. I don't brag on such things."

"Maybe not, but shoot, we've all heard about you," Davey said. "And it's a plumb honor to be related to you, Cousin Pike."

Pike looked over at Nessa and raised an eyebrow. She said, "Charley and Davey are Ed and Tildy Morrigan's sons. You remember Tildy, don't you? She was Aunt Edna's daughter."

Pike barely remembered Aunt Edna, which made her daughter Pike's . . . what? Second cousin? And Tildy's sons would be his third cousins, or were they second cousins once removed? Pike never had been able to keep such relationships straight. All he knew for sure was that these two redheaded youngsters were kin to him, and that was enough.

"I'm glad to meet you, too," Pike said. "Are you boys in charge of this still?"

Obvious pride made them stand up straighter and square their shoulders. "Yes, sir, we sure are," Davey said. "Your pappy Lije gave us the job before he . . . uh, before . . ." He glanced at Nessa. "Sorry, Nessa."

"It's all right," she told him. "Davey and Charley have done quite a few runs. They're very good at it."

"We come by it natural-like," Charley said. "Our last name may be Morrigan, but we're Shannons through and through, ain't we, Davey?"

"Durn right," Davey agreed emphatically.

Pike nodded back down the trail and asked, "Who's standing guard out there?"

"That'd be Lonzo Hightower," Davey answered. "He's one of our pa's sister's boys. Best shot in these parts."

"Yeah, he can shoot the wing off a gnat at a hunnerd yards," Charley put in.

"Of course, you're bound to be a better shot than him, Cousin Pike," Davey added. "After all, you're the famous—"

Pike lifted a hand to stop him. He didn't want these boys hero-worshiping him. Such things had always made him uncomfortable. He was no hero in his own eyes, just a man who'd chosen to ride a dark and dangerous trail and do what needed to be done.

"Like I said, I'm just one of the Shannon boys. And I'm glad to meet you fellas. Keep up the good work."

"Y'all come back and see us anytime, Cousin Pike," Davey said.

As the three riders started to turn their horses, Charley called after them, "You, too, Cousin Nessa!"

She turned her head, gave him a beaming smile that made him gulp and blush again, and said, "Goodbye, Charley."

Pike chuckled as they rode away. When they reached the bottom of the hill, he said quietly, "I reckon that boy thinks he's a distant enough cousin to have a crush on you, Nessa."

"Oh, Charley's harmless," Nessa said. "But I suppose I should be ashamed of myself for the way I tease him sometimes."

Pike didn't spot the sentry, Lonzo Hightower, this

time as they followed the narrow path back to the Brazos. He was glad the still was being guarded. Normally a moonshiner had to worry not only about the law but also about unscrupulous rivals. In Warbonnet County, those threats were one and the same, and somehow, that made it seem even worse.

When they reached the river trail, Nessa turned northwest to follow the river upstream. Along here, the Brazos was a good-sized river, at least where Texas was concerned. It was close to a hundred yards from one bank to the other. Pike tried to keep an eye on that side as well as on the trail in front of and behind them.

As he rode, he took the makin's out of the pocket of his faded red shirt. Working one-handed—his left hand, never his gun hand—he started building a quirley. He had never been a heavy smoker, but he had done it enough he could handle the chore with a single hand. When he had rolled the tobacco and paper into a cylinder and twisted the ends shut, he put it in his mouth, stowed the papers and pouch away, and fished a lucifer from his pocket. He snapped it into life with his thumbnail and started to lift the flame to the end of the quirley.

Before the match got there, something whipped right in front of Pike's face, clipped off the end of the quirley, and scattered tobacco. He knew even without hearing the crack of the rifle that it was a bullet.

CHAPTER 12

Nessa and Fiddler were in front of him. Pike knew from the way they reacted, jerking around in their saddles, that they had heard the shot, too. He spat out the stub that was left of the quirley and shouted, "Go!" at them.

Nessa jabbed her bootheels into her horse's flanks and sent the animal lunging forward. Fiddler just looked around in confusion, though, as if unsure what to do.

Pike leaped his horse ahead and felt something ruffle through the hair on the back of his head as he did so. Another slug coming too blasted close for comfort, he realized. *Much* too close. He yanked his hat off and used it to slap the rump of Fiddler's horse.

Fiddler yelled, "Yow!" as the horse jumped and took off. Pike's dun pounded along in the mare's wake. Pike clapped his hat back on and tightened the chin strap. The shots were coming from somewhere across the river, and as he glanced in that direction, he spotted a spurt of muzzle flame in the brush. The bullet whined past, missing wider than the first two shots had.

Pike drew his Colt. The range was too far for accurate shooting with a handgun, especially from the hurricane deck of a galloping horse, but he triggered three shots anyway, aiming for the general vicinity of the place he had seen the muzzle flash. You never could tell where luck might carry a bullet.

Then he slid the iron back in its holster and leaned forward to concentrate on his riding. The trail twisted and turned with the river. A few yards ahead of him, Fiddler hunched over in the saddle, clinging desperately to the horn with both hands. He wasn't doing anything to steer his mount, but luckily the mare was following Nessa's paint.

Nessa rode like someone born to the saddle, which came as no surprise to Pike. He remembered her riding when she was very young. Their mother had worried about that, but Nessa had never been thrown, as far as Pike could recall. He didn't know what had happened during the years he'd been gone, but clearly Nessa hadn't lost any of her skill as a rider.

Pike glanced to his right, across the river, and saw riders dashing through the trees and undergrowth over there. So there was more than one bushwhacker, and they didn't intend to give up just because they'd missed their first few shots.

Had to be Ramsey varmints over there, Pike thought, either blood kin or some of Doak's deputies breaking the law instead of upholding it.

The trees were thick enough along here to provide good cover, but Pike, Nessa, and Fiddler couldn't gallop into them at full speed. They would have to slow down to weave their way among the trunks, and if they did that, the ambushers would see what they were doing and open fire again.

Pike pulled his Winchester from its sheath and shouted over the pounding hoofbeats, "Nessa! Into the trees! I'll keep them busy!"

It would be dangerous for him to stop and trade shots with the enemy, but it would give his companions time to reach safety.

Nessa turned her head and called back to him, "No! There's cover up ahead! Follow me!"

Pike bit back a curse. Nessa had always been too headstrong and reckless to do what people told her to do, but maybe she was right. He reminded himself that she knew this country a lot better now than he did. Still holding the rifle, he followed, keeping close behind Fiddler's mount so the mare wouldn't be tempted to stop running.

Up ahead, a number of dead trees that had washed down the river during floods in years past had piled up against some limestone outcroppings. The trunks, missing their bark now and weathered to a pale gray, formed a wall of sorts. The rocks added to the barrier. Nessa slowed her horse as she came to them and dropped out of the saddle while the animal was still moving. She carried her carbine with her as she dashed toward the fallen trees.

Pike jerked his Winchester to his shoulder and cranked off four rounds as fast as he could work the rifle's lever, spraying the shots along the opposite bank where the bushwhackers darted in and out of the brush. He wasn't expecting to hit anything, but if he did, it would be a bonus. He just wanted to keep them occupied while Nessa made it to safety.

"Mr. Fiddler!" she cried. "Over here!"

"Whoa!" Fiddler called frantically to his horse as he hauled back on the reins and sawed on the bit. "Whoa, please!"

Even as gentle a mount as the mare seemed to be wasn't going to take kindly to that treatment. She skidded to a halt and reared up on her hind legs as she pawed at the air. With a frightened bawl, Fiddler went backward out of the saddle. He hit the ground hard. From the corner of his eye, Pike saw that both of Fiddler's feet had slipped out of the stirrups. That was pure luck; the little man wouldn't have known to kick them free. But luck or not, at least Fiddler didn't get dragged as the mare bolted on up the trail after Nessa's paint.

Nessa threw herself flat behind one of the logs and thrust her carbine over it. She opened fire, the weapon's spiteful cracks echoing flatly across the water.

Pike dismounted on the run, too, and stumbled a little as he headed toward Fiddler. The little man wasn't moving, and Pike couldn't tell how badly being thrown from the horse had injured him. A bullet sizzled through the air close to him, and another slug struck one of the limestone slabs and sent dust and rock chips flying into the air.

Fiddler began stirring just as Pike reached his side. Holding the Winchester in his right hand, Pike used his left to grab Fiddler's arm. He hoisted Fiddler onto his feet. For a little fella, Fiddler was surprisingly heavy, but Pike got him upright and shoved him toward the fallen trees where Nessa was trading shots with the bushwhackers.

Fiddler looked stunned and disoriented, but the

momentum from Pike's push kept him stumbling in the right direction until Nessa could reach up, grab his belt, and pull him down beside her.

Pike dropped to a knee, raised the rifle again, and slammed four more shots into the brush on the far side of the river. Then he surged up and dived forward, coming to rest on Nessa's other side.

"Ramseys!" she said, sounding like the name tasted bad in her mouth.

"More than likely," Pike agreed. "Fiddler, are you all right over there?"

"I . . . I think so."

"Well, keep your head down and maybe you'll stay that way."

All three of them followed Pike's advice for the next few moments. Shot after shot thudded into the logs or whined off the rocks, but none of them found a way through to the three people who had taken cover there.

Finally there was a lull in the firing from the other bank. Pike raised up enough to send two rounds whipping across the river, then dropped down again.

"How much ammunition do you have?" he asked Nessa.

"Just what's in the carbine. Seven or eight rounds, I'd say."

Pike's Winchester used the same cartridge, a .45-70. He had a dozen extras in his pocket, but that was all. The box of shells in his saddlebags wasn't going to do them any good since the dun had galloped on up the trail with Nessa's paint and Fiddler's mare. Pike was glad the horses were safe, but they sure could have used that ammunition.

"From here on out, don't fire unless you have a clear shot," he told his sister. "We may be hunkered down here for a while, and we need to make these bullets last."

"We're close enough to the still that Davey and Charley must have heard the shots," Nessa said. "They're liable to try to come and help us, and they'll ride right into an ambush."

"Maybe one of them will head down to the ranch headquarters for help."

"I don't know. There's nobody there but Grandpappy."

"And Torrance," Pike said, then his mouth quirked bitterly. "But I'd be wasting my time hoping for any help from him, wouldn't I?"

"I'm sure he'd *want* to help," Nessa said. "He's just not any good at fighting."

"Yeah, claiming that makes a handy excuse for turning your back on trouble."

Pike risked a glance across the river and spotted a man running from one tree to another. With blinding speed, Pike's rifle came up and cracked. On the other side of the Brazos, the running man broke stride, grabbed his leg, twisted around, and tumbled to the ground. Frantically, he crawled behind the tree he had almost reached before Pike winged him.

"Well, that's one of them hit hard enough he's probably out of the fight," Pike said as he bellied down again. "I don't reckon you got a good enough look at them to know how many there are."

"Not really," Nessa said. "Three or four, I'd guess. At least that many."

Pike considered the situation. If it had been him over there, with enemies holed up on this side of the river, he would have sent a couple of men either up-stream or down, around the nearest bend, and had them swim their horses across the Brazos, then try to close in on the quarry from the flank. Even if he had to stay in position by himself while the rest of his bunch tried that tactic, he could keep the enemy pinned down.

"Fiddler, can you use a pistol?"

"I . . . I've shot a gun in the past, but it was a long time ago."

"Yes or no, blast it!"

Fiddler swallowed hard and said, "I'll try. That's all I can promise."

Pike pulled his Colt, replaced the spent rounds with fresh cartridges from the loops on his shell belt, and passed the gun over to Fiddler, across Nessa's back.

"Keep a close watch to your right," Pike said. "If you see any of the varmints trying to sneak up on us, let me know. *Don't* just start shooting. That'll waste bullets. You don't want to use that gun until they're really close."

"But if they're that close," Fiddler said, "won't *they* be shooting already?"

"More than likely. Just keep your head down."

Fiddler moaned. "Keep watch, but keep your head down. Use the gun, but don't use it too soon. Why does being in a gun battle have to be so blasted *complicated*?"

CHAPTER 13

The shooting continued from across the river but became more sporadic. That agreed with Pike's theory that the bushwhackers had split their forces. He tried another snap-shot when he caught a glimpse of a man moving around over there, but he was pretty sure he missed this time. Other than that, the fight settled down into a standoff, which had dangers of its own, especially on a day that got warmer by the minute as the sun climbed overhead.

Sweat trickled along Pike's ribs. Nessa took off her hat and wiped beads of moisture from her forehead. Fiddler said, "Is anyone else getting hot and thirsty?"

"Oh, don't talk about it," Nessa said.

"It's just that there's so much water right there in the river, just a few feet away—"

"I said don't talk about it!"

Fiddler subsided into a shocked silence for a few seconds, then said, "I'm sorry. I understand."

"No, I'm sorry, Mr. Fiddler. I shouldn't have snapped at you."

"You had every reason in the world to react that

way, my dear. What I was saying was just making the situation worse."

Pike said, "Are you watching over there like I told you to, Fiddler?"

"Yes, but I haven't seen any—" Fiddler stopped short, then whispered, "Oh no."

Pike twisted his head in that direction. "What is it?"

"I believe I saw a couple of men in the trees beside the trail. I . . . I think they had rifles."

"If you can see them, they can see us," Pike said. "Where exactly did you spot them?"

"I'm no good at guessing distances. Maybe . . . fifty yards downstream? There's a very distinctive-looking tree close to where I saw them. It has a large trunk at the bottom that goes up a few feet and then splits into two smaller trunks." Fiddler's voice got more excited as he went on, "And there's a man hiding behind it now. I can see his green shirt through the space between the trunks. He . . . he has a rifle! He's pointing it at us—"

"Heads down, both of you!" Pike said. He swiveled on the ground and swung the Winchester over Nessa's back and Fiddler's as well. Nessa knew what was coming and clapped her hands over her ears. Fiddler just cried out in shock as Pike's rifle thundered right above him.

Pike had spotted the tree Fiddler was talking about as soon as he looked in that direction, and he saw the bushwhacker as well when he looked between the split trunks. The man's rifle spat flame, too, but his shot came a split second after Pike's.

An instant after that, the bushwhacker flew backward as Pike's bullet coursed between the trunks and drove into his chest. Pike saw the rifle barrel slant suddenly skyward, then it dropped out of sight along with its owner.

Pike's instincts told him that was one son of a buck who'd never ambush anybody again.

A fierce burst of rifle fire came from across the river, forcing Pike to duck again as slugs chewed into the logs. The men over there—two, by the sound of it—were trying to give the ones on this side of the river a better chance to get in close and attack.

But those hombres didn't know that one of their men was already down over here, and judging by the way the brush was whipping around when Pike risked a look, the other flanker was beating a hasty retreat. When the shooting tapered off and then stopped, he heard swift hoofbeats moving away on this side of the Brazos. The second man had had enough.

Pike wondered if he had taken his dead or wounded partner with him.

He heard horses heading off on the other side of the river, too, the sounds fainter but unmistakable. With hope in her voice, Nessa said, "They've given up."

"Maybe," Pike said, "or maybe they're just trying to be slick. Both of you stay put."

"What are you going to do?"

"Slide out of here and see what I can find."

Nessa put a hand on her brother's arm. "Be careful, Pike."

A reckless grin split his face. "What fun would that be?"

This wasn't exactly fun, though. It was serious business, he told himself as he worked his way backward on his belly. The lives of Nessa and Fiddler might depend on him. If he had been alone, he might have stayed hunkered down until nightfall, just to make sure those Ramsey gunmen weren't waiting for him to show his head. He knew Nessa and Fiddler wouldn't be able to hold out that long, though. So he kept moving and his muscles were tensed against the halfway anticipated slam of a bullet—as if that would do any good.

When he was far enough back that the rocks and logs no longer offered protection from any riflemen on the other side of the river, he rolled over and powered to his feet, then sprinted for the trees. No bullets came after him, but his heart was pounding anyway—and not just from the run—when he reached cover.

Pike pressed his back against a tree trunk and caught his breath. Then he cat-footed through the woods, using all the considerable stealth at his command. He still hadn't seen anyone by the time he reached the split-trunked tree.

Blood had splashed on the ground behind the tree, proof that he had hit the bushwhacker. But there was no body. He suspected the man wasn't dead, just badly wounded, and had been able to make it his horse. That was more likely than his companion hauling off his corpse.

Pike looked around and found the spot where two horses had been tied. He wasn't going to waste his time trying to follow the tracks they had left. He knew who his enemies were. Maybe he didn't know exactly who had pulled the triggers, but Doak Ramsey had ordered the ambush, he was sure of that. Ramsey had had men spying on the Shannon ranch, and they had seized the chance to try to get rid of Pike.

No more shots had come from the other side of the Brazos. Pike felt confident all the bushwhackers were gone. From the trees, he called to Nessa and Fiddler, "Stay where you are for a little while longer. I'm going to find our horses!"

The three horses hadn't gone far, only a few hundred yards up the trail, where they had stopped to graze. Pike's dun and the mare weren't skittish, but Nessa's paint gave him a little trouble, dancing away from him and then coming back, before he got a hand on the reins.

He led the animals back along the trail. When he came in sight with them, Nessa jumped to her feet and hurried toward him. Pike winced a little, wishing she'd kept her head down just a little longer, but no shot came. They were out of danger, he supposed— for now.

Fiddler came after her, pale and sweating. Pike could tell the ordeal had taken a lot out of him. "How are you feeling now?" Pike asked. "You took a pretty hard fall off that horse."

"Sore," Fiddler replied. "Very sore. But I'll live, which seemed rather unlikely for a while there. So all in all, I can't complain." He held out Pike's gun. "I hope it's all right that I'm glad I didn't have to use this."

"Sure." Pike took the iron and pouched it. "I wish nobody had to use guns to settle their differences."

"Really?" Fiddler frowned. "But if that were the case . . . wouldn't you have been out of work in recent years?"

Pike shrugged and said, "Reckon I would have had to find something else to do."

Fiddler didn't understand and Nessa probably wouldn't have, either, but Pike had seen too many men die, too many go down in front of his own gun, in fact, for reasons that in the end turned out to be nothing but greed for more money or power or both. He hadn't lost any sleep over anything he'd done—he had never killed any hombre who wouldn't have been just as happy to kill *him*—but after so long a time, a man had to ask himself why he followed the trails he did.

Maybe that was why he had come home after he got Nessa's letter. Maybe he wanted to fight for something worthwhile for a change . . .

Pike's mouth tightened into a grim line as he pushed those thoughts out of his mind. Standing around brooding never accomplished a blasted thing. He said, "Come on, let's get back to the ranch. You can show me the rest of the stills some other time, Nessa."

"I think that's a good idea," she said. "If the Ramseys came after us this way, they might try to cause trouble for Ma and Grandpappy and Torrance, too."

That was exactly what Pike was worried about. His return to Warbonnet County might have spooked Doak Ramsey enough that Doak would try to wipe out the Shannons while he could. It all depended on how confident Doak was that he was above the law.

And Pike had never known Doak Ramsey to be lacking in confidence for anything.

The three of them mounted up, Fiddler wincing as he did so at the pull of bruised, sore muscles. They rode along the river trail, and when they came to the smaller path that turned off to the still watched by the Morrigan brothers and Lonzo Hightower, they found Davey and Charley waiting there, on foot, cradling their rifle and shotgun.

"I sure am glad to see that you folks are all right," Davey said. "We heard a bunch of shootin' upriver and didn't know what to do about it, whether to come see if you were in trouble or head down the river and warn Miz Shannon and ol' Dougal."

"You ain't hurt, are you, Nessa?" Charley asked anxiously.

"I'm fine," she assured him, "and I'm glad you boys didn't come after us. You might've gotten hurt."

Davey gestured toward the opposite bank and said, "We heard some horses go by hell-bent for leather over yonder." His eyes narrowed. "Ramseys?"

"That'd be my guess," Pike said. "Somebody ambushed us, and I don't reckon there's anybody else in this part of the country who'd be interested in doing that. You fellas had better sleep with one eye open for a while. It could be that Doak Ramsey's decided to go to war against the Shannons."

"What'll we do if he has?" Charley asked.

Pike rubbed his chin, thought about the meeting he hoped to have that evening with some of the other moonshiners in the area, and said, "Ramseys aren't the only ones who can go to war."

CHAPTER 14

Pike listened closely for the sound of gunfire as he, Nessa, and Fiddler headed downriver. He didn't hear any, which was a relief, but the silence in the hot air was no guarantee there hadn't been any trouble at the ranch headquarters.

Everything looked normal, though, as they came in sight of the ranch house, barn, pigpen, chicken house, and smokehouse. Pike pushed his horse ahead of the other two and called, "Grandpappy!" He was ready to draw his Colt if he needed to.

The front door opened and Dougal came out onto the porch. He was limping a little, reminding Pike of Nessa's comment about their grandfather's rheumatism acting up. "What are you caterwaulin' about, boy?" the old-timer asked.

"Is everything all right here?" Pike asked as he reined to a halt in front of the steps.

"Yeah, I reckon, other than this blasted knee of mine achin' to beat the band. We got some rain comin' in the next couple of days, I can tell you that much. The rheumatiz in this knee never lies."

Nessa and Fiddler cantered up behind Pike. Nessa said, "We got bushwhacked!"

Dougal's eyes widened. He let out a surprised exclamation and said, "It was those blasted Ramseys, wasn't it?"

"We never got a good look at them," Pike said, "but nobody else in these parts has any reason to want to ventilate me. Whoever it was shot a quirley right out of my mouth!"

Dougal scowled and said, "I hope you done some damage back at 'em."

Pike thought about the man he had winged in the leg and the blood he had seen on the ground by that split-trunked tree, and drawled, "I reckon we did."

A worried frown appeared on Dougal's face. "Of course, that's likely to just make Doak more crazy-mad than ever."

Pike swung down from the saddle and handed his dun's reins to Nessa, who said, "I'll take care of the horses. Mr. Fiddler, you should go on inside and rest. My ma has some liniment she can rub on those bruises."

"Thank you, my dear. Considering which part of my anatomy took the brunt of that hard landing, I think it best that I apply any medicaments myself."

"Are you hurt, Fiddler?" Dougal asked.

"My dignity, more than anything else."

Fiddler went in the house while Nessa rode toward the barn, leading the other two horses. Pike propped a hip on the porch railing while Dougal sat down in one of the cane-bottomed chairs to ease his aching knee.

"That ambush tells me Doak is ready to raise the ante," Pike said. "I was worried all the way back down here that he might've attacked the ranch at the same time he had men ambushing us. He didn't make the move this time . . . but he might next time."

"What do you reckon we should do?"

"Can you call in some of the cousins and have somebody standing guard here all the time? The house is pretty sturdy. Old Garvan built it so he could fort up inside it and fight off the Comanches. We don't need to be taken by surprise, though."

Dougal nodded slowly and said, "We can do that. Might get some help from those other fellas, the ones who are comin' to that meetin' tonight, too. Ramsey thinks they're all beat, so he ain't givin' them trouble no more."

"Sounds like a good idea. And the men working at the stills need to keep their eyes and ears open, too."

"Nessa was gonna show you the stills—"

"We only made it to one of them, the one the Morrigan brothers are operating. Then the shooting started, and when it was over, I figured we'd better get back here."

Dougal said, "Them twins are a feisty pair, and they got Lonzo Hightower with 'em. Good boys, all three of 'em."

"That's the impression I got. I know they'll put up a fight if the Ramseys come calling." Pike frowned. "But I don't want them to."

"What?"

"I don't want them to fight. If a bunch of Ramseys show up at that still, or at any of our others, those boys need to hightail it out of there. The woods are thick enough they can give the slip to anybody who comes after 'em. We can rebuild a still," Pike said. "We can't replace our people."

With a surly note in his voice, Dougal said, "Aye, you're right about that, I suppose, but the idea of turnin' tail and runnin' sure sticks in my craw."

"If you're outnumbered and outgunned, the smartest thing to do is fix it so you can fight again another day."

"And I'm sure that's what *you* would do if it was you."

"Well"—Pike grinned as he took his papers and tobacco sack out of his shirt pocket—"I hope most folks would be smarter than I've been in my life. Now, I'm gonna build me another smoke, and I hope nobody shoots it out of my mouth this time!"

Men began to arrive at the ranch shortly after supper. At this time of year, the sky remained light until fairly well along in the evening. It was a pleasant time of day. The afternoon heat had started to fade, and often a refreshing breeze blew over the Texas hills, full of the smell of wildflowers, honeysuckle, and rich, dark earth.

Using a cane to take some of the strain off his knee, Dougal met the visitors and ushered them into the barn, where they gathered in the wide center aisle. Pike waited there, and his grandfather introduced him to some of the men. Pike recognized a few of the names and vaguely recalled the men who had lived in the area before he left home, but he had never really been acquainted with any of them until now.

Andy Burnett was a tall, lanky man with a shock of curly, sandy hair under his pushed-back hat. He seemed to always have a grin on his face. Sam Crow was the opposite, short, dark, and serious. He probably had some Indian blood in him, but Pike didn't hold that against him. The days of the Indian wars in Texas had been over for several years, except way out in the Big Bend, where Apaches still raided sometimes, crossing the border from their strongholds in the mountains of Mexico. Will Fisher was a mild-looking man who seemed more like he ought to be a circuit-riding preacher or something like that, instead of a moonshiner.

The Dawson brothers were both tall, a little stoop-shouldered, and prematurely gray-haired. Cloyd was the older by a couple of years, Dougal told Pike. The left side of Hebner's face was covered with puckered, pinkish scars, the ugly aftermath of the burns he had suffered in the fire that resulted when somebody blew up the brothers' still. No one had ever doubted that Doak Ramsey and his clan were responsible for that atrocity, although there was no proof of it.

Dougal had sent out two of the hands who worked for the Shannons to scour the countryside for men who might want to band together and fight back against the Ramseys, as well as sending word of the meeting to the other relatives in the county. Pike figured at least a dozen men would show up, and he hoped for more than that, but he wasn't prepared for the steady stream of men on horseback or driving buckboards and wagons. By the time they stopped arriving, he estimated that close to forty men were packed into the barn. Shadows had gathered thickly enough that lanterns had to be lit. Pike studied the men in the flickering light and saw a lot of anger and determination on their faces.

How long that resolve would last once things started getting bloody, he didn't know. Some men always wilted and faded away when the bullets began to fly.

What he was certain of was that bullets *would* fly and blood *would* be spilled if organized opposition was mounted against the Ramseys. Doak would try to wipe out his enemies as thoroughly and viciously as he could.

Bales of hay had been stacked to create a little platform. Pike climbed onto it and raised his hands to call for attention. The clamor of conversation in the barn gradually died down. Men turned toward Pike and looked up at him.

"Thank you all for coming here tonight," he said in a voice loud enough for all of them to hear. "You know who I am."

"Pike Shannon," a man said. "The gunfighter."

"And outlaw," another added.

"No, I'm Pike Shannon, son of Elijah, grandson of Dougal, great-grandson of Garvan," Pike snapped. "I'm a Warbonnet County man, born and raised, just like some of you."

"Except you haven't been around these parts for a long time," said the man who had declared him to be an outlaw. "You've been off hiring out your gun and killing men for blood money."

"If that's the way you feel, mister, why'd you come here tonight?"

"My name's Clayton Rice. I'm friends with Cloyd and Hebner, and I stand by my friends."

"You're a moonshiner, too?" Pike asked.

"Well . . . no. Just friends with those boys, like I said."

Somebody farther back in the crowd called, "But he's sure *bought* plenty of 'shine over the years, ain't that right, Clay?"

That brought a wave of laughter from the men.

Clayton Rice frowned and said, "I didn't come here to be made sport of, I can tell you that. I'm here because I don't like the way Doak Ramsey and his bunch are running the county, that's why. And I sure as blazes don't like the way the Ramseys have been threatening and hurting good folks like the Dawson brothers."

Now there were calls of agreement from the crowd.

"That puts us on the same side, Rice," Pike said. "I came back here because I got word that my pa had died. No sooner do I ride into the county than I discover that Doak Ramsey is now the sheriff, of all things, and the Ramseys not only run the law and the county government, but all the moonshining in these parts, too! I wound up locked in the county jail, and I don't doubt for a second that old Doak never planned on me getting out of there alive."

Pike looked around at the men in the crowd and went on, "But I'm here, and I figure it's time somebody started fighting back against Doak."

"Some of us have tried to fight back," a man said. "It didn't get us anything except a heap of trouble!"

"That's because you fought back by yourself, or just you and your family," Pike said. "I'm talking about a whole group of us working together."

He saw skepticism and outright suspicion on many of the men's faces, and he couldn't blame them for feeling that way. Most of them came from long lines of pioneers, ancestors who had set out to carve new homes from the untamed wilderness that was Texas in the old days. They were self-reliant to a fault, never asking for help and seldom accepting it because they didn't want to be beholden to anybody.

Pike understood that because he was the same way. He fought his own battles, stomped his own snakes.

But sometimes there were just too blasted many snakes for one man to stomp by himself. That was the way it was with the Ramseys in Warbonnet County.

"Nobody here disagrees that something needs to be done about the Ramseys," Cloyd Dawson said. "But what is it that you've got in mind, Pike?"

"We've got to show Doak that we're willing to fight back, beyond any doubt," Pike said. "And to do that, we've got to hit him where it hurts."

CHAPTER 15

Pike knelt at the edge of a rocky ridge and peered westward along the trail that ran below, at the bottom of the slope. The Brazos River was off to the south about half a mile, flowing between high, sheer banks along this stretch.

"See anything?" Sam Crow called softly from behind him.

"Not yet," Pike replied, "but they'll be along."

He hoped he was right about that. It all depended on Dougal's mysterious informant.

Several days had passed since the meeting in the Shannon barn. A tentative agreement had been struck that evening. Not all the men who had shown up had agreed to join Pike's war against the Ramseys, but all had sworn they would keep what they knew to themselves. Pike trusted them to keep their word because he really didn't have any choice except to do so.

Some of the ones who'd been hesitant could be won over if he could demonstrate a few successes, Pike knew. Today was the first step not only in the campaign to break the Ramseys' stranglehold on Warbonnet County but also to bring more allies into his camp.

After the meeting was over and the rest of the men had left, Pike and Dougal had sat down on the hay bales to discuss the next move.

"There must be some other taverns and road-houses operating in the county with Doak's blessing, if not his outright connivance," Pike said. "Like that so-called trading post where I ran into his deputies yesterday."

"Yeah, Bennett's place ain't the only one, that's for sure," Dougal agreed. "There's probably a dozen scattered around the countryside. And I'd bet a hat that Doak's a silent partner in all of 'em. I expect his deputies were there yesterday pickin' up Doak's cut from Bennett."

"Four men seems like a lot for a job like that."

Dougal snorted. "None of those boys are kin, and Doak don't completely trust nobody who ain't got Ramsey blood flowin' in their veins. One man might give in to temptation and light out for the tall and uncut with the loot he collected. Four men are less likely to do somethin' like that."

"That makes sense. Here's what I'm thinking, though. If Doak is supplying those places with 'shine, he's got to get it to them somehow, doesn't he?"

"Well, sure. He loads the jugs in wagons and has his boys take 'em out and deliver 'em."

"You know that for a fact?"

"Yeah."

"Because the fella you've got working on the inside has been part of those whiskey runs, hasn't he?" Pike guessed.

Dougal frowned. "I told you, the less you know about that fella, the better all around."

"You can't really believe that I'd sell him out to the *Ramseys*?"

"Oh, good gravy, of course not! But if nobody but me knows who the hombre is, then there can't ever be no accidents that'd give him away to Doak."

Pike waved that off and said, "All right, that part of it doesn't really matter right now. I reckon you've got a way of getting in touch with him?"

"Maybe I do," Dougal said guardedly.

"Then you can find out when Doak's going to be sending out more wagons full of 'shine. I imagine he has to do it fairly often to keep those places supplied."

"Warbonnet County is a thirsty place, that's true," Dougal allowed.

"If your man can let us know when that's going to happen, maybe we can see to it that the next delivery doesn't go so smoothly."

A figure stepped out of the shadows near the open barn doors. Torrance came toward them and asked, "Am I hearing right? You plan to ambush Doak Ramsey's moonshine wagons?"

His brother's unexpected appearance made Pike stand up quickly. His hand swung toward the butt of his gun. He stopped when he saw who the newcomer was, but not before Torrance noticed the reaction.

"I suppose I should consider myself lucky that you didn't just shoot me," he said.

"You ought to know better than to sneak up on somebody," Pike said.

Torrance held out a hand toward the barn entrance. "I walked through an open door. How is that sneaking up on anybody?"

"Well . . . you were eavesdropping."

"I heard what you were saying as I walked in. And you haven't denied it, Pike. You're really going to attack the Ramseys? Doak is the legally elected sheriff, you know."

"Maybe the election was legal, maybe it wasn't."

"In the eyes of the state of Texas, it was," Torrance said. "No one has challenged it."

"Because everybody's afraid to." Pike shook his head. "Doesn't matter. When he goes to making and selling moonshine, Doak's breaking the law just like anybody else who does that."

"So you're saying he's an outlaw . . . just like the Shannons."

Dougal said, "Don't you go talkin' bad about your own family, boy. Just because somethin's agin the law, that don't mean it should be. And I wouldn't put it past Doak Ramsey to have made sure that blasted local option election turned out the way it did. He might've figured that if he put all the legal saloons out of business, he could make even more money from moonshining."

That made sense to Pike, and it sounded like the sort of thing Doak Ramsey would do.

"Nobody's asking you to take a hand in this, Torrance," Pike said. "Just go on back in the house and read your books. We'll take care of things."

"You'll wind up in prison . . . or dead. That's what you'll do. And then where will Ma and Nessa be?"

From the doorway, Nessa said, "You can just leave me out of your argument, Torrance Shannon. I'll not have anybody making up their minds about something based on worrying about me. I can take care of myself."

Torrance looked back over his shoulder at her and said, "Followed me out here, did you?"

"Not a bit of it. I was just waiting for those men to leave before I came out to talk to Pike and Grand-pappy."

"What do you want to talk about?" Pike asked.

Nessa strode forward and gazed squarely at him. "Whatever you're planning to do, I want to be part of it." When Pike started to shake his head, she went on, "I traded shots with the blasted Ramseys today, didn't I?"

"Yeah, but that wasn't my idea. That's not the same thing as you coming along when we all know there's liable to be trouble."

"I'm a good rider and a good shot. Better than some of those *farmers* and part-time moonshiners who were here tonight."

"Maybe so," Pike said, "but you're still my little sister and I'm not going to let you get in the middle of some ruckus where bullets are flying around."

"I'm already part of any ruckus that happens be-tween the Shannons and the Ramseys. The Shannon blood in my veins makes sure of that!"

Pike's jaw tightened. Practically speaking, Nessa actually was more of a fighter than Torrance. But de-spite that, Pike knew he wasn't taking her along when he struck the Ramsey moonshine wagons. He wasn't going to put her in that much danger.

She wouldn't accept that argument, though, so he said harshly, "If I took you along, you'd just be a distrac-tion to the other men. Somebody would be worrying about you and wind up getting himself killed because of it."

Her face went pale with anger and hurt. "Do you really believe that, Pike?"

"I know it's true. And that's why I'm not going to let it happen."

"Well . . . well . . . well, you can just go to *hell*!"

Nessa turned and stomped out of the barn without looking back. Pike felt bad about hurting her feelings and making her so angry, but in the long run it would be better this way.

Torrance looked at him and shook his head. "I hope you're proud of yourself," he said. "She's always been your biggest defender, you know. Anytime somebody said something about the way you ran off, she always insisted you had a good reason for it. She claimed you had a good reason for everything you did."

"I still do," Pike said.

Torrance just grunted, said, "I don't want to hear about it," and followed Nessa out of the barn. Pike let him go.

Dougal chuckled and said, "Looks like I'm the only one in the family who's still on your side, boy."

"What about Ma?"

"She just wants peace, so she can grieve for Lije."

"He was your son. You don't want the same thing?"

"Not hardly," Dougal said. "I'm hopin' you'll stir up enough of a hornet's nest that the truth about his death will come out. I want to be able to lay the blame for Lije's death at the feet of those blasted Ramseys, because I know in my guts that's where it belongs."

Pike felt the same way, and he thought about that now as he waited for the moonshine wagons to show up. According to the information Dougal had gotten from his informant, three wagons full of 'shine would be leaving from Warbonnet this morning to make a circuit of all the taverns and roadhouses in the eastern part of the county. If those wagons never made it where they were going, that would turn some hornets loose, all right.

Each wagon would have a driver and a guard, and there would be six outriders, two in front, two behind, and one on each flank. That added up to a dozen men in the caravan.

Pike had fifteen, counting himself, so he had superior numbers and the element of surprise on his side, not to mention the advantage of high ground on this ridge. He had brought eight of his best riflemen up here. Six more men waited on horseback in a grove of trees on the far side of the trail. The bushwhackers would take care of the outriders, and then the horsemen would go after the wagons. Pike would hold himself in reserve to do whatever was needed.

Of course, it was likely that not everything would go exactly according to plan. It never did.

They would find out soon, though, because two riders had just come around a bend in the road about two hundred yards away. They might not be part of the moonshine caravan, Pike told himself, but rather just two hombres on their way somewhere.

Nope. A moment later a team of mules came into view, followed by the wagon they were pulling. The back of the wagon had canvas pulled over it, but Pike had a pretty good idea what was under there. He was even more convinced when two more wagons appeared behind the first one, just as Dougal's informant had said.

Pike turned his head and called quietly to his men, "Here they come. Move on up here and get ready."

Sam Crow and the other seven men eased to the top of the ridge. It was rocky and had clumps of scrub brush growing along it, so they were able to stay out of sight. Each man wore a bandanna that he pulled up to cover the lower half of his face, and their hats were pulled low to obscure the upper halves.

Pike took his hat off and crouched behind a slab of rock where he could still see the trail.

"Keep your guns down for now," he ordered. "We don't want the sun reflecting on any of them."

The day before, it had rained in Warbonnet County, just as Dougal's knee had predicted. Today the sun was back out, quickly drying the few puddles that were left. But it was also a danger, as Pike had pointed out. The men crouched behind cover, holding their rifles down but ready to be brought up and used as soon as Pike gave the order.

Pike watched, waiting for all the wagons and outriders to be out in the open, and as the first wagon rolled past the spot where he was, he heard faint clinking as the jugs in the back jostled one another. That was the last bit of confirmation he needed.

He turned his head toward his men and said, "*Now!*"

CHAPTER 16

Sam Crow and the other men each came up on a knee and lifted their rifles to their shoulders. Pike had told them earlier to spread out their fire among the outriders. Every man here was a good shot. Many of them had grown up helping to hunt for their family's food, in a time when ammunition was scarce and every shot had to count.

The volley that crashed out rolled like thunder over the hills and across the river bottoms. Down on the trail, several riders threw up their arms and pitched out of the saddle as bullets tore through them. Others jerked and sagged but managed to grab the saddle horns and not fall off their mounts. A couple of them even pulled their guns and fired up at the ridge crest. Pike's men had to duck as bullets whipped above their heads.

At the same time, the men waiting in the grove of post oaks burst out of cover and urged their horses toward the wagons at a fast run. Powder smoke billowed from their revolvers as they opened fire, too.

The wagon guards twisted around on the seats and looked for something to shoot at. The one on the lead wagon raked the ridgetop with bullets. One of Pike's men yelped in pain and rolled down the back side of the slope, clutching his bullet-drilled shoulder as blood ran between his fingers.

With a bandanna covering part of his face now, Pike drew a bead on that guard and squeezed the Colt's trigger. The gun roared and bucked in his hand. The guard jolted back against the driver, hit hard. He dropped his rifle into the floorboard at his feet as some instinct or reflex prompted him to stand up and paw at his chest where Pike had shot him. The driver whipped the mules into a dead run. The wounded man toppled off the driver's box and fell under the team's slashing hooves. Then one of the wheels ran over him, causing the wagon to lurch. The driver remained in control of it, though, as it careened on down the trail.

The battle continued between the men on the ridge, the pursuing riders, the surviving outriders, and the other two wagon guards. Shots slammed back and forth, and reeking clouds of powder smoke rose over the trail and the ridge.

Pike saw that he had waited just a hair too late to start the ball. The lead wagon had a narrow window of opportunity through which to escape, and the driver was trying his best to seize it. The vehicle barreled along with the mule team running full out. Another bend loomed about a quarter of a mile away, and if the wagon made it around that turn, it might get away.

Pike growled a curse, slid his Colt back into its holster, and turned to run back down the slope to the place where the horses were tied. He jerked the dun's reins loose, swung up into the saddle, and sent the horse lunging hard up the ridge. They topped it going so fast that Pike came up out of the saddle for a second, and then the dun was pounding down the slope toward the trail.

He felt as much as heard a couple of slugs passing close by his head, but neither of them hit him, so it didn't matter. As he and the dun reached the trail, he turned the horse to follow the wagon that was getting away. Pike leaned forward as he urged the animal to greater speed.

Even with the rain the day before, the trail was dry enough by now and the wagon was moving so fast that the wheels kicked up some dust. Pike narrowed his eyes against it. The wind tugged at his broad-brimmed hat, but the chin strap was tight enough to keep it from flying off his head.

The mule team was running flat out, but even so, Pike's dun was considerably faster. The gap between rider and wagon shrank quickly. The driver must have noticed that he was being followed, because as he clung to the reins with one hand, he twisted around on the seat and with the gun in his other hand threw some lead back at Pike. Pike wasn't worried about any of those shots hitting him. It would be pure luck if they did, and he had learned a long time ago that a man couldn't really fight luck in a situation such as this. He had to just take what it dished out.

The driver jammed his gun back in its holster and turned again to his team, concentrating on getting all the speed out of the mules that he could. He was just trying to get away now and evidently didn't care what happened to the rest of his bunch. Probably he was worried about what Doak Ramsey would do if he lost all that moonshine, Pike thought.

Pike closed in on the wagon. The rolling drumbeat of the dun's hooves filled his ears. As he pulled even with the wagon's rear end, he kicked his feet out of the stirrups and threw himself from the saddle, sailing through the air to land on the canvas covering the back of the wagon.

The jugs of moonshine were loaded into crates under the canvas to keep them from moving around too much. Those open-topped crates didn't give him a soft landing. Some of the jugs broke from the impact of his elbows and knees, but the thick canvas protected him from any jagged edges. It didn't stop the sharp tang of white lightning from surging up around him, though. That was almost potent enough to make him gasp. He got his hands and knees under him, shoved up, and lunged forward.

The driver twisted his head around and snarled when he saw Pike in the back of the wagon. He writhed and reached for his gun again, but as the weapon swung up, Pike's left hand shot out and grabbed the man's wrist. He shoved that arm up as the gun blasted. At the same time, Pike swung his right fist at the man's head. If he could capture this hombre, maybe he could get him to spill some of Doak Ramsey's secrets.

The man wasn't going to give up easily, though. He jerked his head aside so that Pike's fist just skidded above his ear. He dropped his gun and the reins and writhed around so he could make a grab at Pike's throat.

Pike ducked his head and avoided that. He drove

forward and rammed his shoulder into the driver's chest. The man went backward off the seat and thudded onto the floorboards. As he fell, though, his flailing hand snagged the front of Pike's shirt and dragged him over the back of the seat. Pike sprawled on top of the driver, half on the seat, half in the floorboard, upside down enough that it made him dizzy.

The two men wrestled desperately as Pike slid the rest of the way off the seat. The driver got a hand on Pike's face and clawed for his eyes. Grimacing, Pike pulled away. He hammered punches into the man's ribs, tried to drive a knee into his belly or groin. It was Pike who caught a knee in the belly, though, forcing the air out of his lungs. A wild punch clipped him on the side of the head and stunned him for a few seconds.

His opponent took advantage of that to catch him by the throat with both hands and force him to the side. Pike wound up on his back with his head and shoulders hanging off the side of the driver's box as the ground flashed past only a couple of feet below him.

The driver tried to force Pike the rest of the way off, but Pike grabbed hold of the brake lever with one hand and hung on to it for dear life. He slammed his other fist into the driver's jaw again and again, and with each blow the man's grip on Pike's throat loosened. Finally it came free entirely and the man fell against the footboard at the front of the driver's box. Pike jackknifed up, grabbed the man's legs, and heaved. The driver frantically scrabbled for something to hold on to but failed to find a grip. With a terrified cry, he fell onto the wagon tongue, slipped off, and went under the wheels. Pike felt the heavy bump.

With his chest heaving as he tried to drag air back into his lungs, Pike pushed himself up onto the seat. He blinked his eyes, shook his head, and realized that the wagon had left the trail while he and the former driver were fighting. The mules were still running full speed, but now they were heading across open ground toward the bluff that bordered the Brazos River. It was only a couple of hundred yards away.

Pike's eyes widened in surprise, but the reaction lasted only a second. He looked around for the reins, hoping he could stop the runaway team, but the reins had slipped down and were now flapping and fluttering among the mules' legs. If he'd had more time, he could have climbed down onto the tongue, balanced carefully on it, and worked his way out to where he could grasp the harness of the leaders and turn them away from the bluff overlooking the river.

But they were too close to the drop-off for that. He went down into the floorboard on his knees and leaned over the front of the box as he searched for the kingpin that attached the tongue to the wagon's running gear. It was too far back, he saw. He couldn't reach it from where he was. And even if he could, there was probably too much weight pulling against it for him to jerk it loose.

Pike glanced up. Less than a hundred yards to the river now. He was out of time. He stood up, made sure there were no trees or rocks coming up, and leaped off the wagon. For a timeless second, he seemed to hang in the air, then his feet hit the ground and his momentum carried him forward, out of control. As he went down, he tucked his shoulder so he would land on it and be able to roll. The world flipped crazily around him as he went over and over.

He came to a stop on his belly and lifted his head to look toward the river. The mules must have realized at last that they were about to bolt to their deaths, because they swung sharply to the right. So sharply, in fact, that the wagon tongue cracked and came loose from the vehicle. The team turned, but the wagon kept going in the same direction.

Pike scrambled to his feet and ran after the wagon as it trundled toward the edge of the bluff. He wasn't sure what he was going to do if he reached it before it got to the edge. It was unlikely he'd be strong enough to stop it, but at least he could try.

Then he asked himself what he was doing. He didn't want Doak Ramsey's moonshine. Any white lightning the Shannons made would be a lot better than that Ramsey swill. He slowed as the wagon's front wheels reached the edge of the bluff and tipped over it. The rest of the wagon followed.

Pike was close enough to see the wagon turn over in midair as it plummeted the fifty feet to the stream. The canvas came loose and the crates full of moonshine flew everywhere. The jugs themselves came out of the crates and rained down toward the river, pocking the placid surface of the Brazos as they hit. The wagon threw up a huge geyser of water as it struck the river. Droplets pattered down in the aftermath.

Some of the jugs had shattered, and the moonshine they contained was now washing downriver. The ones that survived the fall would sink to the bottom. Anybody who wanted to retrieve them would have to dive into the river to get them. Pike rubbed his chin and started to smile as he thought about that.

Then he swung around and reached for his gun as a swift rataplan of hoofbeats sounded behind him.

CHAPTER 17

Half a dozen men galloped toward him. Pike relaxed and took his hand away from his Colt as he recognized Sam Crow and Will Fisher in the lead. Fisher had been in charge of the riders who'd waited in the trees. The two parts of Pike's force had joined together, indicating that the battle with Doak Ramsey's men was over.

"Pike, are you all right?" Crow asked as the men rode up and reined in.

"Yeah." Pike loosened the chin strap on his hat, took it off, and swatted it against his thigh to knock the dust off it. As he settled it back on his head, he asked, "How about you boys?"

"Kit Sellers caught a bullet through the shoulder, and Jimmy McCoy got a pretty good crease on his side. And Alec Haver was thrown off his horse and wrenched his knee, so he'll be hobbling for a while. But those are all the injuries I know of."

Pike nodded, pleased by the news. All of them had known when they started this campaign against the Ramseys that they might lose their lives, but Pike was glad none of his men had been killed today, anyway.

"What about the other bunch?"

"Two of them are dead," Sam Crow reported. "The ones that got run over by that lead wagon." He had a note of satisfaction in his voice, too. Pike recalled that the Ramseys and their cronies had threatened Crow's teenage daughter. He didn't blame the man for being pleased that some of them were dead.

"What about the others?"

"They were shot up pretty bad but got away," Fisher said. "They lit a shuck out of here when they saw they couldn't win."

Pike nodded. He would have liked to take a prisoner or two, but it hadn't worked out that way. He wasn't going to cry over it.

"They'll tell Doak Ramsey what happened," Fisher went on.

"I'm sure they will. It was never intended to be a secret." Pike shrugged. "He'll just find out a little sooner this way."

"What about the bodies?"

"Leave them where they fell. Doak can come and deal with them."

That was harsh, Pike knew, but he didn't feel like going to any extra effort for men who would have killed him and his family without a second thought. The life he'd led as a hired gun had taught him not to waste any sentiment on the enemy.

Pike looked back across the open ground to the trail, where the rest of his men had gathered around the remaining two moonshine wagons.

"Bring those wagons over here," he ordered. "Then unhitch the teams and push them off the bluff into the river."

Crow and Fisher both looked surprised. "You're going to dump all that moonshine into the Brazos?" Crow asked.

"We don't need it. The white lightning the Shannons make is better."

"I won't argue that," Fisher said. "Might get some use out of the wagons, though."

Pike shook his head. "They're evidence. If a couple of our men turned up with them, Doak might try to use that against them. I've got a hunch that starting out, at least, he'll try to pretend that he's just upholding the law. That's why we covered our faces, so nobody can testify that it was us who jumped the wagons."

"Ramsey will know that anyway," Crow pointed out.

"Yeah, but there's a difference in knowing something and being able to prove it in a court of law," Pike said. It was the same as him knowing in his gut that Doak Ramsey was responsible for his father's death, but not being able to prove it—yet. "We don't want to give Doak any more ammunition than we have to. Shoot, he might even get tricky and call the Rangers in, depending on how long he's willing to pretend to be respectable."

The other men looked uneasy at that. Nobody wanted the Texas Rangers coming after them.

"All right," Will Fisher said. "I reckon that makes sense. We'll get the wagons and dump them and the shine in the river."

"Tell the men who were wounded to stay out of sight for a few days, too, just to make sure nobody gets curious about how they wound up with bullet holes in them."

"When are we going to make another move against the Ramseys?" Sam Crow asked.

"Not right away," Pike said, "but soon. We don't want to wait too long." He smiled. "The more loco we make Doak Ramsey, the more likely he is to make a mistake that'll play right into our hands."

Doak Ramsey was in his office in the county courthouse with the door open a few inches and his booted feet propped up on the desk. He had come in here to try to get some work done. When he had gone to work for the previous sheriff, he hadn't realized how much paperwork went with the job. Now it was one of the banes of his existence—but still a small price to pay for the power and wealth he was amassing.

A man could concentrate on words and numbers for only so long a time, though, so after a while he had opened the lower desk drawer, taken out the jug he kept there, and poured white lightning into a cup. He sipped it now with his feet up, enjoying the familiar, comforting warmth in his belly.

Somewhere in the building, a door slammed, and then rapid footsteps slapped on the polished wooden floor. They came across the outer office, and then the door of Ramsey's private office flew open.

"Doak!" the tall, skinny, balding man standing there said. "I mean, Sheriff Ramsey!"

He was Oscar Causey, some kind of shirttail relative. Ramsey wasn't sure of the relationship. But Causey had been part of the group delivering 'shine in the eastern half of the county today, and he shouldn't have been back from that job yet. Ramsey wasn't expecting the wagons back until the middle of the afternoon.

"Blast it, Oscar, what are you doing here?" Ramsey asked as he swung his feet down from the desk. He didn't know if he was more irritated that Causey apparently had abandoned his duty or that the man had interrupted that cup of white lightning.

Then he noticed the bloodstain on Causey's left sleeve and jumped up to hurry out from behind the desk.

"What happened?"

Causey was pale and he swayed a little, apparently on the verge of collapsing. Ramsey grabbed his uninjured arm to steady him.

"Doak, I . . . I don't know how to tell you this. We got jumped. *The 'shine is gone!*"

Ramsey's grip on the man's arm tightened until Causey grimaced. "What do you mean *gone?*"

"Some of us went back to look, and they . . . they'd pushed the wagons over that high bluff a few miles east of here and into the Brazos. The wagons was all b-busted up and so were the crates the jugs were in. Some of the jugs broke and the 'shine washed away, and I reckon the rest of it's at the b-bottom of the river!"

The words tumbled rapidly out of Causey's mouth. Normally, he didn't stammer. He was so excited and upset he just couldn't get everything out right. Ramsey felt like slapping some sense into him, but he resisted the impulse.

Instead he asked in a low, carefully controlled voice, "Who? Who'd dare to do such a thing?"

"I dunno, Doak . . . I mean, Sheriff. I never got a

good look at any of 'em. They ambushed us from a ridge and then some other fellas rode out from a clump of trees and chased the wagons and they were all shootin' and I got hit and I ain't sure but I think they was wearin' some kind of masks and—"

Causey was babbling. Ramsey grabbed his other arm, the wounded one, although his grip was above the bloodstain. Still, it had to hurt when Ramsey shook the man and said, "Stop it!"

Causey yelped in pain. "Doak, don't—" he began, but Ramsey let go of him and shoved him away.

"Did you see Pike Shannon?" Ramsey demanded. "Was he there?"

"I told you, they was wearin' masks—"

Once again Ramsey interrupted. "Did you see anybody who might have been Pike Shannon? Somebody the right size and shape?"

Causey looked like he wanted to cry. His chin, which was weak and undershot, trembled a little. He shook his head and said, "No, I didn't, but there was so much goin' on and it all happened so fast, and then I got hit and it hurt like blazes . . ."

His voice trailed off as Ramsey put one hand on his shoulder and used the other to pat his back. He took a deep breath and said, "I know, Oscar, and I'm sorry. How bad are you wounded?"

"Not . . . not too bad, I don't think. It just sorta knocked a hunk o' meat outa my arm. I'll be all right, but Doak . . . Philo and Jasper are dead."

Those were two more Ramsey cousins. Jasper Lowe, in fact, had been in charge of the group and had driven off that morning handling the reins of the lead wagon, while his brother Philo sat beside him riding guard.

"The other boys who made it back, are any of them hurt?"

Causey bobbed his head. "Yeah, we got shot to pieces. Ain't a one of us who didn't get nicked, or worse. I tell you, the lead was really flyin' out there, Doak . . . Sheriff. Them bullets was as thick as flies for a few minutes. It's a wonder any of us got out alive, I'd say."

A part of Ramsey wanted to allow the fury raging inside him to explode. He wanted to smash his fists into Causey's stupid face, and then when he was finished with that, he would take out his gun and pistol-whip the idiot until Causey didn't even look human anymore. That was the sort of punishment Causey had coming to him for letting *anyone* steal Ramsey moonshine.

The sure knowledge that Pike Shannon had been behind the attack and the loss of the 'shine and the dead kinfolks just made it all worse.

But Doak Ramsey wasn't going to let Shannon make him crazy. That was probably just what Shannon wanted. He was the sheriff, Ramsey reminded himself, and between that position and the influence he had over the government around here, he ran Warbonnet County. He held the power of life and death in his hands, and no one could stand up to him.

Pike Shannon was going to find that out.

He patted Causey's back again and said, "You go and take care of yourself, Oscar. Get that arm patched up. And later, after you and the other fellas have rested a spell, you go on over to Mollie Dupree's place and tell her I said the white lightning and the soiled doves are on me tonight." He laughed. "She won't even have to kick my cut back to me when I settle up with her, either."

"Really, Doak? You . . . you ain't gonna do anything to us boys for losin' that 'shine?"

"It's not your fault," Ramsey said. "I know *exactly* whose fault it is, and trust me, I'm going to be settling up with *him*, too."

CHAPTER 18

Sam Crow, Will Fisher, and the other men scattered back to their homes and families. In fact, if the law ever came sniffing around, they would have plenty of witnesses ready to swear that they had been home all day. Lying like that might rub some folks the wrong way, but when the law itself was crooked, people had to fight back against that any way they could.

When Pike got back to the house, he found his grandfather and Fiddler sitting in a couple of the cane-bottomed chairs on the front porch, smoking pipes. Their apparent casualness didn't fool Pike. They had known what was planned for today, and he could tell they were anxious to hear what had happened with the Ramsey moonshine shipments.

Pike reined in and dismounted as the two older men watched him. He didn't say anything as he climbed the steps to the porch. Dougal finally couldn't stand it anymore and blurted, "Well?"

"We got all three wagonloads of 'shine," Pike reported. "We dumped everything in the river except the mules. Wagons and all."

Fiddler's bushy eyebrows jumped up. "You dumped

all that perfectly good white lightning?" He sounded like that was an incomparable tragedy to him.

"It wasn't perfectly good," Pike said. "It was Ramsey swamp water."

"Well, admittedly it's not as good as the Shannon recipe, but still, to think of it washing away down the Brazos . . ." Fiddler shuddered.

Dougal said, "I don't know why you'd care. You ain't taken a drink in, what, nigh on to a week now. To tell you the truth, I never expected that."

"To tell *you* the truth, I don't know where I've found the fortitude to remain sober for this long. It's not a usual occurrence, that's for sure." Fiddler puffed on his pipe. "I suppose I want to make sure that if there's anything I can do to help you good people, I'll be able to do it. After all the kindness the Shannon family has extended to me, it seems only fair."

Fiddler *had* been a help around the place, Pike knew. He could handle odd jobs, and he was company for Pike's mother. And he could play rollicking tunes on the fiddle he had brought with him from War-bonnet, which entertained not only the family but also the half-dozen men who lived in the bunkhouse, the hands who helped take care of the horses and the cotton crop but didn't take part in the moonshining.

"Anybody hurt?" Dougal asked.

"On our side, a couple of the boys got winged and another fell off his horse and bunged up his leg. Nothing serious, though."

Dougal squinted at Pike. "What about on the Ramsey side?"

"Two killed, and I don't think any of the others got

away without at least a scratch. Some of them were hit a lot worse than that. They'll be laid up for a while."

"The sheriff is never going to stand for this," Fiddler said. Gloom filled his face and voice.

"I don't intend for him to stand for it," Pike said. "He's been hiding behind the law and his newfound respectability for long enough."

"You're playing with fire," Fiddler warned.

"Doak's the one who's going to get burned."

The front door opened and Nessa came out onto the porch. "I thought I heard you talking, Pike. What happened?"

He went through it again quickly for his sister. When he was finished, Nessa said, "I still think you should have let me come along. I'm a good shot with a rifle. You could have put me up on that ridge with Sam Crow and those other men."

"You can forget about that," Pike told her. "I want you sticking close to home from now on. Doak's going to be riled, and there's no telling what he might do to strike back at us."

"That's what you want, isn't it? For Doak to be riled up?"

Pike nodded. "Yeah. I'm going to keep hitting him where it hurts, too."

"Until all hell breaks loose," Dougal said.

"Sometimes it takes hellfire to burn away what needs to be burned."

A two-man council of war was going on in the sheriff's office in the Warbonnet County courthouse. Sitting in a red leather chair in front of the desk,

Phineas Conway puffed on a fat cigar, blew out a cloud of white smoke, and said, "You can't just ride out there with an army and lay waste to the Shannon place, my boy. You have to remember your position. You're the sheriff now, the upholder of law, order, and justice in this county."

"Pike Shannon is a murderer," Doak Ramsey said, his voice icy. "I got the whole story from Oscar Causey and some of the other boys. Shannon gunned down Philo and then knocked Jasper under the wheels of that runaway wagon. He killed both of them, and he deserves to hang for it."

"I talked to Oscar, too. He said all the men who attacked them were masked."

Ramsey's right hand slapped down hard and angry on the desk. "Blast it, Phin, we all *know* Pike Shannon's to blame. How many range wars has he been in? How many ambushes just like this one has he set up? He's a killer."

"The law requires proof—"

"The law can go to blazes!" Ramsey was on his feet now, glowering darkly across the desk at the corpulent jurist. "Don't go spouting about the law, Phin. Maybe you've started thinking you're a little more high and mighty than you really are, now that you're a judge. But the only reason you're a judge is because *I* put you there! People may respect you now, but it wouldn't take much for them to remember that you used to be nothing but a layabout and a saloon swamper."

Conway's normally beefy face turned pale with rage. His teeth clamped hard on the cigar. The sausage-like fingers of his hands curled into fists.

Then, with a visible effort, he controlled his anger.

Clearly, he didn't like what Ramsey had just said, but he also knew the realities of the situation.

He took the cigar out of his mouth and said, "Regardless, I still advise caution. If you ride out there to the Shannon ranch and try to arrest Pike, he'll put up a fight, even if you have a dozen deputies with you. He won't let you take him into custody. That means, more than likely, you'd have to kill him. And there's a very good chance you'd have to kill the other members of the family, too. Well, not Torrance, I suppose. He's too much of a mouse. But old Dougal, certainly, and that redheaded hellion of a girl. Possibly even Mary Shannon. That would cause a huge scandal, Doak . . . and draw attention that you don't want."

Ramsey sank back down into his chair. "You're talking about the Rangers."

"Indeed," Conway said, even though Ramsey's words had been a statement, not a question. "Right now, our dealings in Warbonnet County at least give the appearance of being honest and aboveboard. You and I were put into office in fair elections—"

Ramsey grunted. "As far as anybody knows."

Conway leaned forward with an intent expression on his bulldog face and said, "I repeat, fair elections, and that's the face we want to maintain. If you launch into open warfare with Pike Shannon and blood runs freely, regular citizens will begin to complain. Newspaper reporters from Fort Worth and Waco might get wind of the trouble and come here. *We don't want that, Doak.*"

Frustration welled up inside Ramsey. He said, "Well, then, what *are* we going to do? We can't just let Shannon get away with what he's done!"

Conway sat back again and puffed on the cheroot. "I agree, he has to reap what he's sown. But you have to go about it carefully and discreetly." The judge held up a fat finger. "Do nothing for the time being. Shannon will be expecting you to strike back at him. When you don't do that right away, he's going to be confused. Confusion in the enemy is always a good thing."

Ramsey narrowed his eyes at the other man and said, "When did you get so blasted philosophical?"

"I've always had a taste for reading, even when I couldn't afford to indulge it. Now, in addition to studying those law books you got for me, I've been plumbing the depths of Machiavelli, as well."

"Never heard of him," Ramsey snapped.

"He wrote a volume on the best ways to defeat your enemies. I'll loan the book to you if you'd like."

"I don't have time to read. I have to figure out what I'm going to do about Shannon." Ramsey grimaced. "But I reckon you've got a point, Phin. I won't rush into anything."

"That's good. I appreciate you listening to my advice, Doak. I know that I, ah, come from humble beginnings—"

"Cleaning out spittoons for nickels and dimes, yeah, I'd call that humble, all right."

Conway seemed to ignore the interruption, although a little muscle in his jaw jumped a couple of times. "If we work together, we can deal with this problem," he went on. "And when Pike Shannon is dealt with, our hold on this county will be stronger than ever."

Ramsey nodded and reached for the jug and a couple of cups in the desk drawer. Let old Phin believe he was calling the shots, Ramsey told himself. He would even follow the judge's advice—for now.

But when the time was right for a showdown, Ramsey wouldn't hold anything back, no matter what Conway said. He would handle the problem of Pike Shannon the best way he knew how.

With fire, lead, and death. Pike Shannon . . . and those closest to him . . . would pay in blood.

CHAPTER 19

Pike knelt in thick brush, and through a narrow gap in the growth he watched a man lean a rifle against a tree and then roll a quirley. The man used a lucifer to set fire to the gasper, then dropped the match and ground it out with his boot toe.

A week had passed since Pike and the other men ambushed the Ramsey moonshine caravan. Pike had expected Doak Ramsey to do something about that before now. Dougal's mysterious informant had let them know that Ramsey had raged around in the sheriff's office when he found out what had happened, promising bloody vengeance on the Shannons. But so far, stomping and cussing was all Doak had done. Not a move had been made against Pike and his family.

In a way, that was more worrisome than if Ramsey had come a-shootin' with an army of deputies. Just what sort of revenge was Doak planning?

Pike couldn't devote too much time to pondering that question. He had to concentrate on his own plans. And that was why he was out here today in the woods.

He looked back over his shoulder and motioned silently to Sam Crow, who was turning into a capable lieutenant. Stolid and unimaginative, maybe, but smart enough to carry out Pike's orders and tough enough to inspire the other men to follow him. He was slick at moving through trees and brush without making a lot of noise, too.

He slipped up beside Pike, who whispered, "There's a sentry beside that tree."

Crow squinted through the brush for a moment, then replied in an equally hushed tone, "That's Amos Ramsey, one of Doak's cousins." Crow's voice was hard as flint as he added, "He's one of the men who threatened my daughter. Said things to her that no man should say to a fourteen-year-old girl."

"Think you can take care of him without killing him?"

Crow's narrowed eyes cut over toward Pike. "What's the idea of not killing these men?"

"We'll kill if we have to," Flint replied. His voice was hard, too. "And I reckon there'll come a time when there's plenty of killing to be done. But until then, I don't want to sink to the same rotten level as the Ramseys. They're animals . . . and we're men."

Crow looked at him for several intense seconds, then slowly nodded. "All right," he said. "I suppose I agree with that. But when that time for killing you're talking about finally *does* come, I'll be more than ready for it."

"Me, too," Pike said. "We'll wait here while you tend to that varmint."

Sam Crow nodded and moved off through the brush, so quietly that he might have been a ghost drifting through the spirit world. In less than a minute, Pike couldn't see him anymore, so he turned his attention back to Amos Ramsey. The sentry had picked up his rifle again and tucked it under his arm.

A few minutes dragged past, and then, seemingly out of nowhere, an arm snaked around Amos Ramsey's neck from behind and jerked him back a step. The forearm clamped hard enough across Ramsey's throat to cut off any shout of alarm. A knife rose, its blade winking in the early-morning sunlight that slanted through the trees.

But instead of that cold steel burying itself in warm flesh, the brass ball on the end of the knife's handle thudded against Ramsey's skull. The blow was swift, precise, and effective. Ramsey dropped his rifle, his knees buckled, and he sagged in Sam Crow's grip.

Crow lowered him carefully to the ground. Pike watched as Crow stood there for a second, looming over the man he had just knocked unconscious, and Pike had a hunch Crow was thinking about how easy it would be to lean over and cut Amos Ramsey's throat.

Instead, Crow looked toward the tree where Pike was hidden and nodded. Then he dropped to a knee and started tying Ramsey's hands behind him, using strips of rawhide he had brought along for that purpose.

Pike waved his other companions forward. Andy Burnett and two other men were with him today. They joined Sam Crow, who straightened as he finished binding Ramsey's hands and feet. He had also shoved Ramsey's own bandanna into his mouth to serve as a gag.

"He didn't know you were anywhere around," Pike said to Crow.

"I would have been ashamed if he did. There are more guards?"

"That's what Dougal was told. He said there were three, spaced out a hundred yards apart from each other."

Crow pointed. "The trail to the camp is there, about twenty yards ahead. Wait there and I'll take care of the other two sentries."

For a second, Pike's first impulse was to bristle at the way Crow was giving orders. Then he told himself not to worry about such things and concentrate on accomplishing the task at hand, instead. Crow was just taking the responsibility for handling something he was good at.

"All right," Pike said. "I'd just as soon not have anybody lurking behind us to cause trouble once we move in."

Crow nodded wordlessly and turned to drift off into the brush again. Pike, Burnett, and the other two men headed for the trail that would lead them to their destination.

They knew from what Dougal had learned that there was a camp here in the thick woods north of Warbonnet, well away from the river, where the Ramsey family had four stills set up. Two stills were operating at all times, at different stages of a run, while the other two had mash getting ready in them. Alternating like that, the setup ensured that white lightning was trickling out of one of the worm kegs almost nonstop. Crews of moonshiners worked around the clock filtering and jugging the corn liquor. It took a lot of 'shine to fulfill the needs of an entire thirsty county, and that was Doak's goal: for the Ramseys to be the only moonshiners in Warbonnet County.

The family had other stills scattered around the county, but this camp was the linchpin of the operation.

Pike, Burnett, and the other two men waited fifteen minutes in the brush beside the trail, which consisted of two deep ruts where wagons rolled, loaded down with sacks of corn and sugar and other supplies on the way in and jugs of 'shine on the way out. Pike was starting to get a mite worried about Sam Crow when the man showed up without any warning, nowhere in sight one second and then standing there and nodding the next to indicate that the job was done.

"Those sentries aren't going to bother us or warn the camp?" Pike asked.

"No. And I did not kill any of them, either. But they will be a long time working loose from their bindings, and they may choke a little on the gags. Their heads will ache when they regain consciousness, too."

"That's their tough luck," Pike said. "Come on."

They stepped out of the brush and followed the trail in the open now. Pike wanted to move quickly. It wasn't long after dawn. The Ramsey men wouldn't be expecting any trouble. The ones who'd been working at the stills all night would have turned in by now to sleep through most of the day. The others probably weren't good and awake yet. Pike wanted to surprise all of them.

The wagon ruts twisted and turned through the trees and brush, following the contours of the rolling landscape, and after half a mile led to a large clearing on the banks of a creek that flowed south to join the Brazos several miles away. The spring-fed stream provided plenty of cool, clean water, which was a necessity for making moonshine. Except for the trail, the trees around the clearing were so dense as to be almost impenetrable. The shade from the canopy formed by their branches meant it was cool here even in the middle of summer like this.

The trees were a mixture of post oaks and cotton-woods, along with a few thick, towering pecan trees among them. Pecans in their shells littered the ground and bushy-tailed squirrels darted among them, gathering the nuts. Those squirrels vanished almost in an instant, flashing across the ground and then scampering up the trees, as Pike and his companions stepped into the clearing. Pike's Colt was in his hand, and the other men held rifles ready.

Pike took in the scene immediately. The stills formed a rough square, with one located at each corner. In the middle, two large tents were pitched to serve as sleeping quarters for the moonshiners. A brush arbor stood in the middle of the clearing as well, with a rough table and some benches under it where the men could sit and take their meals or play cards.

That wasn't the only amusement the moonshiners had to keep them occupied when they weren't working, Pike realized as a lushly built young woman with frizzy brown hair stepped out of one of the tents. She wore only a thin shift that came midway down her thighs, and as she stretched and yawned, the clinging garment didn't leave much to the imagination. She was probably a soiled dove from one of the houses in Warbonnet, Pike thought. Doak must have sent her out here to the camp. A little bonus on top of the cut of the profits these men would draw.

The girl froze with her mouth wide open in the yawn as she caught sight of the armed men striding up to the camp. Pike saw her eyes widen and knew she was about to yell. He wiggled the barrel of his Colt and shook his head. The dove took an unsteady step backward.

Two men were working at one of the stills on the camp's far side. They had their backs turned and didn't know that Pike and the others were there yet. Pike didn't know how many more men were on hand—at least two, maybe more—but he and his companions had surprise on their side.

Or at least they did until a man stumbled out of the woods to their left, yawning and running one hand over his sleep-tousled hair while the other hand pulled up the bottom half of a pair of long underwear, the only thing he was wearing at the moment. He saw Pike and the other men, jerked back, and let out a loud, incoherent shout as he made a dive for the trees. Pike could have shot the man at that moment, but what was the point?

The damage was already done.

CHAPTER 20

The two men at the still on the other side of the camp whirled around. One had an old Remington .44 revolver stuck in the waistband of his trousers. A shotgun lay on a stump next to the other man. Both men grabbed for the weapons, even though they looked confused and probably weren't sure what was going on.

At this range, the man with the Remington was probably the bigger danger. As the man hauled out the long-barreled revolver, Pike shot him in the right shoulder, knocking him back against the still as he screamed in pain. The Remington slipped from nerveless fingers and thudded to the ground. The man fell down next to it and floundered around, the gun seemingly forgotten in his pain.

The soiled dove screamed, too, and turned to run, but she tripped on something and sprawled on her belly. That left her in a pretty exposed and indelicate position with the shift riding up around her hips.

Pike didn't care about that spectacle. His attention was focused on the man scrambling on hands and knees out of the tent where the girl had come from.

He wore a pair of canvas trousers over longhandles and had a gun in his hand. As the man came upright, Pike shot his right leg out from under him, drilling him in the thigh. He howled and flopped back to the ground.

The man with the shotgun yelled and charged forward from his position beside the still. That made him more of a danger as he came closer. Andy Burnett fired his Winchester and the bullet kicked up dirt at the shotgunner's feet. The man jumped in the air, and his finger must have jerked both triggers when he did because the double load of buckshot erupted from the twin barrels with a thunderous roar.

Burnett cried out and the Winchester roared again. This time the shotgunner twisted around as the slug creased his ribs. Pike swung around and said, "Andy! You hit?" He saw a trickle of blood down Burnett's cheek.

"Aw, one of those pellets just pinked me a mite," Burnett answered. "I'm fine, Pike—look out!"

Pike heard a swift patter of footsteps behind him and then a weight landed on his back. The impact drove him forward and almost made him drop his Colt. Bare female legs wrapped around his waist. The soiled dove had jumped on him, and while he was off-balance, she reached around and clawed at his face with one hand. Pike cursed and ducked his head, trying to keep her from scratching his eyes out. She balled her other hand into a fist and hammered at the side of his head, knocking his hat off. She kept shifting her weight as she attacked him, causing him to stagger back and forth.

Even though he couldn't hear it because the girl

kept bawling obscenities at him, he figured the other men were laughing at his dilemma. He probably would have chuckled a time or two if it had been one of them in his place.

Or maybe they were shooting it out with the rest of the moonshiners. He really didn't know because he had his hands full with this unexpected battle. The Colt wasn't going to do him any good under these circumstances, so he rammed it back in its holster and reached up and back with both hands, trying to grab hold of the girl and dislodge her.

He tangled the fingers of one hand in the wild brown hair and heaved. The dove screeched even louder. Pike's other hand found bare flesh and clamped down on it as hard as he could in this awkward position. He bent forward at the waist and hauled her over his head. Her bare legs flew up and over, and she came down hard on her ample rear end.

Pike stumbled back a couple of steps, and as he did, a bullet tore through the air in front of his face. He didn't hear any laughing after all, just the crack of gunshots filling the clearing. He wheeled around, saw that his men had pulled back into the trees and the rest of the moonshiners had retreated to the creek, using the four-foot-tall bank as cover while they blazed away with handguns, rifles, and shotguns. Burnett, Crow, and the other two men returned the fire.

And Pike and the soiled dove were caught smack-dab in the middle.

She was starting to get up. Pike dived at her and forced her back to the ground.

"Keep your head down, blast it!" he shouted. "Or you'll get it blown off!"

Bullets crisscrossed in the air a few feet above them. The dove seemed to realize at last what was going on, because she put her arms over her head and whimpered.

"Take it easy," he told her, raising his voice so she could hear him over the gun-thunder. "Stay down and you'll be all right. They're shooting at each other, not at—"

He was about to say *us* when one of the moonshiners proved him wrong by firing a shot that smacked into the ground only a few inches in front of Pike's face. It threw dirt in his eyes and he felt gravel sting his cheeks. He started to yell at the men for putting the girl in danger but then realized the varmints didn't care if anything happened to her. To them, she was just a whore, after all. Killing her by accident would be perfectly acceptable as long as they managed to ventilate their enemy Pike Shannon, too.

Well, this business had gone to hell in a hay wagon, he thought. Even the best-laid plans had a way of doing that.

The tent where the girl had been passing the time of day with one of the Ramsey crew was fairly close by, but Pike didn't think it would do them any good. Its canvas sides sure wouldn't stop a bullet, or even slow it down. If he could get behind it, though, at least they couldn't see him anymore, and by getting away from the girl, he would draw the fire away from her as well.

"Stay here," he barked at her, then started a fast crawl on his belly toward the tent.

She surprised him yet again by latching on to one of his legs and yelling, "I've got him! Shoot him! Shoot him!"

If she had been a man, Pike would have kicked her in the face. As it was, he settled for kicking her in the shoulder to knock her loose from him. She lay there yelling and crying as he rolled away from her and sprang to his feet. Another slug whistled past his ear. He threw himself behind the tent and snagged it with his shoulder as he did so, pulling it down. It tried to tangle around him, but he made it up again and flung the canvas aside.

The brush arbor was just a few jumps away. He made it with no luck to spare, kicked one of the benches over, and dropped behind it. He drew his gun, raised up long enough to trigger a pair of shots toward the creek, then ducked again.

The moonshiners could get away by leaving one man to hold off Pike's group while the others slipped off down the creek. However, they didn't appear to be making any effort to do that. They didn't want to abandon the stills, he realized. They were too afraid of what Doak Ramsey would do to them if they did.

He frowned in thought, then realized that he had seen a kerosene lantern sitting on the table. He scooted along behind the bench until he could see it. Standing up long enough to grab it would be risky, but he had to chance it. He lunged upright, reached out a long arm, and caught hold of the lantern's bail, then heard slugs whipping around him as he dropped to the ground again.

Over at the still where the two men had been working when the ruckus started, several buckets were sitting on the ground. Pike had a hunch that at least some of those buckets were full of white lightning that had been strained through cheesecloth but hadn't been put in jugs yet. He fished a lucifer out of his pocket, snapped it to life with his thumbnail, and lit the lantern. He waited until the wick was burning well, then risked leaping to his feet again. He ran a few feet to the side to get clear of the brush arbor, then his arm swung back and whipped forward and the lantern flew through the air, turning over once as it sailed toward the buckets of moonshine. Pike could only hope the lantern would stay lit as he dived to the ground behind the bench again . . .

He heard the clatter as the lantern hit something and broke, and then a split second later, a huge *whummmppp!* sounded. Pike looked over the bench and saw a ball of fire swelling until it swallowed up the worm, the thumper, the boiler, and the pipes connecting them.

The utter destruction of the still made the moonshiners at the creek rise up and stare and shout in shocked disbelief. One of them fell as a shot blasted, but he pitched forward instead of back, as he would have if one of Pike's men in the trees had drilled him.

A moment later, as a fiercely crackling blaze consumed what was left of the still, Ramsey's men threw down their guns, climbed the short bank, and trudged out into the clearing. Behind them, covering them with rifles, came Sam Crow and Andy Burnett. When Pike saw the two of them, he realized they had circled around to get behind the moonshiners, and then Pike's fiery destruction of the still had provided a distraction while Sam and Andy got the drop on the men.

As Pike stood up and walked out to meet them, his other two companions emerged from the trees and also covered Ramsey's crew. Several of the men were wounded, but they were all able to get on their feet and shuffle together into the center of the clearing.

The soiled dove sat up, clutched her shoulder, and sobbed. "I think you broke my shoulder," she said to Pike as she glared at him.

"I doubt it," he said. He spotted his hat lying on the ground, picked it up, and put it on. "Move your arm."

"What?"

"I said, move your arm."

The girl raised the arm and moved it back and forth, grimacing as she did so. Obviously it hurt, but she had no trouble making the arm work.

"See, it's not broken," he told her. "But it'll probably have a pretty good bruise on it and be sore for a few days." He spied a dress in the wreckage of the tent. "Get up and get dressed. Then you can head for town if you want to."

"You mean *walk*? We're miles from town!"

"These boys are bound to have some horses around, probably a pen in the woods close by. You can take one of them if you want."

One of the Ramsey men spoke up, saying, "Blast it, Emmy Lou, if you steal any of our horses, you'll be sorry."

"Shut up!" she yelled back at him. "I oughta take all the horses, it'd serve you right, you sorry bunch of—" She stopped short, looked at Pike, and said, "No, wait, you're gonna kill all of 'em, aren't you? So it wouldn't really be stealin' if I took all the horses."

Pike's forehead creased in a puzzled frown. "I thought you were on their side," he said. "You were doing your best to help them kill me."

"That was when I thought they were gonna win," she said, as if that explanation ought to be the simplest thing in the world. "Now that you've got 'em corralled, I don't care what happens to them. I figure I already earned the money I got paid to come out here and keep 'em company." She sniffed contemptuously. "More than earned it, considerin' how bad some of those boys smell."

Another moonshiner said, "You're gonna be sorry for this, you no-good trollop!"

"No, I'm not," she shot back at him, "because I'm gonna take all those horses, sell 'em in Fort Worth, and buy me a train ticket outa this part of the country!" She turned to Pike and waved a hand at the prisoners. "Go ahead. Shoot 'em."

"No, I don't reckon so," Pike said. "But you can have their horses anyway. I kind of like the idea of them having to walk all the way back to Warbonnet, knowing every step of the way they'll have to tell Doak Ramsey all four of these stills are gone."

One of the men exclaimed, "You can't—"

Pike turned to his companions and said, "Light up the others, boys. A moonshine still makes a mighty impressive fire."

CHAPTER 21

Deputy Chuck Hanratty appeared in the open doorway of Doak Ramsey's private office, shuffled his feet, cleared his throat, and announced, "Somebody here to see you, Sheriff." He lowered his voice and added, "You ain't gonna like it."

Ramsey didn't like much of anything these days. It was a constant struggle as he battled the impulse to ride out to the Shannon spread, torch the place, and kill everybody on it. He'd been following Phineas Conway's advice, though, and letting Pike Shannon stew in his own juices.

But even though Hanratty hadn't said who the visitor was, as Ramsey got to his feet, he thought that the pot might be about to boil over.

"Get him in here, whoever it is," the sheriff rasped.

Hanratty nodded and backed out of the doorway. A few seconds later, a bedraggled figure clad only in the bottom half of a pair of long underwear appeared. The man had a blanket draped around his shoulders, but he looked pretty pathetic anyway. He walked gingerly, wincing a little with every step as if his bare feet hurt.

"Ayers, what are you doing here?" Ramsey snapped. "You're supposed to be out at the camp."

"I know, Sheriff, but . . . well . . . the camp ain't there no more."

Ramsey instantly thought of the wagons full of moonshine that had been dumped in the Brazos River a week earlier. Even though he'd been expecting another move against him, the rage that exploded inside him came out in a bellowed, "Shannon!"

"Yeah, it was him, all right," the pathetic-looking moonshiner named Ayers agreed. "All of us seen him, plain as day. He had that half-breed Injun Sam Crow with him, and Andy Burnett and a couple other fellas."

Hanratty had followed Ayers into the sheriff's office. He said, "Wait a minute. You mean they didn't have masks on this time?"

"Nope," Ayers said, shaking his head. "Walked in bald-faced and bold as brass and started shootin'."

"How many killed?" Ramsey asked.

"Well . . . nobody's dead. Everybody except me and Mart Hanks got winged, though."

Ramsey glared at Ayers and demanded, "How come you didn't get shot? And where are your clothes, blast it?"

Ayers looked uncomfortable. He hesitated for several seconds, then said, "They hit us just as I was comin' back from the woods. I'd been up all night workin' on a run, Doak, and I was just about to turn in but had to take care of some, uh, personal business first. So when I seen what was about to happen, I let out a yell and ducked back in the trees. The other boys put up a good fight, but Shannon and his bunch were too much for 'em."

"How come *you* didn't put up a fight?" Ramsey asked. His voice was dangerously quiet.

Ayers looked even more nervous. "I . . . I couldn't," he stammered. "I didn't have no gun, and if I'd waltzed in there unarmed and half-nekkid, I wouldn't'a stood a chance in Hades against those varmints."

"And what about your clothes?"

"They burned up in the fire."

"What fire?"

"The one that destroyed the tents and the brush arbor after Shannon blowed up all the stills."

Just as when Oscar Causey had brought him bad news, Ramsey wanted to take out the anger he felt on Ayers. But killing the messenger wasn't going to change a blasted thing, he knew. The damage would still be done.

"Didn't you have any guards posted?" he asked.

"Yeah, three fellas, just like usual. We found 'em tied up and gagged after it was all over and Shannon and the others were gone. Somebody had Injuned up on 'em and knocked 'em out, I reckon."

"Injuned is right," Hanratty said. "I'll bet it was that blasted 'breed, Sam Crow! We warned him what would happen to that gal of his if he went against us! I say some of the boys ought to ride out to his place and grab her—"

Ramsey stopped the deputy's rant with a curt gesture. "It's gone beyond that," he said.

"Yeah . . . yeah, I reckon maybe you're right. Shannon and his bunch weren't masked this time. That means you can arrest 'em, right, Doak? We can throw 'em all in jail—"

"Not that, either," Ramsey said. "Even if we arrest them, they'll probably have witnesses to lie and claim they weren't anywhere near our camp today."

"Yeah, but with Phin Conway as the judge—"

"A jury decides things in the end, not the judge. We could probably get a trial to go our way, but I'm not going to risk it," Ramsey said. "Besides, Shannon owes me more than that. And he's going to pay. He's going to pay *hard*."

Davey Morrigan dipped a tin cup into a bucket of moonshine and then took a sip of the colorless liquid. He licked his lips and frowned in thought.

"Well?" his brother Charley asked after a moment. Charley had never been the patient sort. "How is it?"

"I'm thinkin', I'm thinkin'."

"You don't have to *think* about moonshine, dad-blast it! It's either good or it ain't."

A grin spread across Davey's features. He had teased his brother long enough, he decided. "It's good," he said. "It's mighty smooth and tasty, and it's got plenty of punch."

Most folks would think that there was nothing good about somebody as young as him sampling white lightning, let alone making it, but they just didn't understand. Moonshining was the family business. Davey and Charley had started helping out around the stills when they were ten years old and had tasted 'shine for the first time when they were twelve.

Neither of them drank a lot, but they had to be able to judge the quality of a run.

"I guess we need to get it in the jugs, then," Charley said. "Ol' Dougal's supposed to pick up the load this afternoon."

Davey grinned at his taller brother and said, "You're just hopin' Nessa comes with him so you can make calf's eyes at her again."

"Dang your hide, Davey!" Charley cried. "You just shut your mouth about that. I . . . I don't know what you're talkin' about."

"Sure you don't," Davey said as he covered the top of another bucket with cheesecloth and got ready to strain more of the moonshine through it. "You're smitten with her, and you know it. You want to be her beau."

"That's a lie!" Charley rubbed the back of his hand across his mouth and muttered, "Anyway, she's older'n us, and our cousin, to boot."

"She ain't *that* much older, only a few years, and we ain't but distant cousins to her. Far enough distant not to worry about it. Not that it really matters, since I reckon Nessa's got enough good sense not to take up with a skinny, ganglin', redheaded galoot like you—"

Davey laughed and ducked as his brother took an open-handed swipe at his head.

"If you want to rassle, wait until we're finished with this run—"

Davey put an abrupt stop to his good-natured ribbing as he saw his cousin Lonzo Hightower step out of the woods. Lonzo, a tall, dark-haired young man a few years older than the Morrigan twins, was supposed to be standing guard over the trail to the camp. He

was the best shot of the trio and usually took that
sentry duty.

Davey had just enough time to wonder why Lonzo
had abandoned his post when he realized that there
was a man behind his cousin, prodding Lonzo along.
Alarm bells began to clamor in the back of Davey's
brain. He had just glanced toward his rifle and
Charley's shotgun, both of which were leaning against
nearby trees, when the man with Lonzo put an arm
around the young man's neck and jerked him to a stop.
The stranger's other hand came into view, holding a
revolver, and he pressed the gun to Lonzo's head.

"What in blazes!" Charley exclaimed. "Davey, look!"

"I see," Davey said. His heart slugged harder than
normal in his chest. He wasn't sure exactly what was
going on here, but he knew it was bad. Mighty bad.

That feeling got even stronger as more men appeared, walking out of the woods. Each of them held
either a rifle or a handgun, and with those weapons
covering them, Davey knew that he and Charley would
be shot to pieces if they made a move toward their guns.

"Just stand still, Charley," Davey said. His brother
had always been the more excitable member of the
pair. "Don't do nothin' to spook 'em."

They were Ramsey men, Davey thought. Couldn't
be anybody else. And there could be only one explanation for why they were here. They had come to
destroy the still. They had done that to other moonshiners throughout the county. All the Shannons and
their relatives knew it was only a matter of time before
Doak Ramsey and his minions got around to them.

So Davey knew that at this point, the best he and
Charley and Lonzo could hope for would be that the

Ramseys would bust up the still, maybe even burn it, but leave the three boys who'd been tending it alive.

A barrel-chested man sauntered out of the trees. Davey's breath froze in his throat. That was Doak Ramsey himself, the sheriff of Warbonnet County. Moonshining was against the law. Maybe Doak would arrest them and order his men to destroy the still, despite the fact that he was engaged in the same business. Davey didn't like the idea of going to jail, but he knew Pike and Dougal would bail them out if that happened.

"You boys are well hidden in here," Doak Ramsey said with a faint smile on his lips. "It took some tracking to find you. But you ought to know, you can't hide forever from the law."

Charley said, "You ain't the law in nothin' but name only, Ramsey. Ever'body knows you're as crooked as a dog's hind leg!"

"Charley, hush!" Davey said.

If what Charley had said made Ramsey angrier, he didn't show it. In fact, his smile widened as he said, "It doesn't really matter what you think, boy, because I'm not here today as a representative of the law."

"You're not?" Davey said. "Then why *are* you here?"

"To settle a score with Pike Shannon. To make a start on settling it, I should say, because it's going to get a lot worse for old Pike before it gets better."

With that, Ramsey drew a gun from the holster on his hip and turned toward Lonzo. The man who had been holding his revolver to Lonzo's head took the gun away, allowing Ramsey to step closer and press the muzzle of his weapon just above the young man's right ear. Lonzo's eyes barely had time to widen in horror before Ramsey pulled the trigger.

The gun boomed and Lonzo jerked as the bullet bored through his brain and exploded out the other side of his skull with a grisly spray of blood and bone fragments. The man who had been holding him up with an arm around his neck let go. Lonzo fell to his knees and balanced there for a second, his eyes still wide but unseeing now, before he toppled forward.

As Lonzo hit the ground, Davey knew with a terrible certainty that he and his brother were never going to leave this clearing alive.

So there was nothing to lose by making a grab for his rifle and trying to take some of those no-good Ramseys with him.

He got a hand on the barrel before bullets hammered his body and knocked him off his feet. Pain flooded through him as he rolled on the dirt. As he came to a stop, he reached for the rifle again, driven by the hatred he felt, but it was a couple of feet from his outstretched fingers. Might as well have been two miles away, for all the chances of him ever getting hold of it.

An agonized spasm gripped him, forced him to roll onto his side, then flop over on his back again. That kept happening. He had no control over his muscles now. The pain was too great.

A shadow moved over him. He blinked and looked up through the tears in his eyes. Doak Ramsey stood over him with the gun in his hand extended down toward Davey's face.

Somewhere far away, somebody was screaming. Davey sobbed as he realized it was his brother. He didn't know what they were doing to Charley, but it had to be something awful.

Davey was still flopping around when Ramsey planted a heavy, booted foot in the middle of his chest to hold him down. Ramsey eared back the gun's hammer and said, "When Pike Shannon gets to hell, you tell him about this, boy. You tell him all about it."

The burst of fire from the gun barrel was the last thing Davey saw. It expanded until it filled the whole world, and beyond.

CHAPTER 22

Pike leaned back in the cane-bottomed chair on the front porch and cocked his right ankle on his left knee. He lifted the cup of coffee in his hand and took a deep breath over it, savoring the rich aroma of the brew, flavored just slightly with a taste of Shannon white lightning. It wasn't noon yet, but drinking didn't count when it was just a dollop in a cup of coffee.

The door opened and Torrance came out onto the porch. He wore canvas work trousers and a cotton shirt, heavy shoes, and a broad-brimmed straw hat. After giving Pike a curt nod, he started toward the steps.

"Where are you headed?" Pike asked.

"I thought I'd go check the cotton fields, see how close the crop is to being ready to harvest." Torrance shrugged. "Maybe pull a few weeds. Somebody's got to work around here."

Pike sat up straighter. "I don't recall that being you very often, when we were both younger."

"Things have changed a lot since those days, in case you haven't noticed."

"Oh, I've noticed." Pike told himself not to let his

older brother get under his skin. He and Torrance had never gotten along, and that was one thing that *hadn't* changed.

Torrance looked like he was about to go on down the steps, but then he paused and said, "You know, now that you're back, if you really want to do something worthwhile you could work with the horses or do something else that might actually make a difference around here, instead of just trying to get yourself and some good men killed."

"What in blazes are you talking about?"

"Did it ever occur to you," Torrance said, "that we could just let Doak Ramsey have the moonshining in this county? Let him control it all! What does it matter? Sure, the cotton market's been rough, and we've lost some horses to rustlers, but some of that is probably just Ramsey trying to intimidate us. If he knew that he'd won, that we weren't going to cause him any more trouble, he'd back off and leave us alone. Times might be a little rough for a while, but the family would pull through. This spread could be an honest farm and ranch again, and our family could be . . ."

Torrance's voice trailed off.

"Something besides a bunch of crooked hillbilly moonshiners?" Pike said as he got to his feet and set his coffee cup on the porch railing. "Is that what you're saying, Torrance? You don't want to have to be *ashamed* of being a Shannon anymore?"

Torrance's jaw tightened as he took a step toward Pike. "I never said that. I'm not ashamed of our family."

"Well, you're sure acting like it, if you think we ought to just knuckle under to a skunk like Doak Ramsey—"

Pike's voice must have been louder than he realized, because at that moment the front door opened again and Nessa came out of the house, saying, "Goodness, what's all the commotion out here? You two bellowing at each other like a couple of old bulls—"

She stopped short as she gasped. She sounded startled enough that Pike looked at her and saw that she was staring along the road toward Warbonnet. Pike looked in the same direction and saw a horse plodding along, little clouds of dust rising around its hooves with each step.

"Nessa, what's wrong?" Torrance asked her.

"I . . . I know that horse," she said. "It belongs to Charley Morrigan. Pa gave it to him last year."

That explained why the animal was walking along the road toward the ranch house and the barn. Most horses would find their way back home if they were turned loose. Pike said, "Did the boys have their horses with them out at that still?"

"I'm sure they did," Nessa said.

"Well, then, this one got loose somehow and came back where it used to live. They'll show up later looking for it."

The words sounded a little hollow in Pike's ears, even as he spoke them. Then the horse turned a little, and he spied what Nessa had already seen.

Something was draped over the saddle and tied into place. At first the thing looked like a blanket roll, but then it took on a more human shape . . .

Nessa leaped down from the porch, skipping the

steps entirely, and as soon as her feet touched the ground, she sprinted toward the road.

"Nessa, wait!" Pike called, but it was too late. His sister didn't even slow down.

Pike was well aware that only the day before, he and his allies had raided the Ramsey camp and destroyed the four stills. They hadn't bothered with masks this time, since Doak Ramsey would know who was responsible anyway. Ramsey had shown an unexpected amount of restraint in not striking back after the ambush on his moonshine caravan, but Pike figured the destruction of those valuable stills was bound to drive Doak over the edge.

That horse—and whatever grim burden it was carrying—might be the bait in a trap designed to catch some Shannons.

And Nessa was racing toward it as fast as she could.

Pike put a hand on the porch railing and vaulted over it, landing gracefully and breaking into a run just as Nessa had done. She had a good start on him, but his legs were longer. As he ran after her, he heard Torrance's shoe leather pounding against the ground in a heavier, slower pace behind him.

Nessa raced through shadows cast by the trees along the road, and her bright red hair flashed as she passed through strips of sunlight. As she came close to Charley Morrigan's horse, the animal stopped and shied away, turning broadside to her so that Nessa got a good look at what the horse was carrying.

She stumbled to a halt and started screaming. Clapping her hands to her mouth in horror muffled the sound but didn't stop it.

In a few more long, fast strides, Pike caught up with

her. He looked past her at the horse and caught hold of her shoulders, turning her and pressing her face against his chest so she could no longer see the grisly sight. He felt her shuddering and closed his arms around her, knowing that his embrace wouldn't be enough to comfort her. And it sure wouldn't make her forget what she had just seen . . .

The bloody, mutilated corpse that was all that was left of Charley Morrigan.

Torrance pounded up beside them. He stared at Charley's body, too, and said in a soft voice, "Dear Lord in heaven." He lifted a tentative hand, as if he wanted to reach out but didn't dare. "Ohhhh, nooo . . ."

"Torrance," Pike said. When his brother didn't respond, he said it again, sharper this time. "Torrance!"

Torrance turned a dull, shocked face toward them. Pike went on, "Take Nessa back to the house. Don't let her come back out here, and don't let Ma leave the house, either. Find Dougal and tell him to come."

Nessa was sobbing now, her back shaking with each teary spasm. Pike tried to turn her and urge her toward Torrance while at the same time shielding her from the view of Charley's body. She clutched at Pike's shirt and didn't want to let go, saying, "No, no, no . . ."

Torrance didn't help matters by saying, "Who could do such a terrible thing? It . . . it looks like somebody took a knife to him—"

"That's what they did," Pike said, his voice harsh now. "I've seen the same sort of thing and worse out in Arizona Territory, after the Apaches got hold of some poor settler or soldier. *Now take Nessa and get her out of here.*"

He managed to gently disengage his sister's grip on

him and maneuver her into Torrance's arms. She looked tiny against his burly form.

"What are you going to do?" he asked Pike.

Unconsciously, Pike let his hand drop to the butt of his holstered gun. As his fingers closed around the walnut grips, his lips drew back from his teeth and he said, "I'm going to find the man responsible for this and kill him."

"Doak Ramsey, you mean."

"That's right. I don't know if Doak did the work himself, but he's to blame for it. And if Charley's dead, I reckon there's a good chance his brother and Lonzo Hightower are, too. Doak's got to pay for them, as well."

"So you're going to murder the county sheriff." Torrance's voice was flat. "You'll probably have to kill some of his deputies, too. And let's not forget Judge Conway."

"Yeah," said Pike, "I reckon Phin's got a bullet coming, sure enough."

Torrance looked at Pike over Nessa's trembling shoulder and said, "And if somehow you manage to survive this . . . this slaughter you're talking about, you'll have every lawman in the state after you, from the Rangers on down. They won't stop until they've gunned you down like a mad dog. Then where will the rest of the family be? The family you claim to care so much about!"

"Damn your eyes, Torrance," Pike grated. "What do *you* think I ought to do about this, if you don't believe I should go after Doak and his bunch?"

"Right now I think you should take that horse to the barn while I help Nessa into the house, and then we need to ride out to that camp where the boys were and . . . and see what we find there."

He was probably right, and Pike knew it. But the righteous anger that blazed inside him was just too fierce to be denied.

"You can tend to that," he said. "I've got work to do."

"Pike, blast it!" Torrance let go of Nessa and started after him. "You've got to listen to reason."

"Be a coward like you, you mean," Pike flung over his shoulder.

"Both of you, stop it!" Nessa screamed at them. "Charley's *dead*! Davey's probably dead! And all you two can do is keep on butting heads like you always have!"

Pike jerked his left hand toward Nessa and said to Torrance, "Get her in the house, like I told you."

He strode on toward the barn, intending to slap the saddle on his dun.

Feet scuffed in the dust behind him. A hand fell on his shoulder and jerked him around. Torrance said, "I won't let you do—"

Pike hit him before he could go on. His fist came up and cracked across Torrance's jaw. Torrance was bigger, taller, heavier, but the blow slewed his head around and made him stagger back a couple of steps.

Pike turned away again, but Torrance caught himself and with a roar threw himself forward, tackling Pike and sending both of them crashing to the ground.

CHAPTER 23

Nessa screamed again as Pike and Torrance rolled over in the dirt, wrestling and slugging at each other. Pike had always thought of his brother as a big soft baby, but Torrance's punches had some genuine power behind them. His fists crashed against Pike's ribs and sent pain shooting through him.

Torrance's weight advantage allowed him to get Pike on the ground and pin him there, too. With Torrance's bulky form pressing down on him, Pike struggled to breathe. The knee that Torrance dug into his belly just made things worse.

The ferocity of Torrance's attack had taken Pike by surprise. Torrance had always gone out of his way to avoid trouble in the past, even to the point of humiliating himself by groveling whenever anyone confronted him. Now Pike was on the verge of losing this fight, simply because he hadn't expected Torrance's actions.

Pike didn't like that idea. He stopped trying to punch his brother, since Torrance was just shrugging off the blows that did land. Instead, Pike cupped his hands and smacked them against the sides of

Torrance's head, too caught up in the heat of battle to even think about the fact that he might rupture his brother's eardrums and ruin his hearing permanently.

Torrance yelled in pain and jerked back, sitting up with his knees still straddling Pike. Pike threw his right leg up, hooked the calf in front of Torrance's throat, and levered him off. Torrance sprawled on his back.

Gasping for breath, Pike scrambled up. He and Torrance made it to their feet at the same time. Torrance lurched forward and swung a roundhouse punch at Pike's head. Pike ducked under it and stepped in to hook several swift punches with both hands to Torrance's midsection. Torrance was stronger than Pike had expected, but his belly *was* soft. He stumbled back a step and doubled over.

Pike clubbed his hands together and swung both arms. The blow smashed into Torrance's jaw and jerked his head to the side. His eyes rolled up in their sockets as he swayed a little from side to side. Pike stepped back to give him some room. Torrance sagged and then crumpled to the ground. He lay there on his side in a huddled heap, breath rasping in his throat. He moaned a little and stirred, as if he was trying to gather his strength to get up again, but then with a sigh, he slumped even more and his head lolled to the side.

He had put up a good fight, but Pike had been in countless bare-knuckles brawls during the past dozen years. His life had been a hard school that taught him to win at all costs.

For one terrible second, as he stared at Torrance's motionless form, Pike thought the cost of winning this battle had been his brother's life. Then he saw that Torrance's chest was still moving in and out and knew that he was just knocked out. Relief flooded through Pike.

He wasn't the only one who believed that Torrance was dead. Nessa came at him, crying, "You killed him, you killed him!" She balled her hands into fists and tried to strike at Pike's face.

He grabbed her wrists and said, "Stop it, you little fool! He's not dead!" He gave her a little shake to get some sense into her head.

"Pike! Vanessa!"

The sharp voice made both of them stop what they were doing. Pike looked around and saw his mother standing there, with a puffing and panting Fiddler catching up to her from behind. Mary Shannon's face was ashen.

So much for not letting her see Charley Morrigan's body until it had been cleaned up some.

Pike let go of Nessa. She turned and dropped to her knees beside Torrance. Taking hold of his shoulders, she rolled him onto his back and leaned over him to slap his face lightly and call his name, urging him back to consciousness.

Mary took an unsteady step toward the horse, which had shied away from the commotion even more. She lifted a hand and said, "Is . . . is that . . . ?"

"Charley Morrigan," Pike said. He flexed both hands, feeling the pain from the wallops he had given Torrance, but the fingers seemed to be working fine and that was what mattered right now. "The Ramseys did that to him."

Fiddler said, "How do you know that?"

"They're the only ones in these parts who hate us enough to do something like that!"

"Well, you're probably right about that," Fiddler admitted with a nod. "I'm sorry, Pike. It was a foolish question."

Pike waved that off and moved to get between his mother and the horse. "I told Torrance to take Nessa back to the house and not to let either of you out here for a while. I'm sorry you had to see this, Ma. If Torrance had just done what I said—"

"Don't blame your brother for this," Mary snapped. "None of it is his fault."

Pike was taken aback by that reaction. He stared at her and asked, "Are you saying it's *my* fault?"

"There wasn't open warfare with the Ramseys until you got here."

"There would have been, sooner or later," he said. "It was only a matter of time until Doak came after the family. And he wouldn't have stopped until he figured the threat was wiped out. We've just taken the fight to him first, that's all."

Mary didn't say anything to that. Maybe she knew he was right, Pike thought. Or maybe she was just so overcome by the terrible sight of Charley's body that she couldn't come up with any more words.

After a moment she was able to speak again. "Bring that poor boy in the house," she ordered.

"I thought we'd put him in the barn—"

"No, in the house. On the bed in the east bedroom that no one is using right now. He'll be cared for properly, not laid on a horse blanket in the barn."

Pike started to warn his mother that the sheets

would get bloody, but he stopped himself. She knew that. She just didn't care right now.

Torrance had come to and was sitting up by now, with Nessa still on her knees beside him. He took hold of his chin in one hand and worked his jaw back and forth. Satisfied that it wasn't broken, he started to push himself to his feet, saying, "I'll give you a hand."

"I don't need your help," Pike said. He went toward the skittish horse, speaking softly and calmly as he approached. The animal settled down and let him take hold of the reins.

"You always did have a good touch with horses," Torrance said with obviously grudging respect.

Pike ignored him and started leading the mount toward the house. The others trailed behind him. When he reached the steps, he untied the ropes holding Charley's body across the saddle and let the young man slide down on his shoulder. There was a lot of strength in Pike's rangy body, which he demonstrated by carrying the body up the steps, across the porch, and into the house.

When he had placed Charley on the bed in the unused bedroom, lowering the youngster to the sheets as gently as possible, Mary followed him into the room and said, "Vanessa and I will take care of this now. You need to see about Davey and Lonzo."

"You know they're bound to be—"

"Just go make sure," Mary said with a steely edge in her voice. "We'll deal with Charley. This is woman's work."

Pike didn't know about that, but he could tell that his mother was in no mood for an argument. He nodded and left her there. Nessa passed him in the hall, headed into the bedroom with a grim expression on her tear-streaked face.

Fiddler and Torrance were in the parlor. Pike said, "Come on, Fiddler. We'll ride out to that camp."

"I can come with you," Torrance said.

He wouldn't be any good if there were still any Ramseys lurking around, Pike thought, but he said, "No, it's better if you stay here, just in case Ma and Nessa need a hand."

Torrance looked like he wanted to argue, just on general principles, but after a second he nodded. He said, "I think Dougal rode out to check on the horse herd. You ought to go by there and let him know what's happened. I'm sure he'll want to ride out to the still with you."

Pike nodded. He was willing to do that. He motioned to Fiddler and said, "Come on. Bring a rifle with you."

Fiddler licked his lips and asked, "Do you think there's going to be more trouble?"

"We'd be fools not to think there might be," Pike told him.

They saddled their horses, Fiddler taking the same brown mare he had ridden before. They found Dougal in the main pasture where most of the horse herd was grazing. The old man was riding around the pasture on his saddle mule and looked surprised to see Pike and Fiddler. Twisted lines of shock and grief replaced that puzzled expression when Pike told him why they were there.

"Charley . . . dead," he muttered as he took off his hat and ran his hand through his long white hair.

"I . . . I can't hardly believe it. That boy was always a caution. Just full of life, him and his brother both."

"I only met them once, but I liked them, too," Pike said. "It's possible the Ramsey bunch caught Charley out by himself somewhere, for some reason, and Davey and Lonzo are all right and wondering where he is." His voice hardened. "Either way, we need to go find out."

"Yeah. Durned right." Dougal pulled his rifle from its saddle sheath and worked the Winchester's lever. "And then we'll go pay a visit to the Ramseys."

Pike didn't say anything in response, but he knew exactly how his grandfather felt. Bloody vengeance was the first thing that had come to his mind, too.

Pike was pretty sure he could have found his way to the still, but Dougal knew every foot of the route, so Pike told him to take the lead. As they headed up the river trail, Fiddler said worriedly, "I don't want you to think that I'm a coward, Pike, or that I don't appreciate everything you and your family have done for me, but I just don't think I'd be much help in a gunfight . . ."

"That's all right, Fiddler. If Dougal and I head for town and a showdown with Doak Ramsey, you'll need to ride back to the ranch and let them know what's going on." Pike paused, then added, "There's probably going to be a couple of bodies for you to take back, too."

"Pike . . . Ramsey has too many men. If you and Dougal go storming in there, they'll kill you. You have to know that."

Pike knew, all right. As his initial shock and rage over Charley's death had begun to fade slightly, he was seeing things clearer. He still *wanted* to charge into Warbonnet with all guns blazing, but it probably was a bad idea. The odds against him would be overwhelming, and it wouldn't do a bit of good for him and Dougal to get killed in such a futile gesture. Difficult though it might be to do, the wiser course would be to wait and plan . . .

Up ahead, Dougal began to curse. The three men reined in, and Dougal pointed to the big black birds soaring lazily through the air on wide-spread wings.

"Buzzards," he said, "and it looks to me like they're circlin' right above the camp." The old man's voice broke. "Only one reason those blasted scavengers would be hangin' around like that."

Pike knew his grandfather was right, but he said, "We've got to be sure," and nudged the dun into motion again. They entered the narrow path that branched off from the river trail. Pike knew the way from here, so he took the lead.

The still had been busted to pieces and then burned. From the looks of it, the bodies of Davey Morrigan and Lonzo Hightower had been tossed onto the flames as they blazed fiercely, fueled by moonshine. Nothing was left of the two young men except charred bones and an unholy stink hanging in the air. They had cheated those hungry buzzards, at least.

Pike hoped they had been dead before they were thrown onto the fire. That seemed likely, because there were no signs that they had thrashed around and tried to escape that terrible fate. Charley had died slower and more hideously, for the simple reason that Doak Ramsey wanted to use his death to send a message.

Well, the Shannons had gotten that message, Pike thought.

From here on out there would be no quarter in this war—on either side.

Chapter 24

The Morrigan twins and Lonzo Hightower were laid to rest in the Shannon family cemetery, on a broad bench of tree-shaded land overlooking the Brazos River about a quarter of a mile away. It was a beautiful, serene spot, and Pike hoped the souls of the three young men would know peace there, despite the awful nature of their deaths.

More than a hundred people were at the burial— most of the family and friends of the Shannons' from all over Warbonnet County. Not all, though. Some had volunteered to stand guard over the stills, so Doak Ramsey couldn't take advantage of the family's mourning to destroy their ability to continue making moonshine. If such a thing were to happen, it would mean that Davey, Charley, and Lonzo had died for nothing.

Early Summerville, the Baptist preacher from Warbonnet, performed the graveside service. Way back over in Ireland, before the Shannons emigrated to America, they had been Catholic, but as the generations passed, in Tennessee, Arkansas, and finally Texas, they had become Baptists, although as moonshiners they weren't real strict about following the Bible verse that talked about how wine was a rager and strong drink a mocker, like most Baptists were. Still, having Summerville there to read from the Good Book and say a prayer over the three boys being laid to rest was a comfort.

When the service was over and a few of the men stayed to shovel dirt back into the graves, Torrance walked toward the house with his mother on one side and Nessa on the other. Pike, Dougal, and Fiddler trailed a short distance behind. As they neared the barn, Pike said quietly, "Fiddler, you go on inside the house. I asked some of the men to meet me and Grandpappy in the barn."

"A council of war, eh?" Fiddler said. "Well, count me in, if you would."

"I thought you didn't want to be part of this fight."

"I said I wouldn't be very *good* at it. I never said I didn't want to be included. Besides, I have grudges of my own to settle against Doak Ramsey and his henchmen."

Pike shrugged and said, "Come ahead, then. I won't turn any man away . . . and I'll understand any man who doesn't want to wade through all the blood that's coming."

Within minutes, a group of at least thirty men had gathered in the barn. Ed Morrigan, Davey and Charley's father, was there, looking pale and grief-stricken but also angry and determined. Barton Hightower, Lonzo's father, brought his other three sons with him. All were in their twenties, older than Lonzo had been. Sam Crow, Andy Burnett, Will Fisher, and the Dawson brothers stood near the front of the group. It was a grim bunch that assembled here, and Pike knew they weren't going to like what he had to say to them.

Before he could speak, though, Fiddler said, "Do you mind if I play a little something before you get started, Pike?" He held up his fiddle, which he must have placed in the barn earlier with this in mind.

Pike nodded and said, "Go ahead."

Fiddler positioned the instrument, tucking his chin down on the smooth wood to help hold it in place. Unlike the raucous strains that usually came from the fiddle when he drew his bow across the strings, this was a more plaintive sound as he began to play. Everyone in the barn fell silent as the tune of "Amazing Grace" filled the air.

When Fiddler was finished, several men murmured, "Amen," as if they'd been in church. Maybe they were, in a way, Pike thought.

Then he said, "We're all here to talk about how we're going to make the Ramseys pay for what they've done."

Barton Hightower said, "There's nothing to talk about. We're going to kill them all. Every blasted one of them."

Pike shook his head. "There's not enough of us to do that, even if we call on every able-bodied man among family and friends, including the ones who don't want to take up the gun." He thought about his brother Torrance as he said that. "Sure, we could kill a lot of them," he went on, "but chances are, they'd wipe us out."

"Then we're not going to do *anything* to avenge my boys' murder?" Ed Morrigan asked in a voice dulled by pain. He lifted a hand and pointed in the direction of the graveyard. "They're out there in the ground, while Doak Ramsey is still walking around on top of it. That's not right, Pike. It's just not right."

"No, it's not," Pike agreed, "and Ramsey's going to pay. I give you my word on that. But I've done a lot of thinking about it and my grandpappy and I have hashed it all out, and I believe we've been going about this the wrong way."

"You mean poking at Ramsey until he lashes out like a rabid dog?" Barton Hightower said. "That was your doing, Pike. And now we're all reaping what you've sown."

Pike grimaced and rubbed a hand over his chin. He said, "I deserve that, Barton. I really do. I never thought Ramsey would go that far."

"Damn right you deserve it."

"But getting more of us killed . . . getting *all* of us killed . . . isn't going to bring back the ones we've lost."

"Then what *are* we going to do?" Sam Crow asked.

"I've been told that maybe we ought to give up, let Doak win, and then he won't bother us anymore."

That brought shouts of anger from several of the men. Pike hadn't mentioned that it was Torrance who'd made that suggestion. Some of them would figure that out anyway.

"Is that what you did in all those range wars we've heard about?" Barton Hightower asked. "Turn tail and run?" His voice was like the lash of a whip. "You must not have been much of a hired gun after all."

Pike shook his head. "I said that was one idea. I didn't say we were going to do it."

"You're just talking in circles," Ed Morrigan said.

"Be honest, Pike. You don't have any idea how to win this war with the Ramseys, do you?"

Andy Burnett said, "They've got the numbers and the law on their side. Mighty hard to buck odds like that."

Pike raised his hands to quell the hubbub that arose. He said, "We're *not* giving up. But right now I'm asking you to go home, go back to your families, and not start any more trouble just yet. Grandpappy and I are figuring this out, but right now we need some time."

"While my boy is dead!" Barton Hightower thundered.

"And my two," Ed Morrigan added, quieter but no less pained.

"I'm sorry," Pike said. He knew it wasn't good enough, but right now it was all he had.

Ed Morrigan just shook his head. Despair filled his eyes. "I guess sometimes the world just comes crashing down around you," he said, "and there's not a blessed thing you can do about it. Man is born to trouble, the Scripture says. That sure is the truth."

He shook his head, turned, and trudged toward the barn doors. The slump of his shoulders testified to his utter defeat.

Muttering in a mixture of anger and disappointment, some of the men followed him. Barton Hightower remained to glare at Pike and say, "You'd better come up with something pretty soon, that's all I've got to say. If you don't, we'll take things into our own hands."

"And finish the job of wiping out this family," Dougal said, his tone one of rising anger, too.

"Better to go out fighting than cowering in the dirt like a whipped dog," Hightower snapped. The gaze he directed at Pike was full of contempt. He turned and stalked out of the barn after the others. The remaining men drifted out one by one until only Sam Crow was left, other than Pike, Dougal, and Fiddler.

Crow looked at Pike and said, "You know I trust you. But you're the one who got us to fight in the first place, and now it looks like you want to quit. You can't blame the others for being upset, Pike."

"I don't blame them. I'm just asking them to trust me, too, and give me a little time."

Crow frowned and said, "There's a dance coming up in Warbonnet in a week. Folks from all over the county will be there, Ramseys and Shannons alike. If nothing's changed by then, there'll be trouble. You can count on it."

"In town, right in the middle of the Ramsey stronghold?"

Crow shrugged. "I'm just telling you what's going to happen. You're a moonshiner, Pike. You know you can only build up the fire under a boiler for so long before it blows up."

With that, Crow left the barn, too.

"He's right, you know," Dougal said. "And you can't blame folks for feeling the way they do."

"I don't blame anybody except Doak Ramsey," Pike said. "He's the one who deserves to have all this trouble laid at his feet." He looked intently at his grandfather. "This fella who's feeding you information from Ramsey's side . . . you're sure he's right that they've got something big in the works?"

"All I know is that he seemed convinced of it. The biggest deal Doak's ever put together, he said. That's why Doak was so upset when you burned his main camp and those four stills. Accordin' to what I was told, he's got enough 'shine cached to go through with the deal, but that'll leave him short goin' ahead with his other customers. So it's mighty important to him that this deal comes off without a hitch."

"Well, find out as much as you can, as soon as you can," Pike said. "Because that's going to be our job—throwing as big a hitch as possible into Doak Ramsey's plan."

CHAPTER 25

Baptists didn't hold with dancing, but they didn't hold with drinking, either, and plenty of them in Warbonnet County bent their elbows on a regular basis. The other churches didn't mind so much if folks wanted to get together and do-si-do.

So the four or five dances held during the year at the town hall and community center in Warbonnet—which was also the Odd Fellows' Hall—always drew a big crowd. Most people who lived in town attended, and the hitch rails along Main Street filled up with horses belonging to the cowboys who rode in for the occasion. The wagons, buckboards, and buggies that brought in families from outlying parts of the county were parked in an open area next to the town hall, and by the time everybody got here, they would be parked everywhere else there was an empty spot along Main Street, too.

The deaths of the three young men a week earlier cast an undeniable pall over the festivities this time, but only to a certain extent. Folks still needed a break from the tedium of everyday life. The hostilities between the Ramsey and Shannon clans involved quite a few people on each side, but practically speaking, they were only a small fraction of Warbonnet County's population. Most of the citizens just stayed out of it as much as possible.

Everyone knew what was going on, though, even if they didn't take sides, so when Pike and his family arrived in town late that Saturday afternoon, they got plenty of curious stares. Some of the expressions on the faces of the townspeople were unfriendly, while others seemed to express tentative support, but for the most part people were just interested and a little bit wary, as if they worried that a pitched battle might break out at any second.

Which it very well might, if some hombres had their way, Pike knew.

Despite advising caution and patience—two things that really went against the grain for him—Pike knew exactly how the others felt, because he had the same almost overpowering urge to strike back against Doak Ramsey and his bunch. Always before, in all the conflicts that had involved him, hitting the enemy hard and fast had been the key to survival.

He'd never had the lives of his own family riding on the decisions he made, though, and that made all the difference. That was one of the hard lessons he had learned over the past couple of weeks.

He and Dougal rode in the lead, with the buckboard following them. Torrance handled the reins, and Mary was on the seat beside him. Nessa and Fiddler rode in the back. Some of the girls they passed waved and called greetings to Nessa, who smiled and returned them.

Fiddler wore a dark gray suit that had belonged to

Elijah Shannon. Despite having large sons, Lije hadn't been a big man in stature, and his clothes came the closest to fitting Fiddler. Mary had suggested that he could borrow the suit, since he didn't own anything really suitable for attending the dance. He'd expressed some reservations about wearing her recently deceased husband's clothes, but Mary had insisted.

"Elijah wasn't always the most practical man in the world," she'd said, "but he wouldn't be upset that someone was getting good use out of his things."

Pike wore a black suit and a black shirt with a dark red bandanna around his throat. Dougal had donned a brown tweed suit coat over his usual overalls in his only concession to dressing up. Torrance had on the trousers from that same tweed suit, as well as a white shirt and brown vest and string tie.

Since she was still in mourning, Mary wore a black dress, while Nessa's gown was dark blue. Being the most staunch Baptist in the family, Mary wouldn't have been doing any dancing even if she hadn't been bereaved, but she came to these events to visit with her friends from town. Nessa didn't dance, either, but she also enjoyed being around her friends. Dougal, whom Mary had accused more than once of being a heathen, and only half jokingly, at that, was the only member of the family who really got out and stomped enthusiastically around the dance floor.

Pike kept watch for any of the Ramseys as he and Dougal led the buckboard toward the town hall. He spotted a couple of the deputies he had clashed with the day he returned to Warbonnet County. One was Chuck Hanratty, the other Billy Ray Briggs, and as the two men walked along the street, Pike noticed that

Briggs was still moving gingerly even though several weeks had passed since Pike kicked him in the groin. The murderous glare Briggs directed toward him made Pike smile faintly. Looked like the deputy remembered him, too. Hard to forget somebody who kicked you in the family jewels, Pike reckoned.

Hanratty seemed surprised to see Fiddler with the Shannons, and then he glared, too. Nervously, Fiddler cast his gaze down at the road unrolling under his feet dangling over the back of the buckboard.

Pike saw that exchange and dropped back to ride alongside the buckboard for a moment. He said to Fiddler, "Looks like Deputy Hanratty doesn't cotton much to you."

"He's a terrible man," Fiddler muttered. "Simply terrible. He tormented me every time I was locked up in that awful jail. That should have been enough to make me stop yielding to temptation, but alas . . ."

"You've been really good about not drinking since you've been staying with us, Mr. Fiddler," Nessa told him.

"Yes, I've surprised myself a great deal. I don't know how long my newfound sobriety will last, but I'm rather enjoying not being soused all the time."

Pike nudged his horse ahead again and rejoined Dougal. They reached the open area next to the town hall a moment later. There were still a few empty spots, so Torrance guided the buckboard into a row of vehicles lined up fairly neatly. As the buckboard came to a stop, Fiddler dropped off the back, carrying the fiddle he had brought along. He hurried to the front to help Mary down.

Trees lined the back and far side of the open area. The sun had gone down a short time earlier and shadows had begun to gather under those trees, but it was still light enough for Pike to see men standing there passing around jugs. The town's ladies kept pretty close watch over the punch bowls to keep them from being spiked, but plenty of drinking went on out here and would continue to do so all evening.

As Pike dismounted, he wondered if that was Shannon or Ramsey moonshine the men were drinking. Probably some of both, he decided.

He and Dougal tied their horses to the buckboard. Nessa hadn't waited for anybody to help her down, of course, but had jumped lithely to the ground despite wearing a dress. She was already walking toward the building with her mother and Fiddler. Torrance climbed down from the driver's seat, rather lumberingly, and said to Pike, "Is there going to be trouble here tonight?"

"Why are you asking me?"

"Because I figure you'd know."

"I'm not planning on starting any," Pike said. "I'm not responsible for whatever anybody else does."

Torrance just grunted, as if to express some doubt about that. He walked on toward the town hall's entrance, but Pike hung back and motioned for Dougal to do likewise.

Quietly enough that no one would overhear, Pike said, "I hope you'll get to talk to whoever your mysterious friend is tonight."

"Maybe," Dougal replied, which didn't help at all.

The inactivity of the past week had been a strain

on Pike. He wasn't used to waiting around and doing nothing when there were enemies to confront. But until they got more information, he and Dougal couldn't plan their next move. He hoped that would change tonight. Since Dougal's informant was somebody who worked for Doak Ramsey, more than likely, there was a good chance the fella would be here this evening. Nearly everybody in Warbonnet County would be.

As the family approached the doors, Pike stiffened at the sight of Doak Ramsey standing with one of his deputies just outside the entrance, where a table had been set up. Ramsey glanced in Pike's direction and reacted with a visible tension of his own. For a second the two men stared at each other with hatred blazing in their eyes. Then Ramsey said something to his man, turned, and walked on into the hall.

The deputy touched the brim of his hat and nodded respectfully to Mary and Nessa. "Mrs. Shannon," he said. He smiled at Nessa. "Howdy, Miss Shannon."

"Deputy," Nessa replied coolly. The young man's eyes followed her as she and her mother went on inside.

Pike saw that and frowned. Unless he was mistaken, that deputy was smitten with his sister, and he didn't like that at all. He figured Nessa was pretty good at handling unwanted attention, though.

The deputy turned his attention back to the job the sheriff had given him. He held up a hand and said to Pike, Dougal, and Torrance, "You fellas hold up for a minute now. The town ordinances say that nobody can be armed at these dances except for duly appointed peace officers. I'm going to have to ask you men to turn over your guns. I'll put 'em in a box I've got back here, and you can have them back when you leave the dance later."

"I'm not carrying a gun, Deputy Eagleton," Torrance said. He held his vest open to demonstrate that.

"Neither am I," Dougal added. He opened his coat the same way Torrance had.

Eagleton looked at Pike. "How about you?"

Pike hesitated. His gun belt was buckled around his hips, of course. He never went anywhere without it. And he didn't like the idea of turning it over, especially to one of Ramsey's men. A glance around told him that several folks were watching, obviously intent on seeing what was going to happen.

Doak Ramsey probably hoped that being asked to give up his gun would keep him away tonight. Pike didn't want to give Ramsey that satisfaction. He unbuckled the gun belt and handed it over to Joe Eagleton.

"I'll be wanting it back later," he said.

"You'll get it," the deputy replied. "You can go on in now."

Pike followed Dougal and Torrance into the hall, wishing he didn't feel so blasted naked without the Colt on his hip.

CHAPTER 26

A lot of people greeted Mary, Nessa, and even Torrance in friendly fashion as the Shannons entered the building. Dougal received a number of hand-shakes and slaps on the back.

The reception given to Pike was decidedly cooler, though. He supposed he couldn't blame folks for feeling that way. As several people had pointed out to him, trouble had really erupted in the county since his return.

They didn't seem to understand that more blood would have been spilled anyway, in time. His arrival and challenge to Doak Ramsey's greed and ambition had just prodded things to a faster pace.

Mary and Nessa took seats in the row of chairs lined up along a wall. Dougal and several other old-timers gathered in a knot to talk. Fiddler had already made his way to the front of the hall where a group of musicians were getting ready to play. He joined them as they tuned up their guitars and fiddles. One of the men had a big bass fiddle as tall as he was.

Pike hung his hat on one of the hooks on the wall inside the door and walked into the hall. He noticed—but pretended not to—as several people moved away from him.

Andy Burnett came up to him, grinning as usual, and shook his hand. "Mighty good to see you here tonight, Pike. Didn't know if you folks would come in or not."

Sam Crow joined them and said in response to Burnett's comment, "Ed Morrigan and Barton Hightower and their families aren't here. Can't say as I blame them."

"Neither can I," Pike said. "Those wounds are still too fresh."

"It was a terrible tragedy," Burnett said, "but life has to go on for the folks who are still here."

"That's right," Crow agreed. "I wasn't going to tell my wife and kids they couldn't come tonight."

He nodded toward a pretty, dark-haired woman surrounded by several children, including a teenage girl who looked like she would be even lovelier than her mother in a few years.

"Ramsey's men have been leaving them alone, I hope?" Pike said.

"So far. I don't reckon even they would try anything in a big crowd like this."

"I hope you're right."

When you got right down to it, though, Pike wasn't sure he would put anything past Doak Ramsey if it would get Doak what he wanted.

Knowing that Ramsey had come into the hall a few minutes earlier, Pike looked around the room now and tried to spot the sheriff. He was surprised and alarmed to see Ramsey walking toward the place where his mother and sister were sitting.

"What in blazes?" he muttered. He hurried in that direction, leaving a puzzled Andy Burnett and Sam Crow behind him.

He came up behind Ramsey in time to hear the man say, "I don't believe I ever offered you my condolences on the passing of your husband, Mrs. Shannon."

"Thank you, Sheriff," Mary said, polite as always but unable to keep her voice from sounding a little stiff and forced.

"It was a tragic accident," Ramsey went on.

The gall of the man! From behind him, Pike said, "*Was* my pa's death an accident?"

Ramsey looked over his shoulder, then turned to face Pike, who was all too aware that he was unarmed while Ramsey had a gun on his hip with the butt cocked forward at a jaunty angle, as usual. The two men stood there with only a few feet separating them. Pike felt the hair on the back of his neck bristle and figured Ramsey's was probably doing the same. They were like a couple of fighting dogs eager to tear into each other.

Ramsey's voice was calm, though, as he said, "What else could it have been? Your father was found at the bottom of Warbonnet Gorge and nobody else was around. He must have fallen in. Unless you think he killed himself by jumping."

Mary said, "My Elijah never would have committed such a sin as to throw away the life the good Lord gave him."

Ramsey looked at her again and said, "No, ma'am,

I don't mean to imply that he did. I was just answering the question your son asked me."

"I can think of another answer," Pike said. "Somebody hit him on the head and *threw* him into that gorge. The fall busted him up so bad nobody would have been able to tell. What do you think about that possibility, Ramsey?"

"It's *Sheriff* Ramsey . . . and I don't think that's what happened, but I reckon we'll never know, will we?"

"Sooner or later, we will," Pike said. "We'll know the truth, all right."

The two men locked hostile gazes a moment longer, then Ramsey turned and nodded to Mary. "You and your family enjoy the evening," he said, then he walked away without looking at Pike again.

"One of these days," Pike said. "And soon . . ."

He might have said more, but at that moment a fat, round-faced man with sleek brown hair climbed onto the little platform where the musicians stood, raised his hands and voice, and called, "Ladies and gentlemen, ladies and gentlemen, if I could have your attention, please!"

Pike leaned over to Nessa and asked her, "Who's that?"

"G. Ellsworth Heath," she replied. "The mayor of Warbonnet Gorge."

Pike cocked an eyebrow. "Another Ramsey relative?"

"A distant cousin by marriage, but definitely in the sheriff's camp."

Pike nodded, not surprised. Mayor Heath went on, "On behalf of the town council of Warbonnet, welcome to the dance, and everybody have a good time tonight! I just want to remind you that there'll be no drinking or fighting here in the town hall."

Dougal had come up beside Pike while the mayor was talking and leaned over to say, "Notice he don't say nothin' about doin' those things outside."

"Now we'll get the music started," the mayor said. He turned to the leader of the group of musicians. "Bob, you and the boys take it away!"

They launched into a sprightly tune, with Fiddler sawing away with the others. Couples quickly paired up and began to swing around the dance floor. Later there would be square dancing, with a caller calling and clapping the beat, but for now folks just danced as they saw fit, most of them doing some sort of variation on a waltz, with different levels of skill. Nearly everyone wore a smile, though. They were having fun, and that was the only thing that mattered tonight.

The town of Warbonnet needed some fun. The whole county did.

And it lasted almost a whole hour.

Pike found out later what happened to start the trouble. One of the Ramseys came up to Lita Crow, Sam's daughter, and asked her to dance. She turned him down, being civil about it, but he took offense anyway, or at least pretended to. Pike wasn't sure but what Doak might have told one of his men to stir up some trouble. Instead of taking Lita's refusal graciously, he'd gotten mad and said some things to her that weren't fit for mixed company. Sam Crow had been dancing with his wife when the Ramsey man approached his daughter, but he saw what was going on and headed in that direction, getting there in time to hear the names the hombre called Lita.

He reacted the way any father would, grabbing the gent's shoulder, jerking him around, and punching him in the mouth.

Several other Ramsey men were close by in the crowd, making Pike even more convinced that the whole thing was staged. They jumped Sam, two of them grabbing his arms while the third man hammered punches to his belly. That went on for only a few seconds before two of Sam's friends arrived and jumped into the fray. Fists flew wildly and the melee began to spread.

Pike didn't actually see any of that when it occurred. One of the dancers had caught his attention. She was a young woman about his sister's age, and she had red hair like Nessa's, although hers was a darker shade, verging from red to dark brown depending on how the light shone on it. And while Nessa had an innocent, wholesome beauty about her, this girl's features possessed a much more sultry cast. Pike thought she was intriguing and wouldn't have minded dancing with her. He was about to go find Dougal and ask if he knew who she was, when he heard startled, angry shouts and looked around to see the commotion breaking out on the other side of the room.

That couldn't be anything good, and if it was something that might threaten his family, Pike wanted to head it off now. He started in that direction, stepping around people when he could and shouldering them aside when he couldn't.

The fight came to him before he could get to it. A hand clamped on to his shoulder and hauled him around. Pike saw a fist flying toward him, and behind it, the ugly, rawboned face of Billy Ray Briggs. Pike tried to get out of the way of the punch, but somebody jostled him from behind and prevented him from doing so.

Too late, he realized he might have charged right into a trap.

He managed to move enough to keep Briggs's punch from landing squarely on his jaw. It brushed his shoulder instead but packed enough force to turn him partway around. Briggs rushed in while he was off-balance. The deputy had a big score to settle, and he threw a hard left that caught Pike in the chest. Pike tried to set his feet, but hands grabbed him from behind and shoved him forward as the sounds of the growing brawl swelled up and overpowered the music.

Briggs aimed another punch at his jaw, and this time the blow landed cleanly enough to knock Pike backward. As he staggered, somebody tripped him. He went down hard and slid across the dance floor.

When he came to a stop, he realized he was lying at the feet of several dancers who had pulled back hurriedly to try to avoid the fight. One of them, he saw to his surprise, was the girl with dark red hair he had been looking at a few moments earlier. She gave him a cool, appraising stare, and he realized he must look pretty foolish, lying on his back on the dance floor like that.

He scrambled to his feet, gave the girl a smile and a nod, said, "Sorry for the interruption, miss," and then charged back into battle.

CHAPTER 27

Billy Ray Briggs was waiting for him. The deputy threw a wild, roundhouse right that Pike ducked under, then followed with a looping left. Pike avoided that blow, too, and moved close enough to hammer a short left into Briggs's ribs. He tried to land a straight right on Briggs's nose, but the deputy recovered enough to block the punch and counter with a right to Pike's solar plexus.

Then, while the brawl swirled around them, the two men stood toe-to-toe and slugged away at each other. They were able to avoid or parry some of the blows, but most of them landed with solid thuds of fist against flesh. The impacts rocked each of them back in turn, and then they surged forward again.

Pike tasted blood in his mouth, and his left eye was starting to swell a little. Briggs's mouth had a crimson smear across it from the blood that had leaked from his split lips. More blood spurted as Pike landed a punch to the deputy's nose and felt cartilage crunch under his knuckles. Briggs reeled back a step.

That gave Pike enough room to lift his right leg and snap it out in a kick that drove his bootheel deeply into Briggs's stomach. Briggs doubled over. Pike hit him on the back of the neck and sent him to the floor, where Briggs lay curled up in a gasping, agonized ball.

Pike didn't even have time to catch his breath before somebody grabbed him around the neck from behind. He smelled raw moonshine fumes on the man's breath as he leaned in and tightened his hold on Pike's neck.

Another man moved in from Pike's front, obviously intent on whaling the tar out of him while the first man hung on to him. Pike grabbed the arm around his throat and raised both legs this time. His double kick caught the attacker in the chest and sent him flying backward to knock down several other brawlers, bowling them over like ninepins.

The kick also made the man holding Pike stagger backward. Pike jerked back and forth, trying to get loose, and deliberately tangled his feet with those of his captor. They both lost their balance and went down. The jolt as they hit the floor knocked the man's arm away from Pike's neck. He rolled free and rammed his elbow into the man's jaw.

A viciously swung boot toe spiked into Pike's ribs and rolled him over as pain burst through him. The man who had just kicked him came at him again, foot lifted for a face-crushing stomp this time. Pike caught it as it came down and shoved up on it as hard as he could. With a startled yell, the would-be stomper went over backward, and he was close enough to the table holding several punch bowls that he landed on top of it and caused it to collapse. The bowls shattered and bright red punch flew everywhere.

Pike slapped his hands on the dance floor and

pushed himself to his feet. He found himself staring across the wreckage of the table and the stunned man lying amid the debris at a young woman with blond curls falling to her shoulders and framing a lovely face. She would have been even prettier if she hadn't been staring down aghast at the front of her light blue dress, which was now dark from being soaked by the punch that had splashed all over it.

She must have sensed Pike looking at her, because she lifted her eyes to him. Those eyes, a light blue like her dress, blazed with anger as she cried, "You . . . you animal! Look what you've done!"

Pike gestured toward the man who had kicked him and said, "It's his fault! What was I supposed to do, let him stomp my face in?"

"You're all drunken brutes!"

She was wrong about part of that, Pike thought. He wasn't drunk. He hadn't had even a taste of 'shine tonight.

Before he could point that out, the blonde glanced past him and then screamed. Pike wheeled around and saw a man swinging what looked like a broken chair leg at his head. He wasn't surprised that more of the furniture had gotten busted up in the ruckus.

He caught the man's wrist before the chair leg could land and whistled a punch to the hombre's jaw. The chair leg clattered to the floor as the man's eyes rolled up and he buckled. Pike shoved him away and started to turn back to the blonde when a whole chair crashed down on his back and drove him to his knees again. He tried to shake off the grogginess that threatened to overwhelm him as he twisted around, grabbed the legs of the man who'd just struck him, and heaved him into the air.

The punishment he had taken caught up to him then. A haze as red as that spilled punch dropped over his eyes, and after swaying for a second, he toppled over into oblivion.

If he had been conscious for anybody to ask him about it, he would have said there was a good chance the Ramseys would take advantage of his passed-out state to go ahead and kill him. Clearly, Doak didn't want to take the risk of doing such a thing with so many witnesses around, because Pike woke up a while later with a pounding head and plenty of aches and pains.

Something cool and soothing dabbed at his face. He forced his eyes open to see what felt so good. It was a wet cloth, held in a slender hand that was tanned like a man's but possessed of a purely feminine grace. His gaze moved from the hand on up a sleek, lightly muscled arm to a bare shoulder and then a very attractive face surrounded by auburn hair.

This girl tending to him was the one he had seen earlier, he realized. The one he'd planned to ask his grandpappy about, just before the fight broke out.

"Hold still," she said when she saw that he was awake. He was sitting on the floor with his back propped against a wall while she knelt in front of him.

"Wasn't planning on going anywhere," he said. His voice sounded a little funny, probably because his lips were swollen from being punched. "Reckon I'm fine right where I am."

She snorted but somehow managed to make it sound appealing. "You're lucky your head's not busted wide open. I saw somebody smash a chair over it."

"No, most of it hit me on the back," Pike said. "Don't know if it would have mattered, though. I've got a pretty hard head."

"So I've heard."

That puzzled Pike, and so did the realization that there was something familiar about her. Had she lived in these parts before he left home? She was about Nessa's age, so she would have been pretty young when he lit out. No doubt she had changed a lot in the dozen years since then. He thought about it while she was wiping more of the blood off his face with the wet cloth, which he now realized was a lace-edged handkerchief. Probably hers.

"What's your name?" he asked.

"Belle."

"Mighty pretty name."

"Be quiet. You're just making your lips start bleeding again."

Pike might have ignored the command, but at that moment another female voice asked, "Is he going to live?"

Belle's lips quirked with amusement. "It looks like he'll survive. He informs me that he has a hard head."

"Well, I don't doubt *that*."

The blonde who had gotten drenched with punch leaned in to peer down at him. She didn't look any happier than she had earlier.

"I hope you're happy, you . . . you ruffian," she said. "You've ruined the dance with your ridiculous brawling."

"I don't reckon I could have done that all by myself," Pike told her. "There were a few other fellas fighting, too."

"That's only fair, Sophie," Belle said.

"Don't you know who he is?" the blonde demanded.

"Of course I do. He's Pike Shannon."

"The man responsible for all the trouble around here," Sophie snapped. "I would think that you'd know that better than anyone else."

With that, she sniffed and turned away. She was pretty, but Pike wasn't sorry to see her go. If he wanted someone to blame him for everything whether it was his fault or not, plenty of folks in Warbonnet County would be happy to do that, he figured.

Still he was curious enough to ask Belle, "Who was that?"

"Sophie Truesdale," she replied. "You wouldn't know her. She's a dry."

"A what?"

"Sophie doesn't believe in drinking moonshine or any other kind of liquor. That's why I said you weren't likely to know her. She's also one of the leaders of the local chapter of the WCTU."

"Don't reckon I know what that is, either."

"Women's Christian Temperance Union," Belle explained. "They have chapters all over the country. The one here was formed when people started talking about having a local option election. Sophie and her friends pushed hard for it. You might say Sophie is one of the reasons Warbonnet County is dry now."

"Oh. I suppose that's the reason she doesn't seem to have much use for me. She knows the reputation my family has."

"She certainly does." Belle cocked her head to the side slightly as she studied his face. "I've gotten about as much of the blood off of you as I'm going to be able to. When you get home, you'd better put something cold on that eye to keep the swelling down. Actually, it probably wouldn't hurt to dunk your whole head in some cold water."

"I'll keep that in mind," Pike said. "I guess the dance is over?"

"Oh yes. It's going to take a while to clean up and repair all the damage."

"Well, for the part I played in it, I'm sorry—"

"*Belle!* What in blazes are you doing?"

The loud, angry voice belonged unmistakably to Doak Ramsey. Belle straightened to her feet. Pike muttered a curse under his breath as he braced himself against the wall and shoved upright as well. Ramsey stood a few feet away, a dark, furious glare on his blocky face and his hand resting on the butt of his gun.

Belle's face was coolly defiant as she gazed back at him. "This man looked like he could use some help," she said.

"Don't you know who that is?" Ramsey demanded.

"I do."

Pike frowned as he studied her face. The familiar feeling he had gotten earlier came flooding back.

Suddenly he remembered a gangling, freckle-faced girl he had seen around Warbonnet years earlier. She hadn't been one of Nessa's friends, though, because she . . .

She was one of the enemy. Pike looked at her now and, unable to keep the surprise out of his voice, said, "You're Annabelle Ramsey."

CHAPTER 28

The look she gave him was just as cool and challenging as the one she had directed at Doak Ramsey a moment earlier.

"That's right," she said. "You didn't seem to care what my last name was a few minutes ago when I was cleaning the blood off your face."

"I *don't* care," Pike said. "You've just changed a mite since the last time I saw you, that's all."

One finely arched eyebrow rose. "I would hope so, as many years as that's been."

Ramsey said, "Belle, get away from him. Shannon, you'd better not have laid a hand on my cousin."

"Well, if he had," Belle said, "that would be my business, not yours, wouldn't it, Doak?"

"I didn't touch her," Pike said. "She was just trying to do me a kindness, that's all."

"A kindness." Ramsey snorted. "Ask her how many men she's done a kindness, Shannon."

Belle paled under her tan. Pike never would have figured that he would find himself defending a Ramsey, even a pretty, redheaded female specimen of the breed, but he heard himself saying, "You'd better shut your mouth, Doak."

Ramsey's eyes narrowed. "I don't reckon you could make me do that on your best day. And you'd better be careful how you talk to me while you're not even wearing a gun."

"We can do something about that," Pike said. "My gun belt's right outside, unless one of your crooked deputies has stolen it."

"Maybe that's what we ought to do," Ramsey replied slowly. "Might be the time has come to settle this."

With her jaw still clenched tightly in anger, Belle stepped between the two men. She had the bloody handkerchief she had used to clean Pike's face balled up in her right hand. She threw it at him, and instinctively he reached up with his left hand to trap it against his chest.

"Here," Belle said. "You're liable to need that to sop up some more blood if you're bound and determined to shoot it out. Besides, it's already ruined."

"I'll say it is," Ramsey sneered, "with Shannon blood on it like that."

Pike ignored him and said to Belle, "I was trying to stick up for you."

"I don't need you to do that. As far as I'm concerned, you and Doak and your feud can go to hell."

She turned and pushed her way into the crowd that was still gathered inside the town hall, many of whom were watching the encounter with interest. Pike quickly lost sight of her.

He saw his mother, brother, sister, and grandfather coming toward him, though, trailed by Fiddler, Sam Crow, Andy Burnett, Will Fisher, and several other men who had thrown in with Pike. As they stepped up, half a dozen of Ramsey's kinsmen and deputies appeared and arranged themselves behind him. Numbers-wise, it was a fairly even confrontation, but Ramsey's backers were all gun-toting hardcases, while the people stepping up to support Pike were unarmed and included women.

Pike's hostile stare dueled with Ramsey's for several seconds, and then Pike shook his head.

"There's not going to be any gunfight here to-night," he said. "I think there's been enough trouble already."

"That's easy for you to say when you've got skirts to hide behind," Ramsey said.

Phin Conway pushed his way through the crowd and stepped up beside Ramsey. The portly judge put a hand on Ramsey's arm and said something quietly to him. Whatever it was, Ramsey looked like he wanted to argue with it, but then he gave a grudging nod and looked at Pike again.

"The dance is over. You and your friends can get on out of here."

"You running us out of town?" Pike wanted to know.

"No, that goes for everybody." Ramsey raised his voice and addressed the people in the hall. "All right, everybody, go on home. There won't be any more dancing or celebrating tonight."

Torrance took hold of Pike's arm. "Come on. Let's go."

"Running out on trouble sticks in my craw."

Dougal said, "Your brother's right, boy. Nothin' to be gained by bein' stubborn." He caught Pike's eye and frowned as he said it, and Pike suddenly got the impression Dougal was trying to tell him something else.

Maybe the old-timer had been able to talk to his spy in the Ramsey camp and had valuable information to pass along.

"All right," Pike said. "We'll go. There'll be another time, though."

"I reckon you can count on that," Ramsey said.

The two factions eyed each other warily as Pike and his family and friends moved toward the entrance. Pike glanced around, thinking that he might see Belle again, but she seemed to have disappeared. He didn't have very many memories of Annabelle Ramsey because she just hadn't meant anything to him back then, but from what he did recall, he wouldn't have guessed that she would grow up to be such a beauty.

No more trouble broke out as they left the building. Joe Eagleton was back at the table where he had been collecting guns earlier in the evening. Pike said to the deputy, "I'll have my Colt back now."

He halfway expected some sort of smart remark from Eagleton or even a refusal to return his gun, but the young man just reached down into the box behind the table, picked up Pike's gun belt, and handed it over, saying, "Here you go, Mr. Shannon."

As Pike took the belt and started to buckle it on, Eagleton added, "Your gun's unloaded. Sheriff Ramsey's orders."

"Special orders?" Pike asked.

"No, sir. We did that for everybody's weapon. Here's your cartridges." Eagleton held out a hand and dropped five rounds into Pike's palm. "I'd be obliged if you didn't reload until you get back to your wagon."

"Sheriff's orders again?" Pike asked.

"No, sir. I just figure there's been enough trouble here tonight. No need to tempt any more to crop up."

Pike just grunted and rattled the cartridges around a little in his hand, then stuck them in his pocket. He nodded and said to his family, "Come on." Crow, Burnett, Fisher, and the others had followed them out of the town hall but were already hunting up their own families so they could go home.

Nothing was said as the six of them walked toward the buckboard and the two saddle mounts tied to it. Pike figured Torrance was itching to bellyache at him for getting mixed up in a fight. The way Pike saw it, he hadn't had any choice in the matter, and anyway, things could have been a lot worse—and a lot bloodier.

Fiddler was the first one to venture a comment. "Well, that was certainly an eventful evening. And quite pleasant . . . up to a point."

Torrance said, "I hope this isn't what we have to look forward to from now on. Fights and killings and no peace anywhere in the county."

"Nobody got killed tonight," Pike said.

"Not for the lack of trying on the part of some people."

"Trust me," Pike snapped at his brother, "if we'd really wanted to—"

"Oh, shoot," Nessa said, interrupting the angry exchange. "I forgot my scarf. I'm going to run back and get it."

"Nessa, wait," Pike said, but he was too late. She was already hurrying back toward the town hall. He blew out a disgusted breath. "I'd better go with her."

"She'll be fine," his grandfather said.

"There are still a lot of Ramsey men hanging around here."

"And Nessa can take care of herself," Dougal insisted.

Pike knew that was true, but the situation still rankled. He didn't argue, though, as Dougal herded the whole bunch of them on toward the buckboard.

When they got there, Fiddler gallantly helped Mary onto the seat. He was always attentive to her, Pike thought, but since she was a recent widow, Fiddler was too much of a gentleman to ever let it go beyond that. Maybe one of these days, if he could stay sober . . .

Pike pushed that thought out of his mind. He liked Fiddler, but he didn't believe the little man would ever stay away from the moonshine permanently. And he wasn't the sort who could drink a little and then leave it be.

Torrance climbed onto the seat beside Mary and unwound the reins from the brake lever. Pike and Dougal untied their saddle horses. Nessa wasn't back yet, and even though only a few minutes had passed, Pike was starting to get worried.

"I'm gonna go find her," he said. He handed his horse's reins to Fiddler, who was already sitting on the back of the buckboard.

"I'll go—" Dougal began, but Pike said, "No, you stay here," and strode off before his grandpappy could argue.

He walked quickly toward the town hall, and as he did, a frown creased his forehead. Nessa had said she was going back to retrieve the scarf she had left behind, but now that Pike thought about it, he believed she hadn't brought a scarf with her tonight. He certainly hadn't noticed one. Why in the world would she have lied about such a thing?

He had almost reached the corner of the building when he saw shadows move along its side. His hand swung toward the Colt, but as his fingers brushed the smooth walnut grips, he realized that he hadn't reloaded the revolver. The cartridges were still in his pocket. He bit back a curse. That was uncharacteristically careless of him, and now it might be about to cost him his life.

This wasn't an ambush, though, he saw a second later. There were *two* shapes there in the gloom alongside the town hall, and as he watched, they merged into one for a long moment and then separated. A boy and girl back there sparking, he thought as he relaxed. That was no threat to him.

Then he heard the girl say something, and even though he couldn't make out the words, he knew the voice. His breath hissed sharply between his teeth. The wild thought that sprang into his mind was confirmed a second later by a flash of red hair in the light that came through a window in the building.

Without thinking about what he was doing, Pike stalked quickly toward them and said, "Nessa!"

She gasped and turned around with a startled, guilty expression on her face, and as she did, Pike came close enough to recognize the man his sister had been kissing a moment earlier.

Deputy Joe Eagleton.

CHAPTER 29

Nessa moved quickly to put herself directly between Pike and Eagleton. She raised a hand, palm out, as if she intended to ward off her brother with it.

"Pike, you go on back to the buckboard—" she began.

"Like blazes I will! Eagleton, step out from behind my sister—unless you're the kind of man who hides behind a woman!"

The deputy moved into the open, standing stiff and straight with defiance and anger. His stance showed that it hadn't been his idea for Nessa to get between him and Pike. She tried to shield him again, but he put a hand on her shoulder and gently but firmly pressed her aside.

"You don't need to get the wrong idea here, Mr. Shannon—"

"I don't see how I could get the wrong idea," Pike cut in, "since I just saw you back here pawing and slobbering on my sister."

"Pike!" Nessa exclaimed. "There wasn't any pawing or slobbering going on! Joe was just . . . well . . ."

"Kissing you?"

"And what's wrong with that?" Her chin jutted up and out as she shot the question at him.

"He's a Ramsey!"

Eagleton said, "Actually, I'm no relation. I just work for Sheriff Ramsey."

Pike flung his left hand out in frustration. "See? He admits it!" He pointed the index finger of that hand at Eagleton. "I saw you looking at her earlier, but I figured she had better sense than to pay any attention to it!"

"I'm right here, you know," Nessa told him through gritted teeth. "And I can make up my own mind who or what I pay attention to."

"Don't tell me that this was your idea."

"Maybe it was, maybe it wasn't," she said, "but either way it's not any of your business. I'm old enough to do what I please."

Pike was still filled with fury, but in the back of his mind, he knew she was right. Plenty of girls around these parts were married by the time they were Nessa's age. And trying to tell a woman what to do was like arguing with a wild mustang. Pike knew that logically, but it was hard to accept when the woman in question was his own little sister.

He noticed she was holding something in her hand and said, "You really did forget a scarf. I thought you didn't have one when we came into town."

"I didn't," she said. "It was a present from Joe. Are you going to try to make me give it back?"

That was exactly the first impulse that leaped into Pike's mind, but before he could say anything, another thought nudged its way into the back of his brain. After considering that for a moment, he said, "No, I'm not going to make you give it back. Like you said, I reckon it's your business."

Nessa stared at him, and even though he couldn't see her face all that well in the gloom, he could tell that she wasn't sure if she should believe what she had just heard.

Eagleton said, "I appreciate you understanding, sir. I really do care about Vanessa—"

"Don't push your luck, Deputy," Pike told him coldly. "Just because I'm willing to admit my sister's a grown woman and can make up her own mind, that doesn't mean you and I are friends."

"No, sir, I suppose not."

"And stop calling me sir! I'm not but two or three years older than you are."

Eagleton shrugged. "Sure. Whatever you say, Shannon."

"Well, I'm glad both of you have enough sense not to turn this into another fight," Nessa said. "Pike, I'll be along in a minute—"

"No, you'll come along now," he said. "You've had the chance to thank the deputy for his present and say good night to him, so let's get back to the buckboard and head home."

She hesitated, and he knew she was thinking about arguing with him some more. But then she said, "All right," and turned to Eagleton. "Good night, Joe. I'll see you again."

"When?" he asked.

"Well, I don't know." Nessa glanced at her brother. "I suppose that depends on how everything else goes."

"Nessa . . ." Pike said warningly.

"I'm coming, I'm coming," she snapped. She stalked off toward the buckboard. Pike trailed after her.

That meant turning his back to Eagleton—a Ramsey man—but Pike wasn't going to show anything other than disdain toward the deputy.

As he walked, though, he dug those cartridges out of his pocket and thumbed them into the Colt's cylinder, vowing not to be that careless again. The oversight hadn't been fatal this time, but there had better not be a next time, he knew.

He wondered if, despite his relatively young age, he was getting too old for gun trouble. He had been in a lot of fights. A man's skills were bound to get duller over time.

When Nessa got to the buckboard, Torrance asked, apparently in all innocence, "Did you find what you were looking for?"

"Let's just go," Nessa said as she pulled herself onto the back of the vehicle next to Fiddler.

Pike was close enough to hear the exchange. He didn't say anything as he took his reins back from Fiddler and swung up into the saddle. Dougal was already mounted on his mule.

Torrance drove through Warbonnet and started out the river road toward the Shannon ranch. Pike and Dougal followed, and as they did, Pike said to his grandfather, quietly enough not to be heard by the others over the clatter of the buckboard's wheels, "Drop back a mite, Grandpappy. We need to talk."

Gradually, Pike let the buckboard pull ahead. Dougal slowed alongside him. When the buckboard was about twenty yards ahead of them, the old-timer said, "Nessa and Fiddler can see us back here lolly-gaggin' along, you know."

"They won't think anything about it," Pike said. "And I didn't want any of them overhearing what I've got to say. I don't reckon you will, either."

"Well, whatever it is, spit it out, boy."

"Joe Eagleton is your source inside Ramsey's bunch, isn't he?"

Dougal drew in a sharp breath and sat up straighter in the saddle. "What makes you think that?" he asked.

"I saw him making calf's eyes at Nessa earlier, when we first got to the dance, and then when I went to look for her back there as we were leaving, I found her and Eagleton sparking in the shadows next to the town hall."

"That rascal! I ought to thrash his hide, gettin' fresh with an innocent young gal—"

"Nessa didn't appear to be objecting," Pike said. "In fact, she was pretty put out with me for interrupting them."

Dougal didn't say anything for a moment. Then, he said, "Still, he works for Doak Ramsey—"

"And he's spying for us." Pike's words weren't a question this time.

Dougal sighed and said, "Yeah, that's true. He sidled up to me one day in Warbonnet when there weren't nobody else around and said he'd like to help us out. I didn't believe him, o' course. I figured he was just actin' on Doak's behalf, trying to set us up for some sort of trap or trick."

"I would have felt the same way," Pike said.

"He swore up and down that he didn't like the way Doak was runnin' roughshod over the whole county, and if I didn't believe him, he'd tell me the next time Doak was gonna be haulin' 'shine and I could check it out for myself." Dougal paused. "I did, and he was tellin' the truth."

"It could've still been a trick. He could've been planting the seeds for a double-cross."

"Well, sure. But then he got word to me that Doak was plannin' to ambush one of *our* shipments and said we ought to take a different trail. So that's what we did. I sent Davey and Charley the long way around with the wagon whilst I watched the trail we normally used. And sure enough, I seen some of those blasted Ramseys come outa the brush and go ridin' off after a while, lookin' disgusted like they couldn't figure out what'd happened. I figured it was possible Eagleton was bein' particular devious, but it was sure startin' to look like he was tellin' the truth."

Dougal fell silent again for a moment, then continued, "By that time I had an idea why he might be doin' it, too. I'd seen him come up to Nessa a few times while we was in town and start talkin' to her. At first she wouldn't have nothin' to do with him because he worked for Doak, but I could tell she started to warm up to him after a while. So maybe he wasn't *all* bad."

"Still, you took a chance trusting him," Pike pointed out.

"Sure. There are plenty of times in a fella's life when

he's *got* to take a chance if he's gonna get anything done. You ought to know that better'n most, the life you've lived."

"That's true," Pike admitted.

"Anyway, then you showed up back here in War-bonnet County and got yourself mixed up in that ruckus at Bennett's place and throwed in jail—"

"And Eagleton was the one who got word to you about that and told you to hustle into town with five hundred dollars to get me out of trouble."

"That's right," Dougal said. "He heard Doak and Phin Conway talkin' about it. So you might say he's the reason you're walkin' around loose today."

"More than that," Pike mused. "I probably never would've made it out of that jail alive if you hadn't got there when you did. So Eagleton sort of saved my life." Scowling into the darkness, he added, "That still doesn't mean I approve of him messing around with Nessa."

"Set your mind at ease about that. Nessa's mighty strong-willed. Eagleton ain't gonna do nothin' she don't want him to do."

"Stop and think about some of the gals you knew when you were young, Grandpappy, and see whether that really sets *your* mind at ease."

Silence reigned for several seconds, then Dougal said, "Dang it, boy, I sorta wish you hadn't reminded me of that." He heaved a sigh. "But that don't change what I found out from Eagleton tonight. I got the details on that big deal Doak Ramsey is cookin' up, and it's a humdinger! Big enough that maybe . . . just maybe . . . we can put the varmint out of business!"

CHAPTER 30

"You ever heard tell of a fella named Solomon Henshaw?" Dougal went on.

"Can't say as I have," Pike replied after a moment's thought.

"Well, he's an even bigger fish up in Chaparral County than Doak Ramsey is down here, at least when it comes to runnin' things in the county gov'ment. But even takin' that into account, he couldn't stop it when the drys raised a ruckus and got a local option election called. It passed by a whisker. Accordin' to the rumors I heard, Henshaw didn't figure it stood any chance of passin', so he didn't bother to cheat hard enough to make sure."

"Why would he care?" Pike asked.

"He owns three reg'lar saloons in Clarkston and Bolivar and half a dozen taverns out in the country. That election cost him a heap o' money. But once it was official, there wasn't a durned thing he could do about it."

Pike nodded. "I'm guessing that didn't stop him from selling liquor, though."

"No, it didn't. The saloons in the towns had to

close down, but the places out in the country are still operatin'. They just have to be quiet about it. Problem is, Henshaw needs white lightnin', and he ain't no moonshiner. He's been buyin' the stuff here and there, some from us, some from Ramsey, some from a few of the other fellas before Ramsey run 'em outa business. But now, accordin' to Joe Eagleton, he's made a deal with Doak to supply him with enough to last all his places a good long while. It'll be the biggest sale Doak's ever made, and there's enough money involved to fill his coffers fuller'n they've ever been."

"And that's why he was so upset about his main camp being destroyed."

"Yup," Dougal said. "He's had them stills goin' around the clock, gettin' ready for the big shipment to Henshaw. Like I mentioned, he's got enough jugs cached to make the delivery, but it'll just about clean him out. Once he's got Henshaw's money, though, he can build up his operation to where it's bigger than it's ever been."

"Without that money," Pike mused, "Doak would be in a pretty bad fix, from the sound of it."

"He durned sure would be."

They rode along in silence for several moments while Pike mulled over what his grandfather had just told him. Chaparral County was just north of Warbonnet County and had a couple of good-sized towns, Clarkston (the county seat) and Bolivar, located on the railroads that had branched out west and south of Fort Worth. If this Solomon Henshaw was the boss of the illegal liquor traffic up there, as well as all the other crime that went along with that, he would be a powerful man—and not one to mess with. That thought made an idea begin to stir in Pike's mind.

"Eagleton told you when and where Doak is going to make that delivery, didn't he?" Pike finally asked. "Henshaw isn't coming down here to get it?"

"That's right. They're gonna meet at the county line, up there by the Bat Hole, at dawn three mornin's from now. Henshaw will have wagons there to carry all the jugs of 'shine away."

"Will Doak be with the men who make the delivery?"

"No, he never goes along on jobs like that, accordin' to Eagleton. I reckon that's Phin Conway's doin'. He wants to make sure him and Doak keep their own hands clean, as much as possible, so if the Rangers ever come in, they can claim it was other fellas who were responsible and they didn't know nothin' about anything crooked goin' on." Dougal paused, then said, "You're thinkin' about stealin' the payoff after the Ramsey bunch makes the delivery, ain't you?"

"Not exactly," Pike said.

"Really? I was sorta hopin' that was what you had in mind."

A grin stretched across Pike's face as they rode along in the darkness. "I think I've got an even better idea, Grandpappy. Listen for a minute, and see if I'm right . . ."

Sunrise was still a couple of hours away. The moon was a crescent-shaped sliver of pale silver, low to the horizon, and cast hardly any light, so what little illumination there was came from the vast sweep of stars in the night sky.

In the shadows under the trees, the darkness was

almost complete. Pike's eyes had had hours to adjust, and despite that, he could still barely see a thing.

That didn't really matter because he and his companions had Sam Crow scouting for them, and Crow knew these woods almost as well as he did the inside of his own home. He had hunted in them for years.

Pike waited where Crow had left him. Behind him were a dozen more men, friends and relatives who had a score to settle with the Ramseys just like he did. Pike had warned them to be as quiet as possible, but he heard them shifting around occasionally. It was almost impossible for men such as these to remain completely motionless and silent. Their lives hadn't depended on that ability, as Pike's often had. Luckily, the sounds they made were small enough that they could be mistaken for night birds and small animals stirring.

Although Sam Crow knew this area better than he did, Pike remembered it from when he was a boy and he had refreshed those memories by paying it a visit the day before, so he could see the terrain in daylight. About a quarter of a mile ahead of his current position, the ground sloped down sharply. It wasn't a sheer drop-off, but almost that steep.

At the bottom of that slope, a trail ran, following a curving route around the hillside. It would have been too generous to call it a road. It was wide enough for one wagon at a time, but that was all. On the trail's far side, the slope continued, but not at such a steep angle.

Steep enough, though, that anyone driving along here had to be careful not to let the wheels slip off the hard-packed dirt. If that ever happened, the wagon likely would tip over and tumble right on down the hillside.

"Follow that trail back to the west far enough and it'll take you to Warbonnet Gorge," Sam Crow had told Pike as they scouted the area. "I kind of suspicion that Ramsey's got a place up in there, way back where nobody would ever stumble across it."

"I thought the brush in Warbonnet Gorge was so thick nobody's ever been able to go more than a mile or two up it," Pike had said.

That brought a shrug from Crow. "That's what people say. But if Ramsey found a way through to the head of the gorge, that'd be a good place to cache a bunch of moonshine, wouldn't it?"

Pike couldn't argue with that, but he also didn't think it would be a good idea to try to strike at any stronghold Doak Ramsey might have back there, deep in the gorge. Out here on the trail, though, the situation would be a lot better.

And according to what Joe Eagleton had told Dougal, this was the trail Ramsey's men were going to use when they hauled out that big load of 'shine.

Pike didn't get nervous when he was waiting for trouble to begin. He was too experienced for that. But he felt impatience stirring inside him now. Sam Crow had been gone for a while. He should have been back by now, Pike thought.

Mere moments after that, he heard a tiny rustle in the brush, followed by a low whistle that most folks would take for a night bird's call.

Pike knew better. He returned the signal, and a few seconds later, Sam Crow seemed to appear out of nowhere beside him.

"They're coming," Crow whispered.

Pike turned his head and told Andy Burnett, who was kneeling behind him, "Pass the word to get ready to move."

He heard the faint whispers as the order passed from man to man. He asked Crow, "How many wagons?"

"Six. We're going to have our hands full."

Pike nodded in the darkness. Joe Eagleton hadn't known exactly how many wagons would be needed to transport the barrels of moonshine Ramsey was selling to Solomon Henshaw. Four or five, the deputy had guessed. He had underestimated.

"Two men on each wagon?"

"Yeah. But no outriders. The trail's not wide enough."

"Riders out ahead or trailing?"

"None that I saw."

Quickly, Pike digested that information. He had fourteen men, counting himself. That meant they would outnumber the Ramsey bunch, but by such a small margin that it was almost meaningless.

"We could blast them off the wagons before they know what hit them," Crow suggested.

"The Bat Hole's only a couple of miles away," Pike replied. "The sound of gunfire could travel that far, especially at night like this. I don't want Henshaw to know that anything's amiss."

"Got to take 'em quiet-like, then," Crow said with a shrug in his voice. "Just like you planned."

"Lead the way," Pike breathed.

Crow moved out again, this time with Pike right behind him. Earlier, Pike had sent back a roll of twine, each man unwrapping some and handing the roll along so they could hold on to the twine and not get separated in the stygian gloom. Crow angled back to the east so they could get ahead of the wagons. Pike knew that, even though under the trees, he couldn't see the stars to confirm it.

Crow moved with surprising speed, but Pike and the others managed to keep up with him. In a fairly short time, Crow whispered that they had reached their destination. Pike brought the men up one at a time and had them spread out along the edge of the drop-off. The trees ended where they were, so more starlight made it to the trail some fifteen feet below them.

Steel hissed against leather as each man drew the knife he had brought with him. Pike had laid out the plan for them earlier, before they ever came out here to lie in wait. When the wagons were in the right place, he would give the order and the men would leap down onto the vehicles to deal with the drivers and guards.

Death dropping out of the darkness without warning, Pike thought. It was cold-blooded, sure, but considering what Doak Ramsey and his men had done to Davey and Charlie Morrigan and Lonzo Hightower, not to mention all the other brutal havoc they had wreaked in Warbonnet County over the past year, all the misery they had sown and the lives they had ruined, they didn't deserve any better.

He heard creaking and rattling a short distance to the west. The sound came from the Ramsey wagons, he knew.

"Get ready," he told his men. "Here they come."

Chapter 31

The wagons rolled into view, trundling along in the silvery starlight, darker hulks against the trail. As they drew closer, Pike made out the shapes of the men on the seats. He was at the eastern end of the line with Sam Crow. The two of them would be responsible for stopping the lead wagon. On this narrow, one-way trail, once it was halted, none of the others could go on.

The rest of the men were paired up as well, two for each wagon, except for Cloyd and Hebner Dawson. Pike told the two of them to remain up here in reserve, ready to jump down and help where and when they were needed.

The trail was rough, so the wagons moved slowly along it. Pike waited until the first one drew even with him and Sam Crow. His right hand wrapped around the bone handle of his bowie knife. He lifted his left hand, put two fingers in his mouth, and gave a piercing whistle.

That signal was what the men were waiting for. They leaped off the edge and hurtled down toward Ramsey's men.

Pike and Sam Crow attacked in silence. Pike jumped

just before Crow did, so he landed on top of the driver while Crow tackled the guard a second later. The heavy jolts drove both men to the floorboards of the driver's box.

They were probably very startled by what had happened, but they were tough, experienced fighters and recovered quickly. The driver managed to writhe around and swing a backhand at Pike's head. Pike leaned away from it and thrust with the bowie. He felt the blade go into the man's body and grate against a rib. The driver spasmed wildly and howled in pain. He tried to keep fighting, but Pike's knife had pierced his heart, and after just a couple of frantic seconds, he went limp.

Only inches away, Sam Crow struggled with the guard. Pike heard several swift thuds and recognized them as the sound of knife thrusts finding their target. Crow stabbed the man at least four times in just a few seconds. The guard fell back with his final breath rattling in his throat.

Pike came up on his knees and pulled his knife out of the dead guard's body. He wiped the blade on the man's shirt, then grabbed the seat back with his free hand and pulled himself to his feet. From there he was able to look back along the line of wagons.

No guns had blasted so far, but just then a shotgun went off with a dull boom, from either the fourth or fifth wagon, Pike wasn't sure which. He grimaced because he hadn't wanted any shooting, but at the same time, he knew the sound of the shotgun wouldn't travel as far as a concentrated volley of rifle fire would have. Solomon Henshaw's men were probably still several miles north of the county line. The chances of them having heard that shotgun were very small.

No plan was without risks, Pike reminded himself. He vaulted down from the wagon seat and hurried along beside the wagons, ready to help any of his men who might need a hand.

As it turned out, none of them did. They finished the grisly job of subduing Ramsey's men. Pike saw Andy Burnett slice a man's throat cleanly and efficiently. The weak starlight should have softened the brutal sight somewhat, but it didn't. The blood that spurted out over the man's shirtfront was still dark and ugly.

Within minutes, it was all finished. The lone guard who had gotten a shot off hadn't hit anybody. Pike's men rolled the corpses off the wagons and let them thud to the ground beside the trail. It didn't take long to drag them off into the trees down the slope, where a ravine waited. Once the bodies were dumped in there and the bank caved in on top of them, they would be well hidden. Given the isolated nature of this area, they might not be discovered for weeks—if ever. Some of Pike's allies had brought along shovels for that very purpose.

"What do we do with this moonshine?" one of the men asked when that grim chore was finished. "Dump it in the Brazos again?"

"You're just tryin' to get the catfish drunk so they'll be easier to catch," Burnett joked.

"Not this time," Pike said. "We're going to finish the delivery for Ramsey."

That declarations brought startled oaths from several of the men. Pike held up a hand to quiet them and went on, "That's right, we're going to sell this whiskey to Solomon Henshaw."

"So we'll get the money instead of Doak," Burnett said. "That's mighty smart thinkin', Pike."

"That's not all. Henshaw doesn't know it, but he's going to be getting a little something extra for what he pays. Dougal's going to meet us up ahead, and he'll have it with him."

Pike left it at that for the time being. The men climbed back on the wagons, the Dawson brothers joining them, and then they drove on, following the trail to the east.

The sky in that direction turned gray with the approach of the new day. After a while Sam Crow, who was handling the reins of the lead wagon with Pike beside him on the seat, brought the team to a halt as Dougal Shannon rode out of some trees ahead of them. There was enough light in the sky now for Pike to see his grandfather approaching with a burlap sack tied onto his saddle. A faint clinking sound came from the sack.

Crow brought the lead wagon to a halt and the others stopped behind him. Dougal rode up and reined in. He had a grin on his weathered face as he said, "I didn't know if I'd see you boys on them wagons or not. Looks like you handled Doak's bunch all right."

"None of them will ever terrorize anybody else," Pike said. "You've got the stuff with you?"

"Yep." Dougal untied the sack from his saddle and lifted it. "Here you go."

He handed the sack to Pike, who climbed down from the seat and went to the back of the wagon. He climbed in and took a small, brown glass bottle from the sack, then used his bowie to pry the lid off one of the barrels. He pulled the cork from the small bottle and poured some of its contents into the moonshine.

"What in the world is that?" Sam Crow asked.

Pike smiled in the gray light. "Castor oil. Dougal and I spent a day riding around to neighboring towns and buying it up from the apothecaries there."

"That 'shine won't be fit to drink, Pike."

"Well, since the Ramseys made it, it probably wasn't very good to start with." Pike moved on to dose the next barrel. "But I'm not pouring in enough to make it taste bad. The fellas who buy this white lightning in Henshaw's taverns and guzzle it down probably won't even notice anything different about it. They just want to get drunk. But they'll figure it out later, when they start running to the privy or the woods."

Crow shook his head slowly and said, "A lot of people aren't going to be very happy with Solomon Henshaw when that happens."

"And Henshaw won't be happy with Doak Ramsey, who'll get the blame for selling him bad moonshine. Because as far as Henshaw knows, we'll be Ramsey's men delivering those barrels."

"That's liable to cause a lot of trouble for Ramsey."

Pike's smile widened into a grin. "Yeah, I know."

The sack Dougal had brought with him held a dozen bottles of castor oil. Dougal passed them out to the other men, who went to work spiking the barrels of moonshine with the vile stuff. At this dosage, not everyone who drank the 'shine would feel the effects of the castor oil, but enough would to cause Solomon

Henshaw to have a grudge against Doak Ramsey. There was a good likelihood that Henshaw would demand his money back—money that Doak wouldn't have.

In that case, Henshaw might try to recoup his losses with blood. Doak Ramsey's blood.

Pike didn't know if it would all play out like that or not, but there was a good enough chance that he considered this ploy worthwhile. When the men were finished with the chore, all the barrel lids were tapped back into place. Dougal took the sack with the empty castor oil bottles and rode back toward the Shannon ranch. The wagons resumed their journey toward the Bat Hole.

That place was famous all over Warbonnet County. Nearly every day at dusk, thousands of bats poured out of a cave in the side of a hill in search of their evening meal of insects. It was something of a rite of passage for youngsters to venture into the Bat Hole, as it came to be called, and gaze up by flickering torchlight at the horde of creepy, leathery-winged critters hanging upside down from the cave's ceiling. All the Shannon boys—Tyree, Pike, and even Torrance—had done that.

The sun hadn't quite risen when the wagons approached the rocky hill, but the eastern horizon was a stunning arch of rose and gold and pale blue. Other than a few high, thin clouds, the sky was clear, heralding the start of a beautiful day. Maybe the beginning of the end for Doak Ramsey's dreams of a moonshine empire, Pike thought as he rocked along on the seat next to Sam Crow.

The Bat Hole was a dark, gaping mouth at the bottom of the hill. Pike saw wagons parked near it, and several riders on horseback were waiting there, too. Henshaw's men were already here for the rendezvous.

Pike had told everyone to let him do the talking, so when the lead wagon was about twenty feet from Henshaw's bunch, he motioned for Sam Crow to stop and then jumped down from the driver's box to stride forward confidently.

"Howdy, fellas," he called to the strangers. "I reckon the same thing brings you boys out on this fine morning as brings us out."

"Doak Ramsey sent you?" one of the men on horseback asked as he edged his mount forward.

"That's right." Pike half turned and used his left hand to gesture at the barrels in the backs of the now-stopped wagons. "And right there is a prime load of the best moonshine you'll find anywhere in the state of Texas. Or any other state, for that matter!"

The man swung down from the saddle and handed his reins to another rider. "Reckon I'll be the judge of that," he said.

"Figured you'd want a taste." Pike smiled as he lowered the wagon's tailgate. He had left one barrel undosed with castor oil for this very purpose. He took the lid off that barrel and caught the tin cup that Sam Crow turned around on the seat and tossed to him. He dipped the cup into the colorless liquid and held it out to Henshaw's man, who had come to the back of the wagon and stood by the tailgate.

The man took a sip, smacked his lips, frowned in concentration, took another sip. Pike's nerves were too strong to allow him to feel antsy while he waited for the hombre's verdict, but he was relieved when the man nodded and said, "Mighty smooth, and it's got a good kick to it."

More of a kick in those other barrels than you know, Pike thought.

The man drank down the rest of the 'shine Pike had given him to sample. He handed the tin cup back and then turned to wave the empty wagons forward.

"Come on, boys," he called. "Let's get this stuff loaded up and back to Chaparral County! There's thirsty men a-waitin'!"

CHAPTER 32

"Not so fast," Pike said, his voice sharp.

The man narrowed his eyes at him. "Is there a problem here, friend?"

"No problem, *friend*, but we all need to remember that this is a business transaction." Pike slapped his left hand on the barrel lid he had just replaced. "Here's our part of the deal. Where's yours?"

The man laughed and said, "Don't worry. I've got your money." He walked back to his horse, reached into one of the saddlebags, and pulled out a small canvas pouch. He brought it back and handed it to Pike, who opened it and saw the bundles of greenbacks inside. "My boss wouldn't try to cheat your boss. But if you want to count it, go ahead. I won't be offended."

Pike hesitated as if considering the offer, but in reality he had no intention of counting the money. The final price in the arrangement reached by Doak Ramsey and Solomon Henshaw was something Joe Eagleton hadn't been able to find out. All Eagleton knew for sure was that it was a considerable sum. So

Pike wouldn't know if the payment was correct or not. He didn't want to risk saying so either way.

"I reckon if Sheriff Ramsey trusts your boss, I do, too," he said. He tossed the pouch up to Sam Crow and waved a hand at the barrels. "They're all yours."

Pike watched as Henshaw's men moved their wagons closer and then started transferring the barrels of moonshine to them. Some of his own companions appeared rather tense as they looked on, and he hoped they wouldn't make Henshaw's men suspect that something might be wrong.

The men from Chaparral County were focused on their job, though, and didn't seem to be paying much attention to anything else. They got the big shipment of white lightning loaded by the time the sun was completely above the horizon and hanging there like a giant orange ball.

"Reckon that finishes our business," the leader of Henshaw's men said to Pike. He had mounted up again and moved his horse over next to the wagon where Pike sat. "If this arrangement works out well for my boss, there's a good chance we'll be seeing each other again."

"More than likely," Pike agreed. The two men gave each other curt nods, then the rider swung his horse around, waved for the rest of his group to follow him, and rode off toward the north. Pike and his companions stayed where they were, watching Henshaw's bunch withdraw.

When the riders and wagons were out of sight, Sam Crow heaved a sigh and said, "I'm just as glad to see those boys go. I don't mind saying, that whole business made me a mite nervous. Every man in that bunch looked like a killer."

"That's what we are," Pike said.

Crow gave him a funny, sideways look. "Yeah," he said slowly. "I guess we are."

With that, he flapped the reins against the backs of the team, turned the wagon, and headed for home.

The look on Sam Crow's face stayed with Pike during the next few days. From the time he had come back to Warbonnet County and found out what was going on, and especially after he'd begun to suspect that Doak Ramsey might have had something to do with the death of his father, the only thing Pike had thought about was fighting back. Because of the life he'd led since leaving home, that meant guns and killing. That was the only way he knew, and he remained convinced that when you were dealing with snakes like Ramsey and his allies, it was the *only* way that truly worked.

However, in order to do that, he had pulled men like Crow and Andy Burnett and Will Fisher into the battle with him. All of them were tough, pragmatic men, willing to do whatever was necessary to protect their families, but Pike had to remind himself that they hadn't ridden scores of dark trails with the Grim Reaper as he had. Sooner or later, the blood they were getting on their hands would begin to bother them, if it wasn't already.

That realization didn't make Pike any less determined to find out the truth about his father's death and deliver justice to Doak Ramsey, but maybe in the future he would try to find ways he could do it on his own.

With that thought in mind, he announced one morning at breakfast that he was going to ride into Warbonnet by himself that day.

"Let me come with you," Nessa said immediately. "We need a few things at the store, and I can pick them up."

"I didn't ask for company," Pike said.

"I know, but I don't see anything wrong with me riding in with you."

Dougal said, "I ain't sure either one of you ought to be goin' into town right now." He gave Pike a warning look. The two of them were the only ones here who knew about the latest move against the Ramseys. Pike had split up most of the money they had been paid by Solomon Henshaw's men, dividing it among the men who had helped him that day as partial repayment of the losses they had suffered at Doak Ramsey's hands. He had kept some to finance future actions against Ramsey. But he hadn't told Mary, Nessa, Torrance, or Fiddler about it.

"I don't think there'll be any trouble," Pike said.

"Then you shouldn't mind me coming along," Nessa responded.

Mary added, "We really could use some supplies, Pike, and I'd feel better if you went with Vanessa."

Seeing that he wasn't going to win this argument, Pike shrugged and said, "Sure." He really *wasn't* looking for trouble by riding into Warbonnet. He just wanted to judge the mood of the town and see if he could tell by that whether his plot involving Henshaw and the doctored moonshine was already paying any dividends. If the Ramsey faction was on edge, it might mean Henshaw was threatening them and trying to get his money back.

"I'll hitch up the buckboard after breakfast," Torrance said.

"I can do that," Nessa told him. "You have your own work to do."

Torrance shrugged. "Fine, if that's what you want."

This wasn't going the way Pike had intended, but at least Torrance hadn't insisted on coming along, too. He told himself to be thankful for that.

After breakfast, while Pike was on the front porch smoking a quirley, Dougal came out and said quietly, "Blast it, boy, what are you thinkin'? You're gonna waltz right into Ramsey's stronghold—and take your sister along?"

"Taking Nessa wasn't my idea, remember? *You* try arguing with that girl when she's got her mind made up." Pike flicked the butt off the porch into the dirt. "Besides, Doak's not going to try anything in town unless he thinks he can make it look legal. Not everybody supports him, and he wants to put on a show of being the sheriff and upholding the law. So I don't intend to give him any excuse to pull anything."

Dougal frowned and shook his head. "I still don't like it. But I reckon you've got your share of the Shannon stubbornness, just like ever'body else in this family."

Pike laughed. "And what's *your* last name, Grandpappy?"

"I never claimed no different!" Dougal declared.

Nessa was ready to go a few minutes later. She was wearing boots, jeans, a man's shirt, and had her red hair tucked up under a hat today. Pike frowned a little when he saw her come out of the house.

"Why aren't you wearing a dress?" he asked her.

"Because I don't feel like it," she answered. "What does it matter to you?"

"Because from a distance you'll look like a boy. Tuck that shirt tighter into your jeans."

Her face turned bright pink. "Are you talking about—"

"You know what I'm talking about. Just tuck it in, if you're going with me. Wouldn't hurt if you let your hair down, too."

"If you think we're liable to be ambushed, maybe neither of us should go."

"We'll be all right," he said. "Just do what I told you."

Reluctantly, she did so, muttering, "I don't know that it's going to make all that much difference where I'm concerned."

"It'll make enough," Pike told her. "Come on."

A few minutes later, they were headed down the road toward Warbonnet. Pike loafed along on his dun beside the buckboard, but despite his casual attitude, his eyes were constantly moving, roaming over the countryside around them for any sign of a possible threat. It was a nice day, a beautiful day, in fact, and a part of him wished he could just enjoy it without having to worry about anybody trying to kill him and those he loved. That wasn't the hand life had dealt him, though.

They didn't encounter any trouble on the way into town. Nessa brought the buckboard to a stop in front of Strickland's Mercantile, and as she wrapped the reins around the brake lever, she said, "I'll be in here for a while, Pike. Is there anything I can pick up for you?"

"No, I'm fine. Wait . . . Better get a box of .45 cartridges." He took a greenback out of his pocket and handed it to her while she was still on the seat. "That'll pay for it, and the other things, as well."

"Ma gave me money for the supplies—"

"No, use that," Pike said. "No reason I can't carry my weight around here."

And no reason he should mention that the money came from Solomon Henshaw's moonshine payment intended for Doak Ramsey, either. Considering the circumstances, that made it blood money, Pike supposed, but his sister didn't need to know that.

"Fine." She hopped down lithely from the seat and looked up at him as he sat on his horse. "Where will you be?"

"Around," he said.

She rolled her eyes and turned to go into the store.

Pike honestly didn't have any plans other than strolling around town and maybe getting on the nerves of Doak Ramsey and his men. As he looked along the street, though, he spotted something he hadn't seen on his previous visits to Warbonnet: a small café with a sign in the window that read FRESH PIES.

Suddenly, the simple pleasure of enjoying a slice of pie and a cup of coffee appealed to him. Surely he could set aside his war with the Ramseys for that long. He rode along the street, swung down in front of the café, and tied his horse to the hitch rail there.

A little bell over the door tinkled as he opened it and stepped inside. In the middle of the morning like this, the place wasn't very busy, only a couple of customers sitting at a table and one at the counter.

Pike came to an abrupt stop as he saw the woman standing *behind* the counter. She wore a crisp white apron over a blue dress, and her blond hair fluffed prettily around her face. The last time he'd seen her, her dress had been soaked with the bright red punch that had splashed all over her during the fight at the town hall.

Sophie Truesdale was her name, he recalled. She was one of the leaders of the faction that had tried to run liquor out of Warbonnet County.

And judging by the glare on her pretty face as she returned his look, she remembered him, too.

CHAPTER 33

"Mr. Shannon." The chill in her voice confirmed not only that she remembered who he was, but exactly how she felt about him, as well.

Pike reached up and pinched the brim of his hat as he nodded politely to her. "Good morning, Miss Truesdale," he said.

"It had been so far."

Irritation welled up inside Pike, but he pushed it back down. A fella had to make allowances for pretty girls, even ones so wrongheaded as to want to get rid of drinking.

She looked like it would suit her just fine if he turned around and walked out of here, but he moved to the counter instead and took the empty stool at the end. He said, "I saw your sign in the window about fresh pies. What kind do you have?"

With obvious reluctance, she answered, "Apple and peach."

"I'll have a slice of apple, then. And a cup of coffee."

She didn't move. "People generally eat pie after a meal, not in the middle of the morning."

"Call it a second breakfast, then," Pike said with a smile.

She still hesitated. He didn't know if she owned this place or just worked here. If she was the owner, she would be well within her rights to tell him to get out. But either way, she must not have felt that she could do that, because after a few seconds she turned and went to a shelf where a stack of saucers sat, as well as a couple of pie plates. She picked up the knife resting across the partially eaten apple pie and cut a slice, then skillfully moved it to a saucer. When she put the saucer in front of Pike, she set it down with a little more force than was absolutely necessary. She grabbed a fork from a drawer under the counter and it rattled down next to the saucer.

"I'll get you your coffee," she said. Her jaw was clenched as she forced the words out.

He started to tell her not to spill the coffee on him when she threw it down in front of him, but he didn't push his luck.

She seemed more in control of herself when she placed the cup in front of him, but her voice was icy as she said, "I'm sorry I don't have any liquor to put in it for you."

"I've got a hunch you're not really that sorry," Pike said.

Her eyes were angry slits as she said, "You probably have a flask of that nasty moonshine in your pocket, anyway."

"Actually, I don't." He smiled as he picked up the fork with his left hand and used it to cut off a small bite of pie. "I've never been one for carrying a flask. I don't mind taking a drink—"

"Of course not."

"—but there's a time and place for it," he finished.

"Some of us happen to believe there's never a proper time and place to become stinking, sloppy drunk."

Pike put the bite of pie in his mouth and chewed slowly as she stood on the other side of the counter glaring at him. When he finally swallowed, he nodded and said, "It's your right to feel that way. And that's mighty fine pie." He picked up the cup and sipped from it. "Good coffee, too."

"Thank you." The words didn't sound the least bit genuine.

The customer sitting several stools away at the counter was a clerk in one of the local stores, by the look of him. He had just a cup of coffee in front of him, and he chose that moment to say, "I'd like some more, Miss Truesdale."

As she turned toward him, a brilliant smile replaced the frown she'd been directing at Pike. "Of course, Mr. Larsen," she said as she picked up the pot from the stove, carried it down to where he was sitting, and topped off his cup. Pike continued eating the apple pie, alternating each bite with a sip from his cup. Every time, he set the fork down and used his left hand to pick up the cup.

Sophie replaced the coffeepot on the stove but didn't return to where she had been standing across from him. She watched him, though, and after several moments her curiosity must have gotten the better of her. She walked along the counter to him, crossed her arms over her apron-covered bosom, and asked, "Why do you just use your left hand? Is there something wrong with your right arm?"

Pike glanced down. His right hand rested easily on his right thigh, where he would have to move it only a few inches to reach the Colt while he was sitting down like this. He said, "Just habit, I suppose. I might need my right arm for something else."

She drew in a sharp breath. "You mean—"

She didn't press him for an explanation because at that moment the bell over the door tinkled again as someone else came in. Pike and Sophie both glanced in that direction to see who it was.

Billy Ray Briggs, the deputy who held a special grudge against Pike, stopped short just inside the door. "You!" he said as he started to claw at the gun on his hip.

Pike didn't want to kill the man and get blood all over the floor for Sophie Truesdale to have to clean up. That surely wouldn't make her feel any more kindly toward him. So instead as he pivoted on the backless stool, he drew back his left arm and whipped it forward. The fork flashed through the air and struck Briggs just under the right eye with enough force to rip a gash there. He cried out in pain and surprise as he took an involuntary step backward.

That gave Pike time to get off the stool and charge at him. When Briggs recovered enough to try to lift the gun, Pike kicked his wrist and sent the revolver spinning away. He followed that with a fast left that crashed into Briggs's jaw and knocked him against the open door. It slammed back against the wall.

As Pike tried to close in and press his momentary advantage, Briggs got his feet set and looped a left at his head. Pike ducked under it, but Briggs brought his right up and caught him under the chin. Pike's head went back and the rest of him followed it. Briggs howled a curse and lunged after him. The deputy's arms swung wide as he flailed punches at Pike, who couldn't block all of them. Briggs landed a knobby-knuckled right fist on Pike's left cheek and made him stagger back against the counter. He knocked over the stool he had been sitting on a few moments earlier.

Behind the counter, Sophie was yelling something, but Pike didn't have time to try to understand it. At least she had some protection back there, and the other customers had already fled, scurrying out the door as fast as they could when the fight started.

Briggs was a crude fighter, relying on strength and viciousness more than anything else, but the sheer, maddened ferocity of his attack had Pike off-balance. The deputy hit him again, and Pike stumbled over the stool he had upset. He made a grab at the counter but missed, landing in a sprawl on his back. Grimacing with hate, Briggs grabbed the stool by two of the legs and raised it, poised to bring it smashing down on Pike's head.

Before the ruinous blow could fall, Sophie reached out, grabbed the half-full cup of coffee Pike had been drinking, and dashed the contents in Briggs's face. The coffee had cooled off some but was still pretty hot. Momentarily blinded, Briggs sputtered and cursed and stepped back, lowering the stool without slamming it down on Pike.

Pike used his leg to sweep Briggs's legs out from under him. Briggs fell and lost his hold on the stool, which clattered away. Pike scrambled to his feet. Briggs got up fast, too, but Pike was ready for him now.

He hammered punches to Briggs's head and body, brushing aside the deputy's attempts to block the blows and forcing him to give ground. Briggs came up against the counter and was stuck there as Pike battered him. His only real break came when Pike glanced past him and saw Sophie standing there behind the counter, backed up against the wall, both hands lifted to her mouth as she stared horrified at the fight.

That sight made Pike hesitate for a second. When he did, Briggs threw a wild punch that clipped him on the chin. By now, though, Briggs didn't have enough strength left to put any real power behind the blow, so Pike shrugged it off. He smashed a left into Briggs's belly and then threw a right that snapped the deputy's head to the side. Briggs's eyes rolled up in their sockets. He sagged and slowly slid down the counter to a sitting position with his legs stuck out in front of him and his head lolling loosely on his shoulders, more unconscious than awake.

Pike didn't have time to celebrate his triumph, not that he wanted to. Heavy footsteps sounded in the doorway. He looked around to see Chuck Hanratty hurrying into the café, trailed by two men. Pike didn't recognize them, but they wore deputy badges so he knew they were more of Doak Ramsey's men.

And all three newcomers carried shotguns. Pike

knew those Greeners could splatter him all over this place, so he lifted his hands to elbow height and made sure to keep them in plain sight. He didn't believe they would gun him down right in front of Sophie Truesdale unless he gave them a reasonable excuse. He didn't plan on doing that.

"What's going on here?" Hanratty demanded. "Folks said there was a fight in—" He broke off as he spotted Briggs leaning senseless against the front of the counter. Lifting the shotgun, he growled at Pike, "If you've killed Billy Ray—"

"He's all right, you blasted fool," Pike rasped. "I just whaled the tar out of him, that's all."

"Is that blood on his shirt?"

"No, it's coffee. The lady here threw a cup of it in his face to keep him from beating my brains out with a stool."

Hanratty's angry gaze swung toward Sophie. "Is that right, Miss Truesdale?"

She swallowed hard and then gave a shaky nod. "Yes, that's what happened, Deputy. Deputy Briggs and Mr. Shannon were fighting, and I thought Deputy Briggs was . . . was going to kill him, so I . . ." Her voice trailed off and she shrugged.

"Yeah, but there's blood on his face," Hanratty snapped.

"I threw a fork at him." Pike smiled tightly. "He interrupted the piece of pie I was enjoying and tried to throw down on me. I figured it was either that or slap leather and kill him."

"You did, did you?" Hanratty advanced toward him with the shotgun leveled. The other two deputies, equally menacing, spread out so they would have a clear line of fire at Pike, too. "Well, it sounds to me like a clear case of disturbing the peace. I reckon you're gonna have to come along to jail with us, Shannon."

And just as before, Pike knew that if he did that, he would never emerge from the Warbonnet County courthouse alive.

CHAPTER 34

In the tense silence that filled the café as the three crooked lawmen pointed their shotguns at Pike, Sophie Truesdale spoke up, saying, "Wait a minute, Deputy Hanratty. That's not fair. Mr. Shannon didn't actually start this trouble."

Hanratty looked surprised as he glanced at her. "Ma'am? You know who this is, don't you? You know *what* he is?"

"A moonshiner, you mean? I know very well who and what Mr. Shannon is." She directed a cool, unfriendly gaze in Pike's direction. "But that doesn't change the facts. Deputy Briggs reached for his gun, and Mr. Shannon simply reacted."

"But Billy Ray's a deputy," Hanratty argued. "He's got a right to pull his iron if he's gonna make an arrest."

Sophie's eyes widened in evident embarrassment. She said, "Oh. Oh, that's right. I . . . I'm sorry. I didn't think . . ."

A smug grin stretched across Hanratty's face. "That's all right, ma'am. You ain't a law officer. You don't have to know all these things. You can do us a favor, though. Go around the far end of that counter, come up behind Shannon, and get his gun for us, would you?"

Without taking his eyes off the men threatening him, Pike said, "Don't do it, Sophie. That puts you in the line of fire."

"There's not gonna be any shooting," Hanratty said impatiently.

"That's where you're wrong, if you think I'm going to jail," Pike said.

"We got three scatterguns pointing at you! You can't beat us, Shannon."

"And you can't stop me from getting one shot off. That one bullet's going right between your eyes, Hanratty."

The deputy didn't look so smug and arrogant now. He knew Pike's reputation as a fast gun and knew he was right about getting a shot off. If Hanratty forced the issue, Pike would die—but so would he.

The door into the café was still wide open so the bell didn't make any noise as another man strode into the building. His heavy footsteps gave everyone pause, though. One of the other deputies looked around and gulped, "Sheriff!"

"Lower those shotguns," Doak Ramsey ordered sharply as he came toward Pike. Hanratty and the other two men pointed the Greeners at the floor and moved back to give Ramsey some room. He stepped past them and faced Pike, then glanced over at the counter. A smile appeared on his face as he nodded to Sophie. "Miss Truesdale. Sorry for the intrusion, but I got a report of some trouble here."

"It . . . it's quite all right, Sheriff," Sophie said. "I know you have to uphold law and order."

"It's not an easy job, but someone has to do it."

Pike wanted to knock those words back down Ramsey's throat, especially since they were said with such a note of arrogance, but he kept a tight rein on his temper. Things could still turn bloody in the blink of an eye.

Ramsey looked down at Briggs, who had started shaking his head groggily. "What happened here?"

"Shannon attacked Billy Ray," Hanratty said. He looked at Sophie and added, "Miss Truesdale says he reached for his gun, but he had to do that if he was gonna arrest Shannon."

"He didn't have any reason to arrest me," Pike said. "I hadn't done anything wrong, had I, Miss Truesdale?"

She looked like she wished they would all just leave her out of this, but she squared her shoulders and said, "Mr. Shannon was just eating a slice of pie and drinking coffee. Roger Larsen was sitting at the counter, too, just a few stools away, and if you go and find him, I'm sure he'll tell you the same thing. Deputy Briggs had no reason to arrest Mr. Shannon." She paused, then went on, "And to tell you the truth, Sheriff, I don't believe that's what he had in mind at all. He looked very much like he was going to pull his gun and kill Mr. Shannon for no good reason."

Hanratty muttered, "He had a good reason, all right. A da—"

Ramsey lifted a hand slightly to silence Hanratty. "Sounds like maybe this was an unfortunate misunderstanding. Is Billy Ray hurt bad?"

"Doesn't appear to be," Hanratty answered grudgingly. "Just knocked silly, that's all."

Movement in the doorway caught Pike's eye. He turned his attention in that direction and was surprised to see Belle Ramsey standing there with a sardonic little smile on her face. She wore a divided brown riding skirt and a dark green shirt open at the throat to reveal a considerable amount of smooth, tanned flesh. Auburn hair spilled around her shoulders, and a brown hat hung on her back by its chin strap.

Doak Ramsey saw where Pike was looking and glanced in that direction himself. He said, "Belle, what are you doing here?"

"I was just on my way past and saw some sort of gathering in here. Are you having a meeting, Doak?"

Her dryly amused tone made Ramsey flush angrily. He snapped, "This is law business. You should move on."

"I don't know, I've got a sudden craving for a piece of pie." Belle sauntered into the café and smiled across the counter at the still-shaken Sophie Truesdale. "Hello, Sophie."

"Hello, Belle," Sophie managed to reply.

Without paying any attention to Billy Ray Briggs sitting on the floor and leaning against the counter, Belle righted the overturned stool, took a seat, and said, "I'll have a slice of peach pie, if you have any."

"Yes, I . . . I do." Sophie looked at Ramsey. "Sheriff, is it all right if I . . . ?"

Ramsey's face twisted in a disgusted scowl. He jerked a thumb at Briggs and told his other men, "Get him on his feet and out of here. Take him back to the office. Fetch the doc if he doesn't come around and start making sense in a while."

The other two deputies lifted Briggs to his feet and half carried, half dragged him out of the café. Hanratty followed them. Ramsey turned to Pike and went on, "As for you, I want you to get out of town, Shannon."

"My sister's over at the store picking up supplies," Pike said. "I'm not going to leave her. Anyway, I never got to finish *my* pie."

"Peach?" Belle asked with a cool smile.

"Apple," Pike told her.

Ramsey struggled visibly with his temper but kept it under control. "When you're done with your *pie*, then," he said, "and when your sister's finished with her shopping, it'd be a good idea for both of you to get out of town."

"Even though we haven't done anything wrong."

"Trouble just seems to follow you around, Shannon," Ramsey responded with a shake of his head. "That's enough for me."

Pike shrugged and said, "Fine. We'll be going . . . when we're done."

Ramsey jerked his head in a curt nod. "Come on, Belle."

"I just got my pie," she said as she gestured toward the saucer Sophie had placed in front of her.

Muttering disgustedly under his breath, something

about arguing with blasted stubborn women being a waste of time, Ramsey left the café.

Since Belle was now on the stool where Pike had been earlier, the saucer with his half-eaten piece of apple pie was still sitting in front of her. She pushed it along the counter and said to Pike, "Here you go, cowboy."

He took a seat and said, "Thanks." Then he looked at Sophie and went on, "I'm sorry for the trouble in here, Miss Truesdale. I appreciate your help, and the way you spoke up for me."

"That's all right," she said. She gave him another fork, since he had thrown the first one at Billy Ray Briggs. "As I told the sheriff, it really didn't appear to be your fault. And while I may not approve of everything you and your family do, Mr. Shannon, I won't stand by while someone is blamed unjustly."

Belle said, "Mr. Shannon's lucky somebody with your moral fiber was around to defend him, Sophie."

The blonde looked annoyed by the ribbing, but she asked, "Would you like some coffee?"

"That sounds good, thanks."

"I could use a refill, too," Pike said.

Sophie poured cups for both of them, then said, "I have to go check on something in the kitchen." She disappeared through the swinging door behind the counter.

When Sophie was gone, Belle said quietly, "I think I got on her nerves."

"She was pretty spooked by everything that happened," Pike said. "And I don't blame her. Things could've gotten messy in here."

Belle's expression turned serious as she said, "I wasn't joking. You were lucky she was here."

"I know."

They ate in silence for a moment, then Pike said, "Your cousin's not going to be very happy with you, socializing with the enemy like this."

"Are we socializing?" Belle asked. Slowly, she licked a bit of peach pie filling off her fork. "I thought we were just eating pie in the same place at the same time."

Pike shrugged. "I reckon you can call it whatever you want. Doak's still not going to like it."

"And I don't always care whether Doak likes what I'm doing."

"I thought he was the head of the family now."

"He thinks so, too." The fork clinked on the empty saucer as she set it down. She swiveled on the stool and stood up. "Don't get me wrong, Shannon. My last name's still Ramsey. I may not fight all the same battles my cousin does . . . but I don't fight against him, either."

"Fair enough," Pike said. "I'll pay for your pie."

"Then we really *would* be socializing." Belle took a coin from her pocket and put it on the counter. "Better keep your eyes open while you're in town."

"Why? Is Doak any more upset than usual these days?"

She frowned slightly and shook her head. "No. Why should he be?"

"No reason," Pike answered easily. "I just thought the way you said that, something might've happened to put another burr under his saddle."

"No, not that I know of." Belle cast a curious glance over her shoulder at him as she walked out of the café.

He might have overplayed that hand a little, Pike told himself as he ate the last bite of pie and drank the rest of his coffee. He had already gotten the impression from Doak Ramsey and the deputies that nothing out of the ordinary had happened. Their hostility toward him was just the usual, run-of-the-mill hatred. Belle's answer had confirmed that.

Which meant Solomon Henshaw hadn't made any moves against Ramsey yet. Doak had to be wondering by now what had happened to the men he'd sent up to the county line to deliver the moonshine to Henshaw's men. At the same time, he'd be confused because he hadn't heard from Henshaw, as he would have if Pike and his friends had hijacked the shipment. To Ramsey's way of thinking, the only explanation that made sense under the circumstances would be if his men had delivered the 'shine as scheduled, then taken off with the money. That would make him mad, but he couldn't blame the Shannons for it.

Trying to figure out how Doak Ramsey's brain worked was a wearying chore, Pike thought as he stood up and got ready to leave the café. Before he could do so, Sophie came back through the swinging door and asked, "Is she gone?"

"Belle, you mean?"

"Miss Ramsey," Sophie said.

"Yeah, she left. The two of you don't get along?"

"She's just very plainspoken. More so than I appreciate at times." Sophie sighed. "But I assume that's because she comes from a much more rough-and-tumble background than I do. It's really not fair for me to judge her. Or very Christian of me, either."

"Well, she paid for her own pie," Pike said, "and so am I." He slid a coin across the counter. "Doesn't look like there are any real damages from that fracas, or I'd pay for them, too. Just some spilled coffee. Maybe I could mop the floor for you . . . ?"

"That's not necessary. Sheriff Ramsey asked that you leave town as soon as possible, and I think that's a good idea."

"Well, all right. I offered." Pike put his hat on. "So long, Miss Truesdale. I'll see you again, I'm sure."

The weak smile she gave him said that she was sure of that, too—and didn't know whether she liked it.

CHAPTER 35

When Doak Ramsey came into the outer office, he saw Billy Ray Briggs stretched out on the worn old sofa that sat against one wall, near the potbellied stove that was cold at this time of year. One of the other deputies had draped a wet rag over Briggs's face. Hanratty, Sullivan, and Whitcomb were lounging around the desks, smoking and passing a flask back and forth.

"Put that 'shine away," Ramsey snapped at them. His tone made Hanratty stand up, and the other two, who were already on their feet, stood up straighter.

Hanratty screwed the cap on the flask and dropped it in an open desk drawer. "Sorry, Doak," he said. "We didn't figure a little middle-of-the-mornin' pick-me-up would do any harm."

"Except that this is the county sheriff's office, and sometimes people come in here who *don't* buy white lightning from us. Blast it, we need to maintain at least a veneer of respectability in this office."

Sullivan and Whitcomb looked confused, probably because Ramsey had used a word they didn't understand in *veneer*. He ignored that and waved a hand at the sofa.

"Is Briggs still alive under the rag?"

"I'm alive, Sheriff," Briggs answered for himself. "It's just that when I stand up, the room goes to spinnin' around me."

"What did Shannon belt you with, a two-by-four?"

"Um . . . just his fists, boss."

Ramsey sighed and shook his head in disgust. "I understand why you wanted to shoot him, Billy Ray, but trying to do it in front of the Truesdale girl wasn't very smart. She believes in law and order, and she carries some influence in this town."

"I'm sorry, Doak." Briggs paused. "But if I ever get a chance to throw down on Shannon when there ain't nobody around . . ."

He left that threat unfinished, but Ramsey knew what he meant. In reality, though, the sheriff thought, if Briggs ever tried to draw against Pike Shannon when no one else was around, it was almost a certainty that Briggs was the one who'd wind up dead. The deputy was no match for Pike when it came to gun speed or fighting ability. Ramsey knew that from the things he'd heard about Shannon.

There was no point in saying that, so he turned toward the inner-office door. Even though he had reprimanded the other men for drinking, he had a bottle in his desk drawer that was calling his name . . .

The door between the hall and the outer office swung open, and three men strode in. Ramsey glanced over his shoulder at them, then stopped and swung around to face them. The obvious leader of the trio walked slightly ahead of the other two. He was medium height, compactly built, but had a sense of power about him. His hair was white under the black hat he wore and his face was tanned and lined from years spent in the weather. Ramsey knew him. His name was Carl McConnell.

He was Solomon Henshaw's right-hand man.

"Sheriff," McConnell said in his gravelly voice. "We got a problem."

"Not here," Ramsey said. "Come on in my office."

For a couple of days now, he had been expecting to hear something from Henshaw, and the silence coming from Chaparral County had been puzzling. When his men hadn't returned from that dawn rendezvous at the Bat Hole with the money, his first impulse, naturally, had been to blame Pike Shannon. He had sent men to search for the ones who were missing, but they hadn't found any sign of them. He had considered sending word to Henshaw and asking him if the moonshine had been delivered as scheduled, then decided against it. He hoped to do a lot more business with Henshaw in the future and didn't want to give the man any reason to question how he ran things down here in Warbonnet County.

That left Ramsey in a pretty sticky predicament, but he hadn't figured out yet what to do about it. He needed the money that deal was supposed to produce, needed it badly, and he had to figure out what had happened and recover it.

Now the arrival of Carl McConnell meant that the situation was probably about to change again.

McConnell followed Ramsey into the sheriff's private office. Ramsey shut the door and said, "Can I get you a drink?"

"Of *your* moonshine?" A bark of humorless laughter came from McConnell. "Not hardly, Ramsey."

Even though he wanted to keep things on an amicable basis, that answer angered Ramsey. He said, "What the hell's wrong with my moonshine?"

"Anybody who drinks very much of it better be mighty close to an outhouse."

"What?" A frown creased Ramsey's forehead as he faced the visitor and hooked his thumbs in his belt. "I don't know what you're talking about."

"We delivered all that white lightning we picked up from your boys a few days ago. Spread it out to the taverns and roadhouses the boss owns."

"So you *did* get it. I was starting to wonder—"

McConnell held up a hand to stop Ramsey. "We got it, all right. And then a day or two later, the fellas who run Mr. Henshaw's taverns started coming in and telling us folks were complaining about how it made them sick. To hear them tell it, anybody who drank much of that 'shine wound up with the trots. People don't like having to make a dash for the privy, Ramsey."

Doak stared in disbelieving silence at McConnell for several seconds before exclaiming, "That's loco! There wasn't a blasted thing wrong with that liquor. It sure as blazes wouldn't make anybody sick like that."

"There are dozens of people in Chaparral County who'd disagree with you. And plenty of them have said they'll never drink at any of Mr. Henshaw's places again." McConnell shook his head. "That makes the boss unhappy. Plenty unhappy."

Ramsey sat back on the front edge of his desk as he struggled to make sense of this. He knew that Carl McConnell had a reputation as a gunman, and the man had a vaguely threatening air about him as he stood there glaring. Ramsey wasn't afraid of him, though. He didn't believe Solomon Henshaw had sent McConnell down here to kill him, and McConnell wouldn't be fool enough to attempt something like that here in the county courthouse.

Besides, killing him wouldn't solve Henshaw's problem.

"What does he expect me to do about it?"

"Well, to start with, you can give back the money you took from him in return for tainted goods."

"That 'shine wasn't tainted," Ramsey snapped. He didn't want to admit that he didn't have the money to return to Henshaw—not that he would have done so.

McConnell shook his head. "I may be tellin' tales out of school here," he said, "but the boss sampled some of it himself. He knows for a fact the stuff made him sick. I wouldn't recommend calling him a liar, Sheriff, not when he's already mad enough to chew nails. You and him had what should have been a profitable arrangement for both of you, until you had to go and double-cross him."

That blunt accusation made Ramsey stand bolt upright again. "I didn't double-cross anybody!" he insisted. "There wasn't a blamed thing wrong with that moonshine when my men delivered it to you." He pointed a finger at McConnell. "Something happened to it after *you* were responsible for it."

McConnell stiffened, too. His hand drifted closer to his gun. "Don't you go accusing me, Sheriff," he said quietly. "I don't cotton to it."

Ramsey was confident he could beat McConnell to the draw, but even if he did, that would mean open war between him and Solomon Henshaw. Warbonnet County versus Chaparral County. Ramsey didn't want that—at least not yet. Maybe one of these days his operation down here would grow big enough that he would need to expand . . .

But that would never happen unless he solved this problem. A thought suddenly occurred to him, and he said, "You met my boys at the Bat Hole like you were supposed to, didn't you?"

"Of course we did. I led the wagons down there myself—"

"Who turned the 'shine over to you?"

"The men you sent with it! They had six wagons loaded with the stuff."

The number of wagons was correct, but that might be the only thing. Ramsey asked, "Did you get any names?"

"Of the men who brought it?" McConnell blew out a disgusted breath. "I'm not gonna waste time asking questions or making small talk during a deal like that. The fella who was ramrodding your bunch gave me a sample of the moonshine, I gave him the money, and then my boys moved the barrels from his wagons to ours. That's all."

"What did he *look* like?" Ramsey asked with a shrewd expression on his face.

"The man in charge?" McConnell shrugged. "Pretty big fella, tall and broad-shouldered. Dark hair. Kind of a rugged face. He struck me as a tough hombre but didn't give us any trouble."

Doak Ramsey felt like he'd been punched in the gut. So his initial suspicions had been right after all.

He just hadn't carried them far enough. The man he had put in charge of delivering that moonshine to Henshaw's representatives was a short, stocky, blond gent named Swenson. But the description McConnell had just given him matched perfectly with that of—

"Pike Shannon," Ramsey breathed. He packed the name as full of hatred as he possibly could.

"What's that?" McConnell said.

"Pike Shannon," Ramsey repeated, louder this time. "The man who's trying to run me out of business down here. He and his friends must have ambushed my men, probably killed them, then took the wagons and did something to the 'shine before they delivered it to you. You said you paid them?"

"Didn't figure they'd turn over the liquor unless I did."

That was a wad of money he'd never see, Ramsey told himself. Pike Shannon had it now. Ramsey didn't know what Pike would have done with it—maybe something as stupid as passing it out among those fools who had thrown in with him—but it was gone, that much was certain.

Unless he could come up with a way to make Shannon give it back.

With that thought nibbling at the edges of his brain, Ramsey forced some confidence in his voice and said to McConnell, "All right, here's what you do. Go back and tell Henshaw that I didn't have anything to do with this, that my enemies are responsible for what happened. But I'm going to make it right, anyway. He'll get his money back, but it's going to take a little while."

"Two days," McConnell said flatly.

"What?"

"Mr. Henshaw said to give you two days to come up with the money." McConnell slipped a turnip watch from his pocket and opened it. "It's nigh on to noon. Close enough to call that good." He snapped the watch shut. "You've got until noon, two days from now, to make good, Ramsey. If you don't, the boss won't be responsible for what happens after that."

Again, Ramsey was tempted to pull his gun and shoot the man. Coming in here, into the sheriff's office, and spouting that high-handed ultimatum . . . ! It rubbed Ramsey the wrong way, and it took all his self-control not to blast McConnell and go ahead and start the war.

But he didn't. He just nodded and said, "I'll have the money."

"All right," McConnell said with a nod. "I'm glad to hear it."

"And when I can prove that I'm not to blame for what happened to that moonshine, then your boss and I can deal again on another shipment."

McConnell shrugged. "That's not my lookout. Mr. Henshaw makes the decisions. I just do what he tells me."

He turned and walked out of the private office. Ramsey followed and watched McConnell gather up the other two men and leave the outer office. Briggs was sitting up on the sofa now, and along with the other three deputies, he was looking mighty confused.

McConnell called back over his shoulder, "See you in two days, Ramsey."

Hanratty said, "What's he mean by that, Doak? Who *were* those jaspers? What happens in two days?"

Ramsey didn't answer. He stalked out of the courthouse and stood on the lawn, looking down the street toward Strickland's Mercantile. He had noticed the Shannon buckboard parked there earlier. It was still there, the two draft horses hitched to the rail in front of the store. Ramsey watched until Pike Shannon came out, along with his redheaded sister, Vanessa, and the vague plan that had been forming in Ramsey's brain firmed up into something solid.

"What happens in two days?" he mused aloud, repeating Hanratty's question. "It won't be that long before Pike Shannon is the sorriest son of a gun there ever was."

CHAPTER 36

From the top of a hill a quarter of a mile away, Doak Ramsey focused the field glasses on the Shannon ranch house. He was tired of watching the place, but he didn't trust anybody else to do the job. The plan he had hatched had to be carried out properly. The future of his whole operation depended on it.

Ramsey and the four deputies with him had been here all morning, and now at midday it was starting to get uncomfortably hot. They wouldn't have to wait much longer, though, Ramsey told himself. Vanessa Shannon would be riding out soon. The girl always took a large wicker basket full of sandwiches and a jug of lemonade to her brother Torrance and the hands laboring in the cotton fields along the river. Ramsey had seen her do that many times in the past while he was keeping an eye on the Shannon place. In a war, it was important to know the enemy's habits.

And Doak Ramsey had never considered this anything less than a war, from the time he had made up his mind to run all the other moonshiners out of Warbonnet County—or destroy them. This wouldn't be the first such move he had made against the Shannons, after all.

A day had gone by since Carl McConnell had delivered his ultimatum on behalf of Solomon Henshaw. The delay, which had eaten up half the time McConnell had given him, had gnawed at Ramsey's nerves. Yet he had needed the time to plan, and it was necessary if his scheme was going to work. There was still time to do what needed to be done.

Ramsey lowered the field glasses and blinked his weary eyes. From behind him, Chuck Hanratty asked, "How much longer do you think it's gonna be, Doak?"

"As long as it takes," Ramsey snapped.

"Sure, sure, didn't mean nothing by it. We're here to do whatever you say, boss."

Ramsey had brought his most trusted men with him today: Hanratty, Ike Ledbetter, Johnny Sikes, and Joe Eagleton. Young Eagleton had the least experience of the four deputies, and under different circumstances Ramsey might not have included him in this bunch, bringing Billy Ray Briggs with him instead. But Briggs was still fuzzy in the head, and anyway, Briggs had come off so badly in his encounters with Pike Shannon that Ramsey had lost faith in him, to a certain extent. He might still make use of Briggs, but if he did, that would come later.

A flicker of movement from the direction of the ranch house caught Ramsey's eye and made him hurriedly lift the field glasses to his eyes again. It took him a second to locate what he was looking for through the lenses, but then the scene jumped into sharp relief and he watched as the Shannon girl crossed the porch and went down the steps.

She was dressed in boots, jeans, and a man's shirt, with a wide-brimmed hat on her head and the basket of food in her hand. She tied the basket's handle onto the saddle and then swung up. Ramsey waited until she had turned the horse and started along the trail that led to the cotton fields where her brother and the other men were working, about a mile away.

Ramsey lowered the glasses and said sharply, "Come on. There she goes."

"There who goes, Sheriff?" Eagleton asked. "You never did tell us exactly what we're doing out here."

"We're going to make Pike Shannon sorry that he ever crossed us and make sure he never does it again."

That was all the answer Ramsey gave his deputies. They mounted up hurriedly when he did and followed as he rode down the hillside on a course calculated to intercept Vanessa Shannon well before she reached the field where her brother Torrance was.

Ramsey didn't know where Pike or the old man might be, but he didn't care. He would be seeing Pike soon enough.

And when he was finished with his vengeance, nobody would ever see Pike Shannon again.

The trail Nessa followed led past a thick stand of post oaks and then a large, rocky outcropping that came down almost to the edge of the trail. She was passing that outcropping when a dozen birds suddenly flew up from the trees behind her. Hearing the flutter of wings, she turned in the saddle to look and saw the birds rising swiftly into the sky. They wouldn't have taken off like that if something hadn't disturbed them, and the same instinct that told her that made her reach for the carbine in the sheath attached to her saddle.

At the same time, she nudged her horse ahead, moving faster in case any trouble tried to come up behind her. These days, it didn't pay to take too many chances in Warbonnet County.

But as the rifle slid out of its sheath, she glanced ahead of her again and spotted men on horseback emerging quickly from behind the rocks. She caught her breath in apprehension. The three riders blocked the narrow trail. Hoofbeats sounded on the path behind her. The men who had ridden through the trees and spooked the birds were closing in on her. She was trapped between the two groups.

The only way out was to open fire over the heads of the men in front of her and try to make them scatter enough for her to ride through them. But even as that wild thought crossed her mind, she recognized the man in the middle of the trio: Doak Ramsey. Law badges were pinned to the shirts of all three men.

They had drawn their guns, too, and Nessa knew that if she started shooting, they would return the fire and blow her out of the saddle. Legally, they would be justified in doing so.

Ramsey reined in, leveled his Colt at her, and yelled, "Drop that rifle, Miss Shannon!"

Nessa jerked her head around to see who was coming up fast behind her. Her heart leaped into her throat as she saw that one of them was Joe Eagleton. The other deputy was the one named Hanratty, and she knew he was a cold-blooded killer like the man he worked for.

Joe's eyes were wide with shock and alarm as he reined in beside Hanratty. Nessa was well and truly surrounded now, but Ramsey and the other men didn't know that she and Joe were friends. Well, more than friends, actually . . .

Maybe Sheriff Ramsey just wanted to talk to her. He was always full of bluster and threats. Nessa had to hope that was the case. She started to slide the carbine back into its sheath.

"Not like that," Ramsey snapped. "Put it on the ground!"

Nessa made a face, but she took hold of the carbine's barrel and leaned over to rest the stock on the ground. She let go and the weapon toppled over with the barrel pointing off toward the side of the trail.

"That's better," Ramsey said, lowering his gun slightly. "There's no need for any trouble here, Miss Shannon. I'm just going to have to ask you to come with us."

"Are you arresting me, Sheriff?"

"Not exactly. But you still need to come with us."

"I don't think I'd be interested in doing that," Nessa said coolly.

Ramsey shook his head. "This may not be an official arrest, but I'm not giving you any choice in the matter. Eagleton, get the girl's rifle."

Joe still looked pretty upset, but Nessa hoped he would play along with the crooked sheriff for now. It would be better if Ramsey and the others didn't know about the two of them. Ramsey would take their relationship as a betrayal, and there was no telling what he might do.

She was relieved when Joe dismounted and moved forward to pick up her carbine from the trail.

"What is it you want with me?" she asked Ramsey.

"Your brother Pike took something that didn't belong to him, and he caused me a lot of trouble. He's going to make all that right and pay for what he did, if he ever wants to see you alive again, girl."

An icy finger traced a path along Nessa's spine when she heard the hatred in Doak Ramsey's voice. He wouldn't hesitate to hurt her, even kill her, she realized, if it meant he would get his revenge on Pike.

But for now, evidently, he needed her alive for whatever scheme he had cooked up. She had confidence in Pike. He would save her somehow.

Unfortunately, Joe Eagleton didn't have that same sort of confidence. He said, "You're kidnapping this girl? You didn't say anything about that, Sheriff!"

Ramsey sneered at him and said, "I don't have to get my deputies to approve of what I do. I give the orders around here, Eagleton, did you forget that?"

"No, but I . . . Well, it just doesn't hardly seem right—"

"Shut up and do what I tell you," Ramsey snapped. "Get back on your horse. We're taking this girl to the gorge—"

"No, sir!" Joe stepped back, all right, but he didn't get on his horse. Instead he lifted the rifle he had picked up and brought it to his shoulder, tracking it back and forth as he tried to cover Ramsey, Hanratty, and the other two deputies at the same time. "You're not taking Nessa anywhere!"

Ramsey stiffened in the saddle and glared at the young deputy. "Nessa, eh?" he repeated. "Sounds to me like you've been getting too friendly with that bunch, kid. Or is it just one of them you're friendly with? A redheaded one?"

"I . . . I'm sorry, Sheriff. But you're gonna leave her alone. Turn and ride off now, and nobody has to get hurt."

"I reckon it's too late for that. Somebody's going to get hurt, all right."

As Joe swung the carbine toward Ramsey and the two deputies with him, Hanratty suddenly jerked his mount to the side without warning. That brought him close enough to shake the stirrup off his left foot and lash out with it. His toe caught Joe under the right arm and yanked it higher as the young deputy pulled the trigger. The rifle cracked but the bullet sailed harmlessly into the blue sky. The next instant, the carbine went flying from Joe's hands as a result of the kick.

"Watch the girl!" Doak Ramsey cried as he spurred his horse forward past Nessa. The gun in his hand spouted flame and smoke as he thrust it toward Joe Eagleton.

"Noooo!" Nessa screamed. She tried to turn her horse and get in Ramsey's way, but Hanratty crowded his mount up beside hers and reached out to loop his arm around her waist. He plucked her out of the saddle, and even though she screamed again and tried to fight, she was no match for his strength.

Ramsey's first shot struck Joe Eagleton in the chest and knocked him back a step. Ramsey kept shooting, the blasts rolling out like thunder as he emptied his gun in a mad rage. The slugs ripped into the young deputy's body and caused him to do a macabre, jittering dance for a second until his feet caught on something and he toppled over backward.

Ramsey was breathing hard as he reined in and lowered his smoking revolver. He stared at Joe Eagleton's bullet-riddled body for several long seconds, then turned to look at Hanratty. Nessa was sobbing now and still struggling fitfully against the deputy's cruelly tight grip.

"Get her out of here," Ramsey said. "Take her to the cabin in the gorge. There'll be people waiting there for her. Take that blasted traitor's body with you, too, and bury it up there."

"What are you gonna do, Doak?" Hanratty asked.

"Go back to town." He took a deep breath and started reloading the Colt he had emptied into Joe Eagleton. "Somebody's got to uphold law and order in Warbonnet."

Those words prompted a hysterical laugh from Nessa. She lifted her tear-streaked face to look at Ramsey. She could tell from the faces of the other men that they were a little surprised by their boss's bloody, violent outburst, but none of them really cared that Joe was dead, that their fellow deputy had been cut down with no warning. None of them wanted to cross Doak Ramsey, for fear that the same fate might await them.

Nessa kept laughing until Ramsey snapped, "Get her out of here!" and then Hanratty rode away with Nessa held in front of him on the horse's back. Behind them, the other two deputies picked up Joe Eagleton's body and slung it facedown over the luckless young deputy's saddle.

Nessa felt sure she was on her way to her own death, but right now she didn't really care about that. She would die without complaint . . .

As long as Doak Ramsey died first.

Pike was the one who would see to that.

CHAPTER 37

Nessa was numb for a while, lost in her grief and shock and the knowledge that Joe Eagleton's body was being carried along behind her. She hadn't been in love with Joe, not yet, anyway, but the affection that had sprung to life between them was real and no less sweet for being so unexpected. Joe had talked about quitting his deputy job so that they could be together openly, but for some reason he wouldn't explain, he had insisted that he couldn't do that just yet.

If he had, there was no way of knowing how far things might have gone between them. All Nessa knew for sure was that her feelings for him were stronger than any she had ever had for other young men.

And now he was dead, viciously, brutally gunned down right before her eyes. Doak Ramsey had been insane, had completely lost his mind as he pulled the trigger of his gun. Nessa would never forget the evil look on the crooked sheriff's face at that moment.

Because of all those terrible thoughts whirling through her head, for a while Nessa paid no attention to where they were going. Eventually, though, she

took more note of where they were and lifted her
head to take a look at the surroundings.

She was still on Chuck Hanratty's horse, riding in
front of him with his left arm tight around her midsection. He hadn't pawed her lustfully as he might
have under the circumstances, but she refused to feel
grateful to him for that. Any decent human being
would have done the same, and she was pretty sure
that description didn't apply to Deputy Hanratty.

A man rode on either side of them. Even if she
could get loose from Hanratty's grip, which was pretty
unlikely, she wouldn't be able to get away. One or
both of the other two deputies would just ride her
down and grab her again.

They were heading west, she realized. It was early
afternoon. Torrance and the hired men working in
the cotton fields would be wondering where she was.
She usually showed up with their lunch before now.
Eventually, they would get curious enough that Torrance would ride back to the house to check on her.
Then he would discover that she was missing. He
might even find her horse wandering along the trail
with the lunch basket still tied to the saddle, unless
Doak Ramsey had taken it with him to delay the dis-
covery that she'd been kidnapped.

The terrain in this direction was more rugged.
Thickly wooded hills bordered narrow valleys where
creeks flowed on their way to join the Brazos. Brush-
choked ravines and gorges slashed across the landscape. The deepest and longest of these was Warbonnet
Gorge, where the body of Nessa's father had been
found. Elijah Shannon had gone up there one day to
hunt and had never come home. His death was still

recent enough that thinking about it was like a knife in Nessa's heart. She knew it was even worse for her mother.

At first Nessa didn't think her captors could be headed for Warbonnet Gorge, but as she recognized landmarks, she realized that seemed to be their destination. Growing up as a tomboy, she had always wanted to go hunting with her father and exploring with her brothers, so she had traipsed over most of the county at one time or another. They weren't far from the gorge, and as she thought about it, she remembered that Doak Ramsey had even mentioned it when he was talking to his men. She had been so shocked by Joe's death and the threat to her that the words hadn't really penetrated her stunned brain at the time—but she recalled them now.

Why in the world would they be taking her to Warbonnet Gorge? There was nothing up there. Men didn't even go hunting there. The brush in the gorge was so thick that a rider couldn't get through it.

That was clearly their destination, though. Nessa saw the mouth of the gorge ahead of them. It ran for several miles into the hills, but only a few hundred yards at this end were passable.

"Are you taking me out into the middle of nowhere to kill me?" she asked Hanratty in a dull voice. She wasn't as numbed by grief and fear as she had been, but she couldn't seem to work up any real anger.

"What?" the deputy said. "Nobody said anything about killin' you, gal."

"Why else would you drag me off like this?"

"If you're asking me what Doak's got in mind, I

couldn't tell you. But I do know he told us to treat you decent."

"Why would he care? He's a madman! You saw what he was like when he shot Joe . . . I mean, Deputy Eagleton."

"Doak doesn't like it when somebody double-crosses him," Hanratty said. "Eagleton was sweet on you, wasn't he? You talked him into spyin' on us for your family."

"I never did any such thing," Nessa said. "We saw each other some . . . I mean, he liked me and I liked him . . . but that's all—"

"Nah, it had to be more than that," Hanratty interrupted her. "He was working against us. That'd explain a whole heap of things. Your brother Pike knew a lot more about what we were doing than he should have."

Nessa fell silent. Maybe Hanratty was right, she thought. Maybe Joe had been trying to help her family without her even knowing about it. He might have believed it was safer for her that way. That sounded like something Joe would do.

After a while, she said, "That still doesn't explain why we're going toward Warbonnet Gorge."

"Just ride and watch, girl."

"Stop calling me girl," she said. Finally, some righteous anger was starting to build up inside her as the shock wore off.

"Well, you *are* wearin' trousers," Hanratty said. "Not much doubt you're a girl, though."

A new fear stirred inside Nessa. Doak Ramsey might have ordered his men to keep her alive, but that didn't mean she had to remain unmolested.

Warbonnet Gorge was fifty yards wide at its mouth, with rough limestone walls that loomed a hundred feet tall on either side. The gorge quickly narrowed down, though, to no more than twenty yards from one wall to the other. Mesquite bushes, briars, and small trees filled it. Hanratty continued riding straight toward that impenetrable wall of brush.

Then the other two deputies spurred ahead, caught hold of some branches while still on horseback, and pulled the brush back. A large section of the growth swung open like a gate. That was exactly what it amounted to, Nessa realized as she stared in amazement. Some of the brush had been cut and then lashed together, with long, thin branches running through it for support, so that it could be moved easily as if all in one piece. From a distance of more than a few yards, the deception was invisible. That would require work, with fresh foliage being woven into it at intervals to make the brushy barrier look like it was still alive, but it could certainly be done.

Now that Nessa knew the opening was there, she looked more closely at the ground and saw marks that could have been left by wagon wheels, as well as hoof-prints here and there. Something *was* up Warbonnet Gorge after all.

Hanratty rode into the previously hidden gap and followed the trail that lay behind it. The other two entered the gorge as well, one leading the horse that carried Joe Eagleton's body, the other closing the camouflaged gate.

The trail, like the gorge, twisted and turned. To Nessa, it looked like someone had come along and widened an old game trail, hacking away the brush to make it passable for wagons and men on horseback.

Even though the afternoon was hot, a slight chill lingered down here between the high stone walls. The sunlight rarely reached here directly. The gloom made her shiver a little.

After a couple of miles, the gorge began to widen, the walls retreating until it was wider than it was at the mouth. The brush wasn't as thick, either. A few open, grassy areas appeared. In one of those clearings, close to the gorge's southern wall, a large cabin appeared, the bottom half made of stone, the upper half of logs. Near it lay a corral, another log building, a big, open-sided shed, and several stills.

Nessa guessed without being told that this stronghold belonged to Doak Ramsey. He could hole up here if the law ever came after him, and until that day, it would serve as a place to make and store moonshine—and keep prisoners, if that ever proved to be necessary, as it apparently was today.

Half a dozen horses were in the corral. Hanratty and the other two deputies headed in that direction, but before they got there, the cabin door opened and a woman stepped outside. She stopped short at the sight of the newcomers. The sun was much brighter here, away from the oppressive walls of the gorge, and she lifted a hand both to shade her eyes and in apparent disbelief at what she was seeing.

Nessa recognized the thick auburn hair, considerably darker than her own hair. Belle Ramsey strode forward and greeted the visitors by saying, "Hanratty, what in blazes are you doing with Vanessa Shannon? Let go of her right now!"

"Can't do that, Belle," Hanratty drawled. "Got to lock her up in the smokehouse. Doak's orders."

Belle wore tan canvas trousers and a dark brown shirt, open at the throat and with the sleeves rolled up over her tanned forearms. She had a gun belt strapped around her hips and a Smith & Wesson .32 caliber revolver with hard rubber grips rode in the attached holster. She rested her hand on the gun's butt as she gave Hanratty a hard look and declared, "That's loco. Why would Doak do that?"

"Maybe you should ask him the next time you see him."

"Maybe I'll do that," Belle shot back. "He told me he wanted me to come out here, said he had a job for me, but he didn't tell me what it was."

"Reckon now you know," Hanratty said. "You can guard the Shannon gal. I guess Doak figured it'd be a mite easier on her if there was another woman around."

Belle frowned. "Could be," she allowed after a moment, "but I'd still like to know what this is about."

"What it's about," Nessa said, unable to stop the words from spilling out, "is that your cousin is a cold-blooded murderer."

"That's not true!"

"He killed Joe Eagleton." Nessa had a hard time forcing the words out of her throat, but she managed to do it. After swallowing hard, she went on, "Ask Deputy Hanratty and the others if you don't believe me. Better still, just look back there behind us."

"Chuck?" Belle said sharply. She frowned in the direction of the horse with Joe's body draped over the saddle.

Hanratty shrugged and said, "Eagleton was double-crossing us. He was really working for the Shannons because he was sweet on this little redhead. When we grabbed her, he got hold of a rifle and tried to stop us. Doak stopped him instead."

Belle looked a little shaken by that news, but after a few seconds, she nodded and said, "All right, bring her on inside."

"Smokehouse, Doak said."

"And I'm saying put her in here! The smokehouse is no place for a woman to be locked up, and I can keep an eye on her just as well inside the cabin."

"If she was to get away—" Hanratty began dubiously.

"She's not going to get away." Belle drew the Smith & Wesson and covered Nessa. "And she'll be mighty sorry if she tries."

For a brief moment there, Nessa had had a shred of hope that maybe Belle wouldn't go along with the deputies. She had dared to think that maybe Belle would feel sorry for her and even help her.

But that had been a foolish thought, she realized now. Belle was a Ramsey, just like Doak. Hanratty and many of the others on Doak's side were in it just for the money, but Belle was blood. She would never betray her cousin, Nessa thought as despair welled up inside her.

Whatever fate awaited her here in Warbonnet Gorge, Belle Ramsey wouldn't help her escape it.

CHAPTER 38

Pike was on his way to saddle his dun when he saw Torrance riding quickly toward the house from the direction of the cotton fields. Torrance bounced a little in the saddle, still not a very graceful horseman even after all this time.

Pike had intended to ride into Warbonnet and maybe stop by Sophie Truesdale's café for another piece of pie, since his previous visit had been interrupted. Torrance had an air of urgency about him, though, so Pike figured he had better wait and find out if anything was wrong.

Dougal and Fiddler sat on the porch playing checkers. Dougal called to Pike, "Looks like your brother's in a hurry."

"Yeah, I thought the same thing," Pike replied, turning his head to speak over his shoulder. He went the other direction to meet Torrance.

Not only the speed with which Torrance approached but also the worried look on his face told Pike that something was indeed wrong. Dust swirled up around the horse's hooves as Torrance reined in and called to Pike, "Is Nessa here?"

"No, she went to take lunch to you and the other fellas a while ago," Pike said. "She's been gone long enough I figured she must've stayed around to give you a hand."

Torrance shook his head and said, "She never got there. After a while I went to look for her, but she's not on the trail between here and the fields." He paused, then added with a grim note in his voice, "But I did find a place where there were a lot of hoofprints, like several horses had milled around there, and there was some blood on the grass nearby."

A cold ball formed instantly in the pit of Pike's stomach at those words. "How much blood?"

"Quite a bit. More than enough."

Pike bit back a curse. He had been ruthless in his attacks on Doak Ramsey's operation, but somehow he had assumed that when Doak retaliated, it wouldn't be against any of the female members of the Shannon clan. Pike had fought with and against some of the worst men in the West, and they had always followed the unwritten rule that decent women were to be left alone in any war. Only a rabid wolf would have gone after a woman.

Maybe Doak Ramsey fit that description after all.

"Let me get my horse," he said to Torrance, "then you're going to show me the place!"

He dashed toward the barn. Dougal and Fiddler had realized by now that something actually was wrong, and they were on their feet on the porch, calling questions to him. Pike ignored them and hurried to slap his saddle on his dun.

By the time he rode out of the barn, his mother

had joined his grandfather and friend on the porch. "Pike," she called, "what is it?"

"Stay here, Ma," he told her. His urgency had communicated itself to the dun, and he had to hold the horse down as he paused beside the porch. "Grandpappy, Fiddler, get some shotguns and keep an eye out for trouble!"

"You need help, boy?" Dougal asked.

"Just keep Ma and the place safe!"

Pike wheeled the dun and rode out along the trail that led toward the river, with Torrance beside him, hurrying to keep up.

They didn't talk as they pounded along the path. For now, there was nothing to say. Pike needed to see for himself the place Torrance had described.

As they approached the spot, Torrance lifted a hand and signaled Pike to slow down. "I reckon we shouldn't track it up any more than it already is," he said.

"You're right." Pike brought his horse down to a walk, and as they reached an area near a grove of trees and a rocky ridge, he reined to a halt and dismounted. He could see the tracks for himself and didn't need Torrance to tell him that they had reached their destination.

The dirt of the trail was packed hard, but not so hard that steel-shod hooves wouldn't leave an impression. Pike studied the tracks. He could tell they were fairly recent, made within the past couple of hours. They were so mixed up, it was impossible to tell how many horses had milled around here. Four or five at least, he decided, probably more. None of the prints were distinctive enough to stand out, although no horseshoe print was exactly like another.

Torrance had dismounted, too, and pointed at a place in the grass close beside the trail. "There's the blood," he said. A note of anger came into his voice as he added, "Looks almost like somebody slaughtered a pig."

Maybe not quite that bad, Pike thought as he hunkered on his heels and peered at the dark stains splattered on the grass and dirt. But he had seen enough violence in his career as a gunman to know that somebody had been shot here, probably several times. Marks in the dirt told him that the body had been dragged back onto the trail, but the bloodstains didn't continue except for a few dark spots here and there. Evidently Torrance hadn't noticed those, but Pike's keen eyes didn't miss them.

That cold ball was still rolling around in Pike's stomach, and his nerves were as frenzied as a bucketful of Mexican jumping beans. Outside, though, he was calm and his voice was cool as he said, "You were right about there being a shooting here"—he held up a hand as Torrance opened his mouth to say something—"but we don't know that Nessa was hurt or was even here when it happened."

"Then why didn't she show up at the cotton field like she usually does?"

"I don't know. But from what I can tell, my best guess is that whoever got ventilated here was put across the saddle and hauled off."

"You mean . . . somebody took them to get medical attention?"

Slowly, Pike shook his head. "Not likely. Not with

that much blood being spilled." He straightened to his feet. "It's less than a mile to where you were working. Did you hear any shooting from this direction?"

"No, but I . . . kind of get lost in my own thoughts sometimes. I get the work done, but I don't really pay that much attention to what's going on around me." Torrance scrubbed a hand over his ashen face. "They killed her, didn't they? Doak Ramsey and his men ambushed our sister and killed her!"

Pike gripped Torrance's upper arm, hard. "We don't know that," he said. "We don't know a blasted thing. But maybe we will if we can follow these tracks."

"Do you think we can?"

Pike hesitated. "Tracking is a lot harder than most folks think, and I'm not an Indian. But we'll give it a try." He looked at Torrance's saddle. "You don't even have a gun with you, do you?"

Torrance rubbed the back of his hand across his mouth. "You know I'm not much of a hand with a gun."

"Go back to the house and get a rifle," Pike said. "I'll wait here for you."

"Should you wait that long before getting on the trail?"

"A few more minutes isn't going to matter."

Torrance frowned at that but didn't say anything. Pike didn't bother to explain. If Nessa was dead, she was beyond help. If she was Doak Ramsey's prisoner, then Doak had a reason for wanting to keep her alive, most likely to use her as leverage against Pike.

Torrance galloped off toward the house. While he was gone, Pike took a better look around and studied the hoofprints more closely. After a while he decided that one horse had moved off toward Warbonnet while the others headed north, away from the trail. That left him facing a dilemma. Which bunch should he and Torrance go after? They couldn't split up. Torrance would be useless on his own.

The drops of blood he found on the trail made Pike think one of the horses headed toward town was carrying the body. Since he refused to believe that Nessa was dead, it made sense to follow the other bunch. She might be their prisoner.

When Torrance came back, he was mounted on a fresh horse and had a Winchester in a saddle scabbard. He said, "It was all I could do to talk Grandpappy and Fiddler into staying at the house. They wanted to come with us. But they saw it was better not to leave Mother there alone."

Pike swung up into the saddle. "All right, let's go."

"Go where?"

Pike pointed and said, "I found enough of a trail to follow for now. We'll see where it takes us."

They started north, away from the trail and along the ridge. They had to move slowly so Pike could spot the signs that their quarry had left behind.

They hadn't gone very far when something rustled in the brush ahead of them. Pike drew his Colt and motioned for Torrance to pull the rifle out of its sheath. If that was a bushwhacker lying in wait for them, Pike thought, the hombre sure as blazes wasn't very good at it. He was making too much noise to ever pull off a successful ambush.

That was because the "bushwhacker" was a horse, Pike saw a moment later as the animal pushed out of the brush and came toward them, tossing its head as if it was glad to see humans it recognized.

"That's Nessa's horse!" Torrance said. He hurried forward. Pike hung back a little, just in case this was some sort of trap.

The horse started to shy. Torrance rode alongside and caught the other horse's dangling reins. He pointed at the wicker basket tied to the saddle and said to Pike, "The lunch she was bringing us is still on there."

Those jumping beans were dancing around inside Pike again. He said, "Any blood on the saddle?"

"What?"

"Is there any blood on the saddle?" he repeated, sharper this time.

Torrance swallowed hard and looked. "No, I don't see any."

"That's good. The horse must have bolted when whatever it was happened back down there on the trail. He came this far and stopped. If they took Nessa with them, she's riding double with one of them, more than likely."

"Does that mean she's all right?"

"We won't know until we catch up to—"

Pike stopped short and jerked his head around as the sound of gunshots floated through the hot afternoon air. A shotgun boomed, followed by another flurry of sharper cracks.

"That's coming from the ranch house!" Torrance cried.

Pike was already galloping back in the direction they'd come from.

CHAPTER 39

When Doak Ramsey got back to Warbonnet, he found Billy Ray Briggs lounging in one of the chairs on the front porch of the Star of Texas Hotel, smoking a long black cigarillo.

Briggs got to his feet as Ramsey climbed the steps to the porch. He didn't exactly snap to attention, but his reaction was similar to that.

"Howdy, Sheriff," he said. "Things have been quiet here in town."

Ramsey had left Briggs in charge in Warbonnet while he rode out to the Shannon spread with Hanratty and the other deputies. He thought Briggs could handle that, since he wasn't expecting any trouble in town.

"You get that chore of yours taken care of?" Briggs went on. Ramsey knew the deputy harbored some resentment about not being included with the others, but he didn't care if Briggs's feelings were hurt. Anyway, he had something to make Briggs feel better now.

"That's right," he said, "and now there's something I need you to do, Billy Ray."

Briggs straightened even more and pitched the cigarillo butt into the street. "I'm ready, Sheriff," he declared. "You just tell me what to do and then stand back. You'll never see a fella more eager to get the job done than me."

Ramsey just grunted. He knew good and well Briggs was saying that because he had come up so spectacularly short in his previous two encounters with Pike Shannon. But if that was what Briggs used to motivate himself, that was fine.

"Come on over to the office with me, and I'll fill you in on it," he said as he turned toward the porch steps.

Briggs hurried after him. They walked to the courthouse and went inside to the sheriff's office on the first floor. Ramsey led the way into the inner office and asked Briggs, "You want a drink?"

Briggs's rawboned face showed the surprise he felt at the question. He wasn't accustomed to the sheriff being this nice to him. He said, "Why sure, Doak." Then he worried that he'd presumed too much and hastily added, "I mean, Sheriff Ramsey."

Ramsey waved that off and took the bottle from the desk drawer, along with a couple of glasses. He poured moonshine in them and slid one across the desk to Briggs. They drank, and the deputy smacked his lips appreciatively over the fiery liquor.

"I want you to ride out to the Shannon ranch," Ramsey said without any more preamble.

Briggs looked surprised again. "You mean we're finally gonna attack the place and burn those varmints out?"

"No. You're going to deliver a message to Pike Shannon for me."

"A message?" Briggs repeated.

Ramsey threw back the rest of the 'shine in his glass and said, "Tell Shannon that I have his sister, and if he wants her to live, he needs to bring all the money he stole from me to the cabin in Warbonnet Gorge before sundown today."

Briggs's mouth hung open as he stared at the sheriff. For a moment he couldn't seem to find any words, then he stumbled out, "You . . . the Shannon gal . . . the cabin in the gorge . . ."

"You've been there," Ramsey said. He controlled the impatience he felt. Briggs wasn't very smart, and that was a big part of the reason Ramsey considered him one of his most expendable men. But even somebody as dumb as Briggs ought to be able to grasp what he'd just been told.

Briggs finally managed to put together a coherent sentence. "I know about the cabin," he said, "but I didn't have no idea you were gonna kidnap the Shannon gal, Sheriff."

"Is that a problem for you, Billy Ray?"

"A problem? No, sir!" A smile that was mostly leer took over Briggs's face. "Fact is, I wouldn't mind spendin' some time with Nessa Shannon my own self—"

"That's not why we're holding her prisoner," Ramsey said. "She's the reason her brother is going to pay back all that money he stole, the money from Solomon Henshaw that was supposed to go to me!"

"Shannon probably divvied that up amongst all those fellas who've been helpin' him—"

Ramsey interrupted again. "Then he can get it back from them, can't he? All I care about is that he comes up with it, and by sundown today, understand?"

"And . . . and that's what you want me to tell him?"

Ramsey poured more moonshine in his glass but didn't offer Briggs a refill. Briggs's mind was already muddled enough without getting him drunk. He didn't really care what happened to Briggs as long as the deputy delivered the message first, but it wouldn't do to have him pass out dead drunk somewhere along the way.

"That's right," Ramsey said. Something else occurred to him. "Oh, and tell him to bring his brother and grandfather with him when he delivers the money."

Might as well get rid of all the troublesome Shannons at once, Ramsey thought. He should have just done that to start with, instead of assuming that murdering old Elijah Shannon would keep the family from causing him any more problems.

Briggs thumped his empty glass down on the desk and declared, "I can handle it, Sheriff. I'll get my horse and ride out there right now and deliver that message for you. And Pike Shannon better do what he's told, for his sister's sake!"

"That's right, Billy Ray."

"Do I come back here when I'm done?"

"Sure, you do that." Ramsey didn't care where Briggs went or what he did. His part of it would be over and done with, and all that would be left was wiping out the Shannons once and for all.

Briggs hurried out of the office. Ramsey sat down and put his booted feet up on the desk as he sipped the moonshine and smiled. When Pike, Dougal, and

Torrance were all dead, Mary Shannon wouldn't have anyone to take care of her or run the ranch. She would have to sell the place, Ramsey mused, and maybe he'd buy it.

A successful horse ranch and cotton farm would be a nice sideline for the King of the Moonshiners, he thought.

Billy Ray Briggs tried to ignore the headache lurking behind his eyes as he rode toward the Shannon spread. The pain had been there ever since Pike Shannon walloped him in the Truesdale gal's café. Sometimes it was worse than other times, but it had never completely gone away. Today it was particularly annoying, but Briggs was determined not to pay any attention to it. He had a job to do for the sheriff, and he didn't want to let Doak Ramsey down.

For one thing, he was a mite afraid of the sheriff, and for another, he looked up to Doak Ramsey more than just about anybody he had ever known. Doak was plumb ruthless about getting what he wanted, willing to go over anybody dumb enough to get in his way, and that was a quality Briggs admired.

So he willed himself to forget the headache, and he wasn't even thinking about it when he reined to a stop in front of the Shannon ranch house. He had looked around the place when he rode in and hadn't seen anybody. It seemed deserted, but he didn't think that was possible. He yelled, "Hey! Anybody home?"

The ranch *wasn't* deserted. The barrels of a rifle and a shotgun suddenly thrust out from a couple of windows in the house and proved that.

"What in blazes do you want?" a loud, rough voice demanded. Briggs recognized it as belonging to old Dougal Shannon.

"I need to talk to Pike."

"He ain't here! And I don't think you got anything to say that any Shannon'd give a hang about hearin'!"

"Don't be so sure about that, old man!" Briggs sat up straighter in the saddle. "Where's that redheaded granddaughter of yours, huh? How about that?"

Dougal turned the air blue with his cussing. The rifle barrel shook from the depth of the emotional reaction, indicating that Dougal was the one holding that weapon.

"Blast your hide!" Dougal roared. "What've you and that devil of a sheriff done with her?"

"Nothin', yet," Briggs replied confidently. "She ain't been hurt. But whether she stays that way is up to Pike and the rest of you good-for-nothin' Shannons." The deputy paused, making sure he had everything he was supposed to say lined up properly in his brain before he went on. "Pike stole a heap of money from Sheriff Ramsey, and he's got to give it back if he wants to ever see that gal alive again. He has to bring the dinero to Warbonnet Gorge before sundown today, and you and that other no-'count grandson of yours better come with him, old man."

"I don't know what in blazes you're talkin' about," Dougal responded. "Pike never stole no money from Ramsey."

"That's a lie and you know it," Briggs said. "Is he in there? Is he listenin' to this?" The deputy raised his voice. "Come out and face me, you coward! Let's settle this once and for all, Pike!"

Briggs knew he was going beyond what Sheriff Ramsey had ordered him to do by challenging Pike like that. He couldn't help it. All the anger he'd been nursing for weeks now, the rage that had only been fueled more by the battle in the café, bubbled to the surface.

"Come on, Pike!" he shouted again. "Or are you scared?"

Briggs jerked his gun from its holster. The pain inside his skull was a living, breathing thing now, hammering relentlessly and demanding to be let out. He howled incoherently in fury, thrust the gun toward the house, and pulled the trigger three times. Gunthunder slammed out.

The men in the house responded. The rifle cracked twice, but the shots had spooked Briggs's horse and the animal was jumping around. Both rifle bullets whined past harmlessly.

Then the shotgun boomed and one of the pellets raked across Briggs's left forearm, maddening him even more. He cursed and slammed two more shots at the house, aiming at the window where the shotgun was stuck out. The bullets jerked the curtains as they passed through the open window.

The rifle blasted again, and this time the slug found its target. Briggs felt it smash against his chest and drive him backward. He tried to grab hold and keep himself from slipping out of the saddle, but he was too late. His fingers slipped off the horn and he toppled to the ground.

The impact of his landing jarred the gun from his hand. He fumbled around and tried to retrieve it, driven by instinct as much as by conscious thought.

He had gotten used to the pain in his head, but now an even worse one filled his chest. It hurt so bad he didn't even notice his head seeming to split apart.

Before he could get his hand on the gun, a big foot in a work boot swept it well out of reach. Briggs was lying on his side. The same foot planted itself on his shoulder and shoved him onto his back. He found himself looking up into the blinding light of the sun, but then a bulky shape moved between him and the light and blocked it. After a few seconds, Briggs realized that it was Dougal Shannon looming over him.

The old man rested the muzzle of the Winchester he held in the center of Briggs's forehead. "I'm about half a second away from blowin' your scum-ridden brains out, you polecat. Give me a good reason not to."

"I . . . I can tell you . . . where to find . . . the girl," Briggs rasped.

"Warbonnet Gorge, you said. But that don't make no sense. There ain't nothin' in Warbonnet Gorge. It's so overgrown, folks can't even get up it."

"There's . . . a way." Briggs licked lips gone painfully dry. "You can . . . find it. A gate . . . hidden in the brush . . . and there's a cabin . . ."

"You're lyin'," Dougal accused.

"N-no. It's true . . . I swear. If Pike . . . takes the money up there . . . Sheriff Ramsey will . . . will turn the girl loose."

Even as he forced the words out, Briggs knew they weren't true. The part about Warbonnet Gorge was, of course, but not about Ramsey letting Nessa Shannon go. Doak planned to kill all of them once he got his hands on that money. He hadn't said as much, but Briggs was sure of it.

And he had done his part by riding up here and setting the bait for the trap. Whether he lived or died now probably didn't matter one blasted bit to Doak Ramsey. That knowledge was a bitter pill for Billy Ray Briggs to swallow.

Then the pain in his head and the one in his chest both swelled enormously. He gasped for air and couldn't seem to get any.

"H-help me!" he gasped.

"You really are dumb as a box o' rocks, ain't you, son?" Dougal asked, and that question was the last thing Billy Ray Briggs ever heard.

CHAPTER 40

Pike's heart was pounding about as hard as the dun's hoofbeats as he and Torrance galloped into sight of the ranch house. The first thing he saw was Dougal standing over what looked like a sprawled body. Pike was relieved to see his grandpappy, but he wondered where Fiddler was. The man on the ground was too big to be the little former drunk.

"Who's that?" Torrance called to him.

Pike let out a startled exclamation as he recognized the motionless man. "It's Briggs!"

"The deputy?" Torrance looked alarmed. "And Grandpappy shot him?"

"Let's find out," Pike suggested.

They rode up and reined in. Dougal looked at them with a sour expression on his face. Pike dismounted and asked, "Did you kill him, Grandpappy?"

"Durned if I know," Dougal replied. "I shot the son of a buck, but I didn't think he was hit bad enough to kill him, at least not that quick. But then his eyes sorta bugged out, and he just up and died." The old man grunted. "Not that I'm complainin', mind you. Good riddance to the varmint."

Pike couldn't argue with that sentiment, but he was still surprised to see Briggs here. Maybe the deputy was still nursing a grudge against him and had come looking for another fight. But it seemed odd that Briggs would show up on the same day that Nessa apparently had been kidnapped.

"He brung us a message," Dougal went on. "No need to look for Nessa anymore. Doak Ramsey's got your sister!"

Pike and Torrance both caught their breath. "Has he hurt her?" Torrance asked.

"Briggs claimed not." Agitatedly, Dougal ran his fingers through his long white beard. "Accordin' to him, Doak wants all three of us to get that money Pike collected from Henshaw's boys and bring it to Warbonnet Gorge by sundown today, or else he's gonna kill Nessa."

"That's loco," Pike said. "There's nothing in Warbonnet Gorge."

"That's what I said, but Briggs insisted there's a cabin up in there and a way to get to it."

Torrance said, "I don't believe it. I've never heard of such a thing."

Pike rubbed his chin and frowned in thought. "It would make a good hideout, though," he said. "Maybe there's something to it. I can't deliver that money to Ramsey, though. I don't have most of it."

"The other men would be willing to give it back, wouldn't they, in order to save Nessa's life?" Torrance asked.

Dougal snorted contemptuously. "You don't actually believe for a second that Doak'd keep his end of the bargain, do you? Your sister ain't nothin' but bait.

Doak figures on gettin' all us menfolks in one place and then wipin' us out. That'd leave your ma and Nessa on their own, and he wouldn't have no trouble forcin' them out."

"He might find that he'd have more trouble on his hands than he expects if he left Nessa alive," Pike said, "but that doesn't matter because we're not going to cooperate with his plan."

"You can't just let him kill Nessa!" Torrance said with an angry wave of his hand.

"Nobody said anything about doing that. But that doesn't mean we're going to waltz right into his trap, either." Pike turned to his grandfather. "First of all, where's Fiddler?"

"That varmint shot him!" Dougal poked the Winchester in his hand at the dead Billy Ray Briggs. "Fiddler winged him with the shotgun, and Briggs fired back."

Pike's eyes widened. "He's dead?" That news was a punch in the gut. Fiddler was an unlikely friend, but he had been a good one ever since Pike had woken up in jail with the little man in the next cell.

But then a familiar voice called from the porch, "No, no, I'm not dead." Pike looked around and saw Fiddler coming down the steps, helped by Mary Shannon. A bloodstained rag was tied around Fiddler's left arm as a makeshift bandage.

Fiddler went on, "I'm wounded rather painfully, but according to this dear lady who tended to my ills, I should survive to play the fiddle another day!"

Pike blew out a relieved breath. "Thanks for taking care of him, Ma."

"Shush, Fiddler's like a member of the family now," Mary said. She seemed to be fighting back tears. "But is it true? Has Vanessa really been taken by those awful Ramseys?"

"Looks like it," Pike said. Quickly, he described the scene he and Torrance had found, then concluded by saying, "We came across Nessa's horse, too, with the lunch basket still tied to the saddle. Somebody ambushed her, that's for sure, and we know now it was Doak and his bunch who carried her off."

"How are we gonna get her back?" Dougal asked.

"The first thing we need to do is round up some help. Doak will have plenty of guns on his side, we can count on that. So we'll need some reinforcements. I'll ride for Sam Crow's place first, and then he and I can spread out to the others and ask them to gather here."

Torrance said, "Then what? Even if you put together a small army, you won't be able to take them up that gorge. If there's a way in, you can bet that it'll be well guarded!"

"I'm sure it will," Pike said. "But if there's one way into Warbonnet Gorge we didn't know about . . . who's to say there might not be two?"

The cabin that was now Nessa's prison wasn't fancy inside, but at least there was a fairly comfortable place to sit at a long, rough-hewn table with bench seats on both sides. There were half a dozen bunks in the place as well, three on each side, and a crude kitchen with a potbellied stove. Over by the stone fireplace were a couple of cane-bottomed rocking chairs, and Belle Ramsey sat in one of them with a rifle across her lap while Nessa sat at the table. Nessa was actually closer to the door than Belle was, but not close enough that she could reach it before Belle had time to shoot her.

Nessa didn't doubt that Belle would do it, too, and she knew the other girl was a good enough shot to wing her. Belle would probably shoot a leg out from under her if she tried to escape.

They were almost the same age, Nessa reflected as they sat in the tension-charged cabin. Belle was half a year older. They had attended the one-room school in Warbonnet, and since both had been on the tomboyish side, they should have been friends. That was impossible when one was named Shannon and the other Ramsey. So they had been rivals instead, always keen to outrace or outwrestle the other, to throw rocks harder and farther, to show off all the cusswords they had learned from their older brothers.

Despite that rivalry and the friction between their families, Nessa had always respected Belle. She wished they were able to be friends, but it just wasn't to be.

Now Belle held Nessa's life in her hands. They were alone in the cabin at the moment. Hanratty and the other deputies had ridden back down the gorge. Nessa had heard them leaving. She hoped they had given Joe a decent burial before they left. The other men who'd been here at the cabin when they arrived, Ramsey relatives and flunkies, were outside working at the stills and handling other chores.

Despite being convinced that it wouldn't do any good, Nessa had to try to get through to the other girl. "I can't believe it doesn't bother you that they murdered Joe Eagleton," she said. "He was just trying to protect me."

"He never should've crossed Doak," Belle muttered.

"It's not safe to do that. Eagleton knew it, just like the rest of us."

"So you're scared of him. Scared to death of your own cousin."

Anger flared in Belle's eyes. "I never said that," she declared. "But I'm not a damned fool, either. I know how things are in this county, Nessa. If you and your family had any sense, you'd know, too. You never should've pushed things as far as you have." She shook her head. "You'd have been better off if Pike had never come back to Warbonnet."

"Pike's just trying to set things right and get justice for our family."

"By destroying mine," Belle shot back at her.

Nessa couldn't really argue with that. Because of Pike, a good number of Ramsey family members and friends had died. It was war, and Pike wasn't the sort to hold back. Maybe that had just made things worse.

Then she reminded herself of her father's death. She had never believed it was an accident, and Pike strongly suspected that Doak Ramsey had been behind it.

Maybe sometimes, there just wasn't any other way to resolve things without a war.

But even as those bleak thoughts went through Nessa's mind, Belle surprised her by saying, "I always thought Joe Eagleton was a pretty good sort, though. When he went to work for Doak, I figured it really wasn't a good idea. I didn't think he was cut out for it. Never expected it to end so badly, though." She paused. "That's what he gets for falling for the wrong gal."

Nessa's face warmed. She and Joe tried to be careful

about displaying their feelings for each other, but clearly, Belle didn't miss much. Then a fresh wave of grief welled up inside Nessa, and she slumped head and shoulders onto the table as sobs made her back shake.

Belle muttered a curse, then said, "You'd better not be putting on a show to try to get me to come over there. You try to jump me and you'll get hurt. I mean it. Besides, you'd never make it out of the gorge."

Nessa lifted her head and tried to blink back the tears. She hated giving in to that moment of weakness. She said, "I'm not getting out anyway. Doak's going to kill me, just as he plans to kill Pike and Torrance and Grandpappy."

Belle shook her head. "He'll keep his word. If Pike just returns that money he stole—"

A bitter laugh came from Nessa and interrupted Belle's halfhearted protest. Belle looked both angry and embarrassed as she went on, "Look, I'll talk to Doak when he gets here. I'm sure he doesn't intend to hurt you. You've just got it in your head that he's some sort of devil."

"What about what happened to Davey and Charley Morrigan and Lonzo Hightower? They were just boys! And Doak slaughtered them!"

"You don't know that Doak had anything to do with that."

"Who else in Warbonnet County would have ordered such a thing? Even if Doak didn't pull the trigger himself—and I wouldn't doubt that he did—you know good and well none of his men would have done that unless Doak told them to."

Nessa could see that her arguments were getting

through to Belle. Whether Belle wanted to admit it or not, she had to know that Nessa was right. Nessa didn't figure she could get Belle to come right out and condemn her cousin, but if she could convince the other girl that Doak intended to kill her, Belle *might* feel enough pity to help her get away—

"Shut up," Belle said. "Just shut your mouth. I don't want to hear anymore."

Nessa's shoulders slumped. She had tried to get through to Belle, but she had failed. Now her doom was sealed. She put her head down on her arms again as they rested on the table. She didn't cry this time, though. She was all cried out.

She wasn't sure how long she sat there like that before she heard the rocking chair creak. Lifting her head a little, she saw that Belle had gotten to her feet. The older girl's forehead was deeply creased in a frown. She had the rifle held at a slant in front of her, across her chest, but as Belle looked at her curiously, she lowered the weapon to lean it against the wall.

She turned back to Nessa and said, "Dry your blasted eyes. I still think you're wrong about Doak, but I'll be hanged if I stand by and let anything happen to you."

"You . . . you mean you're going to help me get out of here?" Nessa warned herself not to hope again, but she couldn't help it.

"Farther along in the gorge, there's a trail that leads to the top. It just about takes a dang mountain goat to go up and down it, but if you want to chance it, I won't stop you. Come on, I'll show you where it is . . . *if* we can get past the others without any of them seeing us."

Nessa stood up and said, "Belle, I . . . I don't know how to thank you—"

"Save it," Belle snapped. "This may not work. And if it doesn't . . . well, all I'll be doing is getting us both killed that much sooner."

CHAPTER 41

Once Doak Ramsey decided on the details of his plan, he didn't waste any time gathering up everything he was going to need for it. A clerk from Strickland's Mercantile was loading the last of three boxes in the back of a wagon when Chuck Hanratty and the other two deputies rode back into Warbonnet.

Ramsey saw them from where he stood on the general store's porch and when Hanratty looked over and spotted him as well, he waved them toward him. The three men reined in, and Ramsey asked, "Did you get that little chore taken care of?" He was referring, of course, to delivering Nessa Shannon to the cabin in Warbonnet Gorge.

Hanratty rested his hands on the saddle horn and leaned forward. "Yeah, we did. Your cousin Belle's lookin' after the little package we delivered." He turned his head to the side and spat. "Buried the other one."

"I don't care about that," Ramsey said, knowing the deputy was talking about Joe Eagleton. "Could have left it to rot as far as I'm concerned, as long as it was out of sight."

The thought of Eagleton betraying him, simply because the young fool had fallen for the Shannon girl, still made anger blaze inside Ramsey. He had put that problem behind him, though, and now had to concentrate on eliminating everyone else who stood in his way.

"Put your horse up and then come back over here, Chuck," Ramsey went on. "You're going to drive this wagon."

"I am? I mean, sure, Sheriff," Hanratty corrected himself quickly. "I'll be back in a few minutes."

While Hanratty was doing that, Ramsey told the other two deputies to go back to the sheriff's office and hold down the fort there. He didn't expect any trouble in town, but he had to maintain the illusion that his office was responsible for keeping law and order in Warbonnet.

Ramsey was already mounted on his saddle horse when Hanratty returned to the general store. The deputy looked curiously at the crates in the back of the vehicle and asked, "What've you got there, Doak?"

"You'll see," Ramsey replied. "You're going to help me with it."

Hanratty climbed onto the wagon seat and untied the reins from the brake lever. "Sure," he said. He backed the team away from the store's porch and turned them into the street. "Which way are we goin'?"

"Right back where you came from. Warbonnet Gorge. Only we're taking the long way around so we can get up on the south rim."

"That's a rough trail, Doak," Hanratty said with a frown. "Why would we want to do that?"

"You'll see when we get there."

Ramsey didn't offer any further explanation, and Hanratty knew better than to press his boss for one. Instead he just handled the wagon in silence.

It took a couple of hours to make the circuitous trip to the south rim of the infamous gorge. Ramsey led the way over the uneven ground as they approached. Occasionally he cast a worried glance over his shoulder at the crates in the back of the wagon. If Hanratty knew what he was carrying, he'd probably have a mighty nasty case of the fantods right about now, Ramsey thought.

Finally they reached their destination. The rocky rim bulged out here, overhanging the gorge below. Ramsey dismounted a few yards back from the edge, let his horse's reins dangle, and moved up on foot to look over the brink.

"Careful, boss," Hanratty called as he brought the wagon to a stop. "That's a mighty bad drop right there."

"I know." From where Ramsey was, he couldn't see the trail that ran below. The rocky wall protruded over it and blocked the view. All that was visible from up here was the currently impenetrable barricade of brush stretching to the other wall.

The mouth of the gorge was about a mile to the east. The cabin lay half a mile in the other direction. It had been a while since Ramsey had been up here, but he was glad to see that his memory of the terrain had been correct. This spot was perfect for what he needed.

"All right," he said to Hanratty as he swung around. "There's a hammer and a chisel in the back. Get 'em and start gouging out holes in a line along here." He swept his hand to indicate an area twenty feet back from the rim. "Make them about a foot deep and three feet apart."

Hanratty couldn't contain his curiosity. "Doak, what in blazes are you up to?"

"You'll see."

While Hanratty got busy with the hammer and chisel, Ramsey pried the lid off one of the crates and reached into the cotton padding to bring out a tube wrapped in greasy red paper. Hanratty glanced over, saw what Ramsey was holding, and yelped, "Holy cow, Doak, that's dynamite!"

"That's right."

"You're gonna blow down the wall of the gorge? But that's loco!" As if afraid that Ramsey might take offense at that bold statement, Hanratty hurriedly went on, "I mean, we got that cabin and all the stills back there a ways, and if you blow the gorge up, that'll all be cut off."

Ramsey shook his head. "We're not going to block the whole gorge. The trail we cut out runs right under here. Pike Shannon and his brother and grandfather will be on it later this afternoon, after they've traded Henshaw's money—I mean, *my* money—for the girl. Then, as they're leaving, we're going to drop tons of rock right on top of them. It won't be enough to fill up the gorge. All we'll have to do then is cut a new trail in the brush and go around all the rubble. The Shannons won't ever bother us again. They'll be buried under there, for good."

Hanratty thought about that and after a few seconds said, "Yeah, that might work, all right."

"It *will* work," Doak Ramsey declared.

"But you got more dynamite than you need to knock down that part of the wall hangin' out over the trail."

"I'm not taking any more chances. Pike Shannon won't ride away from this trap."

Hanratty hesitated, then asked, "What about the gal? Pike's gonna figure on taking her with them when they leave."

Ramsey shrugged. "Then she'll be underneath all that rock when it comes down, too. You're not getting squeamish, are you, Chuck?"

"No, sir," Hanratty answered without hesitation, although he was still frowning.

"By this evening, Mary Shannon won't have anybody left to help her except that old drunk, Fiddler, and he won't be any good to her. I reckon you'd like to get your hands on him again, wouldn't you, Chuck? Seems like you've always enjoyed making him squirm, every time we had him locked up for being drunk as a skunk."

Hanratty's lips drew back from his teeth in an ugly grin. "Yes, sir, that sounds fine to me. Ol' Fiddler, he's gonna be mighty sorry he ever threw in with the Shannons."

"All right," Ramsey said. "Let's get this dynamite planted and the wire strung for the detonator. We want to be ready when the Shannons show up."

Belle backed out of the cabin first, keeping the rifle trained on Nessa as she did so. If one of Doak's men spotted them right away, Belle would come up with some excuse for bringing Nessa out into the open, or so Nessa supposed, anyway.

Several of the men were over at the stills, but none of them glanced in the direction of the two young women. Belle motioned with the rifle barrel and said quietly, "Go on around behind the cabin. There's some brush back there that'll give us cover if we stick close to the wall of the gorge."

Nessa hurried around the building, saying over her shoulder as she did so, "You know you're risking your life, too."

"Trying to talk me out of it?" Belle asked.

"No, just . . . Well, you know what you're doing, I guess."

"I wouldn't be so sure about that," Belle muttered. "Keep moving."

They headed into the trees and brush that grew along the base of the gorge wall. From there, Nessa could still see where the men were working, but the view was considerably obscured. Anyway, they were busy with their own tasks and assumed that Belle was guarding the prisoner.

Nessa glanced back and said, "When I leave, you need to come with me."

"What are you talking about?"

"It's not going to be safe for you here. Doak will know that you let me escape. Even worse, he'll know that you *helped* me. What do you think he'll do when he finds out about that?"

Belle frowned and said, "Doak's not going to hurt me. We're blood kin."

"Are you sure about that?"

Belle didn't make any reply. Nessa didn't know if that was because she didn't want to continue the conversation—or if the older girl truly wasn't certain what Doak Ramsey might do if he discovered her actions.

Having seen the way Ramsey reacted when Joe Eagleton stood up to him, Nessa thought Belle had plenty of reason to worry. But, as Belle had pointed out, she was family and Joe Eagleton hadn't been.

They came to a stop where the rocky wall on Nessa's left was still almost sheer, but as Belle quietly told her to stop, she studied the side of the gorge and saw the faint, steep path zigzagging its way to the rim. All along the gorge, ledges cropped out here and there, some of them several feet wide, but there was no good way to get to them and they wouldn't help anybody get to the top. This path was different.

Although, as Belle had said, it looked more suited to travel by mountain goats instead of human beings!

"There it is," Belle said. "I told you it would be risky. You'll need to be mighty careful. If you'd rather not chance it, we can turn around and go back to the cabin—"

"I'm going," Nessa broke in. "And I still think you should come with me."

Stubbornly, Belle shook her head. "I'll be fine. I'll just tell Doak you jumped me, knocked me out, and got away." Her voice roughened. "And I don't need some blasted Shannon worrying about me!"

"If that's the way you want it," Nessa snapped. She stepped over to the bottom of the trail. It was barely a foot wide and appeared to be like that all the way to the top. She would have to cling to the gorge wall and work her way up slowly, inch by inch, step by step. She rested one foot on the narrow ledge and felt around on the rocky surface until she found a couple of good handholds, then started to pull herself up . . .

A gun blasted, the bullet chipping rock from the wall just a couple of feet over Nessa's head. She cried out involuntarily and jerked back, stumbling onto the ground at the base of the wall. She and Belle both twisted around to see where the shot had come from.

Nessa's heart slugged hard and felt like it was trying to crawl up her throat as she saw Doak Ramsey striding toward them, smoke curling from the barrel of the gun in his hand.

CHAPTER 42

Belle moved quickly to get between Ramsey and Nessa. "Wait, Doak!" she cried. "There's no need for any shooting—"

Ramsey's left arm flashed up and around. He back-handed Belle viciously, knocking her to her knees. She dropped the gun she'd had in her hand and then fell forward onto all fours. She stayed there like that, shaking her head groggily.

For a second, Nessa thought about making a dive for the weapon. She'd handled a Colt before. If she could come up with it, she could blast Doak Ramsey full of holes—

He must have been able to tell what she was thinking, because he leveled his gun at her and eared back the hammer. "Go ahead, girl," he said as a grimace distorted his face and rage made his voice quiver. "You just go right ahead and make a try for it."

Gripped by hate as he was, he might not remember that he wanted to keep her alive until he'd collected the ransom from Pike. Or, if he remembered, he might not care at this moment. Nessa took a deep, shaky breath and stayed where she was, lifting her hands slowly and keeping them in plain sight.

Belle recovered enough to heave herself to her feet. "Blast it, Doak, you didn't have any right to hit me!" she said.

"You were letting this Shannon girl escape! You were helping her!"

"She never did anything to hurt you," Belle said, her face and voice sullen.

"She's a Shannon! That's enough! Whatever happens to her, she's got it coming."

"I could say the same thing about you," Nessa said, knowing she shouldn't defy a mad dog like Ramsey but unable to hold back the words.

A couple of Ramsey's men pounded up on the run, rifles in hand, as they came to see what the shot was about. They stopped and looked confused to see Ramsey standing there with his gun pointed at both Nessa and Belle.

He barely glanced around at them, then ordered, "Keep your guns on the Shannon girl. She moves, blow a knee out from under her." He grinned at Nessa. "I'd just as soon keep you alive for now, but that doesn't mean you can't be in a world of hurt while you're still drawing breath."

The two moonshiners, clearly confounded by this turn of events but not willing to cross Ramsey, trained their rifles on Nessa. Ramsey slipped his Colt back into its holster and advanced on Belle.

She backed away from him. "You stay away from me, Doak," she said. "You lay a hand on me and I'll—"

"You won't do a blasted thing," Ramsey growled, and with that, he lashed out, slamming his left fist into

Belle's midsection. She doubled over, gagging and moaning, and Ramsey brought his right hand looping around to smash into the side of her head. The force of that blow drove her to the ground.

The two guards shifted around nervously, all too aware of what was going on, but they continued to watch Nessa instead of shifting their attention to Ramsey and Belle. With two rifles pointed at her, Nessa couldn't do anything.

Ramsey kicked Belle in the side. She curled up in a ball of pain. He reached down, got hold of the front of her shirt with his left hand, and pulled her up a little so he could slap her with his right hand, back and forth, the cracks ringing out and filling the air in the gorge. Belle moaned again, and he let her slump down on her back.

"Nobody double-crosses me," Ramsey rasped. His face was red with fury. "Especially family."

He reached into his pocket, drew out a clasp knife, and opened it. Not knowing exactly what he was going to do but horrified anyway, Nessa cried, "No!"

Without looking around, Ramsey snapped, "Keep her quiet," at his men.

Then he took hold of Belle's shirt again, jerked her up, and placed the blade's tip against her left cheek. Belle was too groggy from the beating to try to get away and didn't even seem to comprehend what was going on.

Nessa started to scream. The two guards jabbed their rifles toward her. She shrank back against the gorge wall and managed to hold in the cries. When Ramsey started cutting and blood welled out around the knife, Nessa had to close her eyes and turn her head away, but she still seemed to see the terrible sight.

She heard Belle's scream, that was for sure. The agony of having her cheek laid open to the bone had broken through her stupor. She shrieked again, and then the sound trailed off into a moan.

Nessa risked a look. Blood sheeted the side of Belle's face, but she could tell that Ramsey had drawn his knife all the way down across Belle's cheek to the line of her jaw. Ramsey let go of her shirt and stepped back with the bloody knife in his other hand.

"Every time you look in the mirror, for the rest of your life, you'll see what it gets you to double-cross your own flesh and blood," he said. "You'll remember, Belle. You'll never forget."

"N-no," she panted as she looked up at him. "I'll . . . never forget."

Disdainfully, he leaned over and wiped the knife blade on one of her trouser legs. Then he put it away and turned to the other men.

"It's a good thing I decided to ride in here and check on things," he said with a note of scathing anger in his voice. "Otherwise the Shannon girl would have gotten away."

"Belle was supposed to be watchin' her, boss," one of the men said. "We didn't have any reason to think she'd try anything."

"Never put *anything* past a Shannon." Ramsey looked at Belle and grunted. "Or my cousin, either, apparently."

Nessa swallowed hard and said, "Can I help her?"

Ramsey looked at her for a moment, then jerked his hand in a curt gesture. "Sure, go ahead."

As Nessa hurried over to her, Belle said, "I don't need any help." Her voice was thick and distorted because of the injury to her face.

"Yes, you do," Nessa said as she knelt beside the older girl. "You're bleeding pretty bad." She pulled out a bandanna from her pocket, folded it, and pressed it to Belle's face. "Hold this there. We'll go back to the cabin and find something to tie it in place." Nessa paused. "I suppose we ought to clean the wound first, though."

What passed for a bitter laugh came from Belle. "There's a jug of moonshine there. That'll do the trick."

"Yes," Nessa said. "I expect it will."

"One of you go back to the cabin with them," Ramsey told the other men. "Keep an eye on both of them. Belle can't be trusted anymore."

"Sure, Sheriff." The man who spoke nodded and gestured to his companion, who used his rifle to wave Nessa and Belle toward the cabin. They had gotten to their feet, with Nessa helping the older girl stand and then supporting her with an arm around her shoulders. With the rifleman following them, they began making their unsteady way toward the cabin. Behind them, the other man asked Ramsey, "What are you gonna do?"

"I'm going back up on the rim," Ramsey said. "I'll send Chuck Hanratty down here to handle things when the Shannons arrive. It would be nice to see Pike Shannon's face one more time and know that when he rides off, he'll only have minutes to live . . . but when the time comes, he's going to die by *my* hand. I'll be the one to bring death down on him. I've made up my mind on that."

Nessa heard what Ramsey said, and the words sent a chill through her. She knew now that he didn't intend to leave *any* of the Shannons alive, including her. In his arrogance, he probably didn't realize she was still within earshot, or he wouldn't have been so bold about announcing his plans.

But what good would it do her? she asked herself. How could she warn Pike when she was a prisoner here in the gorge? If there was a way, she would tell him not to come, to let Doak Ramsey do his worst to her. But that wouldn't work, either, she realized despairingly, because Pike would never do that.

She couldn't hear anything Doak said now. They were too far away. As the moonshiner herded them toward the cabin, Belle moaned softly and held the bloody bandanna to her face.

"Don't worry," Nessa told her. "Everything's going to be all right."

"You don't believe that for a blasted second," Belle muttered. "Doak always finds a way to get what he wants, no matter who gets hurt."

Nessa couldn't dispute that. She helped Belle into the cabin and sat her down at the table.

The guard loomed in the doorway and pointed his rifle at them. Nessa glared over her shoulder at him and asked, "Can't you give us a little privacy? I need to tend to this wound, and I'm sure Belle doesn't need you gawking at her."

"Sheriff Ramsey said to keep an eye on y'all," the man responded as he shifted a good-sized chaw of tobacco from one cheek to the other.

"Well, you can stand right outside the door. There's

only one window, and it's on the front of the cabin, too. So we can't try to go anywhere without you seeing us."

The man frowned and shifted his chaw again. "Reckon that's true," he admitted. "Don't you try nothin', though."

"We won't," Nessa promised meekly.

The moonshiner backed out of the cabin but left the door wide open. Nessa went over to push it closed.

"Hey," the guard protested.

"Privacy, remember?"

He frowned but didn't argue. Nessa pushed the door the rest of the way shut.

She returned to the table, pulled her shirt out of the waistband of her jeans, and ripped a piece off the bottom of it. The jug of moonshine was sitting on a shelf. She got it and poured some of the fiery liquid on the rag, then eased Belle's hand and the bloody bandanna away from the ugly wound. Trying not to wince, Nessa began wiping at it with the moonshine-soaked rag.

"This really needs to be stitched up," she said, "but it's going to take a doctor for that. You should get back to Warbonnet and get some medical attention as soon as you can."

Belle caught her breath in pain several times while Nessa was cleaning the wound, and after a few minutes she reached up and caught hold of Nessa's wrist, putting a temporary stop to it.

"Did you hear what Doak said?" Belle asked, her voice low enough not to be heard through the cabin's door or thick walls.

"About going back up on the rim to ambush Pike and the others?"

"I think it's going to be worse than an ambush," Belle said. "The way he talked about wiping them out, he's got something more in mind. The best way to be sure of getting all of them would be an avalanche."

Nessa felt her eyes widen in horror. "An avalanche?" she repeated.

"Well . . . a rockfall, anyway. I don't know if you noticed on your way in there, but there's a place between here and the mouth of the gorge where the wall sticks out enough that if anything were to make it come down, anybody on the trail would be crushed. Some dynamite planted up there on the rim would do that, and Doak could set it off . . ."

Every instinct in Nessa's body told her that Belle's speculation was true. That was *exactly* the sort of diabolical thing Doak Ramsey would do. For it to work, though—

"He can't let me go with Pike after all," she said. "He knows I'd warn them."

Belle nodded. "He'll keep you tied and gagged while they're here and tell your brothers that he'll turn you loose after they're clear of the gorge. Pike won't be happy about it, but he won't have any choice except to go along with what Doak says. But they'll never make it that far. And as for you . . . well, not to be too blunt about it, but he'll find a use for you, Nessa. He'll sell you to some house of ill repute up in Dallas, if nothing else."

Nessa's head spun. Even though it wasn't her nature

at all, she felt herself growing faint. She had never been in a situation as desperate as this before.

Then Belle's hand closed on her shoulder and gave her strength. "Finish cleaning up this cut," Belle said as Nessa felt herself steadying. "Then we'll start figuring on how we'll get out of here and warn your brother."

CHAPTER 43

"I know you want to take them by surprise, Pike," Sam Crow said, "but there's just no way to do it."

"There's no back door into that gorge?" Pike insisted.

Crow shook his head. "I've hunted all over both rims and know them pretty well. There's a little ledge where a fella *might* be able to climb down. He'd need to be more sure-footed than I am, though. I wouldn't try it, myself."

"What about the rest of it? Do you believe Ramsey's really got himself some sort of stronghold up in there?"

"It's possible," Crow said as his shoulders rose and fell in a shrug. "There are some places up close to the far end where the brush isn't as thick. You'd have to hack out a trail to get in and out of there and maybe clear off some ground if you wanted to build anything, but it could be done if you didn't mind getting scratched up by briars and branches while you were doing it."

Dougal snorted and said, "Doak wouldn't care

about that. He'd just buffalo some other fellas into doin' the hard work, like he always does."

The three of them, along with Torrance and Fiddler, stood in the ranch yard at the Shannon spread. A dozen other men were gathered there as well, having come in response to the summons spread by Pike and Crow. Will Fisher and Andy Burnett were there, along with the Dawson brothers, Kit Sellers, Clayton Rice, and several others. All were armed to the teeth and ready to ride into battle.

Pike had counted on being able to surprise Ramsey and move in on the cabin in Warbonnet Gorge from two directions at once. If what Sam Crow was saying was correct—and Pike had grown to trust the man completely—then his plan was no good. Even if somebody could make it down that precarious ledge Crow had mentioned, they wouldn't be able to get enough men into the gorge to make a difference without being spotted.

"What do we do now?" Torrance asked. He wasn't armed, but he had insisted on complying with Doak Ramsey's demand and going along anyway. Maybe there was some other way he could help without fighting, he'd said. Pike thought that was one of the craziest things he'd ever heard his brother say, but Torrance was being stubborn about it.

Pike took a deep breath and said, "All we can do is play along with Doak, I reckon, and try to turn the tables on him when he makes his move, whatever it is. One thing we can count on—he's going to try *something* dirty and underhanded."

"I think I should come with you, too," Fiddler said. "I wouldn't be so bold as to claim that I'm a member of the family now, but actually, there are times when I feel like that's true!"

Pike shook his head. "You're staying here with Ma, Fiddler. She'll need somebody around." He turned his head to look at the Dawson brothers. "Cloyd, Hebner, I'd like for you to stay here, too. I don't want the place undefended if Doak tries something really tricky."

"We'd rather fight," Hebner growled. Cloyd nodded his agreement.

"I know that, but I'm asking you as a favor to help Fiddler look out for my mother."

Cloyd grimaced and said, "You make it mighty hard to say no, son."

"We'll stay," Hebner said, adding with obvious reluctance, "I reckon."

Pike nodded in satisfaction and turned back to Sam Crow. "You and the others follow us at a distance. If you hear shots . . ."

"We'll come a-runnin'," Crow promised.

Nessa and Belle had heard hoofbeats outside the cabin and Nessa checked, pulling back one of the shutters over the window enough to see Doak Ramsey ride past, heading back out of the gorge. By now the afternoon heat had started to build inside the cabin, and Nessa used the back of her hand to wipe sweat off her forehead as she returned to the table.

She had torn another piece off her shirt to use as a bandage on Belle's wound and tied it in place with the older girl's bandanna. Belle was pale under her tan and looked shaken but determined. The bandage made it hard for her to talk as she said, "You know what to do."

"Yes," Nessa said. "I don't know if it'll work, but we have to try."

"Just get him in here," Belle said. "I'll handle it from there."

She stood up, moved over to the fireplace, and picked up a piece of wood from the small stack of firewood left over from the previous winter. She went to the door and stood near it, giving Nessa an encouraging nod as she did so.

Nessa opened the door and said to the guard who was standing about ten feet away, "You've got to come in here, mister. Belle's started bleeding worse. It's real bad."

The man started toward the door, looking alarmed, then stopped short and frowned suspiciously. "You might be tryin' to trick me," he said. "Have her come out here iffen you want me to take a look at her."

"She's too weak—" Nessa began, but then a pathetic moan from inside the cabin interrupted her. She went on hurriedly, "See, she's in bad shape. You heard it for yourself!"

The guard was obviously torn about what he should do, but after a couple of seconds he pointed the rifle in his hands at Nessa and said, "You back off now, girl. Go on in there and keep well away from me. I don't trust you, but I ain't gonna take a chance on Belle bleedin' to death, either. Doak may have been mad at her earlier, but he wouldn't want to see nothin' bad happen to her. She's his cousin, after all."

No, Doak wouldn't want to see anything bad happen to Belle, Nessa thought bitterly. He had just mutilated her face, that was all. Belle would carry a hideous scar for the rest of her life—assuming she survived this day, something that Nessa doubted for both of them.

But all they could do was try, as Belle had said, so Nessa kept her hands in plain sight and backed away from the door as the guard had ordered her. He stepped in and swung his head from side to side, looking for Belle. Coming into the shadowy cabin from midafternoon sunlight, his eyes probably had a hard time adjusting.

Belle didn't give them the time they needed to do that. Instead she stepped out from her position against the wall and swung the chunk of firewood with both hands. It thudded into the side of the guard's head. His knees buckled. He fell onto them and dropped the rifle in front of him. Nessa darted across the room and grabbed the weapon while the guard put his hands to his now-bleeding head and groaned.

Belle lifted the firewood over her head and hit him again. This time he went down hard and didn't move.

Nessa started toward the door, but Belle stopped her and said, "Give me the rifle. You get to the horses, grab one, and get out of here."

"We're *both* getting out of here," Nessa said.

"Maybe, but you need to warn your brothers and grandfather not to come into the gorge. I'll cover you and make sure you get the chance, then come after you."

Nessa didn't like it much, but she knew Belle was right. She handed over the Winchester and Belle went out the door first, sweeping the rifle from side to side as she searched for threats. Not seeing any, she looked back at Nessa and nodded.

Nessa rushed out of the cabin and ran toward the corral. None of the horses were saddled, but that didn't matter. She had been riding bareback since almost before she could walk. She wouldn't have any trouble with that.

She believed they both would have made it if one of the moonshiners hadn't stepped out of a storage shed just then, not far from the corral. The man stopped short, his eyes bulging in surprise at the sight of the two girls running toward him.

"Nessa, get out of the way!" Belle called.

Nessa swerved to her left. The man up ahead clawed at the gun on his hip. He got it out and jerked it level. Belle fired first, but only by a hair. The two shots came so close together they sounded like one.

The moonshiner didn't fall. Instead he charged forward. Nessa twisted around and saw Belle on the ground, writhing in pain. Nessa ran to her and saw the fresh blood darkening Belle's shirt, low on the right side. The Winchester lay on the ground beside her on the left.

"Get . . . the rifle!" she gasped at Nessa.

The man's gun blasted again, the bullet kicking up dirt a couple of yards away. Nessa snatched the rifle off the ground, turned and dived forward, landing on her belly. She aimed the Winchester and cranked off three rounds, all of them deadly accurate. The slugs laced into the running man and stopped him like he'd been slapped down by a giant hand. His legs kicked a few times, but that was all he could manage.

Nessa scrambled up and dropped to her knees

beside Belle. The older girl grabbed hold of her arm
and pulled herself up into a sitting position.

"Go!" she told Nessa. "Get on a horse and ride!
Leave the rifle. I'll hold them off."

"No—" Nessa began.

"Just do it!" Belle said. "It's my family . . . that
caused all of this trouble. I see it now . . . gotta do
something to make up for it . . . Just go! Save your
family!"

When she put it like that, Nessa couldn't argue.
She put the rifle in Belle's outstretched hands and
came to her feet. "Thank you," she said.

"Go!" Belle ordered again.

Nessa turned and ran to the corral. The horses
were a little spooked by the shooting, but she spoke
calmly and quietly to them, and they responded to
her. Being raised on a horse ranch had given her the
ability to settle down a horse's skittish nerves pretty
quickly. She climbed the fence, picked out a good-
looking buckskin, and got hold of the horse's mane to
lead it over by the fence. Agilely, she climbed up and
onto the buckskin's back and guided the horse over
to the gate. Then she opened it and rode out, leaving
the gate wide open so the other horses would scatter
behind her and make it harder for Doak Ramsey's
men to pursue her.

As she was doing that, she heard the rifle Belle held
begin to crack. Nessa leaned forward, dug her heels
into the buckskin's flanks as she clutched the horse's
mane, and rode hell-bent for leather down Warbonnet
Gorge, riding not just for her own life but those of
Pike and Torrance and Dougal, as well.

And behind her, the guns continued to go off.

Chapter 44

Pike, Dougal, and Torrance were about half a mile from the mouth of Warbonnet Gorge when they heard the shooting. Pike reined in and motioned for his brother and grandfather to do likewise.

"What in blazes is goin' on up there?" Dougal asked. "Sounds like somebody's tryin' to shoot their way into the gorge."

"Or out of it," Pike said grimly. "Like if Nessa got her hands on a gun and decided to make a break for it."

"She'll get herself killed!" Torrance exclaimed.

Pike heeled his horse into a run and called over his shoulder, "Come on!" He had planned to enter the gorge cautiously, knowing that Doak Ramsey couldn't be trusted, but with those guns going off, they couldn't afford to wait.

Dougal and Torrance followed close behind him. The mouth of the gorge came into view ahead of them, and Pike watched it closely as they approached it. Suddenly a rider burst into the open and galloped toward them. The sight took Pike by surprise, but relief flooded through him as he spotted the long red hair streaming out behind the rider's head. That was Nessa, he knew.

But then who was doing the shooting that continued inside the gorge?

Dougal let out a whoop. "That's our gal!" he called.

Pike yanked his hat off and waved it over his head to attract his sister's attention. Nessa swerved her mount toward them. Pike didn't recognize the horse. She was riding bareback, leaning forward and clinging to the animal's mane. Pike figured she must have stolen it from one of Doak Ramsey's men. If Doak had a stronghold up there in the gorge, it made sense that there would be a corral, too.

"Nessa!" Torrance shouted. "Over here!"

"She sees us," Pike said. He drew his gun, just in case any pursuit emerged from the gorge and came after her.

From the sounds of it, though, whoever was in there had their hands full.

They all brought their mounts to skidding, dust-raising halts as Nessa reached them. She was breathing hard and her eyes were wide. "Pike!" she cried.

He was down off his horse in a flash, reaching up for her as she slid off her mount. He caught her and hugged her tightly, then asked, "Are you all right?"

"Yes, but . . . but Belle . . ."

"Belle Ramsey?" Pike exclaimed in surprise.

Nessa jerked her head in a nod. "Yes. She's in there fighting with Doak's men. She . . . she saved my life, Pike. She saved all of us. There's a trap—"

Pike closed his hands hard on her shoulders. "Where's Doak?"

Nessa turned and lifted her head to gaze up at the

rim of the gorge. "Up there somewhere. Belle and I think he's planning some kind of explosion to take down part of the gorge wall."

That sounded like something Doak Ramsey would do, all right, Pike thought. He stepped back to let Dougal and Torrance hug Nessa as well, and as he did, the shooting inside the gorge came to an abrupt end. In the echoing silence, Nessa gasped and said, "Belle was wounded when I rode out. They must have—"

"We'll find out as soon as we can," Pike promised. He didn't know exactly how Belle was mixed up in all this, but he was shocked that the girl apparently had taken a stand against her own family and helped Nessa escape. He didn't doubt Nessa's story, though.

Right now there were other things to deal with. He said, "Torrance, take Nessa and head for home."

"What are you going to do, Pike?" she asked.

"Deal with Doak, once and for all. This showdown's been too long in coming."

"I'll come with you, boy," Dougal declared.

Pike shook his head. "No. Sam, Andy, and the others will be here soon. We're going to split up. I'll take some of the men up on the rim with me, while you and the others stay down here and guard the mouth of the gorge. You're liable to have to deal with some rats trying to escape."

"They'll run into a hot-lead rattrap if they do," Dougal said.

While they waited for the rest of Pike's friends and allies to arrive, Nessa told them about how she had been kidnapped, including Ramsey gunning down Joe Eagleton, and then what had happened inside the gorge.

"Dadgum, I'm sorry to hear that about Joe," Dougal said with a shake of his head. "He seemed like a pretty good fella who just got in too deep with the wrong bunch. He never was cut out to work for a sorry son of a gun like Doak Ramsey."

"No, he wasn't," Nessa said as she wiped away some fresh tears. "I . . . I don't know what might have happened in the future if Ramsey hadn't killed him." She started sobbing again. "And now we'll never know."

Torrance put his arms around her and patted her on the back, while Pike said, "I'm not surprised Belle turned on her cousin like that, after what he did to her. We owe her for helping you. I hope she's still alive in there."

Nessa turned a tear-streaked face toward him and said, "I don't know how badly she was wounded, but I hope you'll help her if you can, Pike."

He nodded. "You can count on that."

A minute later, the group led by Sam Crow pounded up, slowing when they saw that everyone appeared to be unharmed. "Didn't expect to see you this soon, Miss Nessa," Crow said. "Are you all right?"

She wiped away tears and said, "I will be, Mr. Crow, thank you."

Andy Burnett said, "We heard quite a bit of shooting, Pike. What's going on?"

"Doak Ramsey's got a trap laid for us in there," Pike said as he nodded toward the mouth of Warbonnet Gorge. "And he's up on the rim just waiting to spring it."

"Well, dang, that's where we need to go, then!"

"That's what some of us are going to do," Pike went on. "The rest of you will stay here with Dougal to make sure none of the Ramsey bunch gets away. Andy, you and Sam are coming with me."

Pike called off several more names. Some of the men he didn't pick to accompany him complained, but Will Fisher, who was one of them, said sharply, "Settle down. There's liable to be some fighting for us to do, too."

"I reckon you can count on it," Pike told them. He had mounted again, and he lifted his reins to turn his horse. "Torrance, take Nessa home," he said again. "The rest of you, let's go!"

Doak Ramsey's anger showed in every step he took as he paced back and forth. A few minutes earlier, he had heard guns start to go off, back up the gorge where the cabin and the moonshine stills were located. That damn Shannon girl was causing more trouble again. He would bet money on that.

Maybe his men would kill her this time. He hoped not—she could still be valuable to him—but if they were defending themselves and trying to stop her from escaping, well, he couldn't blame them for that.

He had sent Chuck Hanratty to find out what was going on. He'd planned to let Hanratty handle the payoff anyway, so it didn't matter that the deputy was riding down into the gorge now. Ramsey still had half a dozen men up here with him, just in case anything went wrong with this part of the plan.

But there wasn't much to go wrong with it, he'd reminded himself. All he had to do was push down the T-shaped plunger on the detonator wired to the dynamite he and Hanratty had planted earlier, and all hell would rain down on anyone who was on the trail down there. That would be Pike Shannon and the other men in his family, if everything went as it was supposed to.

Then came the swift rataplan of hoofbeats as someone galloped past, on their way out of the gorge. Ramsey had tried to catch a glimpse of who it was, but between the way the rock bulged out and the twists in the trail, he hadn't been able to spot the rider.

But the shooting continued for several more minutes before coming to an abrupt, ominous end.

Now Ramsey was left to wonder what was going on down there. Part of him wanted to ride around to the mouth of the gorge and then up the trail to find out, but at the same time, he didn't want to miss his chance to drop hundreds of tons of rock on top of Pike Shannon. Everything would settle down, he told himself, and then later he would get the signal from Hanratty— two fast shots, followed by two more—that would tell him to push the plunger and set off the blast.

He walked back to the detonator, which was placed behind a large rock fifty yards from the line of dynamite. That boulder would protect Ramsey when he pushed down the plunger to set off the explosion. All the other men would have withdrawn out of danger at that point.

One of the men was guarding the detonator. He said, "It's gettin' late, Doak. Shouldn't those Shannons be here by now?"

"They'll get here when they get here," Ramsey snapped. "And they'll never go anywhere else, because they won't get out of that gorge alive."

"They won't be able to interfere with your plans after that, will they?"

"They could never stop me," Ramsey said confidently. "They were beaten before they even started. They just didn't know it yet."

He resumed pacing. The man he had spoken to was right—the afternoon was more than halfway along. He had given Pike Shannon a deadline of sundown. That was still a while off, but Ramsey had figured Shannon would be here before now.

More shots blasted without warning, but these didn't come from down in the gorge. Instead, Ramsey swung around and peered off along the rim toward the east. The trail ran for a mile in that direction, then zigzagged down a steep slope to the flats that stretched all the way to the Brazos River. Gunfire from that direction—the direction Chuck Hanratty had gone to reach the gorge mouth—could mean only one thing: unexpected trouble.

"Hunt cover!" Ramsey called to his men. "And be ready to kill anybody who comes riding up here!"

CHAPTER 45

Pike, Sam Crow, Andy Burnett, and their companions were approaching the base of the trail that led up to the rim when a single rider emerged from the post oaks along that ridge, moving fast toward them. The man reined up sharply, though, when he spotted the group galloping toward him.

"That's Chuck Hanratty!" Burnett exclaimed.

Pike's keen eyes had already told him the same thing. He didn't want Hanratty getting away and warning Doak Ramsey, so he spurred forward, urging his dun to greater speed.

He was close enough to see the sudden look of alarm on Hanratty's face. The deputy jerked out his gun and threw a couple of fast shots in Pike's direction. The hurried bullets went wide, though, kicking up dust far to the side. Pike pulled his own Colt and triggered twice, but the hurricane deck of a galloping horse was no place for accurate fire, even for someone as good with a gun as he was. He didn't see any sign that the deputy was hit as Hanratty whirled his mount and raced back through the trees, onto the trail that led to the rim of Warbonnet Gorge.

Pike bit back a curse and followed, waving his men on as he did so. He'd hoped to take Ramsey by surprise, but the burst of gunfire had already ended that possibility.

They might be riding up the trail right into a storm of hot lead, but they had to run the risk. Things had gone too far. This fight wouldn't end until either he or Doak Ramsey was dead.

Pike heard the hoofbeats ahead of him as Hanratty raced back to the rim. Pike pulled the nimble-footed dun around the turns as the trail twisted its way to the top. A glance over his shoulder told him that the others had fallen behind, their mounts unable to keep up with the pace Pike was setting. When he reached the rim, he might be fighting on his own at first, but as caught up in his own emotions as he was, he didn't slow down.

The dun lunged onto more level ground at the top. Pike caught sight of Hanratty riding hard about a hundred yards ahead of him. The yawning chasm of Warbonnet Gorge loomed off to their right, fifty yards away. Pike glanced in that direction and then ignored it as he pursued Hanratty. He had a score to settle with the deputy, too, on behalf of Fiddler, who had suffered at Hanratty's hands while he was locked up in jail.

Pike didn't waste any more ammunition throwing lead after Hanratty. Instead he pouched his iron, leaned forward in the saddle, and concentrated on closing the gap between them. The dun was a strong, rangy mount with plenty of speed and sand. He responded to Pike's coaxing and flashed over the ground, steadily drawing closer to Hanratty.

The deputy twisted around and flung another wild shot in Pike's general direction. Pike was close enough now to see the snarl contorting Hanratty's face.

Hanratty should have been watching where he was going, because the horse suddenly stumbled and went down, its front legs folding underneath it as if they had been yanked up somehow. Hanratty flew out of the saddle, sailing far enough ahead to keep the flailing horse from crushing him. He landed hard, though, and rolled over several times before he came to a stop and started struggling back to his feet.

By that time, Pike was almost on top of him. Pike kicked his feet free of the stirrups and left the saddle in a dive that carried him into Hanratty with stunning force. Both men crashed to the ground.

They broke apart and came up swinging. Hanratty, clearly filled with desperation, landed the first punch. The looping right drove Pike back a couple of steps. Hanratty tried to follow up on his advantage and bored in on him, but Pike caught his balance, ducked under the roundhouse blows Hanratty aimed at him, and hammered a left and right into the crooked deputy's belly. Hanratty gasped and leaned forward, putting him in position for the uppercut that Pike lifted into his chin. Hanratty's head snapped back.

He almost went down again then, but he struggled to stay on his feet and reached back to snatch a knife from its sheath just behind his now-empty holster. He slashed at Pike, who had to jerk back to avoid the blade. Pike darted in before Hanratty could recover and grabbed the man's wrist with both hands. He twisted and shoved, and the knife entered Hanratty's chest at an upward angle that penetrated all the

342 William W. Johnstone

way to his heart. His eyes bugged out and he sagged forward. Pike still had both hands wrapped around Hanratty's wrist, and that was the only thing holding him up. When Pike let go and stepped back, Hanratty pitched forward on his face and didn't move again.

Pike stood there for a second and drew the back of his hand across his mouth as his heart slugged in his chest. A few yards away, Hanratty's horse had struggled back to its feet and didn't seem to be hurt badly by the fall.

While Pike was catching his breath, Crow, Burnett, and the other men galloped up. "You got him!" Burnett said.

"Yeah, but those shots will have warned Doak that we're coming," Pike said. One of the men caught his horse and led the dun over, and as he took the reins, Pike went on, "We're not turning back now, though."

"Not hardly," Crow said.

Pike didn't bother looking for his hat, which had flown off when he tackled Hanratty. He swung up into the saddle, checked to see that his gun was still in its holster, and said, "Let's go."

They rode on, with Pike watching alertly for any sign of an ambush. After passing through a stretch of trees, they emerged onto a long stretch dotted with large rocks. Pike spotted sunlight glinting off something in those boulders. Knowing they were in range, he shouted, "Spread out!"

Guns crashed and powder smoke spurted from behind the rocks, but Pike's friends were already scattering and the bullets whined around them but didn't hit anybody. They returned the fire. Slugs mostly screamed off rocks, but a couple of Ramsey men howled in pain as swift shots found their targets.

Their good luck couldn't hold. Kit Sellers, one of Pike's allies, tumbled out of the saddle as he was hit. Another man followed him a few seconds later. But then the riders reached the rocks where Doak Ramsey's men had forted up, and clouds of gun smoke rolled along the rim as shots were exchanged in a ferocious din. The gun-thunder seemed to shake the earth.

The smoke stung Pike's nose and made his eyes water. No matter how much powder smoke a man breathed, he never quite got used to it. But Pike could see clearly enough to spot Doak Ramsey crouched behind a rock, shooting at him. He felt the wind-rip of a bullet past his ear and left the saddle in a rolling dive that carried him toward the barrel-chested lawman. Another slug plowed into the ground only inches from Pike as he came up on one knee, thrust the Colt out, and fired again. This time the sight of Ramsey jerking back as the bullet hammered into him rewarded Pike's shot.

Ramsey didn't go down, though. He stayed on his feet and triggered again. This time Pike felt the hot breath of the slug almost kissing his left cheek. He twisted to the side to make himself a smaller target. That may have saved his life, since Ramsey's next shot passed only inches in front of his chest. Pike steadied himself and pulled the trigger.

The bullet drove into Ramsey's belly and doubled him over. He staggered to the side, toward the boulder where he had taken cover, and for the first time Pike noticed the detonator behind the rock. He saw Ramsey toppling toward it, knew the crooked sheriff was going to land on the handle, and shouted as loudly as he could over the din of battle, "Everybody down!"

Ramsey fell onto the detonator handle, and the weight of his body shoved it home.

Pike was already diving to the ground. The earth really did shake this time as a series of explosions ripped along the rim. Sheared loose by the blasts, thousands of tons of rock crashed down into Warbonnet Gorge. The mixture of deafening sounds slammed painfully against Pike's ears, and the cloud of dust that boiled up from the gorge blinded and choked him. For a long moment, all he could do was lie there with his ears ringing as he coughed and blinked. Gravel flung high in the air pelted him as it fell back to earth.

As his stunned senses began to recover, he pushed himself to his feet and stumbled toward the rock where Doak Ramsey had fallen. Ramsey lay on his side, groaning as he curled around the wound in his belly. His gun lay not far away, and he reached for it feebly as Pike stood over him.

Pike kicked the revolver away and trained his own gun on Ramsey's pain-contorted face. "You're gut-shot, Doak," he said. "You're dying, and there's not a blasted thing you can do about it. But before you go to hell, know that you're going for what you did to Davey and Charley and Lonzo and to your own cousin . . . and for murdering my pa."

Ramsey grimaced. "Before I . . . threw him off . . . into the gorge," he forced out, "he said . . . you'd come back . . . and avenge him. I told him . . . I hoped he was right . . . so I could kill you, too!"

Then Ramsey stiffened and gasped a couple of times, and his eyes began to glaze over in death. Pike realized no more shooting was going on and looked around to see what had happened. Doak Ramsey was just a lifeless hunk of meat now, no longer worth any interest.

Sam Crow, Andy Burnett, and the rest of Pike's friends and allies—except for the two wounded men— stood there, having come up in time to hear Ramsey admit to killing Elijah Shannon. Pike asked, "What about the rest of Ramsey's bunch?"

"Either dead or hurt bad enough to be out of the fight," Crow reported. "It's over, Pike."

"Not yet," Pike said. "I've got to get down there in the gorge and see what happened when all that rock fell."

"Nessa was clear of there," Burnett said.

"Yeah, but Belle Ramsey wasn't. And hard as it is to admit it about anybody named Ramsey . . . I owe her. Nessa wouldn't have gotten out of there alive without her, and we might have ridden into Doak's trap." Pike grunted. "Too bad he wasn't under all that rock when it fell. Would've made too prominent a tombstone for a skunk like him, though. Better he goes into an unmarked grave where he belongs."

CHAPTER 46

Getting into Warbonnet Gorge proved to be no easy task. After reuniting with Dougal and the other men left near the mouth of the gorge, they found the entrance and the trail Nessa had described, but the explosion and the rockfall had completely blocked the trail part of the way in. Clouds of dust still lingered in the air, too. As they studied the rocks, Sam Crow called, "Pike, take a look at this."

Pike went over to him and saw Crow pointing at a mangled arm and hand that stuck out from under a huge slab of rock. It had belonged to a man, and since the only men in the gorge, as far as they knew, were Doak Ramsey's friends and relatives, it was an easy assumption that this man had been part of Doak's gang of moonshiners.

Dougal said, "You reckon they were all on their way out, trying to get to Doak and give him a helpin' hand after all that shootin' started?"

"Could be," Pike said. "It's possible the rest of Doak's men are buried under there."

"What about Belle?"

"That's what I want to find out," Pike replied grimly. "Sam, you reckon we can get through that brush?"

"We'll be pretty scratched up by the time we do," Crow said with a shrug, "but I reckon it's possible."

"Let's get to it, then."

Several of the men carried bowie knives, so they went to work cutting a path through the growth. It was slow going, and late afternoon had rolled around by the time Pike, Dougal, and the others came out into a more open area and saw the cabin, corral, and stills up ahead. With guns ready, just in case anybody hostile was still lurking around up here, they began to explore. Pike headed for the cabin first, and when he stepped into the doorway, he immediately spotted the huddled shape lying on the floor.

He went to Belle Ramsey's side and dropped to a knee. She was breathing, he saw right away, but, judging by the amount of blood on her shirt and trousers, had been shot several times. The bloody makeshift bandage was still on her face, too.

A jug was sitting on the crude table, so Pike reached out for it, slipped his other arm around her shoulders, and lifted her so he could tip some moonshine into her mouth. She sputtered and swallowed only some of the potent 'shine, but it was enough to make her eyelids flutter open.

Her eyes weren't able to focus for a moment, and when they did, they widened in surprise. "P-Pike?" she rasped. "Pike Shannon?"

"That's right," he told her. "You just take it easy now. You're hurt, but we'll get help for you."

"N-Nessa? She's . . . safe?"

"Yeah, she's fine. But only because of you, Belle. I owe you for that. And for my own life."

"I reckon . . . if you're here . . . Doak must be . . . dead."

"I'm afraid so. I'd say I was sorry, but—"

"Don't be . . . sorry," she said. "He had it . . . comin'."

Pike nodded and said, "I can't argue with that."

"If you saw . . . what he did to me . . ."

"You mean that scratch on your face?" Pike smiled. "That doesn't matter. I reckon you'll still be mighty pretty . . . for a Ramsey."

"You think I care . . . whether a blasted Shannon . . . thinks I'm . . . pretty or not?"

Sam Crow appeared in the doorway before Pike could answer. He said, "Nobody else is here, Pike. Looks like they were all on their way out of the gorge but didn't make it, just like we thought. If any of them did escape, I don't expect they'll stop running anytime soon."

"We can hope not," Pike said. "We've got to get Belle to town. She needs a doctor, and our own wounded men could use some medical attention, too."

"We'll rig up something we can carry her on and take her back to the horses."

While Crow hurried to get started on that, Belle said, "Pike, you think I could have . . . another swig of that 'shine?"

"Sure. But when you get better, you'll have to try something tastier . . . like some Shannon moonshine."

"You talk like . . . our families . . . are friends now."

"Maybe that's not likely, but what I'm hoping is that the war between us is over."

"That's what . . . I hope, too."

He gave her the drink of 'shine she'd asked for, and then when he set the jug aside, her hand moved and found his, and closed on it with surprising strength for a gal who was all shot up.

Pike wasn't sure Belle would make it back to War-bonnet alive, but she was still breathing by the time they got there. He had held her in his arms the whole time as she perched on the back of his horse in front of him, wrapped in a blanket he had found in the cabin. The strong arms of several of his friends took her and carried her into the doctor's residence, which also served as his office.

Pike followed them, and as he stepped up onto the porch, he was surprised to see Sophie Truesdale come out of the house. She wore an apron, not like the one she wore at the café, but different somehow.

"That's far enough," she said as she planted a hand on Pike's chest.

He frowned at her. "I don't think you can stop me, or have any right to."

"Actually, I do," she said. "I happen to be Dr. Faulkner's nurse part of the time, as well as running the café. And speaking in my capacity as a nurse, the doctor doesn't need a bunch of people crowding into the place while he's trying to take care of Miss Ramsey."

"You don't know what happened up at Warbonnet Gorge, do you?"

The blonde's chin came up defiantly as she said, "As a matter of fact, I'm aware of some of the things that have taken place today. I know that your brother and sister are down at the courthouse, waiting to speak with you when you got back to town. I think you should go on down there and see them."

"The courthouse," Pike repeated with a note of alarm in his voice. "What are Nessa and Torrance doing at the courthouse?"

"Why don't you go and find out?"

"Maybe I will," Pike snapped. He started to turn away but paused. "You and the doc will take good care of Belle, won't you?"

Sophie's tone softened a little as she said, "We'll do everything we can for her."

Pike nodded and hurried back to his horse. He had expected to find Nessa and Torrance at home, not here in town. He hoped there weren't more problems he didn't even know about yet.

When he and Dougal reached the courthouse and walked into the lobby, they found Nessa and Torrance there, all right, along with Mary Shannon and Fiddler, which added to Pike's surprise.

There was another man with them, and the sight of him made a tingle of apprehension go through Pike. Tall, rangy, with crisp dark hair, intent gray eyes, and a hawklike nose, the man sported a Texas Ranger badge on his vest.

"Pike!" Nessa exclaimed as she ran toward him and embraced him. "You're all right?"

"Yeah, I'm fine," he assured her. "You and Torrance didn't run into any trouble on the way back from Warbonnet Gorge?"

"No, and when we got back to the ranch, we found

Ranger Scott there talking to Ma and Mr. Fiddler. He said Torrance had sent for him."

The lawman thumbed back his broad-brimmed black hat and said, "Well, it wasn't exactly that way, Miss Shannon. Your brother wrote to Austin and asked the governor for help with the problems you folks have been having around here, and Cap'n McNelty of the Rangers sent me to look into it. Something about a crooked lawman running a moonshine ring and waging war on other families in Warbonnet County?" He shrugged. "That was enough to get me pokin' around these parts for the past week or so without lettin' anybody know what I was up to."

Pike looked at his brother and said, "You did that?"

Torrance frowned. "Somebody had to put a stop to what Doak Ramsey was doing and get to the bottom of Pa's death. I just figured on going about it without burning a wagonload of gunpowder."

"Well, it's over now," Pike said slowly. "Doak Ramsey is dead."

Ranger Scott put his hand on the butt of the big revolver at his hip. "I reckon I'll have to ask you to explain that, mister."

"Wait," Nessa said before Pike could respond. "What happened to Belle? Is she . . . ?"

"She's alive," Pike told her. "Hurt pretty bad, from the looks of it, but I've got a hunch she's too blasted stubborn to die. She's down at Doc Faulkner's."

"I need to go see if there's anything I can do to help."

"I think that's a fine idea," Pike said. "There's a blond nurse guarding the door, but she might let you past."

"Sophie Truesdale?" Nessa snorted. "She won't stop me."

As Nessa hurried out, Mary hugged Pike and Dougal as well, then stepped back, rested her hands on her youngest son's arms, and said, "Is it true, Pike? Doak Ramsey is dead?"

"That's right. But before he died, he admitted that he killed Pa." Pike looked at the Ranger. "Half a dozen men heard him do it, too, but I don't know if you'll believe them since they're all friends of mine."

"Reckon I've already got plenty of proof that your so-called sheriff was a bad hombre," Scott drawled. "Miss Nessa told me she saw Ramsey kill one of his own deputies in cold blood, as well as carvin' up his cousin's face with a knife. If you're worried that I'm gonna come after you for what happened to Doak Ramsey, I don't figure that'll be too big a problem, Shannon." The Ranger regarded Pike intently and went on, "As for the rumors about some other ruckuses I've heard you were mixed up in . . . well, like I say, those are just rumors. Except for the moonshinin'. I've seen the stills and talked to enough folks that I reckon I've got your family dead to rights on the moonshinin'."

"Are you going to arrest me for that?" Pike asked tightly.

"As far as I can tell, *you* ain't done any moonshinin' since you've been back. But your grandpappy has."

Dougal started to bluster, but Scott held up a hand to stop him.

"You'll have to pay a fine, Mr. Shannon." The Ranger smiled faintly. "Somebody'll have to set the amount besides Phineas Conway, though. Seems him and everybody else associated with the late Sheriff Ramsey has lit a shuck outa these parts, once they found out a Ranger had come to town."

"And I ain't a bit sorry to see them rapscallions go!" Dougal declared.

"So consider yourself under arrest, Mr. Shannon," Scott went on, "and don't leave the county until we got all the legal mess straightened out and some honest men running things again. If you'll give me your word on that, I don't reckon I'll have to lock you up."

"You've got my word," Dougal said with a scowl.

Scott looked at Pike and said, "I'd be obliged if you'd hang around these parts, too, until everything gets sorted out."

Pike smiled at his mother. "I can do that. I've been away from home for too long. I'm not ready to leave again."

"All right. Y'all can go back to your ranch."

Pike, Dougal, Mary, and Fiddler left the courthouse. Pike noticed the buckboard now, parked nearby. In his earlier haste to find out what was going on, he hadn't recognized it.

Torrance said, "We'll go down to the doctor's and pick up Nessa."

"And check on Belle," Pike said. "She's not a bad sort . . . for a Ramsey."

Fiddler chuckled and said, "You sound like a man who's on the verge of being smitten, Pike."

"With a Ramsey? That's loco! But I can still admire her and be grateful to her."

"Yes, of course." The little man grew more solemn. "I haven't heard anything yet about what might have happened to Deputy Hanratty."

"He's dead, Fiddler," Pike said. "I killed him myself."

Fiddler drew in a deep breath. "Good. He was an evil man who took great delight in other people's suffering. I hate to say it about any human being, but the world is a better place without him."

At that moment, Pike heard someone call his name and turned to see Ranger Scott striding after them. The lawman came up to them and said, "There's one thing I forgot to say. No more moonshinin'! You reckon you can do that?"

"Why, sure I can, Ranger," Pike answered without hesitation.

Scott squinted and cocked his head a little to the side. "You wouldn't be having a mite of sport and fibbin' to me, now, would you, son?"

Pike smiled and said, "I reckon we'll just have to wait and find out."

CHAPTER 1

Big Rock, Colorado

It had rained earlier in the day, and though the rain had stopped, the sky still hung heavy with clouds, as if heaven itself was in mourning. Phil Clinton, editor of the *Big Rock Journal*, made the observation that this was the largest number of citizens ever to turn out for a funeral in Big Rock, Colorado. The Garden of Memories cemetery was so full that the mourners spilled out of the grounds and onto Center and Ranney streets. The service had been held in the First Baptist Church, which shared the cemetery with St. Paul's Episcopal. And because of Sheriff Monte Carson's popularity, memorial rites were held in St. Paul's even as the funeral was being conducted in the Big Rock Baptist Church.

Father Pyron stood with the mourners, but it was the Reverend E. D. Owen who was conducting the burial service. Monte Carson, dressed in black, and with his head bowed, stood alongside the coffin of Ina Claire, his wife of the last fifteen years.

Sheriff Carson had invited Smoke and Sally Jensen, Pearlie Fontaine, and Cal Wood, all of whom were also wearing black, to stand with him next to the open grave. That was because the four represented the closest thing Monte had to a family.

It was quiet and still and Reverend Owen stood there for just a moment as if gathering his thoughts. In the distance a crow cawed, and closer yet, a mockingbird trilled.

The pastor began to speak.

"We have gathered here to praise God and to bear-witness to our faith as we celebrate the life of Ina Claire Carson. We come together in grief, acknowledging our human loss. May God grant us grace, that in pain we may find comfort, in sorrow, hope, and in death, resurrection.

"Monte, we say to you in the midst of your sorrow and loss that we are grateful that your love for Ina Claire was such that we are all able to share in her quiet gentleness and firm resolve to live her life for you, and others. We take joy and relief in knowing that her suffering has ended, and now into the ever-lasting arms of an all-merciful God, we commit the soul of our beloved Ina Claire. Amen."

Reverend Owen nodded, and six of the leading citizens of Big Rock: Louis Longmont, Tim Murchison, Ed McKnight, Elmer Keaton, Mike Kennedy, and Joel Montgomery, using ropes, lowered Ina Claire into the grave. When the coffin reached the bottom, the ropes were withdrawn, then the six men stepped away. Reverend Owen nodded toward Monte, who stepped up to the open grave and dropped a handful of dirt, which, in the silence, could be heard falling upon the coffin.

"Ashes to ashes, dust to dust, in the sure and certain hope of eternal life," Reverend Owen said.

When Reverend Owen turned and walked away from the graveside, Sally stepped up to embrace Monte.

"We will miss her so," Sally said.

"Thank you, Sally," Monte replied, his voice thick with sorrow.

The funeral reception was held in the ballroom of the Dunn Hotel. Ina Claire had been an orphan and was without any family. She had been married and divorced before she met Monte, but her former husband had died several years ago. The funeral reception was organized by Sally and some of the other ladies in town.

"It's too bad none of Sheriff Carson's family could have been here," Mrs. Carmichael said.

"He doesn't have any family," Mrs. Owen said. "That's why Ina Claire's death is so sad. It has left him all alone."

"But I hear she was suffering terribly with something they call the cancer over the last month," Mrs. Carmichael said.

"Yes, she was. And now, mercifully, her suffering is over. In a way, Monte's suffering is over as well, as he suffered with her."

Smoke and Pearlie had been standing with Monte, but because Smoke thought that their standing together might prevent others from coming up to offer the sheriff their condolences, he put his hand on Monte's shoulder and squeezed.

"In case you need us for anything, Monte, we'll be right over here," Smoke said.

Monte nodded as Smoke and Pearlie walked away.

Smoke had poured himself a cup of coffee and was perusing a table strewn with various pastries when Phil Clinton, the editor of the local paper, stepped over to speak to him.

"You and the sheriff seem to be close friends," Clinton said.

"We are."

"You two have been friends for as long as I have been here. I'm curious. How did you two meet?"

Smoke chuckled as he chose a cinnamon bun. "He was hired to kill me," Smoke said, easily.

"What?" Clinton gasped.

"Once, there was a fella in these parts by the name of Tilden Franklin. He was a man of some importance who had plans to take over the county and he planned on using Pearlie and Monte Carson to help him.

"Then, when I came along and started my ranch, Franklin figured I was in the way. He told Monte and Pearlie that he wanted me killed. Neither one of them would go along with that, and the result was a battle between a lot of Franklin's men, Monte, Pearlie, and me.

"When it was over I offered Monte the job of sheriff here in Big Rock, hired Pearlie on as foreman of Sugarloaf, and those two, onetime enemies, have been my best friends ever since."

Smoke waited until he saw Monte and Sally standing together, then he walked over to join them.

"How are you holding up?"

"I've already been through this once before, Smoke,

when I lost my first wife. It isn't fair that I would have to go through it again."

"I can't argue with that, Monte."

"I know everyone is saying that Ina Claire is in a better place," Monte said. "And I know that she is, especially since she was in so much pain toward the end. The laudanum helped with the pain, but to be honest, it sort of took her away from me even before she died, if you know what I mean."

"I know," Smoke said. "And, Monte, I can fully relate to the pain you're going through now."

"Yes, you lost a wife and a child."

Smoke nodded. "Nicole and Arthur. Murdered." For just a moment the hurt Smoke was sharing with Monte became his own, as he recalled returning home to find his family dead. Smoke went on the blood trail, tracking down and killing the men who had so destroyed his life.

After that, Smoke didn't think he would ever be able to love again. But he met a beautiful and spirited young schoolteacher who changed his mind.

"I got over it once before," Monte said. "I can get over it this time as well."

"You will get over it, but don't force the memories of Ina Claire away too quickly," Sally said. Sally had been standing with the two men, listening to their conversation. "I know that there is a place in Smoke's heart where Nicole still lives. I'm not jealous of that, I love him for it, because it tells me how deeply Smoke can love. In fact, even though I never met Nicole, I can't help but think of her as my sister."

"It's funny you would say that, because Ina Claire once said that she thought of Rosemary as a sister. But you don't have to worry that I'll ever forget her," Monte said. He smiled. "I believe, with all my heart, that the thunderstorm we had earlier this morning was just her talking to me. Lord, that woman did love thunderstorms for some ungodly reason."

Sally laughed. "I remember that a thunderstorm came up during yours and Ina Claire's wedding reception. We had it out at Sugarloaf, and I told her I was sorry that the reception might be spoiled by the storm, but she said, *'No, I love it! It's just God applauding the fact that Monte and I were married.'* For a long time I thought she had just said that so I wouldn't feel bad about the storm."

Monte chuckled as well. "No, she actually believed that. She told me the same thing."

Sally embraced Monte. "Anytime you feel the need for company, you are always welcome at Sugarloaf."

"Thank you, Sally. With friends like Smoke, you, Pearlie, and Cal, I'll get through this."

The obituary in *the Big Rock Journal* the next day was accorded the honor of appearing on the front page of the paper.

Ina Claire Carson

Ina Claire Carson, 36, wife of Sheriff Monte J. Carson, died yesterday after a long battle with the terrible disease of cancer.

Mrs. Carson was raised in the Baptist Orphanage in Jackson, Mississippi. Because she was left there as an infant by persons unknown, she was without family, save her husband, Sheriff Carson.

Although Mrs. Carson was without family, she certainly wasn't without friends. Kirby Jensen, better known to his friends as Smoke Jensen, was there with his lovely wife, Sally. Smoke, Sally, and Smoke's two longtime friends and employees, Wes (Pearlie) Fontaine and Cal Wood, were accorded family positions at both the church and graveside funeral services.

Mrs. Carson was well known and well loved by all the citizens of Big Rock. She was especially renowned for her oatmeal cookies, which she graciously baked for all the prisoners in the Big Rock jail.

Although the atmosphere is Longmont's Saloon was never boisterous, it was generally happy and upbeat. Not so today, as even the patrons who had not attended the funeral on the day before were quiet and respectful. That was because Monte was in the saloon, as were Smoke and Pearlie. Louis Longmont, who owned the saloon, had just read the obituary.

"This is a very nice article about Ina Claire," Louis said. "You and she have been such a wonderful part of our community. I know it will be hard for you, but I also know that you will carry on, providing the steadying influence that will keep Big Rock the fine town it is."

"I have no doubt about it," Mark Worley said. For some time Worley had been Monte's deputy, but six months ago the town of Wheeler was in need of a city marshal, and they sent a delegation to talk to Monte about Mark. Monte gave him the glowing recommendation that got him hired. So far, Monte had not taken on a new deputy. Mark had come to town for the funeral and had stayed an extra day.

"How are you liking it over in Wheeler?" Pearlie asked.

"It's been great," Mark replied. "Oh, I miss all my friends over here, but I've made new friends, and I really like being in charge. Not that I minded deputing for Monte, you understand, but it is good to be the top dog."

Pearlie laughed. "Yeah, well, just don't let it go to your head. You always did think a lot of yourself."

Pearlie was teasing. Actually, he and Mark were good friends.

"I should get another deputy, I suppose," Monte said. "But to be honest, searching for another deputy hasn't been the most important thing in my mind for the last few months."

"Take your time in looking for one," Smoke said. "It isn't like you can't make an instant deputy if there is a sudden need for one."

Monte nodded. "Yeah, that's the way I see it. You, Pearlie, and Cal have helped me out more than once. And I appreciate that, because it means I can afford to be choosy."

"Speaking of deputies, and sheriffs, and all that, I'd better get back to Wheeler and my never-ending battle of fighting crime and/or evil," Mark said with a laugh.

"Thanks for coming over, Mark. I appreciate that," Monte said.

"Smoke, we should get going, too," Pearlie said. "We've got a lot of calves we have to gather."

For a while Sugarloaf had abandoned cattle and raised horses only. But when Smoke's friend Duff MacCallister introduced him to Black Angus cattle, Smoke had gone back into the cattle business. Angus were a little more difficult to raise than longhorns, but they were many times more profitable.

"What did you say?" Smoke asked.

"I said we needed to get back to the ranch. We have work to do."

Smoke looked at the others and smiled. "Would you listen to this man, telling me *we* have work to do?"

"Pearlie, maybe you don't understand, you are the foreman of Sugarloaf, but I am the owner. Do I need to tell you who is in charge?"

Although Smoke spoke the words harshly, he ended his sentence with a laugh to show that he was teasing.

"We need to get back to the ranch, we have work to do," Smoke added.

"The boss man is right," Pearlie said to the others. "We need to go."

Shortly after Mark, Smoke, and Pearlie left, Monte told Louis good-bye, and walked down to his office. There was nobody in jail at the moment, and because he was without a deputy, he was all alone.

He was unable to hold back the tears.

CHAPTER 2

Capitol Hill, Denver, Colorado

State Senator Rex Underhill's house sat but a few blocks from where the new capitol building was to be built. His Victorian house was large with wings and bay windows and gingerbread decorating features. He built the eight-bedroom house in the most elegant part of Denver merely for show. It was a gaudy display of ostentation, especially since, except for his servants, he lived alone in the house.

After Senator Underhill finished reading the obituary of Ina Claire Carson in the Denver newspaper, he laid it beside his now-empty breakfast plate.

He thought of the names he had just read; Monte Carson, Smoke Jensen, Pearlie Fontaine, Cal Woods. It was too bad that the obituary was not for one of them. It would be even better, if it could be for all of them.

"Another cup of coffee, Señor Underhill?" The question snapped Underhill out of his reverie.

"Frederica, I have told you to call me *Senator* Underhill."

"*Sí, señor,* uh, *sí,* Senator. Sometimes I forget," Frederica said.

"You are forgetting too many times, and if you don't start remembering, I'll let you and Ramon go and hire some new domestics, perhaps Americans who understand the language so I won't have to keep repeating things."

"I will not forget again, Señor Senator."

Frederica was a plump woman whose dark hair was now liberally laced with gray. Her husband, Ramon, took care of the lawn, and his hair was all white.

"Are you going to stand there gabbing, or are you going to pour me another cup of coffee?" Underhill asked.

"Coffee, *sí*," Frederica said as she poured a dark, aromatic stream of liquid into the cup.

Senator Underhill eased his harsh admonition with a smile. "What would I do if I let you go, Frederica? Where else would I find someone who could make coffee as good as yours?"

"*Sí*, Señor Senator, nowhere else will you find coffee this good," Frederica said with a relieved smile.

Underhill took his coffee out onto the front porch and sat in a rocking chair to watch the vehicles roll by. Here, in Capitol Hill, nearly all the vehicles were elegant coaches, fine carriages, or attractive surreys, for only the wealthy lived in this part of town.

Rex Underhill hadn't always been wealthy. His father had been a sharecropper barely scratching out a living in Arkansas, and even that was gone after the war. When Underhill left home nobody tried to talk him into staying, because his departure just meant one less mouth to feed.

Underhill survived by a few nighttime burglaries here and there, then he graduated to armed robberies. He robbed a stagecoach in Kansas, killing the driver, shotgun guard, and single passenger. Because he left not a single witness, he was never regarded as a suspect for the crime. He got twelve thousand dollars from that holdup, and he moved on to Colorado, where he became the secret partner of a couple of men—Deekus Templeton and Lucien Garneau—in a scheme to take over most of the ranchland in Eagle County. It was a plan that, on the surface, had failed, miserably.

Underhill glanced at the paper again. He had read the obituary because it was about the wife of Monte Carson. Carson was the sheriff of Eagle County. Eagle County was also the locale of the Sugarloaf Ranch and Smoke Jensen. Smoke Jensen was the biggest reason for the failure of the grand plan to own all of Eagle County.

Underhill was fortunate, however. The principals in the attempt to take over Eagle County were all killed. Underhill survived the plan because nobody knew that he had been involved. Also, he had not only been Deekus Templeton's and Lucien Garneau's secret partner, he had also been their banker, providing some operating funds in the beginning, but holding on to the money from a couple of bank robberies that neither Templeton nor Garneau could afford to deposit in a bank. When the two men died, Underhill profited from their deaths, immediately becoming over forty thousand dollars richer.

That was the money he had used to begin his political campaign. He was a state senator now, an office that put him in a position to take advantage of the many opportunities for enrichment that came his way.

Lately, Rex Underhill had been contemplating another political move, one that would greatly increase his chances to capitalize on his political position. He sold influence now as a state solon. How much more valuable would be the influence of a United States senator?

Rock Creek, near Big Rock

Just under one hundred miles west of where Rex Underhill was having his breakfast, six men were staring into a campfire, having just finished their own. They were camped on Rock Creek at the foot of Red and White Butte, about five miles north of Big Rock.

A little earlier that morning the leader of the group, Myron Petro, had proposed a job he thought they should do.

"It'll be like takin' money from a baby," Myron said. The men to whom he was pitching his idea were his brother Frank, Muley Dobbs, Ethan Reese, Wally Peach, and Leo Beajuex. All of the men were experienced outlaws except for Beajuex, who was the youngest of the lot.

"I don't know how you ever got the idea that robbin' a bank in Big Rock is goin' to be easy," Wally Peach said. "There ain't no way it's goin' to be easy on account of Monte Carson is the sheriff there, 'n he sure ain't easy. Hell, he's one of the toughest sheriffs there is anywhere."

Myron grinned. "Sheriff Carson ain't goin' to be no problem at all 'cause, case you don't known nothin' about it, his wife just died. That means he's so all broke up about it that he can't hardly do his job no more."

"I ain't never seen this Sheriff Carson feller but I've sure heard of 'im," Muley Dobbs said. "'N what I've heard is the same thing what Wally just said. Sheriff Carson's s'posed to be one tough son of a bitch. So, how is it that you know his wife died?"

"I heard talk of it yesterday when I was in Red Cliff."

"Yeah, well, I wish they was some way we could be sure," Muley said.

"All right, s'pose you 'n Beajuex go into town 'n have a look around?" Myron suggested. "You could maybe scout the bank whilst you was there, too."

"Nah, don't send the kid," Frank said. "He wouldn't have no idea what the hell he would be lookin' for. I'll go."

"All right, tomorrow you 'n Muley go into Big Rock, have a look around town, then come back 'n tell me what you've found out. We'll hit the bank day after tomorrow."

That night, as the six men bedded down around the dying campfire that had cooked their supper, they talked excitedly about the money they would soon have.

Leo Beajuex listened, but didn't join the conversation. He had never done anything like this before and he was very apprehensive about it. He wasn't going to run out on them—these men were the closest thing to a family he had. He had met them six months earlier, when he was supporting himself as a cowboy on the Bar S Ranch down in Bexar County, Texas.

Actually, saying that he was a cowboy would be a

considerable overstatement of his real position. Ron Stacy, owner of the Bar S, was a tyrannical boss, especially to someone who was a menial laborer, as Leo was. Whereas the cowboys got thirty dollars a month and found, Leo was paid fifteen dollars. He got the worst jobs on the ranch, and Stacy wasn't averse to physical abuse.

It all came to a head one day when Stacy took a leather strap to Leo because he hadn't cleaned a stall. As it turned out, he had cleaned it, the mess was from a horse that had just been moved into the stall.

Deciding that he had had enough, it was Leo's plan to steal a couple of cows and sell them for just enough money to help him get away. However, while he was in the act of cutting them out, he saw the Petro brothers and the other three men doing the same thing but on a larger scale.

"Boy, if you got 'ny idea of tellin' anyone what we're a-doin' here, we'll shoot you dead," Myron Petro warned.

"Why would I want to tell anyone?" Leo replied. "I'd rather join you."

They rustled forty-nine cows and sold them for twenty-five dollars apiece. That gave them a little over two hundred dollars each, which, for Leo, was more than a year's wages.

There had been a few other, small jobs. They got a hundred and fifty dollars from a stagecoach holdup, and eight hundred dollars from some stolen mules.

So far, at least since Leo had been with them, there had been no shooting. But when the subject came up this afternoon, Frank said that if they had to, they would kill anyone in the bank, as well as anyone on the street who tried to stop them.

Although Leo had come close, he had never killed anyone, and he hoped that nobody would be killed as a result of the job they were planning now.

As the campfire burned down, a little bubble of gas, trapped in one of the burning pieces of wood, made a loud pop and emitted a little flurry of sparks. Leo watched the golden specks as they rode the rising shaft of heated air into the night sky, there to join with the wide spread of stars.

He wondered what would happen in two more days.

Big Rock

The next day Frank Petro and Muley Dobbs rode into town. Even at an easy pace, the ride into town took less than an hour.

"Lookee there," Frank said, pointing to some of the shops and businesses they were passing. "All them buildings has black ribbons on 'em, so that means for sure that somebody died."

"Yeah, but it don't mean for sure that it was the sheriff's wife what died, without we hear someone say it," Muley said. "'N the best place to hear it said is in a saloon, just like this one."

They were just passing the saloon as Muley pointed it out.

"Longmont's," Frank said, reading the sign. "I don't know, it looks a bit fancy for the likes of us."

"The fancier it is, the easier it is to find out information. Besides I'm a mite thirsty, aren't you?"

"A beer would be good," Frank agreed.

"And maybe a couple hands of poker," Muley added.

"No, I don't know, Muley, I've seen you play poker before. More times than not, somethin' gets your dander up, then you go off half-cocked 'n wind up in trouble. We most especial don't want no trouble today, that's for damn sure."

"You don't worry none 'bout me playin' poker. That's a good place to find things out. You just stand up there at the bar, drink your beer, 'n keep your eyes 'n ears open," Muley said. "If you hear somethin' that don't sound right, let me know."

The two men stepped inside, then looked around.

"Whooee, I sure ain't never seen no saloon this fancy before," Frank said.

The long bar that ran down the left side of the saloon was more than just gleaming mahogany. The front of the bar was intricately carved to show a bas-relief of cowboys herding cattle. The hanging overhead lights weren't wagon wheels and coal oil lanterns as was often the case, but cut crystal chandeliers.

"There's a card game," Muley said, pointing to a table where a game was in progress.

"Muley, be careful. Don't go gettin' yourself into no trouble," Frank cautioned.

With a nod as his only response, Muley walked over to the table. "You fellers willin' to take on a fifth player?"

"No need for five players, you can have my seat," one of the players said. "I need to be gettin' along anyhow."

"The name is Muley," the big scruffy-looking man said as he took the chair just vacated.

* * *

A short while after Frank and Muley rode into Big Rock, Smoke and Sally came into town. Sally could ride as well as any man, but they came in a buckboard because Sally wanted to do some shopping and it would be easier to take the purchases back in a buckboard than on horseback. They drove in from the west, following Sugarloaf Road until they passed the depot and Western Union, at which place Sugarloaf Road turned into Front Street. As had Frank and Muley before them, Smoke and Sally noticed that many of the buildings on Front Street had a black ribbon on the door.

"That's nice of them to honor Monte in such a way," Sally said.

"You aren't surprised, are you, Sally? Monte is a popular sheriff and Ina Claire was well liked," Smoke said.

"*Well loved* is a better description."

"I'll go along with that," Smoke said as he parked the buckboard in front of the Big Rock Mercantile.

"I'll be in Longmont's when you're ready to go back home," Smoke said as he tied off the team.

"Really? And here I thought I might find you in the library," Sally teased.

"Sally, has anyone ever told you that sarcasm doesn't become you?" Smoke asked with a little chuckle.

"You mean besides my mother and father and all four of my grandparents? Oh yes, you have as well."

Sally kissed Smoke on the cheek, then started toward the store, as Smoke crossed the street to get to the saloon.

* * *

Owner and proprietor of the saloon was Louis Longmont, a Frenchman from New Orleans, who was quick to point out that he was truly French and not Cajun. The difference, he explained to those who questioned him, was that his parents moved to Louisiana directly from France, and not from Arcadia.

Longmont's was one of two saloons in Big Rock, the other saloon being the Brown Dirt Cowboy Saloon.

The Brown Dirt Cowboy tended to cater more to cowboys and workingmen than it did to professional men, storekeepers, and ranch owners. The Brown Dirt Cowboy provided not only alcoholic beverages and a limited menu, but also bar girls who did more than just provide friendly conversational company for the drinking man.

Longmont's, on the other hand, was more like a club in which ladies were not only allowed, they were made to feel welcome, and assured there would be no stigma to their frequenting the establishment. It also had a menu that could compete with the menu offered by Delmonico's Restaurant, which was just down the street from Longmont's.

Like the other business establishments along Front Street, Longmont's had a black ribbon on the door.

Stepping into the saloon Smoke stood just inside the door for a moment to peruse the patrons.

There were seven men standing at the bar, only one of whom he had never seen before. Three of the tables had customers, and two of the girls were standing near two of the tables, having a smiling conversation with the drinkers. Smoke knew both Becky and Julie and he exchanged a nod with them. He also knew the seated drinkers. There was a poker game going on at the third table, and here Smoke recognized three of the men. Two were cowboys from a nearby ranch and the third was Mike Kennedy. He didn't know who the fourth man was, but there was something about him that gave Smoke a sense of unease.

In addition to those three tables, there was a fourth table. This was Louis Longmont's special table, so designated because nobody but Louis ever sat there unless they were personally invited by Louis.

The pianist was playing, not one of the typical saloon ballads, but a piece by the Polish composer Frédéric Chopin. This kind of music would never be allowed in most other saloons, but it had become a signature for Longmont's.

Tim Murchison, owner of Murchison's Leather Goods, was sitting at the table with Louis, and Smoke, without being invited because Louis had once told him that his invitation was permanent, joined them.